Remember
US THIS
way

Sheridan Anne
Remember Us This Way

Copyright © 2024 Sheridan Anne
All rights reserved
First Published in 2024

Cover Design: Sheridan Anne
Editing: Fox Proof Editing
Formatting: Sheridan Anne

Content Warning

The following list of triggers may also be perceived as spoilers to some. If you do not wish to have the book spoiled, stop reading now!

Your mental health is important to me, so please be mindful of your triggers when reading Remember Us This Way.

This novel deals with some heavy topics -

Loss of loved ones

Grieving/mourning

Self-hate & Self-destruction

On page bullying

On page death of minor

Journey of sick minor, through to death

To those who've had to fight like hell, but never got to see the sunrise.

We love you.

Prologue

ZOEY

Noah stares into my eyes as though I'm the only girl in the world, his dark gaze sending a million fluttering butterflies soaring through the pit of my stomach. A soft smile plays on my lips, and when his warm hand takes mine, he drops down on one knee.

My chest swells with happiness as he clutches his mother's ring between his fingers, and in this moment, I've never been happier. "Zoey Erica James," he says, not daring to take his eyes off mine as the soft spring breeze catches in my hair, blowing my chestnut locks around my face. "Will you marry me?"

His voice doesn't shake, and as I stare down at him, I see the rest of my life flash before my eyes, playing out like a movie. Only my hand falls away, dropping to my side as red-hot anger booms through my chest. "NO!" I huff, stomping my foot and crossing my arms over my chest. "You did it wrong. You're supposed to tell me how beautiful I am."

Noah groans, the frustration clear in his eyes as he scrambles to his feet. "I did not do it wrong," he argues, that temper of his quickly boiling to the surface as his little brother, Lincoln, kicks a goal and cheers to himself across the yard. "That's what they do in all the movies."

"MOM!" I whine, feeling the tears beginning to sting my eyes as I turn to find our mothers watching us from the back patio, my baby sister, Hazel, crying in her bouncer. "Noah's not doing it right."

"Oh, honey," she says with a heavy sigh, a tightness in her eyes that's been there ever since she brought me home from the doctor yesterday. She quickly wipes her face, and I wonder why she's so sad. It's a happy day. Noah and his mom are here. That's her favorite thing in the world . . . mine too. "I think he did a wonderful job. It was a million times better than your daddy's proposal to me."

Noah's mom laughs, watching us with sadness in her eyes as she scoops up my sister and gently rocks her in her arms. "Come on, Noah. Give it another try. Zoey is your bestest friend in the world. Dig down deep and really blow her away."

Noah groans and lets out a heavy sigh before turning back to me, and I smile wide, more than ready to have my bestest friend blow me away . . . whatever that means.

He mutters under his breath before his gaze lifts back to mine. He takes my hand, only this time, he's clearly not in the mood to play along, but it doesn't matter to me. As long as Noah is playing with me, I'm happy. I'm always happy when he comes over. And when he smiles at me . . . maybe that's what it means to blow me away.

Noah holds my gaze and inches toward me, his chest right in front of mine. "Zoey Erica James," he starts again, and my smile stretches wide over my face as he drops back down to one knee. "You are the most beautiful girl in the world. Can you marry me now?"

Elation bursts through my veins, and I squeal, never so happy in my life. "YES!" I boom before throwing myself at him. Noah wraps his arms protectively around me as we crash to the ground, and his mother's ring tumbles into the long grass, probably never to be seen again, but I don't care about that.

I slam my lips down on his, giving him the biggest kiss I can possibly manage. "You're going to be the bestest husband, Noah Ryan."

"Ugh, gross, Zozo," he says, shoving me off him, and as I fall into the dirty grass and stain my dress, he wipes the back of his arm across his mouth, losing my kiss. "This is stupid. You have girl germs."

My bottom lip wobbles as I get to my feet, my butt hurting from when he shoved me off him, but I won't dare tell him that. Noah's so brave. I don't ever want him to see me not being brave too. "I do not have girl germs."

"Uh, yeah you do," he argues back. "You're a girl. You're wearing a silly dress and have flowers in your hair. That makes you a girl, and I don't want stupid girl kisses."

"They're not stupid," I throw back at him, tears welling in my eyes.

"Ugh," he groans, getting annoyed. "Why do we always have to do what you wanna do? Can't we just play tag or something like that? You haven't even seen my new bike yet."

My cheeks burn with embarrassment, and as the tears fall down my face, I turn and run. I run with everything I am.

"Mommy," I cry, only she doesn't look up because she's silently crying into Aunt Maya's shoulder. My tears fall harder at the sight. She never has time for me anymore. She's always busy talking to doctors or crying with my daddy.

Huffing, I go for the door, barging through and passing our daddies in the living room. The game is on, but neither of them seems to be watching it. My feet hit the stairs, and I run faster than I've ever run before.

Noah said my kisses were stupid, but they're not stupid. They're special. Like a gift from me to him. If he gave me a kiss, I would always keep it special.

Barging into my room, I slam the door behind me and throw myself down on my bed, smooshing my face into my pillow and letting the tears flow free.

He's supposed to be my bestest friend.

My tears eventually dry, and while it's barely been a few minutes, it feels like a lifetime. Is this what life is supposed to be about? Boys hurting my heart? Because if that's it, I don't want it. I want to always be happy with Noah. I want him to love me like I love him, but he can't love me if he thinks my kisses are stupid.

A knock sounds at my bedroom door, and I sit up on my bed, watching as it swings open. Noah stands on the other side of the doorway, looking like he just swallowed a whole lemon.

He looks anywhere but at me, and I squint my eyes at him real hard, more than ready to give him a piece of my mind, but I don't know what to say. Noah Ryan broke my heart, and even though we were just playing, it still hurts.

"Your mommy made you come and say sorry, didn't she?"

Noah rolls his eyes and huffs, inching into my room, still refusing to meet my stare. He's never been good at apologizing. He hates it, almost as much as he hates my kisses. "Yes," he grumbles.

Scrambling off my bed, I go and stand in front of him, knowing that when it comes to Noah Ryan and apologies, he sometimes needs a little help. At least, that's what his mommy says. "You broke my heart," I tell him, pouting out my bottom lip. "My kisses are special."

Those dark eyes stare back at me. "I didn't mean to make you sad, Zozo," he says, the ring I'd lost in the long grass now looped over his finger. "I just don't like kisses, but maybe I might like them when I'm bigger."

My heart booms with happiness. "Really?"

He nods, a wide smile stretching across his face. "Yeah," he says before something flickers in his eyes. He steps into me, taking my hand just like he did out in the yard, and pushes the too-big ring onto my finger. "Zozo," he says, squeezing my hand as he leans in to whisper in my ear, a wave of goosebumps spreading over my skin and making the butterflies start to roam again. "You know I love you, right?"

Tipping my head up, I meet his stare, his dark eyes locked so tightly on mine as my heart thunders in my chest. My whole world revolves around this boy, and I've never been so happy. I don't ever want this to change.

"I'm sorry I hurt your heart," he whispers. "I don't ever want to do that again."

"I don't want you to do that either."

A soft smile pulls at his lips, and the way his eyes sparkle has me already forgetting how it hurt. "Can I still marry you?"

I laugh, pulling him into my arms and squeezing him tight, my every dream coming true. "Yes," I tell him. He beams back at me, and then surprising me, he takes my face in both his hands and presses a big kiss to my lips, making my heart beat faster than it ever has in my whole entire life.

And I realize this is exactly what Aunt Maya meant. This is what it means to blow me away, and I swear to myself that every day of forever and ever, I want Noah Ryan to blow me away.

When Noah pulls back and meets my eyes, the look he gives me makes me feel as though I could burst right up into space. "I guess girl kisses aren't *that* bad."

I laugh again and pull him back in for another hug, loving how happy Noah Ryan makes me. "You're my *bestest* friend in the whole world," I remind him.

"I'm your *only* friend, Zozo."

"Nuh-uh," I say, pulling back. "Tarni Luca is my friend."

"Tarni Luca is not your friend," he says, with a huff, his brows pulling down. "She has a face like a butt."

My jaw drops, and I stare at him in shock. I've never heard such a mean thing come out of his mouth, but the second the shock wears off, I laugh. She kinda does have a face like a butt.

"I'm the only friend you need," Noah tells me before walking past me to my bed, grabbing my iPad off the end, and settling against my pillow, already searching for his favorite apps. He pats the space beside him, and I carefully climb up and sit next to him, leaning over to watch what he's doing. "Check this out," he says. "I finally learned how to get past level fourteen."

My eyes widen, watching how amazing he is. He's one year older than me, and I've always been amazed at the things he can do. I've never seen anyone ride their bike quite as fast as he can, and when he plays football, he's the best one on the field. Every time. I love going and cheering at his games. Our moms always let us get a treat afterward.

Noah teaches me how to play, and when I finally get the hang of it, he gets quiet. "Zozo," he murmurs, a strange tone in his voice. He stops playing and looks up at me, his brows scrunched. "Why was your mom crying?"

I shake my head. "I don't know," I tell him in a small voice, shrugging my shoulders. "Mommy and Daddy have been crying a lot lately."

"Do you think something's wrong?"

"Maybe," I whisper, trying not to worry about it. They always tell me I have to be a big, brave girl for my baby sister, and be her protector. I'm not the baby anymore. I have to be a grown-up girl.

"It's okay," he tells me, slipping his hand into mine. "As long as they don't take you away from me, then it's going to be alright."

I trust his word entirely. I always have because he's the smartest person I know and a whole grade ahead of me.

Another knock sounds at my door, and I hear Aunt Maya's voice. "Noah, sweetheart. Are you in here?" she asks, creeping into my room with my parents behind her, finding us on my bed. Noah's mom gives me a wide smile, her gaze lingering on me for just a moment longer than usual before glancing at her son. "It's time to go. Zoey's mommy and daddy need to have a chat with Zo, so we need to scram."

Noah groans. "Really? We were just about to get past level fifteen."

"You can FaceTime each other tonight and finish your game then," she says before stepping up to the edge of my bed and crouching down, placing her hand on my thigh. "Have I ever told you that you're the most beautiful girl I know? You're so brave and strong," she tells me, blinking back tears. "You're my little warrior."

I give Aunt Maya a wide smile, always loving it when people tell me how great I am.

Noah scoots off my bed, and when he gets to his feet, he turns back and looks at me before practically pushing his mom out of his way. He leans in to whisper in my ear. "Don't tell anybody how much I like your stupid girl kisses."

A wide grin stretches across my face, and I beam back at him, making a show of crossing my heart. "Promise."

With that, Noah and his mom make their way out of my room, but Aunt Maya stops to glance at my mom. She pulls her into a tight hug, her hands rubbing over my mom's back as my daddy places his hand on Mom's shoulder. "It's going to be okay," Aunt Maya says, her words making something tremble in my chest. "I'm always here whenever you need."

Noah gives me one last glance before slipping out of my room with his mom, and I'm left looking up at my parents. They give me tight smiles as if trying to pretend that everything is okay, but I see the red around their eyes.

"Hey honey," Mom says, sitting down beside me. Her arm falls around my shoulder as Daddy sits next to me with his big hand on my knee. "There's something we need to tell you."

Chapter 1

ZOEY

The late afternoon breeze sails through my bedroom window as I scan through my closet for the millionth time, searching for the perfect outfit to start junior year tomorrow.

I don't know why I feel so nervous about this. It's not like junior year really matters in the grand scheme of things. I have a great bunch of friends and am usually on top of my grades. I'm the perfect student, and yet the idea of walking into school after a great summer makes me feel sick, or maybe I'm just sad that summer is over, and it's back to real life. Who knows.

Something just feels . . . different.

Grabbing a tank and a pair of high-waisted denim shorts, I hold them up and stand in front of the mirror, my face scrunched as I take it in. It's cute, but it's not really giving me *I'm about to dominate junior year* vibes. Maybe an oversized sweater will be better with these shorts. Only the heat can be a bitch here in Arizona, and I do not want to be the girl with sweat patches under my arms on day one. I would never live it down.

Letting out a huff, I throw the outfit back in the closet, and as I begin to search for another, my phone chimes on the end of my bed. I dart across my room to grab it, skipping over my backpack before I miss the call.

Scooping my phone off my bed, I smile as I find a video call from my best friend, Tarni. Quickly hitting accept, I move back in front of the mirror and hold up the phone as I show off my outfit. "What do you think?" I ask over the sound of my music, laughing as I glance down at the phone to find her standing in her bathroom, an almost identical outfit held up in front of her.

"Pretty damn cute," she says with a stupid grin.

"Yeah . . . I don't know," I tell her. "I was thinking about an oversized sweater, but—"

"Sweat patches?" she rushes out, reading my mind.

"Yes!"

Tarni laughs and puts the outfit down before her face appears up close and personal, her long auburn bangs falling into her eyes. "I swear, Zo, you and me are like . . . twins. Or like . . . what's better than twins?"

"I don't know," I snort, skipping across my room to turn my music down before my eyes widen. "We're a perfect pair, a telepathic twosome. Quick, tell me what I'm thinking?"

"Easy," Tarni scoffs as her phone falls off the bathroom counter and she dives after it. "You're trying to figure out what other names you could call us. And honestly, if double trouble comes out of your mouth next, I'm gonna drop kick your ass all the way to the moon."

A snorting laugh tears from the back of my throat, and I bite my tongue, not surprised that Tarni was able to pluck the phrase right out of my head. She's been one of my closest friends since we started kindergarten, and sometimes I wonder if she knows me better than I know myself.

As I attempt to tell her just how right she is, my phone randomly connects to my Bluetooth speaker. It's been doing this ever since I got the stupid speaker, and it's driving me insane.

"Zo?" Tarni calls out, her voice booming through my speaker and almost deafening me as I race across my room to turn it off. "Zo? You still there? Did you put me on mute again?"

"Hold on," I rush out, knowing damn well anything I say can't be heard. I grab the speaker and flip it over, searching for the little off button that seamlessly blends in with the speaker's design. There should be a big red on/off button on these things with arrows pointing right toward it. "Two seconds. Nearly done."

"ZO?" she calls.

Finding the button, I quickly turn it off, and my room returns to the normal chaos of my day-to-day life. "Sorry, the stupid Bluetooth speaker picked up my call again," I tell her as I place the speaker back in its spot on my windowsill. My gaze lifts as I head back to my closet, but when I see Aunt Maya's car parked in the driveway, I pause. "Oh, hey," I say, lifting my phone so Tarni can see me. "Aunt Maya is here. I better go down and say hi before she ends up in my room for the next seven hours, demanding every detail about our summer."

Tarni's eyes widen, knowing just how serious I am. "Alright. Call me back when you're done. I still need to figure out what I'm wearing tomorrow."

"Sure thing," I say just as Tarni ends the call and disappears from my screen.

Tossing my phone back onto my bed, I burst through my door, skip past my little sister's room, and hit the stairs. I grip the railing to keep from face-planting all the way to the bottom, and the second my feet hit the floorboards, I grip the banister and fling myself around the corner before cutting through the living room.

It's been months since I've seen her. She's so busy with work and everything else that it's always special when she comes over, and nine times out of ten, a quick visit turns into three bottles of wine and a night filled with endless laughter.

Mom and Aunt Maya have been best friends since they were kids, and it reminds me of my friendship with Tarni. I hope when we're old and married with a bunch of kids, we'll still make time for each other.

Following the sounds of Mom's and Aunt Maya's muffled voices, I approach the kitchen. "I just don't know what to do with him anymore," Aunt Maya sighs. "When I got that call, I couldn't believe it. He's spiraling out of control, and no matter what I do, I can't help him. I'm losing him, Erica."

Pulling myself up short, I hover just outside the kitchen, my heart lurching in my chest. They're talking about Noah.

"He'll find his way back," my mom says, her tone so soothing that I almost believe it.

"It's been three years already." Maya's heartbroken words are a stark reminder of everything we lost that day. "I've been trying to give him time, but as each day passes, he just seems to get further and further away."

"I've been hanging on to the hope that he'll just snap out of it," Mom says as I hear her making her way around the kitchen, probably finding the wine glasses. "He did the same thing when Zoey was having her treatments, and he managed to claw his way back."

"No," Aunt Maya sighs. "He didn't claw his way back. Zoey got better and demanded that he snap out of it. She brought him back, but this is different. Linc isn't coming back."

There it is. The knife right through the chest.

Lincoln Ryan. The sweetest boy I ever met. Noah's little brother. He idolized Noah, just like I did. Some days it was like a competition between us as we fought for Noah's attention, and every time I won was like the sweetest victory. Only now, I wish I had stepped back and given Linc that time he so desperately craved with his big brother. If I knew his time was limited, surely I would have seen past my own selfish desires.

Three long years ago, on a cold Saturday afternoon, a drunk driver recklessly decided to get behind the wheel and viciously took Linc's life. He was only eleven and didn't stand a chance. It was the worst day of my life because I didn't just lose Linc, I lost Noah too.

He's never been able to move past the agony of losing his little brother, and it sure as hell didn't help when his father up and left them six months later. Like Aunt Maya said, he's been spiraling out of control, and it's only going to get worse.

My mom couldn't be more wrong; there is no saving him. He's not clawing his way back because the Noah we once knew, the one I wholeheartedly adored, no longer exists.

Noah Ryan broke my heart, and it killed me.

Four days after Linc tragically lost his life, we buried him in East View's best cemetery and had a funeral fit for the sweetest prince that ever lived. We celebrated his life, and then I never saw Noah Ryan again.

"I'm sorry, Maya. I wish there were some way we could help you," Mom says.

"I just wish there were some kind of magic fix button that could make things go back to how they used to be. Before Linc—" Maya cuts herself off, not wanting to finish that thought. She lets out a heavy sigh. "I don't know where we would be if Noah didn't have football to fall back on. It's been a silent savior, but now that he's been kicked out

13

of St. Michael's, I don't know how he's going to cope."

My heart breaks for my old friend, but I'm not surprised. St. Michael's is the fourth private school he's been kicked out of over the past three years. It really doesn't leave many options. Actually, none at all. Not unless Noah plans on commuting hours every day. He's starting his senior year tomorrow, and I can't imagine this is going to look good on his college applications. Assuming it's still his goal to play college football, he's going to have to figure something out, and fast.

"He's the best quarterback in the state. Someone will take him."

"See, that's the thing. After his second and third expulsion, yeah, there was a small chance," Maya says. "This is his fourth, and these private schools are throwing us more and more hoops to jump through. I think we've reached our limit. I almost died when I got the call from the principal letting me know what happened. I've been on the phone with private schools all morning, and no one will take him."

I hear the familiar sound of my mother filling the wine glasses, and something twists in my stomach, sending a chill sweeping over my body. "So what's the plan? Boarding school in Alaska?"

Maya laughs. "Wouldn't that make things easier?" she jokes, but I know there's a level of truth to her statement. "But no. I've been forced to admit that this is the end of Noah's private schooling, but I managed to get him into East View."

My stomach drops right out of my ass, my heart pounding erratically.

East View? Tell me I heard that wrong.

Mom gasps, and I can picture her eyes widening with horror. "With Zoey?"

"Yeah," Maya says slowly. "Do you think that's going to be a problem?"

"I . . . I honestly don't know," Mom says as I step into the kitchen, unable to remain hidden behind the wall any longer. Mom stands facing me, leaning against the counter, and she clocks me the second I appear, but not Maya. She stands on the opposite side of the island counter with her back to me.

"Maybe I should have a chat with my little warrior," Maya suggests.

Mom averts her stare, looking back at Maya, and I keep silent, needing to hear where this is going, grateful that Mom hasn't given me away just yet. "Zoey is . . . she's still very hurt by Noah's distance, and it's taken her a long time to come to terms with it. But Noah, maybe what he needs is to see her again. Maybe this could be good for both of them."

I shake my head, catching Mom's eye over Maya's shoulder. I couldn't possibly think of anything worse.

"That's my hope," Maya says. "If it's not too much for her, I wanted to see if she'd maybe consider helping Noah settle in tomorrow. You know, just give him the basics. Show him where his classes are, give him a rundown of the school, maybe point him in the direction of the football team."

Oh, hell no!

I shake my head a little more vigorously, watching my mother all too closely, seeing the way her eyes go distant as if actually considering Maya's ridiculous suggestions. "You know what," Mom says, a smugness crossing her face. "I'm sure she'd be happy to."

Sweet baby Jesus. What has my mother been smoking?

"Oh, that would be amazing," Maya says as my world crumbles around me. Not only am I going to see Noah Ryan tomorrow, but I'm actually going to have to talk to him. "I know it's going to be hard for them both, but I really think this could be good."

Mom purposefully looks over Maya's shoulder, making it obvious

I've walked into the kitchen. "Oh, here's my little sweet pea now," she says, placing her glass of wine on the counter and walking around to my side as Maya whips around with a wide, beaming smile. Mom throws her arms around me and squeezes my shoulders. "Honey, did you hear? Noah will be starting at East View with you tomorrow."

I'm frozen to the spot, still trying to register the shock, but at the hopefulness in Aunt Maya's gaze, I force down the fear and put on a big, fake smile. "Oh really?" I ask as Maya barges into me, throwing her arms around me in a tight hug. "That's amazing news."

"Sure is," Maya says, pulling back and allowing me the chance to breathe. "I know he misses you."

Liar. If he missed me, he wouldn't have allowed three long years to pass without so much as a hello. Didn't he know I was hurting too? I needed him just as much as he needed me.

"Let me guess. He got kicked out of another school?" I question, trying to sound casual even though I'm slowly dying inside. Just the thought of seeing his face again . . . I'm sure he's changed so much over the past three years. When I saw him last, he had just turned fourteen, but he's seventeen now, and he's not a kid anymore. Not even close.

Maya laughs. "You know him too well."

Ha. What a joke.

"What was it this time?" I ask, moving around the counter and pinching a freshly baked brownie off the cooling rack. "Burnouts on the football field or trashing a classroom?"

"Oooh, so close, but yet so far," she tells me. "My hunk o' hunk o' burnin' love decided it was a great idea to burn down the principal's office."

My eyes go wide, and I gape at Aunt Maya, certain I heard that wrong. "He did what?"

"Yup," she says, just as horrified. "I was just telling your mom that I don't know what to do with him anymore. Now, I know it's a lot to ask, but with him starting at East View tomorrow, I wondered if you could help him settle in. He was always his best self when he was with you, so I hoped that maybe seeing you again would somehow reel him in because this is his last chance. I had to call his father to drop some money on a new office just to keep this from going to law enforcement."

I cringe, hating my need to always be polite. "I'm not sure, Aunt Maya. That's a lot of pressure on my shoulders. I don't think I can just click my fingers and see the old Noah again. Besides, he wants nothing to do with me. Forcing us together . . . I don't know if that's going to be a good idea."

Aunt Maya steps into me, taking my hand the same way Noah used to. "I know you have your hang-ups about seeing him again, and I completely understand. He hurt you, and I see it in your eyes every time you look at me. And if this is too much, if you don't want to do it, then I won't force it. I'm just . . . I'm desperate, Zo. I'm painfully aware that it's a lot to put on your shoulders, but I'm hoping you could somehow bring him back to me. All I'm asking is that you just give it a try, and if it doesn't work, well then . . ."

She trails off with a heavy sigh, not voicing what we all know.

And if it doesn't work, well then, we know he doesn't love you anymore.

I try to ignore the sting of her unspoken words, and seeing the desperation in her eyes, I force another smile across my face, willing myself to be strong, willing myself not to break. "Okay," I finally say in a small voice. "I'll try, but I can't make any promises. If he pushes me away, I'm not going to keep going back for more. I just . . . I don't think I could handle that."

"Oh, thank God," Maya says, stepping into me and giving me

another hug. "Thank you so much. If anyone can get through to him, I know it's you."

Shit. There's that overwhelming pressure again.

"It's okay," I tell her. "Nobody wants to see the old Noah more than I do."

"I know, sweetheart. Let's just hope that he's still buried deep down in there."

"I'm sure he is," I lie.

Maya takes a heavy breath, blowing out her cheeks as she steps back to give me a little space, and I can't help but notice her watery eyes as she reaches for her glass of wine. "Okay," she finally says. "Now that's sorted out, tell me all about your summer break. I feel like I haven't seen you in forever."

Chapter 2

ZOEY

Racing up the stairs, I feel the tears pricking my eyes. This is too much. How am I supposed to face him again? How am I supposed to look Noah in the eye after everything we've been through?

Is it even possible to fall in love at six years old? Maybe even before that? I can't recall a defining moment, just that from my very first memory as a little girl, Noah was my whole world. He was bigger than the sky, and then one day, *poof*, he was gone. My life started and ended with him, and when he walked away, I felt so empty. Everything I knew was gone, and it took me months to find my feet.

Noah slammed a door in my face, and I clung to the handle for three long years, but now a small window has appeared, and I'm terrified of what I might find if I peek through it.

Crashing back into my room, I crumble onto my bed, my head squished into my pillow as I try to calm my racing heart. My hands shake, unease blasting through my veins and poisoning me from the inside out.

Here I was thinking my biggest problem was underarm sweat patches on the first day of school. What a joke.

I knew something was off. The second I woke up this morning, my stomach was twisted in knots. I always had a sixth sense when it came to Noah, and here it was screaming at me to run for the hills.

It's one thing seeing him again, but having to be his guide through East View High? What am I supposed to do when he inevitably tells me to get lost? Drop to my knees in the middle of the school and weep? Scream, fight, or beg for him to love me again? I understand why Maya asked this of me. She's a desperate parent, and she's reached the point where she's willing to risk my heart in order to save him, but where the hell was my backbone when I needed it? Where were my fight-or-flight instincts?

I should have run.

The second Maya showed up and said Noah was enrolled at East View, I should have run and never looked back. It couldn't be too hard, right? Hell, Noah did it without even glancing back.

With tears in my eyes, I slide out of bed and trudge across my room, wiping my cheeks on the back of my hand. I hear Mom and Maya laughing downstairs, already on their second bottle of wine and acting as though they don't have a care in the world. When in reality, these two have had to deal with more in their lives than any parent ever should.

Standing in front of my mirror, I look at myself, like *really* look at myself. I'm not the same girl I used to be. When he last saw me, I was thirteen, scrawny, and didn't have a clue how to do my hair or makeup. But I'm different now, and I try to see the woman he'll see me as tomorrow.

My drab chestnut hair used to be stick-straight and hang limply around my shoulders, but it's longer and thicker now, and my mom let me get highlights and lowlights put in the last time she took me for a cut.

With a sigh, I brush my hair away from my face and tilt my chin from side to side. I don't exactly feel glamorous, even with blush on my cheeks and my new lip gloss and mascara. Dad lost the fight when it came to me wearing makeup, but it's not like I overdo it like some of the girls at school.

My gaze shifts down my body. The last time he saw me, we were too young to look at each other in a sexual way, but now . . . I don't know. I wonder if he'll like what he sees. If I'm the kind of girl he likes.

I don't exactly have an hourglass figure, but it's well on its way. I love my subtle curves. They're just enough for me to feel beautiful and feminine. The boobs came in a little late, but beggars can't be choosers. They're on the small side, but I don't need much. Besides, it's not like I have anyone I want to show them off for.

I have a great group of friends, and while they're all boy crazy, I'm a little more chill. I've had a few silly crushes over the past few years, but nothing that could possibly rival what I had with Noah. Because of that, I haven't even bothered with dating. Besides, what does it even matter? I'm only sixteen. The guys I know aren't exactly A+ material, and if I were to take my father's advice, I wouldn't be dating until I was at least thirty.

Mom and Dad are always on my case about setting a good example for Hazel. They say she'll be following right behind me soon enough, but I don't really see it that way. I feel like she should be free to make her own footsteps, not follow mine. Though, if she wanted to walk beside them, I think I could get down with that.

My gaze is traveling back up my body when my phone rings on the end of my bed. For just a moment, I consider letting it ring out, but when I see Tarni's name across the screen, I realize she's just going to keep calling. Scooping it up, I thank my lucky stars that it's not a video call and hit accept. "Hey, what's up?" I say, moving back to the mirror and continuing my in-depth audit of my body.

"You were supposed to call me back."

"Yeah, sorry," I say. "I was—"

"Who cares?" she rushes out. "Have you heard? Duh, of course you've heard. Maya was just at your place."

The color drains from my face as my stomach sinks, not liking where this is going. "Heard what?" I ask cautiously, hoping that the rumor mill isn't already spinning wildly through East View.

"Are you kidding?" Tarni booms. "Noah freaking Ryan! He's transferring to East View. Isn't that like . . . woah! How could you not tell me the second you found out? I mean, like . . . my mind is blown. This is insane."

Insane is definitely one way to put it.

"I, umm—"

"Holy crap. Can you imagine? Noah Ryan. He's legit the most popular guy in like a fifty-mile radius! The parties that are gonna be partied. God, I knew this year was going to be epic." Tarni finally takes a breath before her tone shifts, almost sounding like a warning. "You're not gonna be . . . weird about this, are you?" she questions. "It's been like three years. That's long enough to be over . . . whatever it was going on between you guys, right? Because, girl, I love you and all, but I can't have you being all sad Zoey again and making us stay home when the parties are going down. That would be social suicide."

I grit my teeth, trying to remind myself just how much Tarni has done for me over the years. She's a great friend, but sometimes she gets carried away and opens her mouth before thinking about the words coming out of it.

"I'm fine," I finally tell her, shrugging it off and not daring to let her know just how hard I'm taking this. "Noah and I are old news. It's been so long, he's basically a stranger to me now."

"Oh, thank God," she says with a heavy sigh. "I just know Abby and Cora are going to be beside themselves when they hear about this. Not to mention, I've already heard the cheerleaders are calling dibs on who gets to screw him first."

I'm taken aback, feeling completely blindsided as undeniable pain slices straight through my chest. I've never considered the fact that Noah could be sleeping around, but I suppose you don't become that popular by not smashing your way through a whole cheerleading team.

I was agonizing about how I've changed over the years, but it didn't occur to me until now that Noah would be older too. All this time, he's been frozen in my mind, still the fourteen-year-old boy I used to know, but when I see him tomorrow, he'll be different. He's a legend in this town, the quarterback at every school he's been kicked out of. Not that I'm keeping tabs on him or anything, but where Noah Ryan is concerned, word spreads like wildfire . . . or like the cheerleaders' legs at East View High.

Just great. Not only do I have to worry about those dark eyes of his showing up when I least expect it, but now I have to be cautious walking around every corner just in case Noah is hooking up with random girls in hallways.

"Ah, shit. That's Cora calling me now," Tarni says quickly. "Did you need a lift to school in the morning, or am I meeting you there?"

"Oh, umm . . . meet me there," I tell her, all too aware of the fact that by the time everyone else arrives at school, I'll have already suffered through the worst emotional trauma after meeting Noah in the student office.

I can't wait!

"Okay, byeeeeee," Tarni drags out before promptly hanging up to take Cora's call. And with that, I stare back in the mirror, knowing without a doubt that I am not even close to being ready to face this.

Tomorrow isn't just going to be interesting; it's going to be a personal tour right through the darkest pits of hell.

Chapter 3

NOAH

Well, this is going to be a shitshow.

Dropping the cigarette butt to the ground, I blow out a cloud of smoke as I stare up at East View High, home of the mighty Mambas football team. But if you ask me, there's not a damn thing mighty about them. They're mediocre at best, though with me, they might just have a shot of taking out the championship, and that's not my ego talking. It's fact. I'm the best high-school quarterback in the state. Most of my stats outrank those in the professional leagues, but it means nothing if I don't have a team to play for.

If life was forgiving and I could choose which team I represented, the Mambas are far from anything I'd select. They don't even reach the top twenty on the list, but unfortunately for me, they're the only chance I have left.

After my latest fuck up, I don't have many options left. It's either make it with the Mambas and work my ass off to try and save what little chance I have of playing college football, or I could just walk away and probably end up behind bars within the next twelve months . . . maybe sooner. Who knows? I've been on a roll lately.

Decisions. Decisions.

Letting out a heavy breath, I stride up the stairs and push through the double doors before letting them fall shut behind me, the loud *bang* echoing up the hallway.

It's time to face the music.

It's time to face *her*.

The hallways of East View High are dead, barely a soul to be seen, but it's still early. I'm not usually the type to show up so early, but with everything happening so fast, I haven't had a chance to meet Coach Martin yet. I don't even know if he's aware I'm coming, but either way, I won't be leaving his office until I get exactly what I want. Whatever means necessary.

My gaze sails from left to right as I get deeper into the school, trying to figure out where the fuck to go. Navigating new schools isn't exactly new for me. Once you've seen one, you've seen 'em all.

I've spent the last three years being the new kid, but it never takes long to settle in and find my people. Besides, they generally find me. When you come fully loaded with a name and reputation like mine, high school becomes a fucking breeze.

Passing some kid with a fucking trombone, I lift my chin and watch as he scrambles to take off, knowing assholes like me generally live to make life hard for losers like him. "Aye," I say, his wide gaze shifting to me, terror blasting through his stare as he takes me in. "Where's the student office?"

"Uh . . . uhmmm. Down the hall. To the right," he says. "Red door."

I nod, and he takes off like some bitch just offered to let him motorboat her beneath the bleachers.

Wanting to get this over and done with, I continue down the hall, scanning the doors on the right until I come across the red door with the words *Student Office* above it. Bringing my hand up, I shove through the door, and as I lift my gaze to figure out where the fuck I need to go, a horrified gasp sails through the office—a gasp I would recognize anywhere.

No.

Zoey James stands in front of me, her elbows braced against the counter, facing the woman in the office. Those big green eyes I used to adore are locked on mine as though she can't believe what she's seeing.

And fuck, neither can I.

I feel like I've just been shot right through the chest.

Zoey fucking James. I knew I would see her today. It was inevitable. She's been going to East View High since the beginning of freshman year, not that I've been keeping tabs on her, but I wasn't prepared for this, not even close.

Her back stiffens, and I watch the subtle way she curls her hands into fists at her sides, trying to hide the fact they're shaking. But there's no hiding from me. I know her better than she knows herself. At least, I used to. That's in the past now, right where it's going to stay.

My heart pounds out of my chest as the world fades around us, so many things left unsaid but never forgotten. Zoey has been nothing but a figment of my imagination for three years, a constant reminder of the agony that lives in the darkest pits of my soul.

I walked away without a backward glance, not even a goodbye, and that's exactly how it's going to stay.

Zoey remains frozen on the spot, and I can almost read her thoughts. They're so fucking loud, they're practically screaming at me—demanding answers, demanding anything that will bring her just a hint of closure. But she's not going to get it from me.

I've always been able to read her. Those bright green eyes give her away—and now is no different. Though, there's no denying that those bright eyes somehow seem duller now.

Unable to handle the intensity of her horrified stare, I shift my gaze down her body and realize just how much she's changed. She's not some scrawny kid in a pretty dress anymore. She's taller now, wears her hair differently, and is more than aware of her body. Hell, she has tits now.

The last time I saw her, she was in a black dress, holding my hand at my little brother's funeral. I've never been able to get the image of her from that day out of my head. *It haunts me.* But the girl standing before me now—this isn't her. I don't know *this* girl. She's changed. She's closed off, hesitant, and pain radiates through her eyes—a pain I know I put there, and one I sure as hell won't be taking away. Besides, Zoey James doesn't need me anymore.

My gaze trails back up, over her denim shorts that show off her toned legs, and to a sweater that falls off her bare shoulder. She crosses her arms over her body, and I narrow my stare, realizing I've made her self-conscious, but that's her problem, not mine.

I know I'm being obvious, but so is she. Her gaze has roamed up and down my body at least four times already, and I can't help but wonder what she's seeing. I'm certainly not the same clean-cut kid she once knew. He was pathetic. Weak. But now? I don't even know. I'm a fucking stranger to myself.

But when it comes to Zoey James, I know she's looking much deeper than what's on the surface—she's trying to get a read on me, trying to figure me out, but I'm not about to let that happen. I'm not hers to save. Not anymore.

It feels like a lifetime of silence before she sucks in a deep breath and raises her chin, determination flaring through her green stare. I shake my head, willing her not to try, but before I can prepare myself, she forces a smile across her face and takes a hesitant step toward me. Her smile is so fake that it leaves me desperate to see a real one—the one that used to be reserved for only me.

She puts herself right in front of me, making my chest ache for a time when life used to be simple and carefree. When life used to be full of love and happiness instead of this dark hell I've been haunted by.

"Long time no see, huh?" she says, her eyes sparkling as if expecting things to be as easy as they used to be—as if the stars will align just by forcing us together. I have to keep myself from scoffing. I've gotta give it to her, she was always so optimistic, but if she hasn't figured it out after three long years, then I don't know what to tell her. What we used to be is over. Done. *Dead.*

I stare at her a moment longer, the silence so fucking loud between us. "What the fuck do you think you're doing?"

Her eyes widen. I'm sure she expected this to go a million possible ways, but this wasn't one of them. A flicker of hurt lingers in her stare, and for the first time in three years, it's a little easier to breathe.

Zoey's taken aback and takes a second to gather her thoughts. "I've been assigned to show you around," she tells me.

Like fuck that's going to happen.

"Don't waste your time," I tell her. "I'm good."

"You're good?" she scoffs, her eyes blazing with the anger I knew was coming. "Three years of radio silence and all I get from you is *I'm good?*"

"What the hell were you expecting?" I spit, stepping even closer and watching the way she has to crane her neck to meet my eye, probably able to smell the lingering stench of cigarettes on my clothes. "You and me—we're nothing. Not anymore. I don't need you, Zoey. I haven't needed you for three years, and I sure as fuck don't need you now. So, let's get this straight because I don't want you trying to recreate something that will never be. I'm only here to play football, and that's it. I'm not here for *you*. At this school, we don't know each other. Whatever the fuck we used to be, doesn't exist anymore. You see me in the hallways, you look the other way. You see me outside, you go somewhere else. I'm not some fucking project for you to save. Got it?"

A breath escapes her lips, and I watch the undeniable pain shooting through her eyes, dulling that bright green I used to love. "Wow, Noah. Haven't you become a giant piece of shit?" she says, taking a step back and grabbing her backpack off the ground. Not meeting my eye, she slings it over her shoulder, more than ready to race out of here. But I'm not surprised, she's always run at the first sign of conflict. What does surprise me is how casually she called me a piece of shit. The Zoey I knew would never talk that way, and I'm not going to lie, her disgust and judgment stings.

Meeting my stare again, she hesitates, trying to figure out if she's going to tuck her tail between her legs and storm away or say whatever the fuck she feels she needs to say. "For what it's worth," she grits out, determination flashing in her hurt stare. "I was only doing this for your mom because she came to me yesterday, begging me to help you out because she's so scared that she's losing you. But you know what? She was right to be scared. You're long gone, Noah. The kid I used to know . . . I can't even see him in there."

Zoey steps around me and storms to the door, and I have to resist reaching out to touch her, hating that part of me that still desperately craves everything that she is. Reaching for the door, she yanks it open but turns back at the last second, her long chestnut hair whipping over her shoulder. "You should have stayed away," she tells me, her voice filled with the type of venom that somehow darkens my already blackened soul. "I was better off without you."

And with that, she flies out the door, leaving a gaping hole right where my heart used to be.

I almost fall to my knees, and if it weren't for the office lady staring at me like I'm a snake making his way into the chicken coop, maybe I would have. I stride up to her, and she keeps her narrowed stare on me, making it clear that we're going to have issues. "Noah Ryan," I tell her. "First day."

"Oh, I know who you are, Noah Ryan," she says, spitting my name like it's poison. "And I am more than aware of just how much you need this school. This is your last shot, and if you think you can come into my office with that big ole chip on your shoulder and treat the students of East View High the way you just treated Miss James, you have another thing coming."

I clench my jaw as she pushes a stack of papers toward me, not daring to take her furious glare off me. "Hear me, boy. I see students like you come and go every day, so don't get me wrong, your football career means nothing to me. What matters is the welfare of the students in this school, and if you're going to be a threat to that then you can walk straight back out that door and exchange this welcome pack for a pair of cuffs. Is that understood?"

"Yeah, got it," I say, scooping the papers off the desk and turning away, not bothered to hear any more of her lecture. Besides, it doesn't matter anyway. Zoey received my message loud and clear. She won't be an issue for me, which in turn means that I won't be an issue for that old bat.

Barging back out into the hallway, I'm pleased to find no hint of Zoey James or anyone else for that matter. It's still early, and if I'm quick, I'll have just enough time to make a pitstop to Coach Martin before having to get my ass back here for homeroom.

Quickly scanning through the welcome pack, I find my locker

number with a padlock, a map of the school, and my class schedule. Then pulling them out of the pack, I dump the rest of the shit in the trash and make my way to my locker.

I quickly set up my lock code, more than aware that at some point, I'm going to have to change it, especially considering it's 0228—Zoey's birthday, February 28. And to think I just made a point that I wanted nothing to do with her. Ironic really.

I was better off without you.

Fuck, those words keep circling my mind. Why the hell do they hurt so much? She's lying. She has to be. I could see it in her eyes. She lost half of herself when I walked away, and she never got it back. She isn't better off without me; she just *wishes* she was.

After dumping my shit in my locker and programming the number into my phone, knowing damn well I'm going to forget which of these bastards is mine, I scan over the map, trying to figure out where I can find Coach Martin.

Students filter in through the doors, and to avoid the attention of being the shiny new toy for as long as possible, I piss off down the hall, pushing through the back doors and out to the football field.

As I cut across the school, I can't help but glance over the underwhelming field. I've been at the best private schools Arizona has to offer for the past three years. They have state-of-the-art training facilities for their students, but this—a bare field with a shitty goalpost at either end—is what you get when you enroll at a public school.

Telling myself that a shitty field is better than no field at all, I barge through the locker rooms and start my search for the coach's office. Finding it right where I expect it to be, I go to knock on the door when I hear shuffling coming from the storeroom directly beside Coach Martin's office.

Taking another few steps, I find the coach buried deep in

equipment, trying to get everything organized and set up for his team. He turns just as I go to knock, and as my hand falls away, he jumps, not having expected anyone to creep up on him.

"Uh, can I help you?" he grunts, moving past me to dump the equipment in the main part of the locker room, freeing up his hands.

"I'm Noah Ryan," I tell him. "I'm starting at East View today."

Recognition flashes in his eyes. "Noah Ryan, huh?" he grunts. "And what do you want with me?"

I gape at him for a minute. This isn't exactly how I thought this conversation would go. Every other coach I've trained with has almost come in their pants at the mere thought of having me on their team. "I'm hoping to secure a spot on the team, Coach," I say, just in case I mistook his recognition for idiocy.

"I get that," he says. "But I also get that you lit your principal's office on fire barely forty-eight hours ago and were kicked out of St. Michael's before the school year could even commence. You might be a star on the field, and I'm sure talent like yours could take the Mambas to new heights, but I'm not willing to jeopardize the integrity of my team for a lost cause such as yourself."

Fuck.

He steps around me, opens his office door, then turns back to me with a tight smile. "Thanks for coming by. It was good to finally put a face to the name," he says, glancing at his watch. "You best get going. School starts in three minutes."

The fuck just happened?

"Umm . . . respectfully, Coach, but that's bullshit," I say, refusing to take no for an answer, hovering in the doorway of his office. "I'm the best fucking quarterback in the state, and between you and me, we both know your job is riding on your performance this year. You need me just as much as I need you."

SHERIDAN ANNE

"I don't need shit from an overprivileged, no-good kid who has no respect for his sport, his peers, or for his own education. I'm sorry, Noah, but the answer is no," he tells me. "Perhaps East View isn't the right fit for you."

"Please, Coach," I say, not above getting on my fucking knees and begging. "I don't think you understand just how badly I need this. East View is my last chance. If I can't play here, I don't play at all."

He doesn't respond, just stares at me, reading the desperation in my eyes.

"Football is all I have," I continue, letting him see just a hint of the darkness living within me. "If I don't have this . . . I don't know where I'll be. I *need* this."

Coach lets out a heavy sigh, and I see a flicker of indecision in his eyes, giving me just a sliver of hope. "You're a risk, Noah. I can't have you leading my team astray."

"I won't."

"I've heard that shit a million times from kids like you. They start heading down a bad path, get involved with the wrong crowd, start skipping training, showing up to school still fucking drunk from the night before, and there's no coming back. They throw away their future and waste my fucking time when their position on the team could have gone to someone else who truly wanted it, someone who would have put in the work."

"I do want it," I growl, frustration burning in my chest as I step back out of his office and begin to pace the hall. If he denies me and it's all over, what's the point of being here in the first place?

Coach Martin leans against his desk, his feet crossed at his ankles. "Okay, here's what I'm going to do," he says. "You can attend training. You work your ass off and keep your attitude away from my team. You attend every fucking class on your schedule and maintain a B+ average, and if you can do that, if you can earn it, then I will officially offer you a position on my team."

A B+ average during senior year? Fuck. That's gonna take some work, but what choice do I have?

"You got it," I tell him, knowing damn well it's going to be a challenge to keep myself out of trouble. Who knows just how bad it's going to be now that I have to see Zoey wandering the halls day in and day out—a constant reminder of everything I've lost.

"Alright," Coach Martin says. "Training runs from three p.m. 'til six. If you're even a minute late, it's over. Understood?"

"Yes, Coach. Thank you."

"Good. Now get out of here, otherwise you'll be late for homeroom," he says. "I'll make sure you have a uniform here waiting for you this afternoon."

I nod, and with that, I get my ass out of there, ready to face down East View High and make it my bitch.

Chapter 4

ZOEY

Noah Ryan can kiss my ass.

I knew he was troubled. I knew he was spiraling out of control, but the stranger who stood before me in the student office was nothing but a monster with a fractured soul. Those dark eyes I used to adore were cold and lifeless, not even close to the ones I used to know.

Noah always had a mean streak, but he'd go out of his way to reel it in when he was with me. The other kids on the playground were terrified to even look at me wrong because Noah was my protector, but not anymore. The hateful, cruel words that so easily fell from his lips . . . shit. They chilled me to the bone.

I couldn't get out of there fast enough.

I ran as fast as my feet could take me, thankful it was too early for students to be crowding the halls, and the second I could, I barged through the door of the girls' bathroom and threw up every single bite of my breakfast. And since then, I've been hiding out in here, too scared to take a single step outside that door, fearing what I might find.

I sat up all night, my heart racing as I tried to imagine what I was going to find this morning, but never in my wildest dreams did I picture that. I thought maybe he'd give me a sad smile, maybe he'd subtly push me away, or maybe he might have even wrapped me in his arms and told me how much he missed me.

God, I wanted him to do that so badly. I *needed* him to welcome me back into his arms, tell me that everything was going to be okay, and take away all the hurt from the past three years. I needed to breathe him in, needed to feel the warmth of his strong arms holding me to his chest, promising me that he would always be right by my side.

But what I got turned my heart to ash.

Don't even get me started on the stench of cigarettes that wafted off him and made my stomach turn. He always swore to me that he'd never smoke, not after his grandfather died of lung cancer. He hated it and would turn up his nose at people smoking in the street. It made me realize that I can't even pretend to know him anymore.

And yet, every piece of me was calling out to him, desperately needing him to make this right.

I hate how much I wanted him, and I hate that after three long years, he still owns every part of me, but what I hate most of all? Despite the words I threw back at him, he could see right through me as though not a single day had passed. He knew the effect his cruelty was having on me, and all he could do was slam the knife further into my chest and revel in my pain as he twisted it right to the hilt.

So why the hell do I still miss him so much?

He was beautiful. Breathtaking even. I've gone out of my way over the past few years not to look him up, not to delve into his world, but as his popularity grew, it's almost been impossible not to know him from afar. Aunt Maya had told me how tall he'd gotten, how he'd filled out, those once boyish muscles now prominent and toned, but nothing could prepare me for seeing him in the flesh.

He was everything I always thought he'd become . . . physically at least. His dark hair was messy and too long, falling into his eyes, but it was always that way. Noah hated getting it cut; he always said it was a waste of time, but really he just hated how everyone would fawn over him and tell him how handsome he was.

I could see the defined ridges of his muscled pecs beneath his black shirt, and while I've never been that girl to go boy crazy and want what I can't have, I wanted so desperately to reach out and touch him.

I can only imagine how that would have gone down.

This chisel-jawed version of Noah is a complete stranger to me. I don't know him, and honestly, I'm too scared to try. All I know is that there's a little boy buried deep inside of him—a little boy I once loved with all of my heart—screaming to get out.

Noah Ryan is stuck living in a hell he created for himself, pushing away anything that could possibly force him to feel, and for the first time in three years, I find myself questioning if I have it in me to save him.

Letting out a heavy sigh, I hear the rush of students outside the bathroom door and realize it's probably time to pull myself together and get on with it. Tarni, Abby, and Cora should be here any minute, so if I don't go and stop by my locker now, there's a good chance I'll be late for homeroom, and I'm not starting my junior year with detention.

Wiping my eyes, I check my reflection in the mirror, hating how red and puffy my face looks after spending the last twenty minutes bawling like some kind of pathetic loser. On the plus side, I need to make a shrine for my waterproof mascara. It held up beautifully.

Hoping to the Hemsworth gods that I can somehow get out of here unscathed, I raise my chin and push out into the packed halls.

But the moment I settle into the crowd and head toward my locker, I realize just how foolish I was to hope for a miracle like that.

The halls are buzzing with the news of Noah's transfer, and a heavy sense of dread sinks to the pit of my stomach. My gaze shifts through the corridor, constantly on guard, terrified of seeing him walk around the corner and pretending I don't exist.

Reaching my locker unscathed, I let out a breath of relief, and my hands shake as I program my code. 0228. My birthday. It's barely even eight-thirty in the morning, and I feel as though I've lived a whole lifetime in the past half hour.

Diving into the empty locker, I toss in my things before finding my class schedule and double-checking where I need to be for homeroom, unable to escape the constant chatter about the amazing Noah Ryan coming from behind me. Getting what I need for my morning classes, I close my locker just in time to hear my best friend's voice rising over the hum of the crowd. "Well heyyyyy biiiiitch," she hollers, Abby and Cora at her back, gossiping animatedly and barely sparing a second to glance up.

I plaster a smile across my face when Tarni flies into me, and as her arms wrap around me, her momentum pushes us both against my locker. "Where the hell have you been all morning? I've texted you like four hundred times. I was gonna grab you a coffee, but then it was like you fell off the face of the earth, so I didn't bother."

"Ah, shit, sorry," I say with a cringe, slipping my phone out of my pocket to find an array of texts, most of them are from Tarni, but two are from Mom telling me she loves me, and one is from Aunt Maya checking in to make sure I made it through my morning alive. "Thanks anyway. I've been a little caught up this morning. I haven't had a chance to check my phone until now."

Tarni scoffs and settles against the lockers, her gaze shifting over the crowd as Abby and Cora creep in to say hello, hovering in front of us. "What were you doing anyway?" Tarni questions. "And don't even think about telling me you were studying because classes haven't even started yet, and I know that's not true."

A small grin pulls at my lips at her mention of our ongoing punchline where I tell her I'm busy with schoolwork just to get out of attending ridiculous parties. "No, I had to drop by the student office," I tell her, hesitating to tell her about my run-in with Noah. "There umm . . . There was an issue with my class schedule that I needed to get fixed up."

She narrows her gaze on me, and I shift my stare to the students passing, hoping she doesn't try to delve deeper into this. Just like Noah, Tarni has always been able to see right through me, knowing exactly when I'm being untruthful. Or perhaps I'm just a really bad liar.

"So," Abby says, glancing down the hallway. "Have you seen him yet?"

"Seen who?" I ask, my stomach doing flips.

Abby's eyes widen, and I watch as excitement flashes through them, assuming she gets to be the one to break the news about Noah attending East View. "Holy shit! You haven't heard yet?" she gasps. "Noah Ryan is transferring here. It's supposedly his first day, but I don't think anyone has actually seen him yet. I overheard these girls outside saying they doubt he's even coming, and I mean . . . if that's true, my heart is going to break. I've been crushing on him so hard ever since I saw him play against East View two years ago. He's so freaking hot."

Well, shit. That's going to be fun to deal with.

"He's definitely coming. Right, Zo?" Tarni says, stepping in a little closer, and at the confused looks on Abby's and Cora's faces, Tarni goes on. "Don't you remember? Zoey and Noah used to be like . . .

bestest friends. Their moms hang out all the time."

Her use of our old saying *bestest friends* makes it feel dirty, and I do what I can to hide the disdain creeping through my chest.

"Oh shit," Cora says. "I completely forgot about that. You guys used to be like really close, huh?"

"Something like that," I tell them, desperately wishing to change the topic, but something tells me that Noah Ryan is going to be the center of attention until he finally graduates and gets his ass out of here. I'm going to have to get used to it.

"So, then he's definitely coming to East View?" Abby confirms.

I nod. "Yep. At least, that's what his mom told me last night."

"Holy shit," Cora says with a dreamy expression. "You're so freaking lucky. You were talking to his mom! You have a direct line to Noah Ryan. Does that mean his family is always at your place and shit like that? You have to introduce us."

Ugh. I couldn't think of anything worse.

I'm just about to tell them where they can shove their introduction when the hallway erupts with excited gasps and shrieks. A path forms right down the center like the Red Sea parting for East View's newest celebrity.

My stomach twists into knots, and as the girls shuffle forward, trying to get just a glance at the famous Noah Ryan, I find myself shrinking back against my locker, trying to hide behind the crowd. But I sense him there, and I hold my breath, preparing for another blow.

This is too much. I can't live my life terrified of seeing his face.

It hurts too much.

My breath comes in hard pants, anxiety gripping my throat and squeezing as my gaze follows the movement of the crowd. Eager bystanders try to peer around one another, but I remain braced against my locker. The bell for homeroom sounds through the halls, yet no one seems to make a move.

My hands start to shake and then finally, there's a break in the crowd and I see him.

Noah Ryan. *My* Noah Ryan.

It's still so surreal seeing him after all this time, and even after seeing him in the student office this morning, my world is rocked again. I catch my breath, my whole body burning from the inside out as I *feel* him, that invisible string between us pulsing with the fiercest electricity. We've always been tethered together, and no amount of distance is ever going to change that.

He doesn't look at me, but I know he *feels* me here. How could he not? How could he possibly deny something so raw and pure? I know he might hate me right now. He might be desperate to push me away and watch his world burn to ashes around him, but there's no doubt in my mind that he still loves me. He will always love me, and no matter how hard he tries, he will never be able to escape it.

Our souls formed an impenetrable bond the day we first met, and since then, it's only gotten stronger. The more he tries to deny it, the more he hurts us both. But something tells me it's that pain he craves. Right now, feeling the pain is the only thing keeping him breathing.

Come on, Noah. Look at me, just once. Let your eyes light up like they used to. Show me you still care.

He goes to stride past us when Tarni does the unthinkable and pushes herself right out in front of him, stepping directly in his path and trying to stop him with a hand against his chest.

I suck in a breath, my heart thundering with a weird sense of betrayal and hurt, not understanding how she could possibly think this is a good idea. Hasn't she been listening to me over the past three years? She knows how much this distance has killed me. I thought she cared.

"Hey, Noah," she purrs, batting her lashes at him as he steps around her, not missing a single stride. Hell, not even bothering to spare her a glance. She's forced to quickly back up, trying not to fall over her feet. "I don't know if you remember me. I'm Tarni. You, me, and Zoey used to be like *bestest friends*—"

His ferocious gaze snaps to mine, the intensity pinning me to my locker as though an invisible hand had physically shoved me back. My breath catches in my throat, my eyes locked on his, held captive as he unknowingly pulls on that tether between us, daring me to make a move.

The moment lasts barely a second, yet it feels like it could have been a lifetime before he finally releases my stare and shrugs off Tarni's touch, not allowing her the chance to finish her sentence. Noah keeps walking, his herd of loyal fans following his every step as Tarni is left behind gaping at him with hearts in her eyes.

Once the crowd starts fanning out, and students scurry to get to homeroom, I stare at Tarni in the middle of the corridor, watching as her gaze slowly shifts back to mine. "Holy shit," she beams as Abby and Cora take off. "Did you see that? Noah Ryan touched my hand."

"He didn't touch your hand," I mutter, that thick betrayal slicing through my chest. "Your hand touched him."

"Same thing," she says before letting out a heavy breath and falling back into me. "Oh my god, is it going to be weird if I fall madly in love with him? You're over that, right? Because dammmmmn. Noah Ryan just became my latest project."

Just great. That's exactly what I need—my best friend crushing on the other half of my soul.

What could possibly go wrong?

I guess I was wrong about Tarni understanding how much I yearn for things between me and Noah to be good again, to go back to how they used to be. She's too busy crushing on him to notice anything else. If she's looking for my permission to pursue him, she won't find it here.

Chapter 5

ZOEY

I hate him. I hate him. I hate him.

Crap, *I love him so much.*

Today has sucked. Every corner I've walked around has been done with shaky hands. The only time I felt safe was during class when I knew I wouldn't see him, but even then, I sat in fear. What if he walked past my classroom? What if I were sent somewhere and passed him? What if we were to do a fire drill and we were all crammed into the hall together? I can't handle the unknown. This is not how I pictured my junior year.

It's just after one in the afternoon, and the school is still buzzing with the news of Noah walking our halls. It's as though they're starstruck, unable to wrap their tiny minds around the fact that they're in the same room as the one and only football legend. I mean, I know he's good, but is he really *that* good? I don't particularly care for football. At least, I used to back when . . . you know. But ever since then, I stopped following it.

I used to go to all of his games and was always the loudest one cheering in the grandstand full of admirers, but I haven't seen him play in three years. He was always amazing, and I'm sure he's only gotten better, especially considering the hype around his name.

My heart races as I approach the cafeteria doors for lunch. I don't want to be here. I should have just grabbed my car keys out of my locker and taken off for lunch. It would have made this so much easier. All morning, my only saving grace has been the knowledge that I could easily avoid him, but here in this cafeteria where the whole football team usually eats, there's no avoiding him now. Especially considering Tarni's newfound love for Noah Ryan, there's no way in hell the girls are going to agree to eat outside. The whole school is going to be crammed into the cafeteria.

Striding through the open double doors, I keep my head down, but as the hairs on the back of my neck stand on edge, I know without a doubt that he's here.

I hear the rowdiness of the football team almost immediately, and even though he hasn't even made it to his first practice, I'm sure that Noah has already found his people. They would have sniffed him out the second he walked through the door, acting as though he's their savior here to give them the best shot for the season.

My gaze remains locked on the scuffed linoleum, and the further I get across the cafeteria, the harder it becomes to resist glancing up.

Don't do it, Zoey. You're not going to see his smile. You're not going to see the old light in his dark eyes. You're setting yourself up for more heartbreak. Don't do it.

I'm right. I don't want to look. I don't want to see what I'm missing or how he so effortlessly falls in line with the other football pigs of East View. I can't watch him welcome these strangers into his life when he couldn't even pretend to do the same for me.

The very thought has a fierce jealousy cutting through my chest, but the second I come to terms with it and refuse to allow it to affect me, a new resolve pounds through my chest. I raise my head, not allowing Noah Ryan to ruin the rest of my day, but the second I do, the second I let my guard down, weakness plagues me, and I snap my stare across the cafeteria.

I look.

My gaze locks on to Noah immediately, almost as though there was a big red arrow in flashing lights pointing him out, or maybe it's the stupid tether leading me right to him. Either way, what I see has me stumbling over my own feet, my chest aching.

Shannan Holter, the captain of the cheerleading team, sits on his lap with her legs squished between his as his hand rests dangerously high on her thigh. She looks as though she's on cloud nine, like there was only one dessert put out for lunch and she was the lucky one who snatched it up first. How though? It's only lunchtime on his first day. How the hell has she snatched him up already? The Noah I know would never have let some skank cheerleader make a claim on him.

God, that hurts. I was prepared to see him with his friends, prepared to see him play again, but I sure as hell wasn't prepared to see him welcome someone else into his life.

An ugliness pulses through my veins, poisoning me from the inside out, and I quickly realize it's jealousy. I was thirteen when he walked away, and while we were definitely flirtatious with each other, it was never inherently sexual. We were too young, only just starting to see each other in a new light. He pulled me down onto his lap a million times before, but it never looked like *that*.

Damn it. Why did I have to look?

"ZO!" I hear my name hollered across the cafeteria.

My head snaps to the left, finding Tarni standing up on a bench, waving her hands to get my attention as Abby and Cora laugh, trying to pull her down. I hastily make my way toward them, unable to keep from glancing back at Noah, only now those piercing eyes are locked on mine.

My heart lurches in my chest, and I pause for just a moment, paralyzed under the weight of his intense stare. But finding myself and remembering that I've survived much worse than anyone in this stupid school could ever imagine, I fix a scowl across my face and roll my eyes before looking away.

Noah Ryan will not see me break. I am stronger than that, stronger than what he could ever put me through.

Making my way over to the girls, I drop my lunch on the table as I take my seat beside Tarni and push my food away, suddenly not so hungry. "What's up with you?" Cora questions. "You look like someone just pissed in your Cheerios."

"Nothing," I mutter, refusing to meet her eyes, hating how easily everyone seems to be able to read me. "I'm fine."

"Oh really?" Tarni grunts, not believing me for even a second. "You've been a moody bitch all day, and my spidey senses are telling me it has everything to do with the man meat across the cafeteria. But honestly, Zo, what gives? You guys hung out like three years ago. And don't get me wrong, I'm only saying this because I love you, but don't you think you're being a little . . . much?"

I let out a breath, wanting nothing more than to take off and pretend today never happened. Tarni just doesn't get it. She never has. "I don't know what you're talking about. I couldn't care less about him."

Abby rolls her eyes. "I'm sorry girl, but I'm not buying it," she says. "It's written all over you. Clearly he means something to you, but I just don't get it. Are you upset because he hasn't tried to say hello?

Because I've got news for you. He's a dude, a very popular dude. He was declared the king of the school before the semester even started. He's not about to come find you when he has the whole world at his feet. If you wanna talk to him, then go say hi. Otherwise, maybe it's time to admit that whatever friendship you had ended years ago and move on."

My hands ball into fists under the table, and I stare at Abby, biting my tongue harder than I've ever bitten it before. I've been friends with her since I started at East View as a misguided, broken freshman, barely two months after Noah walked away from me. Not once during that time have I ever spoken to her about my relationship with Noah. I've specifically gone out of my way not to talk about it because of how much it hurts, and it's just a stark reminder of how far away I've kept these girls. No one in this school really knows me. Apart from Tarni, they don't know the struggles I went through at six years old, the wars I've already battled. All they know is the broken girl they met at thirteen years old, never really understanding the depth of my despair.

Abby shrinks away from my stare, and it's clear her opinion is based solely on what Tarni has told her. Neither of them really understands how much their casual dismissal kills me.

"I agree," Tarni says, her gaze locked on Noah and Shannan. "It's time to move on because this boring, moody Zoey is killing my vibe. You and Noah were only friends anyway. You were little kids. It's not like you were madly in love and on the verge of marriage and babies. Sometimes friends come and go, and that's alright. Doesn't mean we need to get hung up on it. Besides, you have us now, and having three besties will always be better than one gorgeous piece of man meat."

I try to see it from her perspective and force a smile, but the piercing stare from across the room makes focusing on anything else almost impossible. I hate that he can still pull the tether between us without even meeting my eyes.

What's Tarni's problem, anyway? She's always hated when I spoke of Noah in the past. She has gone to great lengths to change the topic, and for a while, I thought maybe she was jealous of the overwhelming, once-in-a-lifetime bond I shared with him, but now I'm wondering if I was wrong. Maybe it wasn't my friendship with him she was threatened by, but more his friendship with me. Was she jealous all these years that he looked at me like an angel descending the heavens while looking at her like the trash I accidentally stepped in? Ever since we became friends at six, he's hated her.

"You're right. I'm being silly," I tell her, but the words feel like venom on my tongue. I don't want this to force a wedge between us because, despite her delivery, she's right. It's time to put it all behind me and try to enjoy junior year. "Noah Ryan is in the past."

"Oh no, no, no, girl," Tarni laughs. "He's far from in the past. I mean, look at him. Someone who looks like that cannot be in the past. I'm sorry to break the news, Zo, but you're gonna have to get used to seeing him around because I wasn't kidding this morning. I need to get closer to him. I've been obsessing all morning! I have to sink my claws into that."

Is she kidding me?

I gape at her, a fierce anger trying to break through the surface as I wave toward the embarrassment across the room. "Don't know if you've noticed," I mutter, trying to keep the bite out of my tone, "but your little boy toy has already been spoken for."

Tarni scoffs. "Who? Shannan Holter? Once he fucks her—and I'm assuming that'll be by the end of lunch—he'll be done with her, leaving all the room for me to swoop in and take what's mine."

Cora laughs. "Yeah, right. She's the captain of the cheer team, and there's no doubt that he'll be announced captain and quarterback of the football team. It's like they're fated to end up together. She's not going to let him slip away now. Consider it a done deal. Noah and Shannan are gonna be East View's newest *it* couple."

God, I hate how right she is. I've never had anything to do with Shannan, and I don't really know her on a personal level, but I've watched from afar, and when she wants something, she gets it. And it's clear from the way she's draping herself all over Noah that she wants him more than anything.

Tarni sighs, realizing Cora is right too, and as she watches them, she narrows her gaze. "What do you think Shannan has that I don't?" Tarni murmurs, playing with her lunch rather than eating it. "Do you think it's the whole cheerleader thing? I could cheer too. They're having tryouts this week."

"Oh God," I laugh. "I'd love to see that. A baby deer stuck on ice is more coordinated than you."

"Shut up," she mutters, rolling her eyes, her lips pulling into a smirk before turning on Abby. "Whatever happened to that guy you were seeing over the summer?"

Abby drops her gaze immediately, her cheeks flushing bright red. "Nothing," she says with a scoff, hurt shining in her eyes. "School started, and he decided he needs to keep up appearances and couldn't possibly be seen with a loser like me."

"What?" I breathe. "No, you're lying. Tell me he didn't really say that?"

"I wish I could," she says, her heart on her sleeve as Cora grips her hand and gives it a gentle squeeze. "He was more than happy to sneak through my bedroom window in the middle of the night and tell me how much he liked me, but the thought of being seen in public with me—no chance in hell."

"I swear," Tarni mutters, her gaze shifting around the cafeteria, trying to figure out the culprit. "Just give me a name, and I'll bust his ass open right now."

Abby shakes her head. "You know I can't," she breathes. "If he knew I was telling people, he'd make my life a living hell. Despite how I feel about him, he's an ass, and he really doesn't care about me enough not to make me the laughingstock of the whole school."

"So you're just gonna go ahead and let him use you for sex instead?" Cora grunts. "Like some kind of cheap ho. Good enough to blow his load all over, but not good enough to see the woman inside? Come on, Abby. You're better than that, and you can't let him get away with it. Name and shame, girl. Name and shame."

Abby cringes and shakes her head, but Tarni knows how to get exactly what she wants, always has. "Okay, don't tell us his name. Just . . . point."

Abby rolls her eyes, and a stupid smirk pulls across her lips as she tilts her head in the direction of the rowdy football players across the room. "He's over there," she says, making a point not to look that way.

We all look up, and I do what I can not to glance directly at Noah, but I simply don't have the self-control. He's preoccupied talking shit with the people around him and thankfully doesn't look up. Though I know he senses my stare just as I sense his.

My gaze shifts over the other players, trying to figure out which one of these assholes could be cruel enough to have pushed Abby aside like that, but the truth is, they all could. Not a single guy on the football team is a decent person. They're all cold and cruel, the perfect fit for Noah.

"Umm . . . is it Lucas Maxwell?" Tarni questions.

Abby shakes her head, her eyes hardening, realizing Tarni is more than prepared to make her way through the whole list until she figures it out. "Uh, gross," she says. "I have better taste than that."

"No, you don't," Cora says, slinging her arm over the back of her seat, her gaze narrowed as she studies her best friend. "It's Liam Xander, isn't it? You've always had a thing for him."

Abby's eyes widen, and realizing how obvious she is, she scrunches her face in regret, not yet ready to face the music as every single eye at the table flicks toward the asshole in question. Liam was supposed to be the star of the school, supposed to be the captain and the quarterback for this season, and Abby is right—he is an ass. But now with Noah here, it'll be interesting to see how that plays out. They're either going to despise each other and cause havoc around the school, or they'll be tight, which could only mean even more bad news for Noah.

Liam Xander isn't just an ass. He's trouble—and not the good kind. If Noah gets involved with him, I hope God has mercy on every single one of our souls.

"Are you shitting me?" Tarni says, wide-eyed, her gaze flicking between Abby and Liam and taking in the way he stands behind one of the cheerleaders, his hands braced on her shoulders as he whispers something in her ear—something filthy enough to make her face flush brighter than the sun. "That's huge! You slept with Liam? Holy shit. You have to tell me all about it."

Abby's cheeks flush, and when a wide grin stretches across her face, I realize the rest of my lunch break is going to be all about Liam Xander's dick. The girls start talking animatedly between themselves, and when Abby recaps their third night together, I zone out.

My gaze lifts back to Noah's table to find him carelessly shoving Shannan off his lap before getting to his feet, and I watch with dread as the one and only Liam Xander gets up with him. They say something I can't even try to hear over the noise of the cafeteria, and with that, the two of them cut through the many tables toward the back exit that leads behind the school, a pack of cigarettes in Noah's hand.

I watch his every step, and just as Liam pushes out the back door and holds it open for Noah, he glances back, that sharp stare locking on mine and knocking the breath right out of my lungs.

The door slams shut behind him, and I find myself heaving to catch my breath. Needing to distract myself, I grab my phone and swipe away my notifications when I remember Aunt Maya's text from this morning.

Opening the text, my gaze shifts over her words, and despite them holding no weight or being particularly meaningful, they still hurt all the same.

Aunt Maya: Hey my little warrior, wishing you all the best for your first day back at school. I know today is going to be hard for you, but stick it out. He'll come around eventually. Hopefully he's not too hard on you. If anyone can help shine a little bit of light on his hurting soul, it's you, Zozo.

Seeing that old nickname of Noah's has tears welling in my eyes, and I fight them back, refusing to let a single tear fall for Noah Ryan, though something tells me this is only the beginning. Not wanting to leave her hanging, I hash out a response and stare at it all too long before finally hitting send.

Zoey: I'm sorry. I really tried, but you were right. Noah isn't the same boy I once knew.
Aunt Maya: That's what I was afraid of.

And with that, I pick up my apple and force myself to take a bite, realizing if I'm about to suffer through an emotional war with Noah Ryan, then I'm going to need all the strength I can get.

Chapter 6

NOAH

The cigarette hits my lips, and I take a deep drag, closing my eyes as the nicotine pulses through my body, easing the fire burning in my chest and making it that much easier to breathe. Fucking ironic. The one thing that's going to kill me is the only thing keeping me grounded. I didn't choose the smoking life, the smoking life chose me, and despite my mother's endless objections, I'm not going to stop. I can't.

"So, we gonna get this over and done with or what?" I ask Liam, my gaze sailing over him, waiting to see how this is going to play out. He didn't bring me out here because he wanted to fuck me behind the school.

He takes a drag of his cigarette before blowing a cloud of smoke toward my face, and I wait patiently, knowing exactly what's coming. Same shit, different scenery. There's always someone who thinks I'm there just to spite them, just to take away their glory. "What are you doing here, man? This is *my* school. *My* team."

"I don't give a shit about your fucking school or your goddamn team. I'm here to play football and keep my ass out of lockup. That's it."

"I ain't buying it. You've been here less than a day and already have the whole fucking school eating out of the palm of your hand. I'm the captain this season. I'm the quarterback, and there's a fucking hierarchy. I climbed my way to the top. I earned it, and you're not about to take it from me."

My brow arches as I take another drag, watching as this fool gets himself worked up, thinking he can even stand a chance against me. "I don't give a shit about being captain. I told you, I'm just here to play. I don't need to be captain to get where I need to go."

"You're a quarterback," he states as if I hadn't worked that out.

I let him see the darkness swirling in my gaze. "And?" I question, arching a brow in challenge. "I'm gonna keep being a quarterback."

"Like fuck you will," he spits. "This is *my* team. *I* set the standard."

I laugh. "You might have set the standard when you thought you were the best player on the team," I tell him. "But there's a new standard now, a much higher standard, and if you can't keep up, then you're gonna spend a shitload of time keeping the bench warm. Trust me, this is my fifth school in three years. I've seen it over and over again. I'm too fucking good. Not even my record can deter the coach from playing me. So, go ahead and fight for it, make a fucking fool of yourself, but you and I both know what Coach Martin is going to say. *You* might be able to throw a fucking ball, but *I* win championships."

Liam clenches his jaw and steps into me, his gaze locked on mine. "I'm not backing down from this."

"Come on, man. What are you trying to do here? You wanna knock me out? Throw a few punches to save your fucking ego?" I ask. "The second I enrolled at East View, your reign was over. You never stood a chance, so instead of trying to destroy what little scraps I might offer you, stand up and take it like a fucking man. You'll still be captain and get all the fucking pussy you want. You're not losing here."

He holds my stare when a loud bang reverbs through the school, and my gaze cuts across to the back door of the cafeteria, the same one we'd walked through only a minute ago. Two of the cheerleaders appear and linger at the door, touching up their makeup and talking, when the one who'd been on my lap glances up. Her eyes go wide seeing us over here, and a seductive grin stretches across her face.

They start walking our way, and I let out a sigh, not remembering her name, despite only learning it a few short hours ago. Not that I care. I don't really want a damn thing to do with her. "You wanna make this right," Liam murmurs beside me, keeping his tone down so the cheerleaders don't overhear. "Then give up Shannan. She's mine."

Ah, Shannan. That's her name.

I laugh. "If you can take her, she's all yours," I tell him, having been around enough of these over-the-top cheerleaders to know when one of them thinks they're going to be the light of my life. Shannan is no different. She wants to ride my success right to the fucking top. It's not going to happen, but if she wants to offer herself up for me, I'm not going to say no. As long as she's aware I won't be going back for seconds.

Liam mutters something under his breath just as the cheerleaders reach us, and I get one more drag before Shannan plasters herself against my chest. Disgust fills me, and I inch back only to have her step with me, not daring to put even a millimeter of space between us, her perfume stinging my nose. "I was wondering where you got to," she says, lifting her chin and hovering her face way too close to mine, waiting for me to kiss her.

I shove her off me, putting well-needed space between us as her desperation threatens to give me hives, but she doesn't get the hint and puts her hand back on my chest, trying to be seductive as she draws little circles over the top of my shirt. "So, I was hoping you'd wanna ditch with me," she murmurs as her friend steps into her side, the two of them looking at me with secretive stares. They look between themselves before Shannan meets my stare again. "Or perhaps you'd prefer to ditch with *us*."

My brow arches as I look down at the girls, and it's fucking tempting.

Liam scoffs, a smug grin stretching across his face as he steps in closer. "Is this a private party or are you looking to even the playing field?"

Well, shit. I wasn't expecting my day to go like this, but there's nothing more important than bonding with a new teammate, especially when said teammate wants to kick my ass for even thinking about taking his position. Though I'm not going to lie, I don't usually like to share.

The girls seem keen on the idea, but they look up at me for approval, and just as I go to respond, Zoey pops into my head, rendering me speechless. "I, uh," I clench my jaw, the idea of bending these two girls over suddenly not so appealing. "Not today."

"Oh," Shannan says, disappointment flooding her eyes, but I honestly couldn't give a shit. If she wants to fuck, she can screw Liam in the teachers' lounge. Something tells me she's no stranger to whoring herself out to East View's most promising athletes.

Taking a dismissive step away, I lift the cigarette to my lips and take another deep drag, not understanding why Zoey is having such an effect on me today. All fucking day, she's all I've been able to think about. The way she looked at me in the student office and the venom in her tone when she spat those lies at me. Surely she knows I wasn't buying her bullshit. Nonetheless, her need to hate me scorched me from the inside out, but when she saw Shannan on my lap, she was jealous. She was so fucking obvious it was almost comical, but what's more, the pain in her eyes made it possible to breathe. It was the sickest form of punishment, exactly what I'd been craving for three long years.

Raising my chin, I blow a cloud of smoke above the girls' heads because, unlike Liam, I'm not always an asshole. "Ah, fuck," Liam mutters beside me, nodding back toward the school.

I glance up to find a man in a suit and let out a heavy sigh. I have no idea who this is, but I've come to learn that the douchebags in the suits are usually the ones who hold the power. "Who the fuck is that?"

"Principal Daniels," Shannan murmurs, fear in her tone. "Not someone you want to be on the bad side of."

Well, shit. Just what I need.

Fury lingers in his stare as he strides toward us, and knowing damn well he's about to demand I put my cigarette out, I quickly take the last drag. He steps right up to us, and I watch the pathetic way the two girls and Liam cower in his presence. "Girls," Principal Daniels says before flicking his chin, silently telling them to fuck off.

Relief flashes in their eyes, and without skipping a beat, they hurry away, leaving me and Liam to face his wrath. "You must be Noah Ryan," he says, sizing me up.

"The one and only," I say as Liam discreetly tries to put out his cigarette as if the guy can't smell the stench lingering in the air around us.

He studiously glances at my cigarette, demanding I follow suit and put it out, then being all too aware of what's at risk, I do just that, dropping it to the ground and stubbing it with my toe. "You missed your appointment with me this morning," he says in an accusatory tone.

Ah, shit. I knew I was forgetting something.

"Sorry, Bossman," I say. "I wasn't aware I had an appointment. I was told to head to the student office, grab my shit, and get ready for the day. I did that."

Daniels presses his lips into a hard line. He knows I'm lying. I know I'm lying. But the question is, what's he going to do about it?

"Yes, Dorris has told me all about your meeting in the student office," he says, narrowing his gaze before fixing a heavy stare on Liam. "What the hell are you still doing here? The bell rang for class ten minutes ago. Get out of here."

Liam spares me a glance before looking back at Daniels. "Yes, sir," he says, going to take off before pausing. "Would you mind writing me up a hall pass? I've got Mrs. Teckler now, and she's a bitch for handing out detentions."

"I think a detention sounds appropriate, don't you think, Mr. Xander?"

Liam glances down and presses his lips into a tight line before letting out a heavy, defeated sigh. "Yes, sir." And with that, he takes off, hands shoved deep in his pockets, and not a single fucking thought for the guy whose threesome he just tried to invade.

I'm left with Principal Daniels, and I prepare myself for the worst. Day one, caught smoking just off the boundary of the school. I'm sure that's going to do wonders for my position here.

"Let's cut the bullshit," Daniels says. "I know why you're here. I've spoken to the Principal at St. Michael's and am aware of just how much trouble you've gotten yourself into. You're not the kind of student I wish to have inside the halls of my school. However, your mother insisted that I give you one last chance. She insisted that under all of the bullshit, you're just a confused, lost soul. And if it weren't for the pure devastation and desperation she expressed during our phone call,

I probably would have declined. You're trouble, Noah. You're a danger to my school and my students, so let me make this very clear. One fuck up, one small step in the wrong direction, and I will personally ensure that you don't see another football field in your life. Do you hear me?"

I swallow hard and nod. This isn't exactly the first time I've been given a speech like this, but it's the first time I think the guy giving it has the balls to actually follow through. "Yes, sir," I mutter, the heaviness of my situation weighing me down.

"Now, your mother told me a little about your situation, and—"

"Excuse me?" The hairs stand on the back of my neck, not liking the direction this is heading.

Daniels presses his lips into a hard line, clearly not appreciating the interruption of what I'm assuming is a speech he's rehearsed at least ten times before coming to me. "You're an angry kid, Noah. You've had it rough. I understand your brother, Lincoln, died in an accident three years ago, and I would like to offer my sincerest condolences. However, I have been made aware that you have spiraled out of control since then. You have pushed away the people who care for you and fallen in with the wrong crowds, and while I appreciate how hard that must have been, I am not going to allow this reckless behavior to continue in my school."

I clench my jaw, not liking this one fucking bit.

"I have spoken to your mother at length in regard to your enrollment here at East View, and if you wish to attend this fine school and graduate at the end of senior year, then there are some stipulations that you will be required to follow."

Shit.

He gives me a hard stare. "First and foremost, the safety and wellbeing of my students is the primary goal here. As I mentioned, I spoke with your mother at length and am aware of your relationship with Zoey James. And following the reports I received from my office staff this morning, I am quite concerned. She is a promising student who has been through a hell of her own, and whether you have a history or not, I will not tolerate the kind of abuse you spouted at her this morning. Her or any other student for that matter. Is that understood?"

My hands ball into fists at my side, the rage almost hitting boiling point. What the fuck is this guy's problem, thinking he can come at me about Zoey? I'll deal with her the way I see fit. Our relationship, or how I handle it, is none of his damn business. The only thing that pulls me up is his comment about her going through a *hell of her own*, and it fucking grinds on my nerves that I don't know what the fuck he's referring to. Has something happened to her over the past three years that I don't know about?

"Got it," I tell him, hoping like fuck that's the end of his bullshit, but apparently, he's only just getting started.

"I get that you need to focus your anger on someone. You need an outlet, but I will not tolerate that anger creeping up on the football field and putting my students at risk. Violence is not the answer. So if you need to be angry, be angry at me. I will take the brunt of it if it means my students will continue having the safety and comfort this school offers in order to nurture their education."

"I'm not a violent person," I spit through a clenched jaw. "I'm not going to hurt anyone."

"Only yourself, right?" Daniels arches a brow and lets out a heavy sigh. "The fire in your principal's office and the clenched fists at your side say otherwise. And until you can prove that I do not need to fear for my students' wellbeing, then I will treat you as a threat."

I nod, the logical side of me telling me this is fair, but that doesn't mean I have to like it. "You don't need to worry about me. I'll be the perfect student. Coach Martin has already laid down the terms of me being on the team, and I'm not looking to fuck that up."

"And yet, you're out here smoking during school hours," he mutters. "You're off to a flying start."

"Would you have preferred I did it on school grounds, in front of the other students? I didn't see a designated smoking area in the cafeteria."

"There will be no smoking on or around school grounds during school hours. Period. What you do following the school day is your business."

"Understood," I murmur. "Are we done?"

"Not quite," he says. "I mentioned stipulations to your enrollment and so far, I've only covered one."

Fuck me. What else could this bastard possibly throw at me that Coach Martin hasn't already done?

He fixes me with a hard stare, and my hands grow clammy, knowing like fuck I'm not going to like whatever bullshit is about to fly out of his mouth. "On top of maintaining a hundred percent attendance record and the B+ average Coach Martin requires, you will be required to see the school counselor on a biweekly basis."

My eyes widen in horror, my heart leaping right out of my fucking chest. "Fuck no."

"Alright then," Principal Daniels says. "Then good luck finding somewhere else to play. You can clear out your locker and return your combination lock to the student office."

With that, he gives me a tight smile before turning on his heel and striding back to the school, and as I watch him go, the panic sets in. I can't fucking sit in a little room and be forced to talk about my brother or Zoey. I won't. I can't fucking do it. But without this school, without this team, I've got nothing.

My whole body starts to shake, and my stomach twists into knots, watching as my future slips further away, step by fucking step. What choice do I have? Without this, I'm going to spiral out of control. I'm going to end up hurting someone, and not just the surface-level bullshit I've been dishing out, but the real, life-changing kind of shit that will live with me for the rest of my life.

I don't want to be this fucking person anymore. I don't like hearing my mother cry at night, and I sure as fuck don't like hurting Zoey and pushing her away. That pain is the only thing I've felt in three years, but if I force myself to feel anything else or to deal with the real issues at hand, it will fucking drown me.

"Fine," I call to Daniels' back, not ready to give up on myself just yet. "I'll see the fucking counselor."

Daniels stops and turns back, his gaze lingering on mine a second too long. "That's what I thought," he says, pressing his lips into a tight line. "Welcome to East View High, Noah Ryan. Let's hope you're a great addition to this fine school."

And with that, he walks away.

Chapter 7

NOAH

Making my way to the football field, I let out a heavy breath, dreading what this afternoon's training session will bring. Day one sucked, but in the grand scheme of things, it could have been worse. It's not over though.

Coach Martin made it no secret that he's no fan of mine. Sure, he might be impressed on the field, but that doesn't mean he wants me on his team. I'm going to have to earn my position. I've burned one too many bridges to expect this to be handed to me like it was in the past.

Liam walks beside me, and I have to resist rolling my eyes at the guy. Ever since those cheerleaders offered to show us a good time, he's clearly decided that sticking with me will be worth the trouble. Suddenly, he doesn't give a shit that I'm here to take his position on the team. He knows damn well he can't beat me, and just like every other position I've stolen over the past few years, they quickly learn it's best just to step aside.

He talks shit about the guys on the team, trying to give me a rundown of the players and what I need to be looking out for, only I don't hear a single fucking word. I have no interest in his opinions. I'll make my own based on their actual skills on the field. After all, Liam's opinions are biased, based on experiences he's had with the players since his freshman year, and considering the kind of guy he is, I can only assume not all of those experiences are positive.

Glancing up at the field, I look over the few players who are already warming up while Coach Martin empties a bag of footballs onto the grass and double-checks the equipment.

It's not as though they're doing much right now, but from what I can tell, they're alright. Not the best, but enough to possibly capture the championship with the right motivation.

A few of the guys are chatting among themselves as they stretch, and I can't help but notice the way they keep glancing my way. Most of them have been hanging out with me today, trying to figure me out, but apart from games, not one of them knows what it's like to train with me. Even Coach Martin is throwing me curious glances.

Liam continues talking shit, probably thinking he's about to be my whole fucking world, when we finally reach the football field. Coach Martin meets my stare and lifts his chin. "Get warmed up," he calls across the field. "I want to see exactly what you've got."

Ah, shit. I should have known training wasn't going to be easy today. Coach Martin is about to push me to my limits, and I can guarantee I won't be walking away from this training session. It'll be more like a hobble.

Liam and I sprint to catch up with the rest of the guys, and as we reach them, they fall in next to us, jogging down the length of the field. We reach the goalposts before making our way back, and as I run, I glance up at the school.

It's nearly deserted. Most of the students ran out the moment the bell sounded for the end of class. There are only a few stragglers dragging their feet, probably on their way to their first after-school detention for the year.

Just as my gaze shifts back to the field, something catches my eye across the school. My brows furrow, finding Zoey fucking James slipping out of the library, her arms filled with books. She makes her way toward the student parking lot, her stare unnaturally focused in front of her, making it damn clear she's doing everything she can not to look down here.

Fuck, she's gorgeous.

All day she's circled my head, and while it's clear that she's still the same girl I once adored, she's changed. For the past three years, I've thought of her as that thirteen-year-old girl, but she's a young woman now, and goddamn, it suits her. She's even got the feisty attitude to go along with it. She's always had a backbone, but there was an innocence about it—not anymore. She's grown into her own and isn't afraid to call out bullshit when she sees it. Though, that's not going to work for me.

I watch her for a moment, every passing second winding me up further. I came here thinking I could read her perfectly, just as I always could. Only the comment Principal Daniels made after lunch has sat with me all afternoon.

She is a promising student who has been through a hell of her own.

What the fuck is that supposed to mean? I've known her since the day she was born. I know everything there is to know about her. I've watched her grow, been there for every bad day she ever had, kissed her knees when she scraped them up, and took the blame every time she was about to get in trouble. If something had happened to her, I would know. Hell, even if something went down over the past three years, my mother would have told me. She goes out of her way to inform me of every single thing Zoey does in the hopes I might have enough interest to bring her back into my life.

Clenching my jaw, I try to keep my curiosity at bay, only the words tumble out before I can stop them. "Yo," I say to Liam, catching his attention before nodding toward Zoey. "What do you know about her?"

Liam scoffs. "Who? Zoey?" he asks, amusement in his tone. "Don't waste your fucking time. She's hot and all, but you can get easier pussy. She's a frigid bitch. From what I hear, Cameron Landry was trying to pop that cherry all summer long and struck out every fucking time. It's become a challenge between the boys. Everyone wants to fuck her just to say they did, but it'll never happen. That bitch will die a virgin."

Burning rage soars through my chest, infecting me from the inside out as I try with everything I have not to react to his bullshit. My hands ball into fists at my sides, and I try to remember what's at stake here, try to remember Principal Daniels' insinuation that I could be a violent person. I'm not, nor do I want to be, so why the fuck do I want to find this Cameron Landry asshole and tear his head clean off his body? I definitely shouldn't want to throttle Liam just for talking about her like that.

Are they blind? Don't they see how fucking precious she is?

Shit. I can't be thinking like this. She's not mine, not anymore.

I try to shake the vision of Zoey belonging with anyone but me from my mind. "I didn't ask if the girl was sucking every cock in school," I spit, unable to take my eyes off her, while secretly pleased that she seems to be one of the only girls in this school with even a shred of respect for herself. "I asked what you know about her."

His face scrunches. "Does it really matter?" he grunts as we hit the top of the field and circle back around. "She's a nobody."

"Just answer the fucking question."

"I don't know what to tell you, man. She's quiet as fuck. She's not someone I pay attention to," he murmurs, shrugging his shoulders. "Keeps to herself. Goes to the occasional party, but never looks like she actually wants to be there, and as far as I know, she's hung out with the same bunch of friends since freshman year. Though I don't get it, she's nothing like the girls she hangs out with. They're all dying to spread their legs, but she's . . . I don't know. She doesn't seem interested. Maybe she's got the taste for pussy."

Fuck, I hate this asshole. It's going to be a pleasure stealing his crown.

Either way, he hasn't told me anything I didn't already know.

Coach Martin calls us all in, and we take off toward him before creating a circle around him, listening as he gives the rundown of today's session. Only I don't hear a fucking word as I watch Zoey climb into her mom's old Range Rover and start the engine.

She backs out of her spot, and a strange pang of guilt rests deep in my gut. I was supposed to be the one to teach her how to drive.

A heaviness settles into my chest as she drives away, and I try to focus on Coach Martin's rundown, catching the tail end of his explanation. He excuses everyone to get started on the drill when he calls for me. "Ryan."

Shit.

I stop and turn back just as the ball in his hands flies toward my chest. I catch it with ease, waiting to hear what he wants. "I've reviewed your more recent games. You're a great player, Noah. However, those games don't tell me shit about your limits. I want to see all you've got."

"Yes, Coach," I say, having expected as much.

"Good. Now get to it," he tells me. "Grab Lucas Maxwell and run drills. He's your wide receiver."

I nod, and he doesn't spare me another glance before focusing on the rest of the team. With that, I find Maxwell and get stuck into it, more than aware of Liam's vindictive stare the whole time, probably hoping like fuck I screw this up.

Chapter 8

ZOEY

Trudging up the stairs to my room, I dump all my crap on my bed, then stare down at the array of books. All this shit here is homework. Already. On day one. How the hell am I supposed to keep up with this? Though something tells me it's only going to get worse from here.

Moving through my room, I step into my closet, reach up to the top shelf, and feel around for my box of treasures. Pulling it down, I place it on my bed, and with shaky hands, I lift the lid off the box, looking down at the framed photograph of myself from another life.

Gripping the photo of me at six years old, I stare at the scared little girl who was in the middle of a torturous chemotherapy treatment. It was the worst time of my life. I've never felt so low, not even after Noah broke my heart, but I survived.

Having childhood cancer was never part of my family's plan, and it definitely wasn't a part of mine, but we fought through it, and I came out the other end stronger than ever. It was almost eighteen months of hell fighting the leukemia that riddled my body. I was so young, but I remember it so perfectly. Mom and Dad would cry when they thought I couldn't hear them. I was so close to losing my battle, but I fought for it because I couldn't stand the thought of never seeing my family and Noah again.

I think being so young at the time was a blessing because I didn't fully grasp the magnitude of what I was going through. I understood that I was sick and could potentially die, but while I was terrified of dying, I didn't understand exactly what that meant or grasp just how much of life I was going to miss out on.

I haven't looked at this photo in a while. It usually brings back a slew of painful memories, but today I felt weak. I felt like I was losing grip on reality. But the little girl in this photo is a fighter, and if she can make it through eighteen months of battling cancer at only six years old, then I can make it through this.

Little Zoey walked so that I could run. Hell, I'm not just going to run, I'm going to fly, whether it's with Noah or without.

Knowing I'm going to need the strength this photo brings me, I walk across my room, press a kiss to the survivor in the frame, and place it right on my desk where I'll see it every morning. Noah Ryan won't break me down. If I can survive leukemia, I can survive him.

Hearing my sister in her room, a smile pulls at my lips, and I make my way down the hall. Hovering in her door, I watch as she stretches across her bed, furiously scribbling in a notebook. When I knock on Hazel's door, her head snaps up. "How was your first day of middle school?"

Hazel's lips press into a heavy pout as she sits up on her bed. "It sucked," she says, shoving her books away. "Everyone is so grouchy, and the teachers are all snappy and mean. Not to mention all the homework. You didn't warn me about that."

I laugh and move into her room, dropping down on the edge of her bed and pulling her into my side. "I didn't want to freak you out."

"Consider me thoroughly freaked out," she huffs. "I mean, have you seen that cafeteria? It's like a jungle in there."

"It's really not that bad," I laugh. "Day one is supposed to be scary. Just give it a little time and you'll find your place."

"Easy for you to say. You had Noah with you all through middle school. No one was going to mess with you. He made sure you were okay, but I'm doing it all on my own. I don't even have any friends yet," she says with a heavy pout that breaks my heart. "If Linc were still here, he would have made sure I was alright, like Noah used to do for you."

Her words are like a knife right through the chest, and I pull her in even tighter, hating how much she's still hurting. Linc was a friend to us all, but because Noah and I were so close, it forced them together. Though he was a few years older than her, he still treated her like the little sister he never had.

I loved them together. They didn't quite share the same kind of bond that Noah and I had, but I could have easily seen them fall in love and live so happily together one day. Losing Linc was a tragedy for us all.

"You know Linc is watching over you, right? He's not going to let anything happen to you. You were his sweet little Hazel Girl."

"I know," she says with a heavy sigh, the old nickname bringing a fond smile to her face. "I miss him."

"I know you do. Me too," I whisper, my hand moving up and down her back, trying to comfort her. It's bittersweet. Don't get me wrong, I've always adored my little sister. Hazel is one of the few loves of my life, but losing Linc made me realize just how precious life really is, and I vowed that I would be the best big sister that I could possibly be.

We used to argue and fight over the smallest things, but not anymore. Linc's passing brought us together, and I'll forever be grateful for that. It just kills me that we had to lose him in order to become closer.

Hazel glances up at me with her big green eyes, so similar to mine. "Is it true that Noah is going to your school now?"

I cringe, unable to hide the hesitation in my tone. "Sure is."

Her eyes sparkle with happiness. "That's amazing. You get to see him all the time now. I bet he gave you the biggest hug ever," she says, not understanding the dynamics of our strained relationship.

"Yeah," I say with a forced smile. "I saw him in the student office this morning and then again at lunch. He found his place with the football team."

"Oh, can we go to his games like we used to?"

"I'm sure he'd love to see you cheering him on at his games," I tell her, knowing damn well he wouldn't feel the same way about me being there. "Listen," I say, needing to change the topic. "Did you want me to drive you to school tomorrow? I could go in with you and make sure you have someone to hang out with. I don't want you to be all alone."

Her eyes widen with horror, and she shoves away from me. "No way. I can't have my big sister walking me into school. Don't you know how not cool that is? But I mean, you could definitely drive me. Just drop me off around the corner."

My mouth drops open, and I gape at the little brat. "First of all, I'll have you know that I am the coolest person you'll ever meet. You'd be lucky to have someone like me walk you into school. And second, if I'm driving you, then I get to go in."

"Forget it. I'll take the bus."

"You know, I could always ask Dad to take you."

Her eyes bug out of her head. "No. No, please don't. You know how loud he likes to sing in the car. Everyone will see."

I laugh and push up off her bed. "Ah, if only you had a cool big sister to drive you instead."

"Ugh," she groans. "Fine. You can drive me, but you're not walking me in."

"Fine, but I'm not dropping you around the corner. I'm stopping right at the school gates."

Hazel groans and lays down on her bed again, picking up her pen to get back into her work. "Fine. Only if the music is turned down."

I grin wide, knowing she couldn't resist. "You got yourself a deal," I tell her, and with that, I make my way back to my room and hit play on my playlist before getting to my homework, refusing to get behind on day one.

I try to keep Noah off my mind, but it's hard. Seeing him today feels as though I've been hit by a train. Everything is scrambled. My thoughts, my heart, my emotions. I'm all over the place. But I'm not going to let him break me, no matter how hard he pushes me away.

I'm just about finished when my phone rings, and I scramble through the sheets to find it. Tarni's name flashes across the screen. "Hey," I say, quickly answering the call before I miss it.

"Hold up," she says. "I'm adding Cora and Abby."

Before I can even respond, Tarni is gone. The call goes quiet for only a moment before she returns, the girls all speaking over each other as though they were already mid-conversation. "Yo, Zo. You there?" Tarni questions.

"I'm here," I say, pushing the rest of my homework aside and getting comfy on my bed, realizing I'm in for the long haul now.

"Abby is holding out on us," Tarni says. "I've been dying to know all the filthy little details about her sexcapades with Liam."

"Ughhhh," Abby groans. "Not gonna happen. It was hot and wild, but now that we're back at school, it's nothing but an old wives' tale.

I'm better off pretending it never happened."

"I'm so angry with him," Cora says. "He's such a player. I don't know what you were thinking getting involved with him in the first place. Surely you knew he was going to break your heart, right? No guy just suddenly changes like that, no matter how tight your vag is."

Rolling my eyes, I put my phone down on my bed and hit speakerphone before getting up and closing my door, not needing Hazel to overhear this. She's a feisty kid who's growing up way too fast, but she doesn't need to be exposed to this. Most of the time, I can't stand being exposed to it. But if I weren't friends with these guys, I'd literally have no one.

Climbing back onto my bed, I drag my homework in front of me again before starting on what's left of my calculus work.

"Men can change," Abby continues. "Whether it's for good or bad, they change."

"I second that," I say, adding my two cents to the conversation.

"Well, Liam isn't changing for the better," Tarni says. "Don't get me wrong, he's hot, but he's not about to quit screwing around and start dating, and if he did, it wouldn't be with a junior. He'd date girls like Shannan Holter."

Abby goes silent, and I feel for her. I hate how oblivious Tarni can be sometimes. She has a habit of not filtering her thoughts before allowing them to tumble out like word vomit. Clearly Abby likes Liam, otherwise, she wouldn't have wasted her summer with him. She's hurting over his dismissal, and hearing how carelessly Tarni shrugs it off as though she'd never be good enough to date someone like Liam must have stung.

Cora laughs, clearly oblivious to Abby's silence as well. "Who knows. From what I heard, Shannan offered to have an orgy with Noah and the whole cheer squad. Seems Liam is old news now."

"Ugh," I groan in disgust before immediately zipping my lips and wishing I hadn't said that out loud. But I couldn't help myself. The idea of Noah lowering his standards to waste his time with girls like Shannan is nothing but an insult to me. How could he want that over everything we had together?

"You're such a prude, Zo. Sex is fun," Tarni laughs, misreading the reasons for my disgust. "When are you going to get over it and just do it? You know, nearly half of the football team have been trying to screw you since the start of the summer. Just pick one and get it over and done with. It doesn't even hurt that much."

Cora laughs. "She's probably holding out for Noah, hoping he'll see the light and start worshiping at her feet again."

I clench my jaw, not liking this topic at all. "I'm not holding out for Noah. I just don't want to screw the first guy who smiles at me."

"Well, you should," Tarni says. "Because just like Liam, Noah isn't going to change, especially not for a good girl like you. He's down with the easy girls who'll give him what he wants without making him work for it."

"You mean girls like you?" I question, my hands shaking.

"Exactly."

"Speaking of Noah," Abby chimes in, her tone hitching as though she's got the gossip of the century. "I heard something about him today."

"Ooh yeah," Tarni says, hanging off Abby's every word. "What is it?"

"So, apparently he used to have a little brother, Landon or Logan . . . something like that, and I don't know . . . five or so years ago, Noah killed him, and that's why he's so fucked up."

I suck in a horrified gasp. "Who the hell told you that?" I demand, anger rolling off me, not only for the disrespect of talking about Linc like that but for spreading such a horrendous rumor. When Noah hears what they're saying, it will tear him to pieces. "That's not even a little close to what happened."

"Hey, don't shoot the messenger," Abby says as hot, rage-filled tears spring to my eyes. "That's just the rumor that's going around. Heard it from some guy in the school parking lot."

Throwing myself off my bed, I pace the length of my room, unable to find control. "His name wasn't Landon or Logan. It was Lincoln, Lincoln Ryan, and he was the sweetest boy I ever met. He was hit by a drunk driver three years ago, and it destroyed his family and mine. Noah adored his little brother and still hasn't come to terms with his death. So do yourselves a favor and don't even mention his name. Shit," I huff, needing to take a breath. "How could you be so cold as to say such a thing?"

"Jesus Christ, Zoey," Tarni says. "Lay off. It's not like she was suggesting Noah did it, just telling us the rumor she heard today."

I shake my head, unable to believe that Tarni is defending Abby right now, especially considering she was there to see the way Linc's death crushed me. She saw the devastation tear through me and experienced it secondhand. She'd even met Linc a handful of times, and now she's just going to pretend like she doesn't even remember his name?

Fuck. I've never been so upset and angry.

Without another word, I end the call, throw my phone on my bed, and get back to pacing. When a knock sounds at my door, I glance up just in time to see Mom poke her head through the opening door. "Everything alright in here?"

"Yes. No," I spit. "I don't know."

Mom walks right in and takes my shoulders, forcing me to stop and meet her eyes. "What's going on my sweet girl?"

"It's only been one day, and the rumor mill is already starting to spin."

"About you and Noah?" Mom questions, sadness in her eyes.

"Well, yes," I say with a heavy sigh. "But that's not what this is all about."

"What's going on?"

Letting out a breath, I collapse onto the edge of my bed and lower my gaze to my hands, Abby's words leaving a sharp sting deep in my chest. "Apparently people are starting to put their own theories together about Linc, and the things they're saying . . . it's horrible, Mom."

"Oh, honey," she says with a sigh, dropping down beside me and pulling me into her arms, the same way I'd done with Hazel. "Usually, I'd tell you to keep your head down and ignore nasty rumors, but you can't ignore this, especially now that Linc isn't here to defend himself. Speak up where you can. Don't let people say nasty things about him. He was such a sweet boy. I couldn't stand the thought of people talking ill about him."

"It's not Linc they're saying bad things about. They're suggesting Noah was the one who did it."

"What?" she gasps.

"Yeah."

She holds me even tighter. "I suppose Noah didn't take that very well."

"I wouldn't know. He took one look at me this morning and acted as though I was dirt under his foot. He said he didn't want anything to do with me, and if I see him in the hall, to walk the other way."

Mom lets out a heavy sigh and rubs my back. "Oh, sweetheart. I'm so sorry. That must have been hard."

"It wasn't my finest moment."

"I bet."

"He's not the boy I used to know," I murmur, my heart falling to pieces. "He's different."

Mom shakes her head. "You see, that's where I think you're wrong. The old Noah, the one we all know and love, is still in there screaming for someone to help him. He's just lost his way, and I have to have faith that he will come back to us. Don't give up on him, Zoey. I know it hurts, but he needs you now more than ever."

"Why does it have to be me?" I say, tears brimming in my eyes. "He doesn't want me around him. He pushed me away three years ago and left me. I had to heal all on my own, and now, seeing him at school, acting as though I never meant anything . . . It sucks. I can't do it."

Mom nods and peers over my head, and I see the moment she finds the photo of me in that hospital bed. She lets out a heavy sigh, no doubt remembering the pain of that time. "That little girl in that photo," she says, adjusting my chin until I see the photo. "She beat all odds, which is how I know you can do this now. Noah might be keeping you at arm's length, but he's hurting, Zoey. He's drowning in grief, and having him here at East View with you is the best thing that could have happened to him. He might not be able to see it, but I do. He needs you, and despite how much you deny it, I think you need him too."

With that, Mom stands and squeezes my shoulder before walking to my door. She pauses and glances back at my photo, a sadness in her eyes. "You were such a fighter, Zoey. I know it can sometimes make you uncomfortable keeping this photo out on display like this, but I love it. Yes, it's a reminder of the hell you suffered through, but it's also a reminder of how hard you fought. You're a survivor, Zoey, and that should always be celebrated."

I give Mom a tight smile, unable to help glancing back at the photo, looking at the heavy, tired bags under my eyes and my sunken cheeks. I was as sick as anybody could ever be, but there was also such a bright light in my eyes, a fire that burned within me, and that fire pushed me to fight . . . that, and Noah.

He may not know it, but he saved me all those years ago and I'll never forget it.

But Mom is right, he's drowning in grief, and if he was able to give me the strength I needed to survive without even realizing it, then it's only fair I do the same for him now.

Chapter 9

NOAH

Another fucking day at East View High. I wonder what fresh bullshit is in store for me today. I suppose it really wasn't that bad yesterday, apart from the whole Zoey thing. If she wasn't here, then I might even try to give this school a chance.

What other choice do I have? It's this or nothing, and after the hell I've already put my mom through over the past few years, I can't afford to slip any further. I know I'm hurting her, but I can't seem to stop or pull my shit together and make the hurt go away.

Every fucking day without Linc only kills me more, and I feel myself slowly dying inside. It's like the walls are caving in, and every breath I take turns me further into stone. It's going to kill me, and then what? I'll really be leaving Mom and Zoey. But at least the hurt would stop, and the darkness would fade, but what kind of hell would I be leaving behind?

After locking the doors of my ZL1 Camaro, I stare up at the school, my hand slipping into my pocket and closing around my pack of cigarettes. As I make my way toward the school and go to pull the pack out of my pocket, I see Principal Daniels, his narrowed stare locked on me, waiting to see how this is going to go down. Not prepared to get my ass kicked out of here so soon, I release the cigarettes and stride up the front steps, his stare not wavering from mine for even a second.

He nods as if knowing exactly what I was going to do, and I simply walk past and push through the front door of East View High, ready to face another day.

As usual, eyes fall on me, only today is different. They seem to be whispering among themselves, looking at me as though I have some kind of fucked-up secret that was just exposed. It's not the first time I've walked into a school to find everyone talking about me, and it sure as hell won't be the last. When you have a reputation like mine, if people aren't talking about you, then you no longer matter.

Ignoring the stares, I barge through the girls trying to get my attention, but I can't help scanning the hall, searching for the one person I'm not supposed to want. I hate being at the same school as her, having to see her every day and remember the pain I caused her, but I can't let her in to see just how far I've sunk. I'm not the same guy she once loved. It would be best if she just moved on and forgot about us.

Reaching my locker, I put in the code—0228—and as I open the door, Liam falls into the locker beside me. "Yo, dude. You didn't tell me about your brother. Tough break, man."

My head whips toward him, my lethal stare locked on his. "The fuck did you just say?"

Reading the rage in my tone, Liam's hands fly up in innocence. "Woah, chill out," he laughs. "I didn't mean to hit a nerve. But if you're all fucked up over me just mentioning it, you should know, the whole fucking school is talking about it, and it ain't pretty."

Dread fills my veins like poison, pulsing through my body and destroying everything in its path. I grab Liam, pressing into him as I slam him flat against the lockers. "What are they saying?" I growl, my hand gripping a little too tight around his throat.

"You don't wanna know, man. Just let it go."

"What. Are. They. Saying?"

Eyes gravitate toward us from every direction while Liam tries to shrug it off, acting as though we're cool here.

He lets out a sigh and meets my stare. "There's a million different versions of the story," he finally tells me. "Some are saying your little bro got hit by a drunk driver, others are suggesting you did it."

"FUCK!"

"Come on, man. Nobody actually believes that shit," he says just as my fist flies right by his face and slams into the locker beside mine, leaving a dent in the metal.

Liam shoves a hand into my shoulder, demanding my attention. "Don't fuck this up, Noah," he spits through his teeth, not even flinching at my rage. "If anybody wants you out of this damn school, it's me, but for some fucking reason, I don't wanna see what happens to you if this shit doesn't work out. So pull your shit together. They were going to find out sooner or later."

I clench my jaw, my hands balling in and out of fists, my heart racing as the darkness threatens to consume me. And just this once, I wish it would. I try to shake it off as I step away from Liam when I see that familiar wave of chestnut hair stepping into the girls' bathroom, and I know without a doubt that she has everything to do with this.

Without a second thought, I throw my hand out, slamming my locker closed before taking off after her. Walking into the girls' bathroom, I find a bunch of girls fixing their makeup in the mirror and Zoey at the very end, clutching the sink with her head down, tears staining her beautiful, rosy cheeks.

The girls whip around at my entrance, their mouths dropping open, and before they can say a damn word, I point back toward the door. "GET OUT."

They run, grab their shit, and take off as though someone just announced that Liam was offering his dick up to the most willing participant. Zoey barely glances up, but I watch the way her body tenses, knowing damn well I'm coming for her.

I stride through the bathroom, and her body stiffens as I reach her. It's clear by the tears on her cheeks that all the talk of Linc has gotten to her, but she has no right to cry for him. She did this.

As I step right into her, Zoey's head whips up, meeting my stare. "What are you—"

Before she finishes the angry sentence, I grab her arm and shove her back against the wall, pinning her with my body, her hand braced against my chest, trying to force just an inch of distance between us. "I warned you," I growl, the fury burning through my lethal stare, ignoring the way her familiar scent overwhelms my system. "I told you to keep my name out of your fucking mouth and then you go and throw Linc's name around like it means nothing."

Her jaw drops, and she stares up at me in horror. "Do you even hear yourself? What the hell is wrong with you?"

"Me?" I scoff.

"Yes, you, asshole," she seethes, trying to shove against my chest to give herself space, but I'm not going anywhere. "I said what I had to say to keep people from speaking ill of Lincoln. If you knew what they were saying—"

"I don't give a shit what they were saying."

Zoey arches a brow, and I do what I can not to breathe her in. "Sure. You don't care what they are saying, yet the second you hear one little whisper on their lips, you come in here to abuse me. I set the story straight, Noah. They were saying you *killed* him, and I know you're determined to forget he ever existed, but I'm not, and I wasn't about to let them spread shit like that and leave a stain on Linc's memory. So, talk it up all you want, Noah, but I see right through you. You don't fool me."

I push into her, and her hand shifts from my chest to my arm, her fingers digging into my skin as her nails leave little half-moon indents. "I don't give a shit who you think you're trying to protect. I told you to stay out of my fucking way."

Someone walks into the bathroom, and I tear my gaze away from Zoey's, ready to tell them to fuck off, when I find Shannan standing by the door, staring at Zoey with an arched brow, her lips pulling into a wicked smirk. She takes in the scene, and I see the very moment she thinks she knows what the fuck is going down.

"Interesting," she muses, her gaze shifting back to mine. "When you're done playing with the trash, come find me. I have just the thing to get your mind off the bullshit."

Shannan turns her gaze back to Zoey, and I realize that without even trying, I've just painted a target on Zoey's back. I inch away from her, putting space between us, but not enough for her to slip away. Shannan laughs, her filthy stare lingering on Zoey. "Good luck, Zoey. You're gonna need it."

And with that, Shannan turns her back and strides out of the bathroom, leaving us alone.

"Great," Zoey mutters, shoving hard against my chest and forcing me back a step. "Do you have any idea what you've just done? Shannan is going to eat me alive."

"Not my problem."

Zoey scoffs and steps around me before looking me up and down, her judgmental gaze sending me spiraling out of control. "Look at yourself, Noah. Your act is getting old. You look pathetic," she tells me, stepping right back into me and lowering her voice. "You're broken, and I know you're hurting, but pushing me away isn't going to help you. You're a mess, and you're only making things worse for yourself."

My hands ball into tight fists at my sides, my jaw clenching with rage. "Don't act like you have any fucking idea who I am. You don't know me, not anymore."

Zoey scoffs. "Maybe you're right, but I know that Linc would despise this asshole you're pretending to be. He'd be so ashamed of you. I mean, sure. The whole bad boy, *I don't give a shit* vibe really suits you. It's hot, and I'm sure every girl across the state wants to be the one you take to bed, but it's a lie. You look like a joke, Noah."

Disgust filters through her stare, and I fucking hate it. It's one thing to push her away, but seeing how I disgust her? That fucking hurts, but it's the hurt that keeps me breathing. I need it more than she'll ever know.

Zoey turns her back and stalks toward the exit, and just when I think she's twisted the knife enough, she turns back. "For the record, I know pushing me away makes you feel like you hold some kind of power over me. Or maybe it's some messed-up way to punish yourself, but it's not just me you're hurting. Hazel misses you too." A tear rolls down her cheek, and she refuses to wipe it away. "I don't know. Maybe you're trying to punish me because it makes you feel something, reminds you that you're still alive and *he's* not, but stop punishing her. She was too young. She lost her only friend in the world. I can handle it. You can push me away as much as you want, but please, Noah, stop hurting her."

Undeniable guilt soars through my chest, and I watch as Zoey turns and storms out of the bathroom. The morning bell sounds through the school, calling everyone to homeroom, but I can't fucking move. I can barely fucking breathe.

The overwhelming mix of rage, guilt, and pain pound through my body, and I turn toward the sink, gripping it the same way Zoey had been doing when I first walked in, gasping for air. And when I glance up at myself in the mirror, I don't even recognize the asshole staring back at me.

Zoey was right, I'm a fraud—a fraud who Linc would despise. He would be ashamed of me, but I'm so fucking lost in the dark. There's no way back for me now, no way to save myself. All I can do is try to get through the rest of high school without fucking things up more. After that, I can disappear. I can start fresh and try to forget about the pain that plagues me.

Walking out of the bathroom, I make my way to homeroom, unable to keep myself from glancing back down the hall at Zoey as she rifles through her locker, hating this hold she has over me.

The second I turn back, the whispers hit, and I hear Linc's name on the tongue of those who never knew him, those who only care for a fucking story. They call me a killer. Some say I pushed him in front of that car, others claim I was the one behind the wheel, and as I reach homeroom and go to push through the door, it becomes too much, and I find myself turning back.

I barge through the crowded bodies, my mind spinning, and I feel myself slipping even further into the darkness. Before I know it, I push through the door of an unfamiliar room and stare wide-eyed at the woman across from me. "Are you the school counselor?" I ask, my chest heaving with heavy breaths, and my skin burning from Zoey's touch.

"You must be Noah Ryan," the woman says. "I was wondering if I might meet you today."

My brows furrow and she goes on. "Close the door and take a seat," she says in an overly nice tone. "I think we may have a lot to talk about."

And with that, I kick the door shut behind me and drop into the chair opposite her desk, ready to fucking break.

"Alright, Noah. I'm not here to tiptoe around the issues. I've heard the rumors on my way in, and I can only assume you're here to talk about your brother," she tells me. "Now let's get one thing straight. I've been doing this a long time, and if you walk through my door to talk, then that's exactly what we're going to do. This is not an hour where you get to waste time and skip classwork. If you're meeting with me, then we're going to get to the root of your issues. I want to help you, Noah. But I can only do that if you're ready to be helped."

I swallow hard and nod as she goes on. "Alright, let's talk. What's going on?"

Clenching my jaw, I prepare to say the one thing that's haunted me for the past three years, the one thing that plunged me into this world of darkness and has trapped me there. The one thing bad enough to force me to push Zoey away and keep her at arm's length. "Those rumors," I tell her, my voice wavering as the guilt and agony become too much to bear. "They're right. I killed my little brother."

Chapter 10

ZOEY

After shoving my books into my locker, I go to close the door when Tarni crashes into me, her arms flying around my shoulders and keeping me pinned. "Where have you been all day? I couldn't find you this morning."

"I've been around," I tell her, feeling frustrated with our friendship. The comments the girls made on the phone last night still circle my mind.

"Come on," she grumbles, letting me go before falling against the locker and waiting for my undivided attention. "Don't tell me you're still pissed about yesterday? It's not like Abby knew anything about Lincoln. She was just telling us what she heard."

I give Tarni a blank stare. "She was using the death of a child, one who I happened to be extremely close with, as a form of entertainment. Not to mention, suggesting Noah was responsible was just wrong. I get that she was just repeating what she heard, but that wasn't cool, and the fact that you didn't have my back was an asshole move. You know how close I was with Linc."

Tarni gapes at me before amusement crosses her face. "Are you shitting me? What is up with you? Ever since Noah showed up, you've had your panties in a twist. You need to relax. You know Abby. If she thought there was anything really serious going on, she never would have said anything. You snapping at her like that made her feel like shit, and you know I always have your back, but I wasn't going to make Abby feel even worse."

"Oh great," I say, rolling my eyes. "So I'm the bad guy for standing up for Linc?"

"I never said that. I just think you need to relax."

"Well, that's not about to happen," I tell her, grabbing my lunch and starting to make my way down to the cafeteria, dreading what I might see after Noah's performance with Shannan yesterday. "Noah heard everyone talking about Linc this morning and cornered me in the bathroom. He thought I was the one who told everyone, and—"

"But you were," she says, cutting me off. "You told us what really happened."

"Yeah, I know that, but he assumed I was the one who started it when all I was doing was correcting the story and making sure no one was disrespecting Linc in the process. But that's beside the point," I tell her. "He was getting all up in my face. He looked like he wanted to tear my head clean off my body, and then Shannan walked in—"

"Oh, shit," Tarni gasps, her eyes going wide. "If she thinks you're trying to get close to Noah, she'll bury you, but if she thinks you're an enemy of his and she can score points with him by putting you down, you're fucked."

"Tell me about it," I mutter. "Do you remember the hell she put Lucy Stonebridge through last year just for thinking of trying out for captain of the cheer squad? They bound her to a chair and shaved her head. I can't have that shit happening to me."

"I don't know what to tell you," Tarni says, shrugging her shoulders as though she couldn't care less. "What did you think was going to happen when Noah showed up? He's by far the most popular guy in school. Every girl wants to be with him, and once people find out about your history, you're going to be seen as a threat. And now that they see how adamant Noah is about hating you, you're an easy target. Shannan's going to use that against you. But be prepared, you know she's only going to fuck with you right in front of Noah for his approval, and honestly, I can't see him stepping in to do anything about it. Not now at least. Kinda sad though," she adds as we push through the doors and into the cafeteria. "The old Noah would have walked through the darkest pits of hell to make sure you were the happiest girl in school. Not anymore. This Noah doesn't give a shit about you."

She laughs to herself and walks ahead of me, beelining for our usual table, and for the first time in a long time, I feel my pace slowing, not sure that I really want to sit with her today. But where else am I supposed to go? I have other friends in the school, but they all have their own groups they sit with at lunch. Hell, I don't even know if I could call them friends. More like acquaintances.

Tarni, Abby, and Cora are my group. It's been that way since I started at East View High, and I don't want to mess with a good thing. They're just going through a new phase. Their preferences are shifting. We're all getting older, and their likes and dislikes are changing, which can only be expected, but unfortunately, all they seem to care about is getting the attention of douchebag guys, and it's not something I want to waste my time obsessing about. I feel like they're going on this new ride and have left me behind, but I'm not sure it's a ride I particularly want to get on.

Perhaps it's time for me to move on and find a group of friends a little more my speed, the type of girls who aren't going to spread rumors about a dead child while suggesting that the dead child's brother was the one who killed him.

Shit. It's East View High. I don't even know if that type of girl even exists here, otherwise, I'm sure I would have gravitated toward her years ago.

My gaze shifts to Noah at the back of the cafeteria, and unlike yesterday, where I hesitated to look his way, I suddenly don't care if he sees the judgment in my eyes. I hope he does, and I hope he knows just how disappointed I am in him.

Mom was right. Noah is hurting. He's a lost soul trapped in a world of darkness, screaming for someone to save him, but he's also a complete asshole. Why do I have to love him like this? It's one thing having him here, but this morning was bullshit. Why can't I seem to let go of the past? He's made it crystal clear that what we used to have doesn't exist anymore, so why am I clinging to it so hard? I need to let him go.

As if sensing my gaze like a tug on that invisible tether, Noah's head lifts, and those dark, haunted eyes come directly to mine, holding me captive. His eyes have always been dark, only today, they're clouded by shadow. He looks like shit, like today has been hard on him, and I'm not surprised after all the talk of Linc this morning, but this isn't right. There's something more there. Guilt, sadness, overwhelming pain. He's on the edge, ready to break, and knowing he needs me more than ever, my body jolts, desperate to run into his arms and tell him that everything is going to be okay.

My hands twitch at my side, ready to throw caution to the wind and run to him, but I hold back, knowing he's not ready. Not yet. Especially considering the way he's looking at me now.

I can't fault Tarni. She was right. Noah looks at me like a leech who won't let go. This new version of him doesn't give a shit about me. I just hope that the old Noah is still buried in there somewhere. I've barely gotten past Linc's passing, and to find out the old Noah doesn't exist would feel like losing him too.

Noah's gaze narrows, daring me to try something, but I can't handle any more of his abuse today. I have a high pain threshold, but tolerating Noah's constant rejection isn't something I'm capable of. It's wearing me down, and soon enough, it'll drown me. But at least then Noah and I might be on the same level for the first time in three years.

"You coming?" Tarni calls back at me.

Tearing my gaze away from Noah, I look back at Tarni to find her walking backward toward our table, staring at me like I'm some kind of inconvenience. What the hell happened to my best friend? She's always been blunt, but over the summer we'd never been closer. Now, she's almost as much of a stranger to me as Noah.

"Yeah, I'm coming," I tell her, wondering just how lame it would be to go and eat lunch in my car.

As I catch up with her, I can't help stealing one last glance at Noah. His gaze is trained heavily on his table, ignoring the other football assholes around him, and I know he senses my stare, but he refuses to look up again or allow me the chance to see inside.

He's hiding in plain sight, and it's so blatantly obvious how much pain he's in. It leaves me wondering how the hell nobody else can see it. He's screaming for help, and the people surrounding him can't seem to hear it.

God, why the hell does he do this to himself? Doesn't he understand just how much it kills me to see him hurting like this?

Taking another step toward my table, a hand shoves hard into my shoulder, forcing me to an agonizing stop. My head whips back to find Shannan Holter standing right in front of me, that same wicked smirk

I'd seen this morning resting on her lips. "Why are you looking over there?" she questions, moving in dangerously close. "There's nothing there for you."

"I don't know what you're talking about."

"Sure you do," she sings, her voice hitching higher and gaining the attention of everyone in the cafeteria, especially Noah's "You're in love with Noah Ryan, but guess what? He doesn't want you. I saw the way he looked at you this morning. You're trash."

She laughs, and the rest of the school seems to laugh along with her as humiliation pours over me.

"Trash," she repeats, her grin widening as she leans in even closer.

I roll my eyes and go to step around her, but she steps with me, blocking me and forcing me to stay to play her ridiculous little game. "Don't you have orphaned puppies to kick or candy to steal from children?"

"It seems I have a break in my schedule," she says, her eyes dancing with amusement as I feel Noah's heated stare like lasers on my back. "But don't you worry about that, I have more than enough time for you."

"Seriously?" I say, my lips twisting in disgust and boredom. "This is really the kind of bullshit that gets you off? Don't you see how pathetic this makes you look? The popular cheer captain picking on the typical good girl. You're such a cliché, Shannan. It's lame and embarrassing."

She scoffs, not affected by my words in the least. "What's cliché is the way you're drooling over Noah. Now, that's what I call embarrassing. Look at you, Zoey. You're pathetic, but don't you worry, I'm going to dedicate my whole senior year to making sure you know just how fucking pathetic you really are."

My gaze flicks back to Tarni, watching her from our table as she watches me in return, not doing a damn thing to help me. Then, letting out a sigh, I look back at Shannan. "Perfect, can't wait," I say with a forced smile, realizing this is only the beginning. I go to step around her again, and this time she lets me, only I pull back and meet her stare. "By the way," I say, matching her loud tone. "You've got a big chunk of spinach right there between your two front teeth."

Humiliation washes over her face, and she quickly ducks her head to pick at the spinach. I waste no time walking away, but the rest of the cheer squad gathers around, creating a circle around me. "Trash. Trash. Trash," they chant as I desperately search for a break in the circle, needing a way out, but there's no denying the synchronicity of the cheer team is on point. They're good at what they do.

"Trash. Trash. Trash." The chanting gets louder, the rest of the school joining in as they gather around. I search for Tarni in desperation, finding her across the room, but she just shakes her head. She's not willing to take on a crowd this size, and the more the circle closes in around me, the more my claustrophobia turns to panic.

"TRASH. TRASH. TRASH."

Air becomes harder to pull into my lungs with each heaving breath I take, and as I desperately search for a way out, I find Noah still sitting at his table, watching the fresh hell surrounding me. Despite the crown on his goddamn head, despite being the only one with the power to put this shit to rest, he just sits there and watches as I become the school outcast, ridiculed for simply caring about the boy I used to know.

This is his doing. He might not be the one chanting, but he's just as guilty, and I'll never forgive him for allowing this to happen.

"TRASH. TRASH. TRASH." The chanting is at an all-time high, the people moving in closer, and I spin around, frantically searching for an escape. Tears begin to well in my eyes. The laughter and taunting come from every angle, and unable to bear it a second longer, I barge right through the crowd, shouldering past the students as they laugh at my back.

People grab at me, pulling my hair, spanking my ass, and the tears finally fall, staining my cheeks as I reach the doors and race out into the hallway. I run toward my locker to get my things, stumbling and struggling to catch my breath, but the lock shakes in my unsteady hands as I try to enter the combination.

Finally getting it open, I reach in to grab my bag and check my keys are right where I left them, and as I slam my locker closed, I hear someone running after me. "Zoey," Tarni calls from up the hallway.

"Leave me alone," I spit, hastily wiping my eyes.

"Come on," she groans, catching up with me. "Don't be mad at me. There was nothing I could do. It was a fucking mob. What did you expect?"

"Anything," I cry, slinging my bag over my back. "Anything would have helped."

With that, I turn away and run for the exit, more than ready to get out of here. Barging through the doors, I break out through the front gates and get halfway to my car when I see him standing there, waiting for me as though he has every right.

I shake my head, not ready to face him after that humiliation, but I refuse to walk away now.

Noah leans against my Range Rover, his big arms crossed over his strong chest as his stare bores into mine. I continue storming toward him, my jaw clenched as the overwhelming anger, frustration, and humiliation claim me. "What the hell do you want?" I demand, walking around him to unlock the car and shove my bag in the passenger's side.

He shakes his head, clearly having no damn clue why he bothered to come down here, but it's obvious to me—guilt.

"I just—"

"No," I snap, moving back around to the driver's side and reaching for my door. "You don't have the right to come to me. Not anymore. And especially not after the bullshit you've thrown at me the last two days."

I go to open the door, but he reaches past me and slams it again, demanding my attention. "Hold up a fucking second."

I whip around, the tears so hot in my eyes. "No, Noah. You had your chance," I yell, shoving my hands into his chest as the anger overwhelms me, but he's like a brick wall, refusing to step away. "You used to be my hero. *My bestest friend.* I thought the whole world shone through your eyes, but I couldn't have been more wrong. What happened in there . . . That's on you. You had the power to make it stop, but you didn't because you're too fucking scared of feeling anything. You're a coward."

He steps back, looking at me as though I just slapped him across the face, and without another word, I pull my car door open and slip inside, locking the doors behind me. I watch him for a second, the two of us held captive by one another's stare, and when he inches back and looks away, deciding not to fight for this, I shake my head, never so disappointed in my life.

And with that, I start the engine and back out of my spot, desperate to leave him behind.

Chapter 11

ZOEY

This week has sucked, and not just the normal kind of end-of-week sucking that I usually get hit with. No, this week has been torturous. I'm only one week into junior year, and I'm officially the school outcast thanks to Shannan and her need to get in Noah's pants. Though from what I can tell, the more she messes with me, the more Noah seems to pull away from her, so there's that. It doesn't stop her from trying even harder though.

I've had my locker vandalized, an iced coffee thrown over my Range Rover, red food die thrown at the back of my pants in a pathetic effort to make me look as though I'd gotten my period. Not to mention, everywhere I've gone, every class I've taken, I've heard the word *trash* chanted over and over again.

I can't escape it.

Tarni hasn't exactly been the best of friends this week either. After Tuesday, she chilled out and was mostly being her normal self. They all were. I think they might have had a little sense knocked into them and realized just how insensitive they were being about Linc.

But Tarni . . . I don't know. She's been hesitant with me. It's as if she's trying to put distance between us because I'm the school reject and being seen with me doesn't do her any favors. What happened to the lifetime of friendship? Where's the loyalty? I've stuck by her side since we were six years old, and now, when I need her most, she's nowhere to be seen. Though the second school is over, she's more than happy to chill at my place or spend hours talking on the phone. Only in public, it's as though I don't even exist.

Great friend she is. If only I had other options.

The second the bell sounded after school today, I couldn't wait to get out of there and start my weekend. I need the freedom from school more than my next breath. Not to mention, the thought of not having to see Noah for two whole days is amazing.

It's funny, there was once a time when I would have fallen apart at the thought of not seeing him all weekend. How things have changed. My only saving grace is that since I called him out on his shit on Tuesday, he seems to be leaving me alone. I haven't spoken a word to him, but don't get me wrong, I still feel his overwhelming stare every time I walk into a room.

I feel as though he's stolen my power.

Before I found out he was coming to East View, I was excited for the school year to start. I was ready to dominate junior year and make it my bitch. I was prepared for the slew of work I'd have to get through and all the extra credit to ensure I got into a good college. I was ready for it all, and now, I feel more unprepared than ever. I've already missed so much work and gotten behind on my assignments, all because I'm so completely consumed by everything Noah Ryan.

I need to get a grip.

Crashing down on my bed, I slip beneath the blankets and pull them right up to my chin, more than ready for a night of Netflix and chilling by myself. My phone buzzes from my bedside table, and I reach over with a groan, knowing damn well I should be using tonight as a chance to catch up on my missed work, but I just can't find the strength to do it.

Grabbing my phone, I swipe my thumb across the screen, unlocking it and glancing down to find the group chat with Tarni, Abby, and Cora.

Cora: So……… I know Liam is a bit of a touchy topic right now, but please tell me we're going to his party tonight.

Tarni: Hell yeah, we're going. It's the first party of junior year. There's no way we're missing it.

Tarni: Get your drinking on, bitches. We're partying tonight!!!!!!!!!!

Abby: Seriously? Why does it have to be Liam? Aren't there any other parties tonight?

Tarni: You down to partaaaayyyyyy, Zo???? God knows you could use a shot or two.

Cora: Nope. Already checked. It's Liam or nothing! Choose your poison.

Abby: Fine. But you whores better keep me away from him. Heartbreak and alcohol don't mix, and I refuse to be the sad bitch crying at his feet and begging him to take me back.

Tarni: Ewwww…..

Tarni: What are we wearing? I'm thinking my little black dress, something just short enough to see my ass when I bend over.

Cora: You're such a whore!

Tarni: YO, ZOEY?????? ARE YOU ALIVE???????? I know

you're seeing these messages! I see YOUUUUUUU!

Letting out a sigh, my fingers hover over the screen, knowing Tarni is bound to call me if she doesn't hear from me soon.

Zoey: Yeah…I don't think a party is the best idea for me right now. Especially with Shannan on the loose. That's just asking for trouble.

Tarni: Don't be boring! Shannan's going to be so far up Noah's ass, she won't even notice you there. She'll probably fuck him in the bathroom, and the second she gets him out of her system, it'll all be over. Trust me, this is a good thing.

Abby: I mean, not unless he's the best screw of her life and she turns into a thirsty hoe for him, hanging off his dick every chance she gets.

Tarni: True! But if she's hanging off his dick, at least she won't be hanging off Zoey's!

Zoey: Me and my dick would like to be excused from the narrative.

Tarni: It's too big to be excused!

A few moments pass, and I feel as though I've gotten away with it until another text comes through.

Tarni: Come on, girl. Tell me you'll come. You love a good party, and don't even pretend that you're not dying to let off a little steam. We can do shots, and by the end of the night, you won't even remember that Noah Ryan exists.

Damn. I don't know if that's a good or bad thing.

As I try to respond, Hazel barges through my bedroom door with her arms full of my makeup, hair products, and nail polishes. "PAMPER PARTY!" she calls, barely able to see me over the things piled high in her arms.

She waltzes into my room and dumps everything down on my bed before giving me a wide smile. "Mom says if you're going to be boring all night then the least you can do is be boring with me and turn me into the most gorgeous princess who ever lived, and by gorgeous, I mean sexy as hell."

I laugh and roll my eyes before sitting up in bed to make space for Hazel. "Give me a second," I tell her, scooping my phone up again and hashing out a quick reply.

Zoey: Let me think about it.
Tarni: FUCK YESSSS!!!!!!

Rolling my eyes, I hit play on my playlist and boost the volume just enough to frustrate Mom for calling me boring. Dropping my phone into my lap, I reach across my bed and haul the stack of makeup closer. "Alright," I say. "What do you want me to do?"

"Everything," she says, her eyes sparkling with undeniable joy.

"Okay," I laugh. "But you have to do my makeup too. And my hair and nails. If you get to be a sexy as hell princess, then I get to be one too."

"I like the way you think," she says, holding out her hand as serious as can be. "You've got yourself a deal."

I shake her hand and get to work, and over the next hour, I transform her into the most dazzling princess that ever lived, going as far as to clip in all of my hair extensions and hitting her with as much glitter as her face can possibly take. After raiding my closet and trying on every dress I own, Hazel stands in front of my mirror, staring at herself as though she can hardly believe it.

"I'm beautiful," she breathes. "Every prince in the kingdom is gonna want a piece of this ass."

I laugh while choking on my own spit, wishing like hell I could scrub that sentence from my memory. Then grabbing my phone, I open my camera, having done this enough times to know she won't go away until she's had a full photoshoot to go along with it. "Give me a twirl, Princess Hazel," I smile, loving that while she's definitely too cool to have her big sister walk her into school, she'll still let me spoil her in the privacy of our home.

Hazel laughs and spins around, watching the way her dress flies out, and I clamber off my bed before tackling her to the ground and holding the camera up for the best selfie we've ever taken, only the little brat sticks her tongue out and licks the whole side of my face.

"Ewwwww," I groan, grabbing her face and holding her down before dragging my slobber-filled cheek down the side of hers, sharing the love.

"NOOOOOO!" she howls. "You'll ruin my makeup."

She shoves me away and gets to her feet before checking her reflection in my mirror, and as she falls even more in love with herself, I trudge back across my room, more than ready to put all the makeup away before my bed turns into a cosmetic massacre.

"Nuh-uh," Hazel sings, her eyes brimming with excitement. "It's my turn."

Ah, shit. I'd almost forgotten.

I'm manhandled into my desk chair, and I sit as still as possible, getting poked in the eye over and over again. It takes a lifetime, but I don't dare move as I watch the concentration in Hazel's eyes. If I move even an inch, and she gets even the slightest idea that I've ruined her look, then all hell will break loose.

Next up, she goes to plug in my hair straightener when I shake my head. "No way am I letting you use that on me," I tell her as a vision of charred hair and burn marks assault my mind. I tip out a packet of pins and slide them across the desk toward her. "I'm thinking half-up half-down."

Hazel pouts, and as she works on my hair, I hit up the nail polish, going for jet black to match Noah's soul. Hazel busily chats about the boys at school, and I zone out, my mind stuck on Noah, and before I know it, she grabs the armrest of my desk chair and spins me to face her. "Beautiful," she says, her eyes shining so damn bright. "Dazzling. Stunning. A work of art. I didn't know if I could pull off the impossible, but the great Hazel James has done it again!"

Gripping the armrests on either side of the desk chair, I hoist myself to my feet and strut across the room to check out the train wreck otherwise known as my face. As I step in front of the mirror and take one look at myself, my jaw drops, absolutely blown away. "Holy shi—"

"MOM! ZOEY SAID A BAD WORD!"

"ZOEY!" Mom reprimands from downstairs.

"Shut up, you," I hiss at my smug sister, turning back to my reflection and really taking it in. She's done my makeup flawlessly with the perfect smokey eye, liner, and even a few single false lashes to make my eyes pop. My gaze shifts over my face, and I'm lost for words, seeing how she's even contoured my cheeks and jaw.

"Where the hell did you learn to do this?" I ask, positive I was about to find that a rainbow had thrown up on my face, but it's the exact opposite. I've never seen myself like this.

Hazel shrugs her shoulders, and shyness creeps into her eyes. "I don't know," she says, refusing to meet my stare, sheepish for the first time in her life. "I guess I've been watching a few makeup tutorials on TikTok."

"A few?" I scoff, turning to take in the cute twist she's put in my hair. "There's no way you learned how to do this just by watching a few tutorials. I can't even do this."

"Alright, fine," she grumbles, throwing her hands up in resignation. "I watch them all the time and practice on Mom. I'm obsessed!"

I can't help but laugh as I glance over myself one more time, feeling like a whole new me. I've always been confident in myself and felt beautiful, but I've never felt quite like this. I feel incredible. It even makes me consider going to Liam's party, but that could only end in disaster.

"You need an outfit," Hazel declares.

I roll my eyes and barely get to groan before she grabs my hand and hauls me across my room and into my walk-in closet. She starts throwing clothes at me, and I try not to get smacked in the face. "Do I really have to dress up? It's late. What's the point? I'm only going to get back into my pajamas afterward."

"Don't be silly," Hazel says, stopping her riffling as she peers up at me, her eyes sparkling with mischief. "You're going to Liam's party."

My eyes spring wide, and I gape at my little sister, momentarily lost for words. "I, umm . . . what? How do you know about Liam's party? Wait . . . How do you even know who Liam is?"

Her smug grin widens, and I realize this has all been a ploy to get me out of the house. "Liam's cousin's best friend's little brother is in my history class and couldn't stop talking about it, and seeing as though Liam is like . . . the coolest guy in school, I figured that meant Noah was going, and if Noah is going, you *have* to go."

I gape at her a little longer, trying to wrap my head around everything she just said. "First up, Noah outranks Liam on the coolness scale by a mile. Liam only tries to be cool, but he's really not. And second, I'm not going to that party."

"What?" Hazel shrieks. "Why not? I did your hair and makeup and everything. All you need to do is get dressed and go. Don't even try to tell me that your friends aren't going because I know Tarni, she wouldn't miss a cool party."

I shake my head, not prepared to tell her about the shit I've been getting from Shannan all week. She doesn't need to bear the weight of that. "No, it's a bad idea."

Her face falls, her brows creasing. "I don't understand," she says. "Things were supposed to get better when Noah came back."

"It's complicated," I tell her, desperately wishing she was right.

"What's complicated about it? You love him, don't you?"

"I . . . That's not an easy question to answer."

"Yes, it is," she says. "What's hard about it? You either love someone or you don't."

"It's just, I think you're asking a different kind of question. Do I love him? Yes, I've always loved him. Since the day I was born, I've loved him, but I think you're asking if I'm in love with him, and that's where it gets complicated."

"You are though, right?"

I shrug my shoulders.

"I . . . I really don't know, Hazel. He broke my heart when he put distance between us, and I don't think it ever really healed."

"Well," she muses, her brows creased in thought. "Is he in love with you?"

I shake my head, desperately willing myself not to cry, hating how much this innocent conversation hurts. "I used to think he was, but then, how could he abandon me the way he did if he were? People who love each other don't hurt each other like that."

Her lips press into a hard line, and she looks up at me with those big, sad eyes. "But he was already hurting after Linc died. Maybe he just doesn't remember how to love you."

Reaching out for her, I pull my little sister into my arms and hold her tightly against me. She's always held on to hope that Noah and I would somehow come back together, and I suppose that's my fault for allowing her to believe that he could come back to me. But after this week from hell, I don't think it's possible. I'm losing hope that the old Noah is capable of emerging out of the darkness. It's consumed him too much. He's lost for good. "I wish it were that easy," I tell her, hating the thought of breaking her heart. "I don't think it's possible to forget how to love someone, but I think he's trying really hard to forget."

"I don't want him to forget," she murmurs into my chest. "It was always so fun when Noah and Linc came over."

She lets out a heavy sigh that breaks my heart before pulling back and looking up into my eyes. "Do you . . . Do you think he stays away because of me? Maybe he doesn't like me."

"What?" I ask, horrified. "Not even a little bit. Noah loved you so much. I think he's just hurting so much from losing Linc that he can't see how much he's hurting everyone else. It's consuming him, and he needs to work through all of that before he can even try to be his old self. I just worry that it'll be too late."

"Too late?" she grunts. "It's already been three years. How much time does he need?"

"Tell me about it!"

"You know this only means you have to go to that party even more now."

"Huh? If anything, it means I need to stay away."

"Nuh-uh," she says, stepping out of my arms and digging back into my closet, searching through my clothes. "You need to go have a great time and ignore him like he doesn't even matter to you, and then he's going to be all drooly with big hearts in his eyes and come racing back into your arms."

A booming laugh tears from my chest. "That easy, huh?" I ask, unable to deny that having a good night out without having to think about Noah Ryan sounds like the best time ever.

"Uh-huh. That easy," Hazel confirms, finding my black thigh-high boots and high-waisted leather miniskirt. She shoves them at me. "Here, put these on while I find a cute top."

What in the fresh hell has happened to my sister? One week of middle school has turned her into a fashion guru.

Excitement drums through my veins, and I find myself following directions as I hastily get dressed, pulling on the miniskirt and boots before looking in the mirror, almost horrified by how sexy I look. I've never matched these two items before because . . . Well, I'm not a sexy girl. I can do pretty outfits or cute, but I've never been able to pull off sexy before.

"Woah," I murmur, taking it in as Hazel tosses me an oversized sweater that hangs off my shoulder. I quickly pull it on and stare at myself in awe.

"There's no way you can't go to that party now," Hazel says, her eyes brimming with beaming excitement.

"Fine," I grumble, unable to deny how right she is. It would be a shame to waste an outfit like this. "But I'm only staying for a little while. The second Noah even thinks about ruining my night, I'm out."

"YES!"

Hazel races from my room, and I hear her out in the hallway, all but hanging over the banister and calling downstairs. "MOM. IT WORKED! SHE'S GOING TO THE PARTY. YOU OWE ME TEN

BUCKS!"

"Thank God," Mom calls back. "Movie night for us without Grandma Gertrude up there."

"HEY!" I yell back, shoving my head out my door. "I heard that!"

Mom laughs, not even a hint of regret in her tone. "You were supposed to."

Rolling my eyes, I grab my phone and shove it into my bra before strutting downstairs and finding Mom in the kitchen. I cross my arms over my chest and give her a hard stare. "You planned this," I say.

She turns around and takes one look at me. "Wow, honey. You look—"

"Grown up," my dad cuts in from across the kitchen, his eyes wide and filled with horror. "I don't like it."

Mom shakes her head, her lips pulling into a wide grin. "Don't listen to him, sweetheart. You look incredible. He's just jealous that he can't pull off boots like that."

"You're damn right," Dad says. "Have you seen these calves? I'm practically built like a linebacker."

Ignoring their ridiculousness, I try to get back on track. "You know damn well that this Grandma Gertrude had no plans on going to that party."

"I know," Mom says. "But you'll be seventeen in five months, and you've barely lived. These are the years you're supposed to enjoy yourself. Go out with your friends and make memories because one day, you'll wake up and realize you're old and wish that you could have taken advantage of the small things."

"What are you saying, Mom? You think you're old and boring?"

"Who? Me?" Mom grunts. "No, not at all. I'm talking about your dad."

"Hey!" Dad mutters, but Mom completely ignores him.

I laugh and step closer to Mom. "Seeing as though you orchestrated this whole thing, I only think it's fair that you drop me off."

"Deal," she says. "But there's going to be rules. I know you're a smart girl and know better, but remember to never accept drinks from a stranger, and absolutely no alcohol. I want you home by midnight, and if you're in trouble or you don't feel safe, always call us."

"I know," I say with a groan.

"Good, then let's go. I've been dying to get you out of the house, and I swear, if you don't come home with some exciting stories for me to live vicariously through you, then you're not partying right."

Oh God. Maybe having Mom drop me off isn't such a good idea after all. If she even gets a hint of a good time, she'll be the one taking up space on the dance floor, and before I know it, she'll have Aunt Maya and all her college friends crashing Liam's party and turning it into an over forty rager.

With that, we make our way out to the car, and as Mom starts the engine, I pull my phone out of my bra and send off one final text.

Zoey: Hazel twisted my arm. I'm coming, and I'm ready for a good night!

Tarni: HELL YEAH!!!!!!!

Fifteen minutes later, I stand in the doorway of Liam's home, looking in at the array of crammed bodies. This was such a bad idea, but I can't find it in me to turn around and walk back out. Besides, Mom hit the gas the second the door closed behind me, making it impossible to change my mind.

People stare at me, their eyes dragging up and down my body as if not even realizing I'm the girl they've been calling trash all week. I try to ignore them and push past the insecurities their taunts have created in me.

The music is so loud that I can't hear myself think, and without Noah or Shannan in sight, that's exactly what I need to relax and actually enjoy my night. Making my way through the door, my gaze shifts over the eager partiers, and I barely get five feet into the fray when I find Tarni, Abby, and Cora dancing like nobody's watching, drinks in hand.

I make my way toward them, a genuine smile spreading across my face for the first time all week. I'm just about there when Tarni glances over Cora's shoulder, her big blue eyes coming right to mine.

"Hooooooooly shit," she beams, her jaw dropping as she takes me in. "Who are you, and what the hell happened to my best friend?"

I laugh as I crash into my friends, their arms slinging over my shoulders as they drag me into their little circle. Indicating down my body, I meet Tarni's stare. "It's too much, isn't it?"

"Hell no, girl," she says, taking one last sip of her drink before shoving the almost full cup into my hand. "It's perfect. You look like you've come to make a fucking statement, and that's exactly what we're going to do. Now, let's get you fucked up."

I grin back at her, and with that, I lift the cup to my lips while sending a silent apology to my mom, knowing damn well that I'll be breaking a few of her rules tonight.

Chapter 12

NOAH

It's just after ten when I finally show up at the East View High party just outside of town. I wasn't planning to come tonight, but Liam hasn't quit bugging me about it. The second he told the world his parents were out for the weekend, he started planning the first party of the semester, and naturally, every last person in East View showed up.

I've spent most of the night chilling with a few of the guys from St. Michael's, but since moving schools, they haven't been able to hold my attention, not since coming back here to this place. I've been here a week, and to say it's been a dumpster fire is an understatement.

Tuesday with the rumors about Linc and Shannan's mob attack on Zoey were a tipping point. It threw me right over the edge, and the guilt for not protecting Zoey like I always promised I would has eaten at me all week. The school has turned her into an outcast, and while she's held her head high and suffered through it all week, I haven't been man enough to step up and put a stop to it. If I did, I'd have to admit that I actually care.

Fuck. The school counselor has been earning her paycheck this week.

Shannan has gone out of her way to make life hell for Zoey, but despite how Zoey just sits there and takes it, I know that she'll eventually bite back, and when she does, Shannan better run. Zoey has always had a backbone, but she keeps it hidden like a secret weapon.

I don't get what Shannan's angle is though. Is she trying to impress me or get my approval? Because it's not working. If anything, it's just showing me how fucking awful she is. Sure, I might have thought about fucking her when I first got to East View, but now that she's messing with Zoey, there is no way in hell I'll touch her. Liam can have her.

I don't even know why I care so much. Maybe it's out of habit or a way to protect Linc's wishes. He would hate the way things are between us now, and that's on me. He'd hate it all. My relationship with Mom, my relationship with Zoey, the way I've let down Hazel.

Fuck, he'd hate that most of all. I need to make it up to Hazel.

Zoey was right, Linc would be so ashamed of me, and that thought kills me. Zoey's been right about a lot of things. How I'm too scared of my own feelings, how I'm a fucking coward. I hate how easily she can read me. When I first got here, I thought the ball was in my court, that I was the one who could see right through her, read her so perfectly, but it's been the opposite. She's becoming a mystery to me, while after three long years, she still knows me better than I know myself, no matter how hard I try to push her away and hide it. She makes me vulnerable.

Trying to push the thoughts of Zoey aside, I walk up the pathway toward Liam's home. It's pretty big for East View standards. His family clearly has money, but not the type of money they can just easily throw around and show off. Most families are like that around here. Middle to upper class. It's why the majority of the kids around here drive expensive cars. If it weren't for the over-the-top fees of the local private schools, I can guarantee most of these assholes would have been enrolled there instead.

My family is no different. Well, it used to be before Linc died. My father left us after that, and the guilt eats at him, so he overcompensates by throwing money at me to avoid having to deal with the fact that he's a piece of shit. I'm not complaining though, that money bought my Camaro and paid for the killer matte black paint job. It also kept me out of jail, so there's that.

People have spilled out on the front lawn of Liam's property as the music blares from inside. There are kids sitting on the roof just outside the bedroom windows and spilled drinks from one end of the front porch to the other.

Clearly this party has been in full swing for a while, and I'm surprised it hasn't been shut down yet. Though from my experience, the cops tend to let us party as long as our noise is contained and we're not bothering anyone. They only need to worry when we're not partying, and everyone is out on their own.

People I don't recognize say hello, and when I stop for a second, someone shoves a beer into my hand. I talk with one of the guys on the team, pretty sure his name is Jason something . . . Maybe Harding? I don't know, but all that matters is he's a good player, and so far, he hasn't let me down in training. I haven't had a chance to get to know him yet, and from what I can tell, he seems to have his head screwed on, apart from the fact that he just fucked one of the cheerleaders in the bushes outside Liam's home.

Come to think of it, was this the asshole who spent his summer trying to get between Zoey's legs? Or was that Cameron Landry? I don't fucking know anymore.

Dropping my cigarette to the lawn, I quickly stub it out with my toe before finally heading inside. The house is crammed with bodies, most of the guys are standing around and watching the girls dance while calling out crass comments. The floors are sticky, and I keep to the edges of the room as I scan Liam's home, not willing to risk walking through the girls just yet. I need a few drinks before I can lower my standards enough to put myself through that shit.

A game of beer pong is set up on the dining table, and I find Liam at the head of it with a girl under his arm as he throws the ping pong ball across the table, directly into the cup at the other end. Everybody breaks into cheers as Liam hollers and takes a swig of his beer before dropping his lips to the girl's and furiously eating her face.

Not giving a shit if I break up their little celebration, I step into Liam's side as people call out to me, wanting my attention. "Hey man," I say as he pulls away from his girl.

"Yo, you made it," Liam cheers, grabbing my hand and pulling me in to clap me on the back. "I was starting to think you'd bailed."

"On the first party of the year? Nah. Just had shit to do first."

"Fuck yeah," he says, nodding to some kid who scurries into the kitchen to grab me a beer, despite the one already in my hand. "Let's get you fucked up. There's a party to be had!"

I grin, not really in the mood to get fucked up, but after the week I've had, I could use the drink. The kid returns and offers me a beer, and I take it gingerly before cracking the top. Lifting the rim to my lips, I take a quick swig and scrunch up my face. This shit tastes like piss, but I'll drink it anyway.

Liam bails on his game, and we head outside to where the rest of the football team is chilling by the firepit. The guys welcome me with open arms, and before I know it, another beer is shoved into my hands. The loud music flows out to the yard, but it's muffled enough that we can actually hold some form of conversation, not that the guys are interested in talking when there are girls draping themselves all over them.

Shannan hovers like a bad stench, but I'm not about to make a scene by telling her to fuck off, not yet at least. As long as she doesn't try to get naked and grind all over me. She's fine to pretend she means something here. Besides, she's dancing with her friends, and so far, the rest of the guys seem to appreciate her efforts. Me on the other hand, I couldn't be less interested.

I fuck around with the boys for an hour before getting up and making my way toward the back door, but I only get a few feet away when Shannan steps directly into my path. "Where are you going?" she purrs, her hand plastered against my chest.

"None of your damn business," I say, pushing her hand off me.

Shannan shakes it off, and as I go to step around her, she steps with me. "Come on, don't be like that," she says, reminding me just how persistent she is, only when I look at her, all I see is the bitch who's been making Zoey's life a living hell all week. "Why don't you come dance with me?"

"I don't dance," I say, attempting to get around her again.

She puts her hand up on my chest again and steps even closer, pushing up on her tippy toes to whisper in my ear. "That's okay," she murmurs. "I can dance enough for the both of us. Unless you'd rather just skip all the bullshit and take me upstairs instead."

Fucking hell. This chick doesn't give up.

I pull back and look down at her, my face scrunching in disgust. It's one thing getting with the cheer captain, but hearing that kind of desperation is the biggest turnoff. "I'll pass," I say, shoving her off me again. "Fuck Liam instead. He'll give you what you want."

Shannan gapes at me as I walk past her, and I can guarantee that she's never been rejected before, especially by one of the football players, but I've got better things to do than play pass the cheerleader.

Making my way inside, I head for the kitchen and find another beer before cracking the top and lifting it to my lips. I've already had a few, too much that I won't be driving home tonight, but not enough to fuck me up. Not yet at least. There's still time. After all, pushing away the people I love isn't the only thing that helps numb the pain.

Wanting to avoid Shannan's bullshit for a while, I make my way through Liam's home, cutting through the throng of partiers and stopping to say hi to the few people I've gotten to know this week.

The music is so loud, I barely hear what anyone is saying, and I zone out, glancing around the party. Couples are hooking up in the hallways and lingering on the stairs while sloppy, drunk girls fumble around, knocking into each other. Girls squeal and laugh as they spill their drinks everywhere while random guys make asses of themselves trying to hit on them.

A familiar laugh sounds over the music, and my gaze shifts back toward the dance floor, and I suck in a breath when I find Zoey dancing with her friends, and fuck me, she's breathtaking. I can't tear my eyes off her.

She's got a drink in her hand, and it's clear from the light flush in her cheeks that she's already had a few too many. She dances so carefree, more relaxed and happier than I've ever seen her before. She's simply stunning, and for just a moment, something thaws in my frozen heart.

Her body moves to the music, and goddamn, it's hypnotizing. In those boots and that tiny skirt, I've never wanted her more. I've always looked at her as a kid, and well, that's because we were kids, but now? Fuck! No wonder every guy at school has been desperate for a taste.

A wide smile spreads across her face, and I watch as her friend, Tarni, holds up a bottle of straight Vodka and pours it right into her cup. "Alright, girl," she calls over the music, leaning into Zoey. "Which one of these assholes is gonna pop that cherry?"

Oh, hell no. Over my dead fucking body.

Zoey laughs and glances around the room as if actually looking for someone to fuck, and a deep anger swirls through my veins. Only as she looks around, those big green eyes find mine through the darkness, her smile so fucking bright it hurts.

She doesn't respond to Tarni's question, just simply keeps watching me as she continues to dance, and I can't look away, the two of us locked in a trance. Zoey laughs to herself, sipping her drink as she moves to the music, her wide stare drawing me in.

I've never seen her like this before—like a fucking angel sent right from the heavens—and for the first time in three pain-filled years, I don't feel plagued by darkness.

I inch toward her as she dances for me, and for some reason, nothing can hold me back tonight, and as I watch her, it feels as though we're the only people in the room.

My heart thunders.

Zoey doesn't dare take her eyes off mine, and I wouldn't have it any other way. It's where those eyes have always belonged.

It feels so damn right.

She finishes what's in her drink, and I take another step toward her, that deep, sultry gaze beckoning me, daring me to take everything I've ever wanted. She tosses her empty cup over her shoulder, and it hits the guy behind her, but she doesn't seem to notice, her attention solely on me.

The guy turns around and steps into her, his arm slipping around her waist and forcing her attention up to his gaze, stealing those eyes away from me. He leans down and murmurs something into her ear, and the way she smiles up at him and laughs has a fierce jealousy pulsing through my veins.

My heart races, and I can't help but watch as he pulls her into him, that perfect body of hers folding against his like it should be doing to mine.

My hands ball into fists at my sides, and while I've done absolutely nothing to deserve her, I'm not ready to watch someone else sweep her away.

I have no right to try and hold on to her after the last three years of pushing her away. It'd make life a shitload easier if she just pretended I didn't exist, but this . . . no. I can't fucking stand seeing her like this.

I force my stare away, needing another drink, and this time, it's going to be something a lot stronger than a fucking beer. I turn away and stalk back toward the kitchen, my hand slipping into my pocket for a cigarette.

How the fuck could I let her get to me like that?

Zoey James has me weak, and I don't like it.

Just before stepping out to the kitchen, I glance back and find her through the crowd, needing to know if this was all for show and if I still had her attention, but instead, my rage hits an all-new high.

The guy tries to kiss her, and I watch as she turns her face away, shaking her head and trying to tell him no, but he doesn't listen. She pushes at his chest, but he holds her tighter, his arm locking around her waist and keeping her pinned against him. His other hand trails down to her ass, squeezing tight, and her soft cry for him to stop is like a knife right to my chest.

Zoey looks around for help, but her friends are nowhere to be seen, and then she looks for me across the room, but I'm already there, having crossed the dance floor in a matter of seconds, moving toward her before I can even fully comprehend what's happening. Her eyes widen, finding me right behind the guy, and before she can say a word,

I grip his shoulder and whip him around.

He barely has a chance to see what's coming before my fist flies toward his face. The force of my punch throws him back, and Zoey jumps aside, narrowly avoiding being knocked out by his flailing arms.

The asshole comes back at me, roaring with anger before his friends rush into his side, pulling him back. They clearly have more sense than he does at the moment. "Leave it," one of his friends urges. "That's Noah Ryan. You don't wanna start shit with him. It's not worth it."

The guy fights against his friends, trying to tear out of their grasp, roaring at them to release him, but I couldn't give a shit about him as I turn to Zoey, anger booming through my chest. "You're drunk," I spit at her. "Go home. You don't belong here."

Chapter 13

NOAH

Zoey glares at me, venom pooling in her furious stare, but I turn away, hoping like fuck she has enough sense to get out of here before that asshole gets his hands on her again. The second I step away, Shannan moves back in front of me, and the moment she sees Zoey at my back, her eyes fill with heated anger.

Shannan looks between me and Zoey, and I see the very second she foolishly convinces herself that Zoey has tried to take something that belongs to her, something that was never hers to start with. A low groan rumbles from the back of my throat, knowing how this is going to turn out before she's even said a single word.

Shannan fixes me with a hard stare before shifting her wicked gaze to Zoey and stepping around me. Her friends have her back within seconds as they surround Zoey. "Well, tonight just got a little more exciting, don't you think, Zoey?" Shannan says, her gaze sailing up and down Zoey's body as she looks back at her with disdain. "You've got a lot of balls showing up here."

"Seriously?" Zoey laughs, waving around her at the overwhelming show of cheerleaders surrounding her. "Is this supposed to intimidate me? You're a joke, Shannan."

My brows arch. I've only been here for a week, and so far, Zoey has proven over and over again that she's not the type to back down, and it blows me the fuck away. She always needed my protection when we were kids, and since I've been gone, she's had to learn how to fend for herself, and damn, it fucking suits her. But unfortunately for Zoey, Shannan isn't the type to back down either, and what's worse, she likes to play dirty.

"I'm the joke?" Shannan throws back at Zoey. "Look at you, constantly throwing yourself at Noah. You're pathetic. Tell me," she adds, her hand waving up and down Zoey's body, taking in her outfit and makeup. "Did you do this for him? Did you do your hair and makeup and pick out some whorish outfit in the hopes he might take pity on you and take your pretty little V-card?"

Zoey's gaze flickers to me, embarrassment shining in her eyes, and it leaves me wondering if maybe she did do all of this for me. Was she hoping to get my attention? Because she already had it.

I see in her eyes that she's waiting for me to step in, but I can't. I've gotten too close already, and I made it clear on day one that I wanted nothing to do with her. The divide between us feels like it's closing in already, and if I allow myself to open that door, I won't be able to turn back. Besides, she made it perfectly clear in the school parking lot that it was too fucking late for me to try. If I step in now, Shannan will retaliate, and things will only get worse for Zoey.

Zoey doesn't respond, and my stomach starts to feel uneasy as Shannan pushes harder. "He doesn't want you, Zoey. You're trash, and he's way out of your league. Face it, you're going to die a virgin."

Ah, fuck. Somebody tell me this bitch didn't just say that to her.

She couldn't be more wrong. Zoey is fucking gorgeous, and soon enough, she's going to meet someone and fall madly in love, and when that happens, it'll destroy me, but it'll be for the best.

"I'd prefer to die a virgin than have screwed my way through the whole football team before the end of school. Tell me, do you have a rotating roster or is it a first-in, best-dressed kind of situation?" Zoey argues, stupidly giving Shannan exactly what she's looking for instead of just walking away.

"Oh my god," Shannan laughs as people crowd around, the same way they'd done in the cafeteria on Tuesday. "You really are a frigid bitch, aren't you? What's the matter? Scared the big, nasty cock is gonna bite you?"

Zoey's cheeks flush, clearly not comfortable, and my hands ball at my sides, feeling sick to my stomach. I want to put an end to this, to finish this once and for all, but I won't fight Zoey's battles.

She's not mine to protect anymore.

Shannan inches forward. "Cat got your tongue?" she purrs. "I think it's time for you to leave. You're not welcome here."

"Careful," Zoey says, narrowing her gaze at Shannan. "Your insecurities are showing."

A smile pulls at the corner of my lips. She's never been so right in her life, but clearly Shannan doesn't appreciate being outed like that. "You're trash, Zoey," she throws back at her before saying it again, louder. "Trash. Trash. Trash."

The other cheerleaders join in, and the chanting quickly starts to drown out the music until the whole fucking room is chanting at her, Tarni included.

"Trash. Trash. Trash."

Zoey looks around in a blind panic, searching for a way out. Her eyes meet mine just as Shannan hits her with the final blow, tossing what's left of her pink drink all over Zoey's outfit. She gasps as the cool liquid assaults her skin, and as if on cue, every last cheerleader around the circle does the same, and the contents of my stomach start to rise in my throat.

I run for the bathroom, my stomach clenching and twisting with agony, feeling like the biggest fucking disappointment for not stepping in.

Fuck, I hate how much I love her, but goddamn, she deserves so much better than this.

Bursting through the door of the bathroom, I slam it behind me before emptying the contents of my stomach into the toilet, heaving as I struggle to come to terms with just how low I've sunk.

I'm a piece of shit.

I should have stepped in, no matter what it cost me mentally, even if it meant making matters worse. How can I go on knowing I didn't have her back when she needed me?

Linc must fucking hate the bastard I've become. *She* must hate me.

With nothing left in my stomach, I flush the toilet and move toward the sink to rinse out my mouth and splash water over my face. I hang my head over the basin limply and watch the water drip, too ashamed to look into the mirror. I wish I never fucking came here tonight. But that wouldn't have changed the fact that Zoey was here, drunk, with that asshole, and if I hadn't been here to stop him . . . I don't even want to think about what could have happened.

Wanting to get out of here, I move across the bathroom and open the door, only to step out and crash right into Zoey, soaked from head to toe in sticky pink shit. She glares up at me, and before I get a chance to step around her, she shoves her hands into my chest, forcing me back into the bathroom.

Zoey pulls the door closed behind her, and as she looks back at me, I see the tears in her eyes. She moves past me to the sink and grabs the hand towel before holding it under the water and wringing it out.

She starts cleaning the sticky liquid off and meets my stare through the mirror. "Are you happy now? Is this what you wanted?" she asks, indicating down her body. "Is it not enough for you to kill me every fucking time you look at me, but you have to make sure I'm thoroughly humiliated? You have to make sure my life is a living hell just for being someone you used to know?"

Her words are like a knife right through the back.

Unable to handle the hurt in her stare, I look away. "I had nothing to do with that."

"Right," she laughs, pulling her soaking hair over her shoulder and trying to wash out the pink mess. "Because Shannan just wants to humiliate me for the fun of it and not because she thinks I want to ride your dick like a fucking cowgirl."

My eyes widen, never having heard her talk like this in her life. I know she's always had a stubborn streak, but she's always been respectful with her language, refusing to curse unless it was detrimental to the situation. But this is the alcohol speaking.

"This is all on you, Noah," she continues, sounding like a broken record and telling me everything I already hate about myself. "She's only getting at me in the hopes of winning your approval because for some fucking reason, you haven't bent her over and given her what she wants yet. You are the only person in this stupid school who has the power to do anything about this, and you just stood there like a fucking idiot. Do I really mean that little to you now?"

The tears stream down her cheeks, and my fingers itch to reach out to her and take away her pain, but I can't. I don't get to have the best of both worlds. I don't get to be the asshole who hurts her and the one to take away her pain. That's not fair.

She rinses out the towel and wrings it again before dragging it up and down her arms, mopping up as much of the sticky drink as possible, but the only thing that's going to help her now is a shower. When she finally gives in, realizing it's useless, she grips the sink and hangs her head, much like I was only a moment ago.

"Congratulations," she says, her broken tone cutting right through my chest as she glances up and meets my stare once again. "I hope that watching me suffer sparks some kind of light in your cold, dead heart."

Fixing her gaze back to her own reflection, she hastily wipes her eyes before storming to the door, refusing to look back at me. She grips the handle, and I will myself to back down and keep my mouth shut, but I can't help myself. "Where the hell are you going?"

She pauses, the door half open as she looks back at me with furrowed brows. "Where do you think I'm going?" she scoffs. "I'm going home, asshole. Isn't that what you spat at me? *Go home. You're drunk. You don't belong here.*"

And with that, she storms out into the party, and I clench my jaw, anger swirling through my chest.

Don't go after her. Don't go after her. Don't go after her, you fucking idiot.

"FUCK!"

I go after her.

I storm out of the bathroom, following the mop of dripping chestnut hair through the crowded bodies. She walks up ahead, and I watch as people laugh at her back, the word trash echoing through the crowd. She passes her friends, Tarni, Abby, and Cora, and I watch the moment Tarni notices her and slips further into the crowd, not wanting to be seen with Zoey after everything that just went down.

My jaw clenches, and I shake my head. I always told Zoey when we were kids that Tarni was a shit friend, and she never believed me, no matter how obvious it was. Zoey figured I just wanted her to myself, and yes, I suppose I did, but I was also being honest. Tarni is a piece of shit. She's not nearly good enough for Zoey.

I continue after her, watching as she slips out the front door, not even bothering to tell anyone that she's leaving, not that her friends would care anyway. I expect her to walk down the street a little and call her parents, maybe her dad. She wouldn't dream of calling her mom to come get her this late.

I follow from afar, wandering down the street and keeping enough distance for her not to notice me, only she doesn't stop. She just keeps walking, and I realize that she had no intention of calling her parents at all. She's walking the whole way home.

What the fuck is wrong with this girl?

Not able to stomach the thought of her walking through the streets by herself in the middle of the night, I keep walking, no longer giving a shit if she knows I'm here or not.

We walk for ten minutes when she finally takes enough notice of the space around her to realize someone is here, and I watch as her body tenses and she picks up her pace. A smirk pulls at my lips, but I stay silent, not prepared to put her out of her misery. Hell, if I were some creep in the night, I'd be the one in danger. With the mood she's in, I wouldn't be willing to cross her.

I can almost feel how her heart races as she strides up the street, and after a minute, she finds the courage to glance back over her shoulder. Her gaze comes right to mine, and the second she makes me out in the darkness, she doubles over with relief. "Holy shit, Noah," she yells back at me, bracing her hands on her thighs and blowing the air from her lungs. "What the hell is wrong with you? What kind of asshole stalks girls through the street like that? I thought you were trying to kill me."

I stay silent, slowly creeping in closer, and she sends me a wicked glare before giving me her back and storming ahead. She doesn't want to accept that I'm walking her home, but I don't give her much of a choice.

We walk in silence with at least another twenty minutes to go. Had we driven, it would have taken ten minutes this time of night, but I've had too much to drink to even think about offering. And to be honest, I don't think I could cope with being in a confined space with her again tonight. I need some time to cool down and pretend her words didn't tear me to shreds.

The minutes tick by when I hear her soft tone filling the night. "Do you remember that day we were at the park with Linc? You were tossing a ball around while I sat in the grass. You were giving him such a hard time, making him run from one end of the park right to the other. Any other kid would have gotten frustrated and told you to go screw yourself, but he thought it was great," she says, the memory so fresh in my head. It's one that I play on repeat every day of my life. It was one of the last times just the three of us were together.

Zoey lifts her hand and wipes her eyes, and I listen as her voice wavers. "Do you remember what we were talking about between Linc's groaning?"

I swallow hard, hating just how fucking well I remember it. That was the day I realized that we were so much more than just best friends. I was in love with her and knew that I was going to spend the rest of my life by her side. Don't get me wrong, I always knew she was it for me, but there was something about the way the sun lit her face and the way she smiled at me. "I told you that you were the greatest love of my life," I tell her, the words so hard to say out loud, but I know I meant every fucking word, maybe I still do. "That I would make you the happiest girl in the world and protect you with my life."

Zoey scoffs. "I was so foolish to believe you," she tells me, making my chest ache with the idea that she no longer has faith in what I felt for her. "Maybe it was because I was so young, and you were all I knew. You were my whole world, Noah. I never could have dreamed that you'd be the person I'd need protecting from."

Fuck me. Her words bring me down to my knees in the middle of the sidewalk, and I gasp for air as she continues up the street, discreetly watching me fall apart over her shoulder. She's always known exactly what to say to make me feel, to bring me back to life, and that's why I've fought so hard to stay away. She's the greatest weapon against me when I don't want to feel anything at all.

She's always been my whole world, even now, and despite how hard I try to hide it, how hard I push her away and tell her it means nothing, she can see right through my bullshit. And this only proves just how right she is.

Zoey doesn't stop walking or wait for me to pull myself together, not that I deserve that, but I'm sure as fuck not going to leave her to walk home alone.

Forcing myself back to my feet, I follow after her, watching her silhouette down the street, not daring to close the gap and give her the power to use my own words against me again. That old me, he doesn't exist anymore, but that doesn't mean I don't grieve for the man I used to be or the life I used to think I'd have with Zoey. It kills me to pull away from her, but it's the only way I can survive.

I wasn't lying all those years ago when I told her I would protect her with my life. If it came down to stepping in front of a bullet for her, I'd do it in a heartbeat. I wouldn't even need to think about it. But with people like Shannan, she needs to learn to stand on her own two feet, and she has. Over the past three years, she's grown in a way I wasn't expecting. She's so damn strong. I always knew she would be, and I regret not being there to see the way she came out of her shell, but she only had to learn how to do that because I wasn't there like I promised.

Fuck, I'm such a piece of shit.

My hand digs into my pocket, and I pull out a cigarette, lighting it quickly before taking a deep drag and blowing out a cloud of smoke into the dark Arizona sky. The nicotine hits my system, and I close my eyes, feeling myself finally start to calm.

I follow her the rest of the way home and watch as she storms up her front porch and through the door, ignoring her father watching her with concern. I can't help but take a moment, staring up at her home as I stand in the shadows. So many memories live inside this house.

A moment passes, and when Zoey's bedroom light turns off, her silhouette fills the bedroom window. Taking the final drag of my cigarette, I drop it to the ground, stub it out with my toe, and turn on my heel to get the hell out of here.

I barely get two steps away when a familiar tone tears through the night. "Why are you following my daughter home, Noah?" Zoey's father, Henry, asks.

Fuck.

Turning back around, I find Henry James standing on his front lawn, his hands buried in his pockets with disapproval written across his face. "She's drunk and stubborn, sir," I tell him, not bothering to sugarcoat it. "She left the party without telling a soul. I couldn't let her walk all the way home alone."

Mr. James holds my stare for a moment, his gaze narrowed. "You abandoned her three years ago when she needed you the most, so let me be very clear with you, Noah. Zoey doesn't need you anymore. She clawed her way back without you, and I am not about to let you drag her back down into that pit of despair. Do you understand me? I may not have seen you over the past few years, but I have followed you. I've kept an eye on you, Noah, and you are a troubled child. I have seen the type of trouble you get yourself into, and the lack of respect you have for authority. You're heading down a dangerous path, and I don't want you leading my daughter down it with you. When it comes down to it, you and I both know that she will follow you blindly. You're not good enough for her, Noah. Not anymore."

"Believe me," I say with a nod, taking a step back as a lump forms in my throat. "I know."

"I appreciate you making sure she got home okay," he says. "But this is the last you will see of her outside of school."

I stare at him, knowing without a doubt that I can't accept that. The idea of never seeing her. . . fuck. I know that's what I asked for, what I've needed these past few years, but I always knew that at some point, we would find our way back to each other. But having her this close and never being able to see her? No, I won't accept that.

"With all due respect, Mr. James. No," I tell him. "There's too much history, and you know damn well that Zoey isn't just going to walk away. I see it in her eyes. She thinks she can somehow save me, and you and I both know that means she's never going to give up. You can try and keep her away from me all you like. I'll fucking beg you to, but you can't. I know you're just trying to look out for your daughter. I'd do the same if I were you, but this needs to be her decision. Zoey and I . . . We're two halves of the same whole, and no matter how much I try to pull us apart and burn that tether between us, we'll always be forced back together. It's inevitable."

I glance up at the home before me, finding Zoey hovering in her bedroom window, watching over me and her father with a deep curiosity in her eyes. I hold her stare for only a moment, so many silent messages passing between us, just like they used to, and with that, I bow my head and walk away before I throw myself through the door and fall to my knees, begging her to forgive me.

Chapter 14

ZOEY

Gently pressing a kiss to the photo of me as a child in the hospital, I pull the frame away and glance down at the little version of me. "Wish me luck," I say, the nerves pounding through my body and making me want to hurl.

Monday mornings suck at the best of times, but this is the first Monday morning after Liam's disastrous party that I'll see Noah, and I can't think of anything worse. Friday night started out great. It was fun . . . until it wasn't.

Having at least twenty cheap cocktails thrown on me wasn't exactly the type of good time I was looking for. Though to be honest, I was drunk enough to be able to shrug off the humiliation. Had that happened any earlier in the night, I would have crumbled right there on the dance floor. The fact that it happened right in front of Noah didn't help. Not to mention his inability to be the hero I always needed him to be. But it wouldn't be Shannan if she didn't strive for maximum effect.

Forcing him into the bathroom to tear him to shreds was one thing, but the walk home was pure torture. I shouldn't have said anything about that day at the park three years ago. I don't know what I was trying to achieve. Maybe I wanted to see if he remembered, or maybe I just needed to remind him how it used to be. But hearing him recite those words killed me. He remembers it all just as deeply as I do, and despite that, he's still capable of denying that I mean a damn thing to him, and I think that's what hurts the most.

Had he forgotten it all or buried it so deep that it was impossible to recall, I might be able to understand how he could so easily push me away. But it's right there for him, tormenting his mind in the same way it does mine, yet I need him now more than ever. I don't understand how he can keep pushing me away when he still feels it. He can deny it all he likes, but I heard it in his broken tone as I watched the agony drive him to his knees in the quiet street. The idea of hurting me is killing him inside, but maybe that's what he needs. I think he wants to feel numb to our past because the memory of his brother is woven intricately through each memory of us, and if he lets even a sliver of light shine through the darkness, he'd be left to deal with Linc's death, and I don't think he's even a little bit ready to come to terms with it.

All I know is that when it comes to Noah Ryan, tiptoeing around the issue isn't going to work. He needs to be pushed to the edge and then thrown right over. I need to make him break, but he's not going to do that easily, and he's sure as hell isn't going to allow me to lead him there.

I have to force this, and I have to bring him to me to make it happen. But that's not going to be easy. Noah Ryan has never been easy to navigate, but if anyone can do it, it's me. At least, I hope it's me. If some other girl is holding a piece of his heart hostage, it's going to destroy me. How could he let another where I belong? I've never even been remotely interested in dating or sex because, for me, it's always been Noah.

Am I saving myself for him? Maybe. I don't know. The thought of being intimate with him like that . . . wow. I can't even think about it without goosebumps spreading across my skin. I know there's something special there, and I just hope he has the strength to claw his way back to me because, despite how much I want to hate him right now, we both know that we belong together.

I fear I'm his last shot, and I hate the thought of this monster he's allowing himself to become. That's not the real him. He's sweet and caring . . . mostly. He was always an asshole with a mean streak, but never to me. His popularity forced him to be like that, learning how to keep people at arm's length when they wanted to use him for a step up in the world.

Putting the photo frame back down on my desk, I let out one last shaky breath before reminding myself that I'm stronger than any of the bullshit. Anything Noah, Shannan, or the rest of the cheerleaders can throw at me means nothing, and the only reason they continue to torture me is because they're still trying to break me, but it won't happen. Not today at least.

Grabbing my things, I race downstairs, pleased to find Hazel already waiting by the door for me. "What took so long?" she says, glancing up at the clock on the wall. "We're going to be late."

"Not if I can help it," I say, flying out the door with Hazel on my six.

After quickly locking the door behind me, we scurry to the car, and within seven minutes, we're pulling up at Hazel's school with barely seconds to spare. She races through the front gates, and I hit the gas, only having a few minutes to get my ass to school.

Pulling into the East View High parking lot, I search for a space and find only one available—right next to Noah's matte black Camaro.

Great. I thought I could turn today around with my glowing pep talk this morning, but deep down, I knew today was going to be a disaster. I've barely put my Range Rover in park when I hear the bell sound through the school, and I suck in a breath. "Ah, crap," I mutter, grabbing my things and flying out of the car.

I hurry through the front gates and into the school, finding most of the students already well on their way to homeroom. Having barely seconds to spare, I quickly stop at my locker and key in my code before tearing the door open and scrambling through my things.

"HOLY SHIT," I hear Tarni from right down the other end of the hallway. "YOU'RE ALIVE!"

My head whips up, and I catch the slightest glimpse of her grinning at me, walking backward before disappearing around the corner. I laugh to myself. I didn't exactly stop to say goodbye to the girls on Friday night before stupidly taking off from the party with a stalker, and in hindsight, that probably wasn't the smartest choice to make. If Noah hadn't made sure I got home alright, who knows what could have happened to me. My dad made sure to remind me of that bright and early Saturday morning, drilling into me the dangers of drinking and how stupid it was to leave the party without a safe way home. To be honest, I think he was hurt that I didn't even think about calling him to come be my hero.

I felt sorry for myself all day Saturday and then spent Sunday with Mom and Hazel and never got a chance to text the girls, but now that I think of it, I don't think I ever got a message from any of them asking where I'd gone on Friday night, not even on Saturday making sure I was alright.

That realization has a pang of hurt residing in my chest, but I don't have time to dwell on it now.

"Get to homeroom," Principal Daniels says to the few stragglers still lingering in the hall.

I cringe and get a move on, making it to homeroom just moments before the door closes behind me. Letting out a sigh of relief, I drop into my seat and as Mrs. Pembroke goes through attendance, my mind spins, trying to figure out how the hell I can bring Noah to me.

I need to get him alone, trap him, and force him to talk.

So far, every time we've been alone, I've been on the defense, coming at him with hurt and anger, but clearly that isn't working. Though there's no doubt that I'm starting to break through his walls. The stranger I saw in the student office last Monday never would have followed me home, or maybe he would have, and I was just too blinded by my own pain that I couldn't see that.

Either way, this isn't going to be easy.

I spend the day in a haze, staring out windows and zoning out when the whispers and snickers hit me in the hallway. For the most part, Shannan and her tribe of assholes leave me alone today, but there's no mistaking the word *trash* that seems to follow me around the school like a bad smell.

My day passes in a blur of schoolwork, and during lunch, I sit with the girls. My mind is too preoccupied to hold a conversation, but they don't seem to notice I'm even here, and honestly, I'm starting to question why I even bother.

The end-of-lunch bell sounds through the school, and just as I stand from the table, watching Noah walk out of the cafeteria, it hits me.

I know exactly how to force him to me, and it's probably the most moronic thing I could ever think of. Maybe even dumber than getting drunk at a party and trying to walk home alone.

No. No, this is too stupid. Too risky. I can't. Scratch that. I'll go back to the drawing board.

But then . . . shit.

I have to. What other choice do I have? I have to push him while I still can because if I leave this too long, he's going to fall in with the people here and then seeing me every day will get easier. I need to strike while those old memories and feelings are swirling around in his head. I can't risk giving them a chance to settle. I can't risk this becoming our new normal.

Making my way out of the cafeteria, I walk to my locker, my gaze set on Noah down the hall, wondering how the hell I'm going to pull this off. Though one thing is for sure, it's going to have to wait until after school. There's no way I'll get away with doing this now.

My hands start to shake, and I force the plan to the back of my mind, needing to concentrate on my last two classes before the end of the day.

Nerves pulse through my body, and despite my need to focus and actually learn something, all I seem to be able to do is stare at the clock, watching the seconds tick by. By the end of my last class, a bead of sweat is trailing down my spine, and I've almost convinced myself to bail on the plan, but I keep reminding myself that this isn't for my twisted enjoyment, despite how exciting it might be. I need to do this to help Noah. At least that's what I'm going to keep telling myself. I mean, the fact that it's going to get him where it hurts is kind of nice too. It's going to be the sweetest victory. Assuming I can pull it off, of course.

Not knowing how long this might take, I pull my phone out and hold it discreetly beneath my desk before shooting a text to Hazel.

Zoey: I'm going to be a while! Could you catch the bus?
Hazel: The bus? Gross! Worst chauffeur ever!

Zoey: I am not your chauffeur!!!!
Hazel: That's not what Mom says!
Zoey: You're such a brat! Can you catch the bus or not?
Hazel: I suppose so.
Zoey: Perfect. I'll see you at home.

Putting my phone away, I concentrate on the last few minutes of class, furiously taking notes, knowing the second I'm out of here, everything the teacher has said is going to fall straight out of my brain. Then as the bell sounds for the end of school, a vicious wave of anxiety cripples me, my chest heaving with nerves.

I remain in my seat as the students pack up and bail around me, my hands gripping the sides of my desk, not sure if I have the lady balls to pull this off. If I get caught . . .

This is a bad idea. A really bad idea.

Crap. Crap. Crap. Crap on a cracker.

"Everything alright, Zoey?" my biology teacher, Ms. Lennon asks, her bag slung over her shoulder, more than ready to get out of here. Though I suppose she can't leave while there's still a freaking-out teen taking up residence in her classroom.

I swallow over the lump in my throat and force a smile. "Umm, yes," I say, my tone wavering and making it clear that I am anything but alright. "All good."

Ms. Lennon's brows furrow, and she watches me a little too closely as I scramble to pack up my things and get to my feet. "If there's anything you need to talk about, or just need a friend, my door is always open," she says, following me out of the classroom and pulling the door closed behind her before searching for her keys. "You know that, right?"

My forced smile shifts into a real one as fondness spreads through my chest. I've noticed the teachers watching me ever since the whole trash thing started in the cafeteria last Tuesday. I think they're waiting for me to break, but either way, it's nice of her to offer. "Thank you," I tell her. "I'll keep that in mind."

Ms. Lennon gives me a wide smile, and with that, I take off, knowing it's now or never. I can only hope this crazy little stunt doesn't end with a pair of handcuffs strapped tightly around my wrists.

Chapter 15

ZOEY

Needing the school to be almost deserted, I stop by my locker and take extra long to collect my things, slinging my bag over my shoulder before closing the door. Glancing up and down the hallway, it occurs to me that Tarni didn't even bother to hang around and say goodbye like usual, but the second the thought enters my mind, it's already gone.

At least ten minutes after the bell sounds, I make my way outside. My hands shake violently as I shove them deep into my pockets. Then, without a soul in sight, I let out a nervous breath before finally making my break for it.

I slip out of the building and make a sharp right, taking the long way around to keep hidden from anyone still lingering outside the school. I hear the football team on the field getting started with their drills, and I realize this could be my only chance. I step out from behind the building and slip into the boys' locker room, my face scrunching at the foul, lingering stench of stale boy sweat.

I can happily say that until this very moment, this is the only room in the whole school that I hadn't been in—and for good reason. There's nothing particularly exciting about it, apart from one tiny little thing—Noah's keys to that fancy Camaro that's sitting so lonely out in the student parking lot.

And now all I have to do is figure out which one of these lockers belongs to him.

Creeping deeper into the room, I glance around, hoping like hell there's no one left in here. The lockers are dirty with the players' things scattered from one end of the room to the other. Half of their lockers have been left open, while only a few of them have bothered to keep their things tidy.

Noah was always the neat and tidy type. He never liked people touching his things and made a point to always make sure everything had a spot. With that snippet of information, I look closer at the few tidy lockers, knowing one of these would be his. Red varsity jackets linger at most of the lockers, but there's only one of the clean lockers without a jacket.

Bingo.

Noah's only been here a week, and this school isn't put together enough to have a spare varsity jacket on standby to give him. I'm sure that will come later, but for now, he's the only football player without one.

Striding across the locker room, I grip the little combination lock and stare down at it, wondering what four-digit code he would use.

I start with his birthday, and when that doesn't work, I mentally kick myself for not trying Linc's birthday first. How stupid could I be? What other code would he possibly have? My heart pounds, and I try to get this done as quickly as possible, but when the lock still doesn't open, my brows furrow. Maybe this isn't his locker after all.

Glancing around, I try to figure out which of the others could be his, but none of them make sense to me. This is the only one that stands out. It just feels . . . right.

This has to be it, but what other code would he use? He's not the type for coming up with random numbers and calling it a day. He'll forget them. No, he's always used something meaningful, something he'll remember. He always used . . . crap. He always used my birthday, the same code I use now.

Curiosity pulls at my chest, and as I grab the combination lock again, I look down at it as though it might bite me. My heart races, and I don't know why, but I push the building anxiety away before finally entering my birthday—0228.

The combination lock clicks open, and my jaw drops as I stare at the open lock. There's no way that actually just happened. I know he used to use my birthday when we were kids. It was his code for everything, just as mine used to be his, but I assumed he would have changed that years ago. The fact that he's still using it . . . I don't know how to feel about that.

Is there a part of him still hanging on to me, or was he just too lazy to figure out another number combination to use? Probably option number two.

Not wanting to hang around and get caught in here, I hastily pull the locker open, and the second I do, I'm hit in the face with Noah's cologne, and it's everything. My eyes roll and my knees go weak, but I push it aside, searching through his things until I hear the familiar jingle of car keys.

I pull them out of the locker, but they feel heavier than I was expecting, and I glance down, sucking in a breath as I find my favorite Z keyring.

"That rat bastard," I mutter under my breath, shaking my head and realizing that he must have stolen it.

My keyring went missing last year, way after Noah had stopped talking to me, and I know for a fact that it was put away safely in my jewelry box. And then one day—*poof*—it was gone. I accused Hazel of stealing it, and she screamed at me, telling me she was innocent, but I wouldn't hear it. I owe her an apology. How the hell was I supposed to know that Noah freaking Ryan snuck into my room and stole it? As far as I was aware, he hadn't set foot in my home since before Linc's funeral. Hell, I wonder what else he's stolen over the years.

That assface has got another thing coming.

Not having the time to get all worked up about it now, I shove the keys into my pocket and scram.

After sneaking out of the locker room, I backtrack to the main part of the school, just so I can walk straight out the normal doors and not cause any suspicion. Who am I kidding? It's already suspicious that I'm walking out of here so much later than the rest of the students, but I could come up with a million excuses as to why I'm loitering on school property that would be more believable than the truth.

Just as I did every day last week, I walk to the student parking lot, keeping my gaze locked heavily on the ground in front of me, refusing to glance up at the football field, not wanting to see *him*. He's bad for my health, and until I can get the image of him falling to his knees at the idea of me needing protection from him out of my head, I need to play it smart.

Making my way down to my Range Rover, I feel his laser-sharp stare on the side of my face, but I do what I can to ignore it as I put on a show of unlocking my car and opening the door. My hands shake. I'm going to have to time this just right. Noah is fast, and if I fumble even a second, I'll be screwed. When I pulled up this morning, I was frustrated to find the only available spot right next to Noah's Camaro, but now, having it so close is nothing but a gift from the Hemsworth gods.

I feel myself growing sweaty, and I know it has absolutely nothing to do with the blistering Arizona sun and everything to do with the fact that I'm about to steal Noah Ryan's car.

Yep. I really have lost my mind.

Climbing into my Range Rover, I keep the door open as I spare a glance toward the football field, my face concealed by the tinted windows. Noah's gaze lingers on me a moment, but when he's scolded by Coach Martin, his stare falls away, and I watch as he jogs back down the field, catching the ball before immediately tossing it away.

Wanting to use every second of his distraction to my advantage, I quickly grab a few things from my car before scrambling out of it, keeping my body concealed by the Range Rover.

My heart hammers erratically in my chest, and I take a shaky breath before making a run for it. I scramble over to Noah's car, hating how my head bobs over the top of the stupid thing. But damn, it looks nice up close and personal.

Hastily digging into my pocket, I pull out the keys and quickly dive into the driver's seat. Then as I close the door behind me, I spare another glance at the field to find him still running drills with his teammates, none the wiser. But the second I turn the key in the ignition, he's gonna know. The whole fucking team will, and when that inevitably happens, I'm gonna have to get my ass out of here quickly.

Under the cover of the dark tinted windows, I take a second to glance around the Camaro, making sure everything is where it's supposed to be. I grab the seat belt and quickly fasten it into place before reaching under the seat and pulling the lever to drag it as far forward as it will go.

After fixing the mirrors, I let out a shaky breath before taking the key and inserting it into the ignition. My whole body sweats, my nerves running rampant and almost convincing me to bail. But I've come this far, and while this is definitely for my own benefit, it's also for Noah's. I need him to come back to me, to give me a chance to get close to him, and if grand theft auto is how I'm going to do that, then that's exactly what I'm going to do.

A wave of determination comes over me, and as I grip the key tighter between my fingers, I glance up at the field, waiting until Noah is in prime position. After all, if I'm doing this, then I want to make sure I can see his face at the exact moment he realizes I'm stealing his car. I want to commit his rage to memory and spend the rest of my life reveling in it, and if I happen to see a little bit of shock and disbelief in his eyes, then I'll add it to my list of growing bonuses.

Noah makes his way back up the field, and I watch as he raises his gaze to my Range Rover again. Realizing he hasn't got the faintest clue what's about to happen, I grin to myself. His brows furrow, probably wondering why the hell I'm still here. When he reaches the very top of the field and goes to turn back around, a wicked smile tears across my face, and with a quick twist of my wrist, the Camaro's engine roars to life, rumbling through the school.

Fuck yeah. This is better than I could have ever dreamed.

Noah's head whips up mere milliseconds before the rest of his team takes notice, and my grin only widens when I read the "OH FUCK NO," on his lips. He breaks into a sprint toward the parking lot, jumping the chain link fence with ease, but I put the Camaro in reverse and hit the gas. The tires screech as I spin the wheel, and I'm thankful that the rest of the parking lot is mostly deserted apart from a few cars belonging to Noah's teammates.

Hitting the automatic button for the passenger's side window, I wait the few seconds it takes for it to lower all the way down while pressing my foot on the clutch and putting the car back into gear, never more grateful my father insisted I learn to drive a stick shift. Then as Noah barrels toward me, his ferocious gaze locked on mine, I hold my hand up, my middle finger flying high as I hit the gas again, peeling out of the parking lot.

The second all four tires are off school property, I hit him with the final blow and show him exactly what I can do. Bringing the Camaro to a stop, I watch Noah as I press the clutch. He shakes his head as if reading me perfectly, and with that, I hit the gas, the very same way Aunt Maya taught me, and I revel in the sweet sound of tires squealing against asphalt as I show him the most stunning burnout I've ever performed.

Noah's mouth drops, and I don't hang around to hear what he has to say about it before adjusting my hold over the pedal and shooting down the street. A giddy laugh tears from deep in my chest.

Checkmate, Noah Ryan. Check-fucking-mate.

With the engine purring so beautifully beneath me, I put the other window down before reaching over and silencing the angry calls coming from a number that hasn't graced my phone in a long time. After all this time, it's nice to see that my number is still programmed in his phone.

Then knowing damn well Noah doesn't have any good music in his car, I grab the emergency CD I stole from my Range Rover and slide it into its new home before trying to figure out how to make it play. I could always connect my phone to Bluetooth, but then how the hell would I irritate the shit out of Noah when I finally take pity on him and allow him to have his car back?

Music blasts through the speakers as I cruise through the streets of East View, and it's impossible to wipe the smile off my face. His car smells so much like him. It's intoxicating.

I get halfway home before thinking better of it and turning around, heading back toward the park that Noah and I once called our spot. It's going to be a long walk home—a walk I never considered to be long whenever I was walking it with Noah—but it's worth every second of it. Though with my Range Rover stuck at school, I'll have to bug Mom or Dad for a lift back there tomorrow. Maybe even Tarni, but then . . . maybe I won't bother asking her because that's only going to bring questions that I'm not ready to answer.

Reaching the park, I bring the Camaro to a stop right in the middle of the small parking lot, and I sit there staring out at the familiar terrain for far longer than I should. My mind takes me back to all the memories this place once held. So many amazing times filled with laughter and teasing. It was another world back then, back when Linc was still here, and we didn't understand the true meaning of hurt.

Realizing Mom and Dad will be coming home from work soon, I initiate the second portion of my grand plan as I flip through the songs on the CD, trying to figure out which one would be most appropriate to burst his eardrums when he gets back in the car. I try to find something upbeat, something with plenty of bass and drums just to add an extra punch, but when I pass something completely different, something that holds a message within its lyrics, my finger pauses on the skip button, and I know this is the perfect song.

Nerves settle in my chest, the message in the song far too deep for me to be able to speak the words out loud, but I know he will understand. He's always known that when I can't find the words, I communicate through the music I listen to, something not many people have been able to pick up about me. But Noah did. He was always so observant.

Not wanting to linger on it or give myself a chance to change my mind, I go about screwing with his car, being as inconveniently irritating as humanly possible. I turn on the hazard lights, put the windshield wipers on full blast, and crank the volume to the max. Then just to be extra, I change the angles of the side mirrors and adjust the rearview one. Leaving the center console and glove box open, I start the song right from the beginning and cut the engine with a sigh. I wish there was some way to record his reaction when he finally gets back in his car.

I squeeze my way out of the car, leaving the seat as far forward as it can possibly go. Then before locking the doors behind me, my fingers trace the lines of my Z keyring as if holding on to something he coveted could somehow make me closer to him.

I begin my journey home with my head a mess of emotions, but what else should I have expected? Wild, unruly emotions seem to be my new normal at the moment. It's almost been twenty minutes before I grace Hazel with my presence, and I barely even get a hello before she promptly ignores me and goes back to practicing her winged eyeliner in the bathroom mirror.

Trudging into my room, I drop Noah's keys on my desk, and as I go to walk away, I think better of it. Scooping the keys up again, I steal my Z keyring back, grinning at the smug pride that swells in my chest.

Settling on the end of my bed, I get stuck into my homework until I hear Mom and Dad coming home from work. I make my way back downstairs to find Dad struggling with an armful of groceries. "What's going on?" I ask, striding into the kitchen and eyeing Dad as he dumps the bags on the island counter, taken aback by the amount he managed to carry in one load. "What's with all the groceries?"

"Aunt Maya is coming for dinner," Mom tells me as she unloads the wine—because we all know that's the most important part.

"Oh cool," I say, a fond smile pulling at the corners of my lips as I help Dad with the groceries, still wondering why the hell we need so much when it's just Aunt Maya.

Hazel strides in and drops her bony ass on one of the island stools, clearly not in the mood to lend a hand. "Did I hear you say that Aunt Maya was coming?" she asks, her gaze lingering on the groceries as if wondering what yummy snacks she can hide and steal.

"Sure did," Mom says as a strange note appears in her tone. She swallows hard before sparing me a glance. "She said Noah was coming."

My mouth drops at the same time the bag of carrots slips out of my hand, spilling out across the kitchen floor. "Ummmmm . . . what?" I say, my eyes wide as I gape at my mother, my heart racing a million miles an hour. Noah can't be coming over here. Not after I just stole his car. I gave myself a mental pat on the back for my checkmate, but now he's pulling a move like this? I thought I'd won this round, but it seems I wasn't even in the running.

Crap. He's going to be in my house again. Sitting across from me at the table. I'm going to have to pretend that his very presence isn't making me want to fall to pieces, all while his car keys are burning a hole in my desk upstairs.

Shit.

What could possibly go wrong?

"Uh," Dad says behind me, nervousness ringing in his tone. "Are you sure he's actually coming?"

"Yes," Mom says, eyeing Dad through a narrowed gaze. "Why do you look like you suddenly have the overwhelming urge to go get a rectal exam?"

My gaze sweeps to my father, and I narrow my stare the same way Mom does. She's right. He doesn't look entirely thrilled about the idea of Noah having dinner with us. "I . . . I. Ummm . . . ahhhhh."

"Dad," I prompt, crossing my arms over my chest, completely forgetting about the spilled carrots while noticing that Hazel is the only one who seems remotely excited about the idea of Noah coming over. "What did you do?"

"Nothing," he says, eyeing me with the same suspicion. "Why are you acting so shady about it?"

"No reason," I throw back, immediately averting my gaze. Only my curiosity gets the best of me, and I look back up to find him nervous again.

Dad meets my stare, his gaze tightening as if he's about to burst from the seams. "Okay," he finally says. "I'll tell you mine if you tell me yours."

"What?" I screech. "No way. I'll definitely get in trouble for this one."

He shrugs and gets back to packing away the groceries, knowing damn well the curiosity is eating at me. "Fine," he says as though he doesn't have a care in the world. "Have it your way."

I groan, my resolve quickly crumbling and burning to ashes at my feet, desperate to know what could possibly have Dad so on edge. "Ughhhhh. Okay. I need to know. Tell me everything."

Excitement shoots through his gaze, and he whips back around to face me, holding his pinky finger out at me. "Promise you won't get cranky at me, and I'll promise you won't be in trouble."

"Cranky?" I ask, looping my pinky finger around his and shaking on the deal as my tone lowers, my gaze narrowing on my father. "What did you do?"

"Well," he starts, having the nerve to look a little sheepish. "On Friday night, after he stalked you home from the party across town, I sort of gave him the *come near my daughter again and your life won't be worth living* speech."

"What?" I demand, gaping at my father, all but stuttering over my words, unable to string a proper sentence together. "I . . . What? Are you insane?"

"I was just looking out for you, Zo. You're my little girl, and he's trouble, but for what it's worth, he straight up told me no, but it was a respectful no. It was like he was saying, *I see your protective-father obligations, but I know what's best for your daughter.*"

Mom sputters around the rim of her wine glass, choking on the liquid goodness while trying to act as though she's not listening in on our conversation, but all I can do is continue to gape. I remember Dad standing out in the yard on Friday night talking to Noah. I was so focused on everything that happened; I didn't give it a second thought. I figured they were just saying a quick hello, perhaps Dad was thanking him for making sure I had gotten home alright. But never in my wildest imagination did I think that my father would have warned him to stay away from me, let alone have Noah blatantly refuse.

What in the fresh hell was that about? I don't know how to feel.

"Out with it," my father says. "What did you do that's got you so nervous about seeing He-Who-Shall-Not-Be-Named?"

Ah crap.

I wince, glancing up at Dad. "Promise you won't get mad?"

He stares at me as if he's never been more offended in his life. "I pinky promised," he declares. "Does that not mean anything to you?"

Rolling my eyes, I let out a heavy sigh and hope like hell my parents can somehow look past this and see the funny side of it all. "I, uh . . . Well, I need to have a real conversation with Noah, away from . . . everything, and if I just asked him to come over here and lay everything out on the table, he would have said no. I have to work up to that, and to be able to get there, we need to be forced together, over and over again. And so . . . I may or may not have found a way to draw him out."

Hazel laughs, a smirk pulling at her lips. "Well, whatever you did worked because he's coming for dinner for the first time in over three years."

"What did you do?" Mom pushes, no longer pretending that she's not listening.

"Well, I umm . . ." I wince. "I sort of stole his car and did a burnout down the street in front of the whole football team."

"YOU DID WHAT?" Mom sputters as Dad gapes at me, his eyes going wide with pride.

"In his Camaro? Wow. How was it, sweetheart?"

"Henry!" My mother scolds him before flicking her gaze back to mine. "Wait. I didn't see his car in the driveway. Where is it?"

"I might have dumped it at the park and then walked home, but don't worry," I rush out. "The park is safe. It's not like anything is going to happen to it. Plus, I still have the keys. I just . . . felt that after three years of radio silence, he deserved a little payback while on the road to redemption."

Mom shakes her head. "I worry about you, Zoey."

"What?" I say as a slow grin stretches across my face. "Try and tell me he didn't deserve it. Besides, if I'm the one putting myself at risk trying to help him, then shouldn't I get a little something for my troubles?"

Mom scoops up her wine again, taking a long, healthy sip. "As far as I'm aware," she mutters to herself, "you two were made for one another. Now go set the table. They should be here in an hour."

Scurrying out of the kitchen and into the dining room, I get ready to set the table when I hear mom turn on my father. "Now you," she says. "Where do you get off butting into Zoey and Noah's business?"

"What?" Dad responds. "She steals a car, and I'm the one getting in trouble? Where's the sanity in that?"

"Oh God," Mom says. "I knew I should have bought more wine."

Chapter 16

NOAH

S he stole my fucking car.

Innocent little Zoey fucking James stole my car, and not only that, but she did a burnout right up the main street in front of the school.

What in the fresh hell was that?

I stare at her across the dining table, my fingers drumming on the hard wood, unable to look away. I don't know if I want to get in her face or applaud her for a job well done. If it had been anyone else or any other car, I might even go as far as to say that I was impressed, maybe even a little turned on. Okay, a lot turned on, but this is Zoey, and I shouldn't be thinking of her like that.

Showing up here, I quickly realized my Camaro wasn't in the driveway, and my anger has been boiling beneath the surface ever since. What the fuck did she do with it? Knowing Zoey, this is all part of her master plan. She has more in store for me, and I'm playing right into the palm of her hand. But what else am I supposed to do? She's holding my car hostage and I'm not about to let her get away with it.

She glares right back at me as our parents try to hold some semblance of a conversation. They're either oblivious to the tension in the room or going well out of their way to ignore it. But to me, all that exists right now is Zoey and the smug grin resting on her full lips.

Fuck, I want to kiss them so bad, but not like the way I used to. I've kissed her thousands of times before, each one just as amazing as the last, but they were the kind of kisses an innocent boy gives to the girl of his dreams, nothing but a respectable peck here and there. But the way I want to kiss her right now. That's different. I want to claim her, kiss her so fucking deeply that her knees crumble, and I have to grasp her waist just to keep her on her feet.

Damn it.

I knew transferring to East View High and seeing her again was going to screw with my resolve. Zoey James is not mine anymore. I tore her to shreds, and I sure as hell don't have the right to think about her like this or want her in a way I never have before. Especially considering the way I've hurt her.

Being back here, surrounded by the walls that hold so many of our childhood memories, has brought a surge of nostalgia swirling within me. This is where I first realized how deeply I loved her. It's where I stood out in the yard as a seven-year-old boy and got down on one knee, proposed to her, and told her she was the most beautiful girl I ever knew. We were only playing then, but there was such a profound truth to those words. Not the proposal bit, but the part about Zoey being beautiful. She always has been. Undeniably so.

Officially, I haven't been here in over three years. Unofficially, I've snuck through Zoey's bedroom window more times than I care to admit. Usually only when things are at their worst, or when I feel like I'm about to spiral. I come here and sit in her room, and by the time I leave, I feel grounded again, as if just being closer to her could somehow make everything better. Not that I'll be telling her that.

Fuck, had she caught me during those dark moments, or if I had set my eyes upon her and seen that light that always seems to shine so brightly, I know I would have crumbled.

There have been a few times where I've sat on the roof outside her bedroom window as she slept, staring out at the street, refusing to peer in at the broken girl inside. I know she feels like I've put this distance between us, and she's right, I have, but in some way, I've always been right here, she just never knew it.

My fingers continue drumming against the table as I refuse to break our stare. With every passing second, it feels as though that invisible string between us pulls just a little bit tighter, but soon enough, it's bound to snap.

Irritation burns through me. I hate that just the sight of her is screwing with my head. I'm trying to keep her at arm's length, not draw her back in. There's a reason I pushed her away, and despite how every last piece of me is screaming to have her back in my arms, I need to keep this distance. Her father was right on Friday night. I'm a troubled kid. I'm heading down a path I won't be able to claw my way back from, and I refuse to drag her down with me. The darkness has consumed me, and while she shines brighter than any star in the sky, my darkness will drown her.

Tension rolls off me, and the longer I relentlessly hold her stare, the faster her resolve begins to crumble. There's a silent challenge lingering in the air between us, but neither of us is willing to say a word or give in. She never could handle the intensity of my stare. I have to give it to her though, she's putting in a good effort.

The sound of cutlery against the plates mixes with the conversation flowing around the table. I don't miss the way Zoey just sits there, letting her food go cold, too preoccupied with this current battle for dominance that seems to be going down between us.

When she stole my car after school, she turned this disastrous game into a cold-blooded battle, and if that's the way she wants to play, then so be it. I'm not afraid to get my hands dirty. The only question is, can she handle it?

Zoey blindly reaches in front of her, closes her hand around her glass of water, and lifts it to her lips. Just as she tips the glass and takes a sip, I lift my foot under the table and brace it against her chair, right between her knees. She sputters into her water, her eyes widening before she chokes and breaks her stare.

"Oh, honey," Erica rushes out, gently clapping her hand on Zoey's back and rushing in with napkins to mop up the spilled water. "Are you okay?"

"Yeah," Zoey says, her glare sharpening back on me as she reaches between her legs and shoves my foot off the end of her chair, then she goes as far as to use her feet to kick me even further away. "Must have gone down the wrong way."

It's almost ironic. Three years ago, we used to do the exact same thing, only the looks we were secretly giving one another across the table were very different. Either way, I think it's clear to say I've won this round. And to think just how easy it was.

Clearly irritated with me, Zoey lets out an almost inaudible huff and forces a fake smile as she turns toward the conversation, leaving me almost gasping for air. Only there's a different James daughter now demanding my attention.

Hazel stares at me, narrowing her gaze, and it's clear that she's the only other person at the table actually paying any attention to what's been going down the past fifteen minutes.

Hazel doesn't say a word, just watches me, only unlike her big sister, there's no disdain or confusion swelling in her green eyes, just plain old curiosity. A smirk pulls at the corners of her lips, and with that, she lifts her hand, her fingers hovering in front of her eyes before turning them on me, the universal sign for *I'm watching you.*

A wide grin stretches across my lips, and I almost let out a real laugh, something I don't recall doing for . . . actually . . . I have no idea how long it's been. That move had Linc written all over it. He used to give me that bullshit all the time, and I hated it, but now, it only makes me realize just how much I miss it. Then just because she's asking for a different kind of trouble of her own, I tear off a small piece of bread from the roll on my plate and brace it against the edge of my fork. With their parents' attention firmly on the she-devil sitting across from me, I pull back the fork and launch the bread forward.

It arches high across the table, and I watch as Hazel's eyes open. Without a second to dodge out of the way, it hits home, slamming right against her cheek.

Her mouth drops in mock horror, and she quickly scrambles for the piece of bread, only to dunk it in her water before loading it onto the end of her fork. Eight-year-old Hazel from three years ago would have already burst from the seams with laughter, but she's eleven now, and she knows better than to draw attention to us before getting a chance at sweet revenge.

Seeing exactly where this is going, I give her a hard stare and shake my head, warning her that this isn't a war she wants to start with me, and before I can even get my warning across, she launches the soggy bread. It hits me square in the jaw, and the way it clings to the side of my face is too much for her to handle before a loud, snorting laugh booms across the table.

All eyes turn to Hazel, wondering what the fuck has gotten into her as I fake a look of innocence and flick the soggy bread off my face.

My mom smiles wide at Hazel before turning her gaze toward me and holding my stare. As she realizes I had everything to do with that laugh, her face creases with the brightest smile, one I haven't seen since before losing Linc.

Something flutters in my chest, and I do what I can to crush it back down, letting my gaze fall away.

Fuck, I miss Linc.

The last time I sat in this very spot, he was sitting right here with me, the four of us all cramped on one end of the table so we could fuck around away from our parents' watchful eyes. My father was sitting on my mother's right, looking at her as though she was his whole world. Funny how tragedy can show people's true colors. He split six months after Linc died without a care for how Mom and I were supposed to get through it all alone.

I suppose I'm no better than my father. Only instead of leaving, I just mentally checked out. I was a ghost for Mom to have to deal with day in and day out, causing trouble and giving her hell. Shit, I've really been an asshole. If I knew how to apologize and make it up to her, I would, but I've never been any good at that shit. The only person who seemed to fully understand that about me was Zoey. She never held it against me and always helped me through it when I needed it, but now . . .

"What's going on down there?" Erica, Zoey's mom asks, her gaze settled on me. "You look like you just went somewhere."

I clench my jaw, not particularly willing to entertain this, especially now with everyone's attention on me, but despite everything, Erica has always been too good to me. She was like a second mom until I split. "Nothing," I murmur, my gaze falling away. "Just noticing how there's a lot of empty chairs at this table now."

Erica gives me a sad smile, her heart falling out on her sleeve. "Yes.

However, since the last time your mom came for dinner, there's now one less empty chair, and to me, that's cause for celebration," she tells me. "You have no idea how wonderful it is to see you sitting around my table again Noah, even if all you want to do is trade glares with Zoey all night."

Well, shit. Maybe our parents were paying attention after all.

Erica gives me a smug grin as if she's in on a secret that I know nothing about, and when my mom breaks the silence, I couldn't be more grateful. "So, my little warrior," she says to Zoey, making my brows furrow at her use of that old nickname, something I haven't heard in what seems like a lifetime. "How's school going? Still kicking ass in all your classes?"

Zoey scoffs. "Kicking ass is not exactly how I would put it," she says before explaining herself. "It's been one week, and the homework and assignments are already piling up. I thought they might ease us into it, but apparently, my teachers are the *throw them straight in the deep end* type."

"Ah, that sucks," Mom tells her. "Just give it a little time. I'm sure you'll find your groove."

"Let's hope."

Erica smirks toward her daughter. "I'm sure if you didn't spend your afternoons talking on the phone and committing grand theft auto, you would have plenty of time to get on top of that pile of homework."

Zoey reaches for her glass of water again, sparing me a quick glance before lifting it to her lips. "I don't have any idea what you're talking about," she says dismissively as if my car keys aren't currently burning a hole in her pocket. At least, that's where I assume she's keeping them. She's not going to make it easy for me to get them back.

Mom and Erica share a glance, and it's clear they already know every detail about Zoey's afternoon activities, and it grinds my gears that Mom didn't think to even mention it to me. Though I don't know why I'm so surprised. Mom and Erica gossip like a bunch of old ladies. They live for it, and as for Zoey, she tells her mom everything, even knowing that most of the time, anything she tells her mom will somehow get back to me through mine.

Moving right along, Erica glances back at me. "How are you settling in at East View? I'm assuming Coach Martin was thrilled to have you join the team?"

A harsh scoff rips from the back of my throat, and I find my leg stretching out under the table and settling right beside Zoey's, her bare skin resting against mine, and damn it, she doesn't even try to pull away. "Thrilled is one way to put it," I mutter. "He thinks I'm more trouble than I'm worth, but he's also thirsty for the championship trophy, so he's putting up with me. He's making me work for it though."

"Good," Zoey's father says, barely able to meet my eye after our little chat out on the front lawn on Friday night. "What good is a coach who doesn't push his players to their limits? He might be hard on you, but he's making you a better player."

I press my lips into a hard line and nod. "He's holding me to a hundred percent attendance and a B+ average as well. If I start to slip, I'm done."

Zoey leans back in her chair, crossing her arms over her chest, her dinner still untouched. "The way I heard it, Coach Martin isn't the only one putting limitations on your enrollment," she adds, but how she knows about my conversation with Principal Daniels doesn't sit well with me. Our conversation about my enrollment was private, especially considering the end result was forcing me into counseling, and it sure as fuck isn't something I want to openly discuss at her dining table.

I don't respond, just hold her stare, daring her to push me on this.

Electricity pulses between us, her leg practically burning hot against mine, and that tether tightens between us once again.

"Speaking of school," Mom says, defusing the situation before it gets ugly. "Have you guys had a chance to hang out much?"

Zoey sputters again, and I can't help but wonder if she's going for a record. "That's a joke, right?" she asks, gaping at my mom and pulling her leg away from mine, sending a searing pain through my chest that I can't quite understand. "Noah and I certainly aren't hanging out at school. I'm the straight-A student who spends her days memorizing every single lyric of Taylor Swift's ten-minute version of 'All Too Well,' while Noah is a heathen who spends his days burning schools down. We don't exactly run in the same circles."

"You only wish we did," I murmur, earning a spectacular eye roll out of her.

"Would it really be so terrible if you did hang out?" Zoey's mom suggests, taking a sip of wine. "I know there's social circles and a hierarchy at high school that I can't even begin to understand, but you guys don't need to lower yourselves to those standards. Your friendship has spanned over your whole lives. Perhaps it'll be good to reconnect, and instead of glaring at each other across my dining table, you could find comfort in one another like you used to."

Zoey glances at her mother, and I watch her a little too closely, hating the way those bright green eyes seem to darken, unshed tears welling, but she refuses to allow them to fall. She shakes her head, this time not even bothering to spare me a glance. "That ship sailed a long time ago," she murmurs before standing and clutching her plate. "If you'll excuse me, I'm not very hungry."

Zoey walks away, taking her plate with her, and I watch as she dumps it on the kitchen counter before hightailing it to the stairs and taking her ass back to her room. I listen to every step she takes until I hear the familiar sound of her bedroom door closing behind her.

A heaviness weighs down on my shoulders. I'm not going to lie, the idea of falling back into our old patterns and dragging her kicking and screaming back into my life fills me with the kind of elation that no man should ever be so lucky to possess. But she's right, that ship sailed three long years ago. We can't go back to how it used to be. Too much has changed. I broke her heart and tore her to shreds, and despite the way she holds her head up high, I can still see just how broken she is.

The rest of dinner passes in an uncomfortable silence, at least for me anyway. Mom and Erica hound Hazel about how she's settling into middle school, and I curse myself for being so fucking self-centered that I didn't even realize she was starting this year. I can't help but think back to what Zoey said to me in the school bathroom, how my avoidance of her is also a punishment for Hazel, and seeing how grown up she's become and how much of her life I've missed, I see just how right Zoey was.

The guilt eats at me, and after dinner, I make my way up the stairs. Music trickles from beneath Zoey's closed door, but I slink right past it until I'm leaning in the open doorway of Hazel's bedroom.

My gaze shifts around her room, taking it all in and realizing just how different Hazel is compared to Zoey at her age. There are makeup and hair products spread out from one end of the room to the other, but when Zoey was eleven years old, her room was filled with . . . me. Our photos were stuck up on the walls, and she had a collection of teddy bears I'd won for her at every fair we'd ever been to piled up in the corner.

Hazel relaxes back on her bed, holding her phone above her head, and from the sound of it, she's listening to a makeup tutorial. Clearly not having noticed me in her doorway, I gently rap my knuckles on the frame and watch as her head snaps up.

Hazel peers at me from her bed, abandoning her phone on the blanket and sitting up, her gaze narrowing as she crosses her arms over her chest. "Well, well. If it isn't Noah Ryan coming to beg for forgiveness," she chides, proving that while she's certainly very different from her big sister, there are also a lot of striking similarities. "I never thought I'd see the day."

"Ha. Ha," I say, laying the sarcasm on thick before pressing my lips into a hard line. "You hate me too, huh?"

Her gaze falls away, and sadness creeps into her eyes as she sits there, not knowing what to say.

I let out a breath and stride into her room, sliding her desk chair out and dropping onto it. I lean forward, bracing my elbows on my knees, not really knowing what to say either. "I'm really sorry, Hazel," I tell her. "After Linc died, I didn't know how to handle it. I still don't, and I pushed away everything good in my life. I was drowning in my own grief. Linc was . . . you know. And Zoey—" I let out a breath, needing to figure out what I'm trying to say and how to explain something so complicated and deep to an eleven-year-old. "Your sister made me happy. She was everything good in my life, and I wasn't ready to feel that happiness. The guilt I felt for even thinking about smiling when Linc was gone ate at me, so I pushed her away. I distanced myself from everyone without a thought about who I was hurting in the process."

Hazel pulls her legs up on her bed, crosses them, and tugs the blanket over her lap, unable to look up and meet my stare. "I lost Linc too, you know?" she murmurs. "He was my best friend. You had Zoey, and I had Linc, then he was gone. But you were gone too, and Zoey was sad all the time, so I had no one."

"I'm sorry, Hazel," I tell her, probably one of the sincerest conversations I've had in over three years. "I was selfish. I was thinking about my own pain when I should have been thinking about all the people who needed me. I've hurt a lot of people over the past few years."

"But you're back now," she says in a small voice, as if not quite sure, and honestly, I'm not sure either. "Things can go back to how they used to be."

"I don't know," I tell her. "Like Zoey said at dinner, that ship sailed a while ago. I hurt her really badly, and to be honest, even if we were ready for it, I don't know if I'm capable of making it up to her. But I promise, I won't be a stranger to you. I've missed three years of your life, and if Linc was looking down on me, he'd be ready to kick my ass for allowing that to happen."

"I can kick your ass for him," Hazel suggests in all seriousness before a ridiculous grin stretches across her face, her eyes shining just the way Zoey's used to.

"Oh really?" I laugh, feeling part of the darkness starting to chip away. I lean back in her desk chair, feeling the ease of our old friendship falling into place. "And how the hell do you think you're going to do that? You're all but three feet tall."

"I am not," she argues, and the music from Zoey's room hitches a little higher as if trying to drown out our conversation.

I nod my head in Zoey's general direction. "Does she do that a lot?"

"What? Listen to music so loud it bursts her eardrums? Yes. Just be happy she's not screaming the songs at the top of her lungs like she usually does."

Warmth spreads through my chest, feeling as though I'm getting a little insight into Zoey's life for the first time in three years, something I lost the right to know, and fuck, it wasn't until this very moment that I realize just how much I miss it. All the little things that make her happy, the things that put a smile on her face or make her feel content. I've been missing it all, and while I still know all the big things, there's so much about her I don't know anymore. She's grown up without me, and that realization stings.

"Wanna know a secret?" I ask, feeling as though I don't need to hide here, not with Hazel.

"Umm, yeah," she says, slightly leaning forward as though she's about to hear the gossip of the century.

I press my lips into a hard line, having known this since day one but never having the strength to actually say it out loud. "I miss her."

Hazel scoffs, disappointment flashing in her eyes. "That's your big secret?" she grunts, rolling her eyes and resting back against her headboard. "Anyone could have told you that. It was all but stamped across both of your foreheads at dinner. You're so obvious that I'm going to change your name to Captain Obvious. Actually, what's higher than a captain? Colonel? Colonel Obvious. Wait . . . that doesn't have the same ring to it."

Rolling my eyes, I kick my feet out and cross them at my ankles. "Alright, kid," I say. "Catch me up on the Hazel James highlight reel from the past three years, and don't spare any of the gory details."

Chapter 17

ZOEY

Gripping the door handle, I slowly pull it open and hold my breath as I peer out into the hallway. My gaze swings from left to right as I listen out, making sure Aunt Maya and Noah are gone.

It's late, and I've been hiding out in my room way too long to be considered polite, but for some reason, I don't think anyone is going to hold that against me tonight.

I was stupid to assume I could do this, stupid to give him a reason to need to come here. What was I thinking? I thought I was strong enough to face him, but the second his leg brushed against mine under the table, everything within me broke. I needed his touch more than I needed to breathe, and I think on some level he knew that. Or maybe he needed the touch just as much as I did.

But then Mom had to go and push it, and while I get that she thought she was helping, all it did was crush me, and every snide comment I'd been planning to unleash on Noah suddenly didn't seem so important. *I* didn't feel important, not anymore.

My gaze sweeps toward Hazel's door, and I listen a little harder. Noah was up here earlier. I could hear the soft murmuring of their conversation, muffled by the walls. I'm not going to lie; I've never been so jealous of my sister in my life. Actually, I don't think I've ever been jealous of her, but seeing how easily she held Noah's attention and was able to get a whole conversation out of him only added insult to injury.

I've never longed for something more.

It guts me that we don't have that anymore, that I can't just go to him and tell him all about my day and hang on his every word like I used to. And despite him sitting right across the table from me during dinner, I've never missed him more. Having the distance so blatantly rubbed in my face only makes him feel that much further away.

This whole night has only served to mess with my head. It used to be me who he'd launch little bits of bread across the table at. We always thought we were being so discreet, having ridiculous bread wars at the other end of the table from our parents, thinking no one was watching. Only we couldn't have been more wrong. They were always watching us. Always waiting for the moment we realized that we were so much more than *bestest friends*. But what they didn't know is that we'd known it all along, and those precious moments when things were starting to shift would happen in private—a soft brush of his fingers over my arm or when I'd catch his stare lingering on my lips like he'd die without them.

No longer able to hear clinking wine glasses or Mom and Aunt Maya's shrill laughter downstairs, I let out a heavy breath, though, for the life of me, I can't work out if it's filled with disappointment or relief. I had hoped tonight would play out differently, but that's on me. I should have known better than to allow myself to hope.

Certain Aunt Maya and Noah have left for the night, I venture out into the hall, and as I pass Hazel's room, I don't look up, terrified that she'll be able to see the jealousy in my eyes.

Stepping into the bathroom, I tear my clothes off and dump them into the hamper before stepping into the shower and allowing the warm water to cascade over me, willing it to wash away the stain Noah has left on my heart. Unfortunately for me, it seems that stain is permanent, and I have a sinking feeling that the only person capable of scrubbing it clean is the one person who refuses to get close enough to try.

Stepping out of the shower, I grab my towel and quickly dry off before wrapping it around my body and tucking the end between my barely existent breasts to keep the towel firmly in place. I brush out my hair and then as a yawn rips through my body, I stride out of the bathroom and head back to my room, more than ready to find my comfiest pajamas and call it a night.

Music spills from my bedroom, and when I push back through my door, I come to a screeching halt, finding Noah standing at my desk, his car keys hanging from his fingers as he leans back, his foot crossed over the other, as casual as can be.

My eyes widen as my hand flies to my towel, gripping it hard, more than aware that I am very naked beneath this shred of cotton.

Noah's gaze slowly trails up and down my body, and I try to ignore the flare of desire that pulses through his eyes, but when he blinks and opens his eyes again, I'm met with the usual darkness. "What the hell do you think you're doing?" I snap. "Get out."

He doesn't even pretend to make a move, simply crosses his big arms over his chest, looking bored. His gaze bores into mine, making my heart race faster than ever before. A strange curiosity flashes in his eyes, and I wait a moment, realizing whatever this is doesn't have anything to do with the keys in his hand.

His tongue rolls over his bottom lip, deep in thought, and from what I can tell, it looks as though he's suffering through an internal battle, debating whether he's going to ask me whatever's been plaguing his mind.

"Spit it out, Noah," I say, my gaze darting to the back of my bedroom door to where my robe usually hangs, only the one day I actually need it, it's not there.

Noah's gaze singes me from the inside out, and I try to hold on to my composure as he finally gets to the reason he's here. "Why does my mom call you her little warrior?" he questions, a strange tone to his deep voice, something I'm still not used to hearing.

My jaw slackens, and the shock of his question has my hand falling away from the top of my towel. "You're kidding, right?" I breathe, my brows furrowed as a deep slice cuts straight across my chest, letting my agony fall out on the ground for the world to see.

This has got to be a joke. How could he not know?

My gaze flickers to the photograph of me that's half hidden behind his big body, and I will the tears to stay at bay. He was there for all of it. Held my hand through the chemotherapy. Is he so far gone to have forgotten all of that?

I shake my head in disbelief. "You know what?" I say, trying to hide the hurt I know he sees in my eyes. "Figure it out yourself."

"Zo—"

"No," I cut him off, feeling myself starting to fall to pieces. "I'm not doing this with you." I point to the keys in his hand. "You got what you came here for, so just go. Leave me alone."

As if forgetting all about the keys in his hand, he glances down, studying them for a moment and not even pretending to make a move to leave. "Where's my keyring?" he questions, his tone thick with authority, demanding a response.

I groan, realizing we're playing the Noah game tonight and that he's not leaving until he's gotten exactly what he came for.

I shrug my shoulders and return my hand to the towel, gripping it with everything I have. I arch a brow, not willing to allow this to go down however he thinks it will, even if I don't quite know how I want it to go down.

"You mean *my* keyring?" I question, pleased to find he has enough sense not to push me on the whole little warrior thing. "Tell me, just how many times have you snuck in here and stolen my shit? Better yet, *why* do you steal my shit? Is your little dark soul so depraved of human contact that you need to take my things just to feel something?" I stride toward him, my gaze narrowed on his. "Or did you finally realize that you pushed away the one good thing you had left and now you're desperately clinging to any piece of me you can get your hands on?"

Noah clenches his jaw, and I know without a doubt that I've struck a nerve. "You certainly think highly of yourself."

He holds my stare, much like he had during dinner, and the air is knocked right out of my lungs. He's so intense and demanding. His presence alone fills the room with a thick tension, and I have no idea what to do with it.

Raising my chin, I stand just an inch away. So close that I can feel his warm breath brush across my bare shoulder. Lowering my voice, I keep my eyes locked heavily on his. "Tell me I'm wrong."

Noah doesn't respond, just continues staring as the heat and tension become almost unbearable between us. Goosebumps spread across my body, and I know he sees it. He feels it too. Moving this close to him was a mistake. A colossal one.

My hands shake, and yet for some reason, I can't find it within me to move away.

"Where's the keyring, Zoey?" he grumbles, that deep tone filling my room as his stare holds me captive.

"You're not getting it back," I tell him, forcing my stare away and breaking his hold on me. I cross my room, certain that if he were to look a little closer, he'd notice the way my whole body shudders under his intense stare. "Feel free to see yourself out."

Striding into my walk-in closet, I kick the door shut behind me, but when I don't hear the familiar click of it closing, I glance over my shoulder to find Noah walking in behind me. My back stiffens, and the second he closes the door, there suddenly isn't enough oxygen in the room.

I turn to face him, ready to tell him to leave, but as he continues toward me, his heated eyes full of determination, the words catch in my throat, and all I can do is watch as he closes the distance between us.

My chest heaves, rising and falling faster than ever as my hands shake at my sides. The tension ramps up, almost to the point of physical pain, and my body screams to reach out and touch him. I've never quite felt something so intense in my life. All that exists in the world is him. His dark, intense eyes, his scent filling my small closet, the space closing between us.

My heart thumps erratically, but he just keeps coming, those deep, haunted eyes not daring to look away from mine.

I back up a step, then another, until my back hits the overflowing row of clothes hanging in my closet. I'm desperate to keep the distance between us as I read the intention in his eyes. He's just as lost as I am, breathing just as heavily, but he's not stopping, not daring to look away and break this connection between us.

"Noah," I breathe, a soft warning that neither of us truly hears.

He takes the final step into me, and I press my hand to his chest as if I could somehow force the distance between us, but we both know I'm not about to do that. I feel the rapid beat of his heart beneath my palm, and a thrill shoots through me, realizing he's just as affected as I am. He swallows hard, his gaze shifting over my face before finally dropping to my lips.

My stomach swirls with butterflies as the tension in the small walk-in closet becomes unbearable, and I can't help but wonder if he feels it too.

Of course he feels it. How could he not?

His hand lifts to my bare shoulder, his fingers gently caressing the skin as he trails them right down to my wrist, leaving goosebumps spreading across my body, my skin burning from his electric touch.

Noah's hand falls away, and just when I think this heated moment is going to slip out of my grasp, I feel his fingers slipping beneath the fold of my towel before brushing against my bare waist. His fingers tighten, holding me there, and despite being completely naked beneath this towel, I trust him with everything I am, knowing he would never push me past my limits.

Noah's thumb brushes against my waist as shivers trail over my skin, and feeling brave, I allow my hand at his chest to slowly trail down his body, feeling the tight ridges of his muscles below. His chest heaves, mirroring my own heavy breathing, and as my shaking hand finds the hem of his shirt, I slip it beneath the fabric and feel his warm skin under my fingers.

I almost whimper, having imagined this very moment for years.

I've seen him without a shirt so many times, hugged him, held him, even kissed him, but it never felt like this. He's different now. He's not a boy. He's filled out with stacks of defined, strong muscle from hours of intense training. He's a man now, and for the first time in our lives, he's looking at me like I'm more than just the girl he used to know. He's looking at me as though I'm the most desirable woman he's ever seen.

My hand trails right up his body, moving beneath his shirt and exploring every inch before me. His skin is so warm, and a part of me wonders if that has something to do with his proximity to me, but then every train of thought slips from my mind when he moves impossibly closer, inching into me as his fingers tighten on my waist.

I know I should push him away, tell him to leave, and I know the second I do, he'll obey it like gospel. He's waiting for me to be the voice of reason, to be the smart one and stop this before we cross a line neither of us can come back from. Because we both know that when he eventually walks away, it's going to destroy us both. Yet, there's not a single part of me willing to tell him no.

"Zozo," he whispers, and then before I even get a chance to bask in the bittersweetness of hearing my old nickname on his lips, he dips his head down to mine and kisses me.

My eyes close as I melt into him, his lips effortlessly moving against mine as though that's where they've always belonged. I open up, allowing him to kiss me deeper, and when his tongue sweeps into my mouth, those damn butterflies cause havoc in the pit of my stomach.

He kissed me so many times when we were kids, but it's never been like this, never been so full of intense passion, desire, and need. It's everything I always knew it would be and more. Everything I'd always hoped for, and damn it, I kiss him back with everything I have, not knowing when I might ever get to do this again.

My pulse beats so heavily in my ears that I don't hear anything apart from the soft, needy groan rumbling through his strong chest. My hand roams up over his shoulder and hooks around the back of his neck as my fingers glide up into his hair, desperately wishing this moment never has to end.

I feel like I'm home. Like the other half of my soul has finally returned to set me free, and it's the most phenomenal feeling in the world.

It's enchanting, magical, and undeniably breathtaking.

Noah's hand at my waist slides right around my back and pulls me right in until my chest is pressed firmly against his. Then just when I thought it couldn't get better, he steps us right into the overcrowded rack of clothes, parting them to make space, but he doesn't stop until my back is up against the drywall. My clothes fall back into place, crowding around us like a heavy curtain, dimming the light until it's nothing but just me and him.

Noah doesn't dare stop kissing me, and it's as though he's been starved for me, and every lavish swipe of his tongue feels like the sweetest surrender. It's as though he's trying to make up for the past three years in one mind-blowing kiss.

The longing and hurt that's built and built has finally reached its limits and explodes around us. It's cocooning us in this moment and forcing us to act on our most basic needs for each other. That undeniable attraction and overwhelming hunger have taken complete control, and I don't ever want it to stop.

When he pulls back, we're both panting, and a part of me just expects him to walk away, only he stays right here with me, refusing to let me go. His forehead drops against mine, both our hearts still rapidly thrumming. "Zoey—"

"Don't ruin it by speaking," I beg him, terrified that he's about to hit me with a long list of why we should never have done that, because if he did, it would surely kill me.

My eyes remain closed, soaking up the feel of his arm wrapped securely around my waist. I've never felt so safe in my life because I know nothing bad could ever happen to me while being locked in his arms. It's like the old Noah has come back, and I don't ever want to see him leave.

His body presses hard against mine, his thumb still stroking over my bare skin at my waist, and then his lips are back on mine. Only this time there's control, and his lips only linger a moment before pulling back. He takes a heavy breath and puts just an inch between us before taking my chin and forcing my gaze to meet his.

There's a longing in his eyes, and I realize it's taken him great restraint to pull back, but there's also a lightness I haven't seen in over three years, making those dark eyes I've always loved just that little bit brighter. "Zoey, who the hell taught you to drive a car like a fucking idiot?" he questions, his deep tone like a warm caress that wraps right around me.

A real, heart-warming smile tears across my face, and I feel the apples of my cheeks pushing right up into my eyes as I laugh. My fingers ease out of his hair, slowly trailing back down until my palm presses right against his chest, feeling his heartbeat, and committing it to memory in case I don't ever get the chance to do this again.

"Who do you think taught me how to do that?" I say, just as the person in question calls out from downstairs.

"Noah, honey. Are you up there?" Aunt Maya's booming tone fills my home. "It's time to skedaddle."

I fix him with a heavy stare, my silence answering his question, and he nods. "I should have known," he murmurs before going quiet for a moment, not the least bit bothered by the fact his mom is waiting for him downstairs. "It kinda hit me just how much of your life I've missed," he tells me. "I always thought I'd be the one teaching you how to do shit like that."

I don't respond because honestly, I had always thought the very same thing, and the fact that never got to happen still feels like a million knives recklessly plunging straight through my chest.

"Noah?" Aunt Maya hollers. "You hear me, kid? Get your ass

down here and drive your momma home."

He still doesn't make a move to leave, and I find my chest starting to heave, terrified of the moment he walks away, but all he does is hold my stare, his eyes conveying a million messages of pain and unease.

My vision blurs with tears as the inevitable agony swells inside me. "You don't need to hurt like this anymore," I whisper into the small, tension-filled closet, his haunted gaze not moving from mine for even a second. "*He'd* want you to find peace."

"Zoey," he starts, his hand slowly dropping from my waist and making me feel colder than ever before.

"Don't say it," I beg, feeling the rejection growing between us. "Just . . . When you finally realize that you deserve to be happy, come back to me."

He flinches at my words as though I'd physically slapped him, and the agony in his eyes is almost unbearable. "I'm sorry, Zozo," he murmurs, before leaning back in. He presses a gentle kiss to my temple just as the tears spill over and roll down my cheeks, and before I even get a chance to reach for him, he's gone.

The closet door clicks closed behind him, and my heart breaks all over again.

Chapter 18

NOAH

Walking away from Zoey James after discovering how sweet she tastes is the hardest thing I've ever had to do, especially knowing that she's still up there in her closet, probably on the ground with tears streaming from her beautiful green eyes.

I saw the second she realized that this changes nothing, and damn it, I wish it could. I watched her break right in front of me, desperately wishing I could take her pain away. If I could be the man she deserves, I'd hold her until our dying days, but that's not possible.

That kiss though.

Fuck, I've kissed plenty of girls over the past three years, each one of them for the sole purpose of trying to dull the ache in my chest, but not one of them made me feel as though I could breathe again. Not one of them was Zoey. It was everything I knew it would be, and damn it, I've never wanted to do something so badly again. If I could be back up there kissing her right now, I would.

I don't know what I expected to come out of tonight, but that sure as hell wasn't it. When I followed her into her closet, I expected her to scream at me. I wanted to give her the chance to get it all out, to say everything she needed to say, but she didn't stop me or push me away, and the second my lips came down on hers, I felt the darkness lift. Don't get me wrong, it was still hovering close by, ready to infect me all over again, but for those few minutes with my lips against hers, I felt like I was finally the man she always needed me to be.

When you finally realize that you deserve to be happy, come back to me.

Those words haunt me as I make my way downstairs and meet my mom by the front door. *Come back to me.* Shit. I wish it could be that easy. But there's no denying it, the three years of distance have done nothing but make my need and attraction for her all that much stronger.

In that closet, all that existed was her. Her touch on my body, her lips on mine, her soft, breathy moan as my arm wrapped right around her back and pulled her against my chest. It only proves how much she belongs with me. We've always been two halves of the same whole, and when we came together, it was like our souls coming home. It was nothing but a stark reminder of everything I'd given up and the pain I'd caused her.

It was never my intention to hurt her, but she has to understand that it's best this way. If I were to finally give in to those urges, to be her whole world like she is mine, I would eventually drag her down. Zoey James was born to fly, and I . . . I was born with nothing but poison in my veins.

Reaching the bottom of the stairs, I give Zoey's parents a forced smile and thank them for dinner, grateful neither of them bothered to ask where I've been. They know without being told, so what's the point of coming up with a lie?

Glancing at Mom, I find her with one hand braced against the wall to keep her upright. "Shit, Mom. Just how many glasses of wine have you had?"

"Is that really any of your business?" she questions, trying to fish her car keys out of her purse, and after trying for far too long, I take the purse and grab the keys myself.

"Fuck me," I mutter under my breath. "Can you even walk?"

Mom bursts into laughter, and it's only seconds before Zoey's mom is snickering right along with her, needing to grip her husband's arm to keep from toppling over. "I guess we're about to find out," she tells me, bouncing her brows and grinning like a child.

Letting out a heavy sigh, I reach around her and open the door before pressing a hand to her lower back and leading her out. I rarely see her like this, and that's mostly because she's always had to be her own designated driver. I haven't exactly been here to ensure she gets home safely. But clearly, she took advantage of her opportunity tonight.

After leading her out and getting her settled in the passenger's seat, I drop down into the driver's seat and recline it all the way back, not knowing how the hell she could stand sitting so close to the steering wheel.

Backing out of Zoey's driveway, I head home, and the drive is silent for a few minutes before Mom lets out a sigh and gives me a sad smile. "You broke her heart again, didn't you?" she questions.

I keep my stare focused on the road, knowing if I were to meet her saddened eyes, I'd surely break. "She deserves better, Mom," I murmur, my voice barely audible in the silent car. "The sooner she's able to figure that out and move on, the better. I'm only going to hurt her."

"What could possibly be better than you and the bond you two share?" she asks me. "You're selling yourself short, Noah. I think sometimes you forget that I know what's on the inside. I know your heart, the real you, and while you're hurting and buried deep in this pain, eventually, you'll be able to overcome it. I just hope that when that time comes, you haven't pushed her so far away that you'll never be able to get her back."

I don't respond, not really knowing what to say, and after a few moments of intolerable silence, Mom hits me right where it hurts. "She still loves you, you know?" she says, reaching over the center console and gripping my hand, giving it a firm squeeze. "Even after all the distance and hurt, I still see it when she looks at you. You haven't lost her yet, and maybe if you'd let her, she'd be able to pull you out of this sea of despair."

"Mom," I sigh, a subtle warning in my tone, begging her to stop.

"I'm sorry, my love. I just worry about you," she says, trying to force an encouraging smile. "I see how much pain you're in, and it kills me."

"I know," I say, squeezing her hand. We keep driving, and we're just reaching our street when I glance over at her, she's deep in thought, and I know without question, she's thinking about a possible future for me and Zoey. She thinks about it more than I care to admit, but I suppose that's what happens when one of your children dies too young without getting a chance to live life to its fullest. She doesn't want that for me. She wants to make sure I'm happy and that I get everything I've ever wanted in life, and she and I both know all too well that has everything to do with Zoey James.

"Mom," I say as I bring the car to a stop outside the house that hasn't felt like a home in three long years. "Can I ask you a question?"

Her brows furrow, and she turns to look at me, giving me her undivided attention, not even daring to reach for the door handle. "At dinner, you called Zoey your little warrior. And I know you used to call her that all the time, but I don't really understand why. When I asked

Zoey, she looked at me like I'd slapped her across the face."

"Ooooh," she says, scrunching up her face. "That probably wasn't your best move."

"Mom," I groan. "Just put me out of my fucking misery and tell me what that's all about."

Her face falls, and for just a moment, I think I see pity flashing in her eyes. "Oh, honey," she says with a heavy sigh, reaching out and squeezing my hand again, this time refusing to let go. "Do you really not remember?"

"Remember what?"

"When Zoey was six, she was very ill."

"Of course I remember that," I say with a grunt, frustrated that I'm still missing the point. "We were at the hospital with her all the fucking time. I'd sit in her bed with her playing her stupid girly games on the iPad. But she was just sick for a while, and then she got better."

"You were only seven at the time and didn't fully grasp what was happening," she explains, a heaviness plaguing her eyes. "I was trying to shield you from the magnitude of what was going on. I didn't want to tell you just how sick she really was, Noah. I didn't want you to shoulder that burden so young. If you knew just how severe it was, you would have been the most heartbroken seven-year-old boy to ever walk the planet. I didn't want to frighten you, and Zoey needed your positivity. I supposed I just assumed you would have learned all about it at some point."

My brows furrow, and I pull my hand back from hers, curling my fingers into my palms. "What are you talking about?"

"Those times Zoey was at the hospital, honey," she says, swallowing hard. "She was undergoing chemotherapy. She had cancer."

"What?" I question, my whole body going rigid. "She didn't have cancer. I know everything there is to know about her. I know her better than her own fucking parents. Even after being away from her for three years, I still know her better than anyone. I'd have known if she had cancer."

My mind starts to whirl, memories of Zoey in her hospital bed, weak and connected to all sorts of machines. Sometimes she'd have to run to the bathroom and throw up, other times she was too weak to even lift her head before getting sick. Her mom and the nurses would quickly clean her up, but there were times like that I wasn't allowed near her. I was pissed. They told me the type of medicine she was taking meant that I couldn't be there, and I was too young to even question it. I wasn't a doctor. I didn't know any better, but I knew if they said it was helping Zoey, I would have done anything, even if it meant not being there to hold her hand. At times like that, I would FaceTime her instead. But childhood cancer? I would have known.

Not in the sixteen years that I've known her have I ever heard that word tumble from her mouth. Sure, every now and then her parents would mention the time she was sick, but they always talked about her being a survivor, being strong, and . . . *a warrior.*

Fuck.

I never even thought to ask because all that mattered was that she was okay. That she was healthy and strong and still smiling back at me. Her illness didn't matter. It was in the past, and she kicked its ass. But cancer?

How the hell did I not know? Am I that fucking self-centered or just naive?

The horrendous realization has me tumbling out of the car, and I hurry up the path to the garden before throwing up everything in the pit of my stomach. Mom gets out of the car and walks around to the driver's side to close the door I'd left wide open.

She makes her way up the path and moves in beside me, rubbing her hand over my back like she used to when I was sick as a kid. "It's okay, Noah," she soothes. "Zoey is okay. She's been in remission since she was seven and a half and hasn't stopped living since."

The agony is too much to bear, and I drop to the sidewalk, bracing my head in my hands. "I stopped her living," I say. "I stole three years of her happiness. How is she supposed to forgive that?"

Mom shakes her head, kneeling down beside me. "That's for Zoey to decide," she tells me. "But you're never going to find out while you continue to hold her at arm's length. She's been through enough. Don't continue to make her suffer. She wants to be part of your life, and I know you, Noah. You'd sooner lay your own life down than see her get hurt again."

I don't respond, not able to find the words or even figure out how to feel about any of this, and as I sit in agony, Mom makes her way toward the door, leaving me alone to deal with this overwhelming grief. She's just about inside when I glance back at her. "What kind of cancer?" I ask, my voice coming out strained.

She gives me a tight smile, hovering in the doorway. "It's called ALL. Acute lymphocytic leukemia," she tells me.

"Leukemia," I say, the word sounding so alien on my tongue. Of course I've heard of it before, but I never thought to do any research. I never knew I needed to. When someone hears the word leukemia, you automatically think the worst. "That's blood cancer, right?"

"Yes. It's an aggressive form of blood cancer that starts in the bone marrow. I'm certainly no doctor, and it's been quite some time since I've looked over the facts, but my understanding is that due to some form of mutation, patients with ALL create an influx of cancerous blood cells, and instead of dying out as they should, they continue to grow and multiply, essentially crowding the healthy blood cells."

I swallow hard and nod, itching to do some research and fully understand exactly what it is Zoey had gone through as a child while I sat beside her, fucking clueless, probably complaining that we couldn't go outside and play.

"And it's aggressive?"

"Yes," she says, not willing to sugarcoat it. "However, Zoey had amazing doctors, and her symptoms were caught early on, so she had the best chance to fight it. She really is a warrior, Noah. She responded well to her chemotherapy, and after eighteen months, she was in the clear."

I let out a shaky breath and nod, having heard what I needed to hear. "Okay," I say, getting back to my feet and trying to smother the fear that pounds through my veins despite having nothing to worry about. This was all in the past. Nearly ten years ago. I don't need to fear for her, and if she knew I was right now, she'd probably be pissed.

Zoey isn't the type to use her battles as a crutch. She grows from her experiences and uses them as a weapon to draw strength. I can only imagine what kind of strength she'd gain from this. Like Mom said, she's a warrior.

And me? Fuck, she's so much stronger than me.

Glancing back at Mom, I blow out my cheeks, finally able to get a firm grasp on my control. "I, uh . . . I need to head out," I tell her. "Don't wait up for me."

Her brows furrow. "It's late," she scolds. "Where could you possibly be going now?"

Digging into my pocket, I pull out my car keys and dangle them before me. "I have a car to go and find," I remind her.

"Ah," she says with understanding, a smirk playing on her lips. "I'm not going to lie. I'm impressed that she managed to pull it off without getting caught. That Zoey certainly is full of surprises."

She sure as hell is.

With that, Mom heads in, hopefully taking herself straight to bed, and I make sure the door is locked before turning on my heel and stalking down the street. Pulling out the pack of cigarettes hidden within my pocket, I quickly light one up and take a deep drag, the nicotine settling my system.

I never got around to asking Zoey where the hell she had dumped my car. That's the whole reason I was in her room to start with, apart from getting my keys of course, and a part of me was disappointed. I thought she would have at least tried to hide them, but they were just dumped right there in the center of her desk. But once she walked in wearing nothing but a towel, every train of thought I had systematically derailed, and I suddenly couldn't give a shit where my car was. But I didn't need to ask anyway.

Like I told my mom earlier, I know Zoey better than anyone. Everything she does has been thoroughly thought through, so if she was going to dump my car somewhere, it would be somewhere meaningful. And where better than the one spot we used to say was ours?

The park.

It's at least a fifteen-minute walk, but I really don't mind. The fresh air is probably the best thing for me tonight. My head is a fucking mess right now. The kiss. Zoey's comment. Leukemia. I don't know how to handle it, but one thing is for sure—while the kiss was absolutely everything, and I've replayed it a million times over, I keep coming straight back to her cancer.

Despite it being nearly ten years ago, the overwhelming need to hold her plagues me, to reiterate that she's okay and put me at ease, to apologize for not looking beneath the surface and digging deep enough to know what was really going on with her. But I no longer have the right. So, for now, I have no choice but to settle with my mom's assurances that she's better now.

Reaching the park, I quickly find my car in the deserted parking lot and make my way toward it while shaking my head, knowing damn well Zoey was the one to pull my windshield wipers up like that. I can just imagine the stupid smirk on her lips as she did it.

Walking around to the driver's door, I groan at the lipstick on the window. Not because it's there, but because of the picture of a hand she's drawn, a hand that's specifically flipping me the bird. I'm going to have to remember to scrub that shit off before school in the morning.

Unlocking the door, I'm hit with more of Zoey's ridiculous little pranks, each one getting under my skin just the way she'd hoped they would.

Well played, Zoey James.

Well fucking played.

After sliding the driver's seat all the way back and fixing the positioning of my rearview mirror, I close the center console and finally shove the key into the ignition. The second I turn the key and the engine kicks over with a deafening roar, my car comes alive like it's fucking possessed.

"What the fuck?" I grunt, physically jumping as music blasts from the speakers while the windshield wipers fly back and forth across the windshield so fast that I fear they might actually fly right off.

The hazard lights flash, lighting up the space around my car, and I quickly get everything under control, turning down the music just enough to not burst my eardrums.

Once my heart is firmly back in my chest, I hit the gas, unable to help sparing a glance toward the park I haven't been able to visit since the day Linc died. There are so many memories here with both Linc and Zoey, each one of them better than the last.

My heart aches for everything I've lost, and as I peel out of the park and back onto the main road, I force the thoughts from my mind and focus on the song playing through the speakers. It's not one I recognize, and my brows furrow as I glance down at the screen.

It's a song called *Fall Out Of Love* by Alessia Cara, and as I take in the heart-wrenching lyrics, I realize that Zoey left this song playing for a reason. Like I said, she doesn't make a move without it being carefully thought through. And this right here is nothing but a message.

The singer asks when I fell out of love, but it might as well be Zoey's voice blasting through the speakers. Every time the lyrics repeat, it hits me harder than the last. This is Zoey's way of asking me when she stopped being my whole fucking world, but surely she knows I've never stopped loving her.

I was maybe seven when I realized I was going to spend the rest of my life with her, but I was around twelve or thirteen when that love for her really started to develop into something a little more serious. I didn't just want to spend my life with her, I wanted to make her my whole world. I wanted to love her in a way no one ever loved before. I wanted to be her protector, the person who put a smile on her face, and the reason she woke up in the morning. And until Linc died, I was just that.

God. I wish I could be that for her again.

The song comes to an end, and as I sail through the streets, I find myself starting it over, because I'm nothing if not a sucker for punishment. I drive for another ten minutes, and when I come to a stop and stare out my window, I find it's not my house I'm looking up at.

It's Zoey's.

Chapter 19

NOAH

Considering Zoey is now more than aware of my stalker tendencies when it comes to her and my antics over the past few years, I don't bother wasting time knocking on the door. Instead, I climb straight up the side of the house and to her window.

I'm not exactly in the mood to deal with her father tonight, not that he's a bad guy or anything, but I haven't got a single doubt that he would tell me to fuck off. Well, maybe not quite that way, but the idea would be there, demanding I speak to Zoey at school rather than keep her up. And I'm damn sure he's not going to approve the idea of sneaking in through her bedroom window instead. So, for now, this little visit will be kept on the down-low.

Glancing into her room, I find her curled up in bed, her blankets pulled up to her chin as she lays on her side with one arm scooped beneath her pillow.

I shouldn't be here. I should be giving her space after everything that went down tonight. That kiss meant something, but then I also broke her heart all over again, and that pain has got to be sitting fresh in her mind. Just as raw and painful as it's always been.

Gripping the bottom of the window, I pull it open, having to give it a slight wiggle to get past the mangled lock that Zoey and I broke when we were kids. Sliding it up, I slip inside her bedroom, and the second my feet hit the ground, a fearful gasp sails across the room. "It's just me," I tell her, not wanting her to assume the worst, but I know she did. What else would she think seeing a man climb through her window in the middle of the night?

Zoey lets out a sleepy groan, needing a moment for her heart to stop racing, and when she does, she scrambles up her bed, sitting a little higher against her pillows and staring at me through the darkness. She grips her blankets to her chest, much like she'd held on to her towel to keep it from falling down. "What are you doing here?" she murmurs, sparing a glance toward the digital clock on her bedside table. "It's almost midnight."

I creep closer, inching in as she watches me like a hawk, and even through the darkness, I can see her red-rimmed eyes, no doubt caused by my need to walk away from her tonight. I hate that my actions caused tears to fall from her beautiful eyes, but what fucking choice did I have? "Nice song selection," I tell her.

She glances away, a smugness creeping into her eyes. "I don't know what you're talking about."

I scoff before taking another step. "Leukemia, Zoey," I state, letting her hear the torture in my voice, the torment I've felt since those words came out of my mother's mouth.

Her gaze falls away, and a flicker of shame flashes in her eyes before she forces a small smile to spread across her lips as if somehow trying to make this easier for me. "You didn't waste any time looking for answers, huh?" she whispers as sadness fills her tone.

"How the hell could you not tell me?"

"Why would I?" she questions, adjusting herself against her pillow to get comfortable. "You always wanted to protect me from the things that would scare me, and I wanted to protect you from the ugliness of this." She pauses for a moment, her gaze shifting away from mine. "You were the only person who didn't look at me like I was a ticking time bomb, and I needed that more than you could ever know. I needed my bestest friend, and maybe it was selfish of me not to tell you exactly what I was up against, but I needed the real, unapologetically amazing Noah that I loved with everything I had. If you had started looking at me the way that everyone else did . . . I wouldn't have survived."

Unease pounds at my chest, and I clench my jaw. The thought of little Zoey not surviving cripples me. "Don't fucking say that."

"Noah," she whispers. "It's true. You're the reason I'm still here. You saved me. You got me through it. During those torturous chemotherapy sessions, I remember thinking all I had to do was get through that and when I was done, I would get to see you again. It's your optimism and that stupid smile that forced me to fight."

I shake my head. "I knew you were sick, and that it was bad, but I never thought . . ." My words trail off, not able to bring myself to say the rest of that sentence out loud. *That I could have lost you.*

She just sits there in the comfort of her bed, looking at me as though not knowing what to say, but this is Zoey fucking James, she's always known the right things to say. "I guess I just assumed that at some point, your mom or someone would have told you."

"*You* should have told me."

Zoey scoffs. "And there's a lot of things *you* should have done too, but you don't see me sneaking through your bedroom window to dig up the past."

"Zo," I whisper, inching closer. "I'm not asking you because I want you to have to relive all of that bullshit. I just . . . I need to fucking know."

"I don't want you hurting for me, Noah," she says. "You're already hurting enough for the both of us."

Pain rockets through my chest, and I drop down on the edge of her bed, keeping just out of reach so that I can't be tempted to throw myself at her and pull her into my chest, right where she's always belonged. "Tell me about it," I beg her. "Every last excruciating detail, and don't even think about trying to spare my feelings. I can handle it."

"The same way you're handling your feelings now?"

"For fuck's sake, Zoey," I groan, unable to bear being left in the dark a second longer. "Please just tell me. Do you have any fucking idea how it feels to learn that there was this huge, monumental thing that you went through, something that could have easily taken your life, and I just stood by, fucking clueless?"

"You didn't just stand by, Noah," she tells me. "You knew enough to help me through it, and that was everything I needed. We were only kids. You were seven when I was diagnosed. I barely understood what was happening to me, and it's not like any of our parents were willing to put the weight of that on your shoulders."

Leaning forward, I brace my elbows on my knees. "Please, Zoey," I whisper, my voice trembling.

Zoey nods, grabbing the spare pillow from beside her and hugging it to her chest as if that can somehow offer her just a snippet of comfort, and damn it, I've never needed to be the one to offer her that so badly in my life. "I was six," she says. "I don't really remember much of it."

"Just tell me what you do know."

She nods again, and as her words flow through the dark room, my head falls into my hands, taking in every last detail. "It all happened really quickly. One minute I was at the doctor's office because my mom thought I had the flu, and the next, I was in a hospital bed, connected to a million different machines with nurses fussing over me. I remember thinking that I just wanted to get out of there and see you," she says. "At the beginning, the tests were really scary. I didn't understand what was happening or why I had to go to the doctor's office all the time. They would always take blood tests and then there was the bone marrow biopsy. That one was terrifying, and while I had been given local anesthesia, I remember screaming. Not because it was painful or anything, I was just . . . scared."

She takes a deep breath, worrying her bottom lip, but I remain silent, taking in every detail. "People seemed to cry a lot," she continues. "I had people I never really knew holding me in the street and wishing me well. Actually, a lot of that I've worked hard to try and block out over the past ten years, but those memories just seemed to have stuck. Our moms were the worst at it. Every time they'd look at me, they'd burst out crying, but you would roll your eyes as if they were being ridiculous and then we'd end up laughing."

My lips press into a hard line, somewhat remembering that. It seemed everyone we talked to knew that Zoey was sick, and I remember thinking they were all exaggerating and making her feel like she was broken. I hated it. Especially considering she was trying to get better, and all those assholes were going out of their way to remind her just how sick she was. She didn't need that. She needed me.

"Fuck, Zo," I mutter.

"I can stop," she suggests. "If it's too much—"

"No," I tell her. "Keep going."

"Okay," she says, her voice a little shaky. "After the diagnosis came, we were pretty much straight in the hospital to start my chemotherapy treatment. There were three rounds of it over the course of eighteen months. And they really sucked, Noah."

Her voice trembles, and I find myself reaching out, my hand dropping to her foot that's hidden beneath the blanket, and she flinches, pulling her foot away. "Don't," she warns me, her tone filled with pain. I meet her stare, my brows furrowed. I thought she wanted this from me, wanted to feel me coming back to her. Seeing the confusion in my stare, she explains herself. "Not like this. The old Noah, the one I loved and needed, he's already gotten me through this. He's already given me what I needed. This new you, this stranger sitting at the end of my bed, I don't need or want his pity."

"I don't pity you, Zoey," I say, pulling my hand away and accepting her reasoning without question. "Never."

"Okay," she whispers with a slight nod before pressing her lips into a hard line. Something softens in her eyes as if deep in thought, and for a fleeting second, I see that six-year-old girl who so desperately needed me by her side. A moment later, she throws her blanket back and crawls across her bed, climbing straight onto my lap and straddling me.

She sits far enough back, her ass resting against my thighs with plenty of space between us, not at all like the way my body was pressed against hers in her closet earlier tonight. I keep my hands down, not daring to touch her despite the overwhelming need to do just that.

Then with her gaze locked on mine, she raises her hand to the neckline of her pajama top and pulls it aside, pointing out a small scar just below her collarbone, one I've always known was there but never thought to ask why. "This is where they put the port for my chemo," she tells me. "The first round was brutal. I remember it making me sick all the time, and I would cry non-stop. I'm pretty sure that first round I was only in there for a few weeks and then I got to go home."

"I remember," I tell her just as someone appears in Zoey's doorway.

My gaze flicks across the room to find Zoey's mom, clearly having heard voices in here, and I wait for her to tell me to leave, but instead, she just hovers, listening to Zoey's recap of her chemotherapy.

"The second round was intense," she murmurs, clearly not realizing her mom is listening as she focuses her whole attention on me, her gaze far away as she recalls those painful memories. "But I think I was better prepared because I knew what to expect. Only, that round was a lot longer. I can't be sure exactly how long that hospital stay was. Maybe a few months? I don't know. The details are fuzzy now."

"And the third?" I ask.

"The third wasn't quite as bad," she tells me. "By that stage, the first and second rounds had already killed all the cancerous cells. I was pretty much in the clear, but I still had to complete the full treatment. They call it the maintenance round. It's like when you kill a bug, and then you step on it again just to make sure it's really dead. You know, just in case."

I nod. "Just in case."

Seeing Erica's slight movement out of the corner of my eyes, I glance back to watch as she wipes a stray tear from the side of her cheek, and seeing my gaze, she gives me a sad smile before slipping away.

"Exactly," Zoey says, her gaze dropping as her hand comes up and gently presses against my chest, gripping the soft material of my shirt and rolling it between her fingers. "I hated those long stays in the hospital, but I knew that when I got home, you were going to be there, and it didn't matter to you how sick I was. You just sat by me the whole time, not caring when I fell asleep in the middle of a game. You just pulled my blanket up and made sure I was comfortable."

The corner of my lip pulls into a broken smile, and I can't resist reaching up and gently brushing my fingers down the side of her face, watching as she tilts her head into my touch. "I remember the day my mom told me you weren't sick anymore," I tell her, the memory forcing my smile to widen. "She had guests over, but I made her kick them out just so we could race over here."

Zoey's eyes sparkle with a fondness that warms my cold, dead heart. "I remember," she whispers. "You came storming through the door and nearly knocked Hazel on her ass. But then you kissed me right there in the living room, right in front of my parents."

A cocky smirk stretches wide across my face. "Damn fucking straight, I did."

Zoey laughs as her hand falls from my chest, dropping between us, and as the silence stretches on, I find myself desperate to fill it. "I'm sorry I'm making you relive it all," I tell her as my control begins to slip, and my hands gently move to her thighs. "Losing Linc was the hardest thing I've ever had to go through. It fucked me up in a way I'm not sure I'll ever come back from, but if I lost you . . . I'm not sure that I could survive it."

Her brows furrow, and she watches me for a moment before leaning in and wrapping her arms around me. Her face burrows into the curve of my neck, and I can't help but reach around her and pull her into my arms, her body pressed right against me. She breathes me in, her chest rising and falling in sync with mine. "Is that why you pushed me away?" she murmurs against my neck.

I close my eyes, not knowing if I have the strength to tell her the depth of the reasons why I needed to force the distance between us. "That and other things," I tell her, wanting to offer her at least something to help her understand, even if it's only a little bit.

"I'm sorry I didn't fight harder for us," she tells me.

My brows furrow, and I move my hands to her arms, gently pushing her back so that I can see her beautiful face. "What do you mean?"

"After Linc," she tells me, tears pooling in her eyes. "When you first pushed me away. You needed me more than ever, and I was too blinded by my own hurt to see that. I should have tried harder and refused to let you push me away. You were always right there by my side when I needed you, and when you needed me, I was too broken to see it. I didn't fight for you."

"Zoey—"

"No," she says, cutting me off. "If Hazel had been hit by that drunk driver, and I'd told you to leave me alone, you would have told me to shut up and just held on tighter. That's what I should have done for you."

"You're right. If it had been Hazel and you were the one pushing me away, I would have broken down your fucking door and refused to go, but it wasn't Hazel. It was Linc. And whether you fought harder or not, whether you physically held on to me and refused to let go, I still would have pushed you away, but it would have only hurt more."

The tears spill over her eyes, and I reach up to wipe them away. "Don't cry, Zozo," I tell her. "You know I never could handle your tears."

"Can't help it," she mutters.

Letting out a breath, my hand curls around her back again, pulling her in, and she falls right back into me. Her arms lock around my shoulders, and her face burrows into the curve of my neck. "I'm sorry I hurt you tonight," I whisper. "That wasn't my intention when I came into your room."

"I know. I shouldn't have let you get that close," she says, her fingers roaming up into my hair, just as they had inside that damn closet. "Don't get me wrong, that kiss was . . . I don't even have the words for what that was, but the second you followed me into the closet, I knew what you were going to do, and I knew you were still going to pull away, but I didn't stop you, and that's on me. You gave me every chance to tell you no."

"It was selfish. I shouldn't have walked in there," I tell her before scoffing. "I should have walked away the second I got my keys, but you know just as well as I do, I've never been able to control myself when it comes to you." I pause, my hand moving up and down her back. "I just don't want you getting the wrong idea about what's going on here."

"What *is* going on here?" she questions, pulling back to meet my stare. "Because I've never been so confused in my life. I'm assuming you're just going to pretend that you didn't rock my world in my closet and go straight back to treating me like *trash*."

"Fuck, Zoey," I say, my chest aching as she uses that filthy word. "You know I never meant for that to happen."

"I can handle Shannan," she tells me. "What I can't handle is having to watch as she throws herself all over you, knowing damn well you can't stand her."

"I haven't touched her," I say, not understanding why I feel it's important for her to know that.

"I know," she says. "The whole school would have known if you had."

I groan, knowing just how right she is before pressing my lips into a hard line and meeting her saddened stare. "And as for you and me?" I ask.

Zoey shrugs her shoulders, and the sadness in her eyes only increases. "You know what I want, Noah. That's never changed," she tells me. "I stand by what I said in that closet. When you're ready to come back to me, I'll be right here waiting. Just promise that if there ever comes a point where you change your mind or decide that I'm not what you need, let me go because I'll never be able to pull away on my own."

My arms tighten back around her, and I clutch her tightly to my chest. "You'll never not be what I need," I promise her.

"Then I'll never stop fighting for you."

I close my eyes, my forehead tipping against hers as we sit there in this warm silence, our arms wrapped tightly around one another. Then when a yawn tears through her, I scoop her up into my arms and lift us off the end of her bed. I take two strides to the top of her bed and slide her back in between the sheets, pulling the blanket right up to her chin, just the way she likes it. "Go to sleep, Zozo," I murmur, leaning down and pressing a kiss to her temple.

I pull back, and before I can convince myself to stay, I turn and make my way back across her room, my fingers clutching the window. "I'll miss you, Noah," she says, and the way her tone makes this feel like goodbye tears me to shreds, but it's nothing less than what I deserve.

Glancing back, I see her eyes shining in the darkness, one perfectly round tear rolling down her cheek. "I'll miss you too, Zo." And with that, I climb back out through her window and sit right there on the roof until the sun peeks up over the horizon.

Chapter 20

ZOEY

THREE YEARS AGO

My feet drag along the path toward the park as the hot Arizona sun bears down over me. There are a few weeks of summer break left, and then Tarni and I will be starting at East View High together. I've never been so excited. Well, that's not entirely true. I'm excited, but I'm also kinda nervous.

Starting high school was supposed to be easy because I thought I'd have Noah there to calm my nerves. It's what we always planned. He was going to be at East View a year before me, and when I followed, he would be there to hold my hand, but things don't always go according to plan. The second he showed promise on the football field, his father made sure he was enrolled in the best private school in the area, but it's fine, I still see him all the time. It just means that during school hours, I'm not going to have anybody to swoon over.

He's fourteen now, and over the last two years, he's gotten so tall, and that boyish grin is starting to morph into something else. When he looks at me, it makes my stomach flip-flop. I love it so much. *I love him so much.*

I don't think it's normal for kids our age to already know what they want in life, or who they want, but I've known for a while now that Noah is my person. We've always been best friends—*bestest friends*—but lately, it's felt like more than that. Things are changing between us, and I don't really know where we stand.

He's always kissed me since we were kids, but he does it more often now and thinks of ridiculous reasons to stop by my house to see me. If someone asked me to define our relationship, I don't know what I would say. I think he's my boyfriend, but it's not like we've ever had a conversation about it, and I don't want to be wrong. God, that would be so embarrassing.

Tarni walks beside me, her arm looped through mine, and as she blabbers on about some guy coming to East View with us in a few weeks, I find myself cringing. Noah asked me to meet him in the park, which is fine, we do it all the time, but the second he sees Tarni tagging along, he's not going to be happy. He's never really liked her, but I don't understand why.

When Tarni and I get to the park, I quickly scan the field, and finding it empty, we make our way over to the swings, sitting down and talking about all the crazy things that have happened over the summer.

We're only here for a few minutes when I finally see him on the opposite side of the park. His gaze instantly comes to mine, a wide smile spreading over his lips, and as I smile back, I feel something pull between us, like an invisible string. It's always been this way, but I've never had the guts to ask if he feels it too.

Noah's gaze quickly flicks toward Tarni, and his steps falter, but Tarni doesn't pick up on his hesitation the way I do. I always notice everything he does. I know him better than I know myself, and though he's not going to hold it against me for bringing her with me, he's definitely not jumping for joy.

Despite his silent objections to our tag-along, I jump off the swing and make my way toward him. Tarni follows but is stuck a few paces behind, unable to catch up to my quick strides.

I meet Noah in the middle of the park, and he immediately throws his arm over my shoulder, pulling me right into his side, but if we were alone, he would have slid his other arm around me in a tight hug and dropped the sweetest kiss to my lips. "What's she doing here?" he mutters under his breath.

"What was I supposed to do? I promised that we'd hang out today," I tell him. "Besides, how many times do I need to tell you that she's really not that bad? Are you ever going to give her a chance, or do I have to put up with this for the rest of my life?"

"Hell no. I'm not wasting my time giving her a chance. You already know how I feel about that," he grumbles, dragging me toward the field as Tarni falls in step beside us. Noah lowers his tone. "Besides, why would I do that when I have everything I need right here?"

I roll my eyes. "I think that was the cheesiest thing you've ever said."

Noah grins wide, and as that boyish charm lights up his whole face, my knees go weak. "Oh yeah?" he challenges. "You haven't seen anything yet."

Oh, God.

Noah leans in, his lips hovering by my ear as a familiar figure appears at the other end of the field. "HEADS UP!" Linc roars just in time for us to see the football hurtling right toward my face.

"FUCK," Noah grunts, shoving me out of the way as I scream, certain I'm about to have my face rearranged by a ball. I tumble aside and trip over Tarni's feet, falling right to the ground as Noah's arms strike out like lightning and catch the ball with ease. He tosses it aside and quickly scrambles to scoop me up and set me back on my feet, shoving Tarni away in the process.

I cringe as I look down at my scraped knees, willing myself not to cry. I hate crying at the best of times, but I won't do it in front of Noah. He can't handle my tears.

"Shit, Zozo. Are you okay?"

"I'm fine," I say, shaking it off. "It's nothing."

"It's not nothing," he spits, turning his anger on his little brother as Tarni attempts to get close to see the damage. "What the fuck, Linc? You hurt her."

"I didn't mean to," Linc responds, jogging toward us and offering me a sheepish smile. He's not very good with apologies, but I know he's sorry.

"What are you even doing here?" Noah demands as Tarni's phone rings and she steps away to answer it, leaving me to deal with the brothers. "I told you to stay home. I was just coming to hang out with Zoey."

"You always hang out with Zoey. You never have time for me anymore," Linc whines, instantly making me feel like crap. Noah and I have been spending a lot of time together. We always do. "I just wanted to toss the ball around with you for a while. Besides, we all know that Zoey is going to get bored and end up sitting down, and then you're gonna wish you had me here."

"Linc," Noah groans.

"Why do you have to be such an ass all the time?" Linc grunts, his gaze falling to the ground.

"Get lost, Linc," Noah grits through a clenched jaw. "You're so fucking annoying. Go home."

Linc clenches his jaw, glaring at his big brother, and when they do this, they always look so similar. I can tell that when Linc is older and they're both grown, people will mistake them for twins.

Linc's bottom lip pouts out just a fraction, but he won't break in front of Noah. He's so stubborn. He wants Noah to see him like one of the big kids, but he'll always be his little brother. I don't know, maybe things will change in a few years when Linc can hold his own against him, but until then, it's always going to be a power struggle.

"You're a shitty brother," Linc grumbles, devastation flashing in his eyes, and with that, he turns on his heel and stalks away.

"Linc," I call after him, but he doesn't stop. I love Linc as much as my little sister, but now that things have shifted between me and Noah, it changes the dynamics between us all. Noah and I aren't just playing ball anymore, he's flirting, accidentally touching my hand, and pretending to tumble right into me just so he can put his hands around my waist, and just when I think he'll let me go, he'll kiss me. It's not exactly something Noah wants to do around his little brother, but Linc doesn't understand that yet.

Linc's rigid figure grows smaller with the distance, and Noah picks up his discarded ball as if nothing happened. "Did you really have to do that?" I ask Noah, swatting at his chest as Tarni continues her phone call, probably oblivious to anything going on here. "You were mean."

"He'll be fine," Noah grunts. "Mom was planning on taking him and Hazel to see a movie this afternoon, and if he's not home when she gets home, he'll miss out."

"Then why didn't you tell him that?" I question, rolling my eyes, feeling as though I'm never going to understand how a boy's mind works. "If he knew he was going to have a movie date, he would have run home."

Noah shrugs his shoulders, not seeing the issue. "It was supposed to be a surprise."

"You're impossible, Noah Ryan."

"Don't pretend like you don't love it."

Rolling my eyes, I snatch the ball off him and throw it up into the sky, only as I go to catch it again, his big arm shoots out and collects it before I even get a chance. I give him a blank stare. "Why are you so adamant about it being just you and me?" I ask. "We're just tossing a ball around."

A wicked grin stretches across Noah's face. "Did you see me walk in here with a ball?" he asks, indicating to the one now in his hand. "Linc brought this. Not me." My brows furrow, and he lets out a groan. "I had no intention of tossing a ball around with you today, Zo. I was going to drag you into the woods and make out with you instead, but then you had to go and bring Tarni freaking Luca."

My jaw drops, and I gape at him, watching the way my shock only makes his grin wider.

"What do you say, Zo?" he murmurs, stepping in closer, his fingers brushing along my arm. "Get rid of the tag-along."

My gaze flickers toward Tarni, watching as she paces through the overgrown grass, mindlessly chatting on her phone, completely unaware of her surroundings. "What am I supposed to say?"

"I don't know," he grunts. "Just tell her to fuck off."

"Noah!" I gasp. I hate when he talks like that, but I think it's something he picked up from the boys at his fancy private school. Or maybe it's just a high school thing. Maybe it's just a Noah thing, and I'm just going to have to get used to it.

"What?"

I roll my eyes and go to tell him he's an idiot when his phone rings. He dives deep into his pocket, pulling it out to find Linc's name on the screen. He decides to ignore it, but I snatch the phone off him and quickly answer it before Noah can steal it back. "Linc," I rush out. "It's fine. You can come—"

"Help," Linc croaks out.

"Linc?" I ask, my brows furrowed as I meet Noah's gaze. "What's wrong? What happened?"

Linc sputters, crying out in pain. "Help," he cries. "I can't . . . I can't breathe."

My eyes widen, fear brimming in my chest as I grab Noah's hand and start running faster than I've ever run before, leaving Tarni behind. Noah screams something at me, but I don't hear it over my panic. "What happened, Linc? What happened?"

"Zoey?" Noah demands, needing answers.

Linc sputters in my ear. "A car. It . . . It came out of nowhere."

His words fade away, and it sounds as though he's choking on something, and I cry out to Noah. "I think he's been hit by a car."

Undeniable fear flashes in Noah's eyes. I've never seen anything like it before. "FUCK," he roars, his feet pounding against the sidewalk as he drags me along with him toward the road that leads back to his house.

Realizing I'm only slowing him down, I pull my hand out of his. "Go," I urge him, the fear of Lincoln lying somewhere along the road crippling me, making it hard to breathe. "You're faster. Go, Noah."

He doesn't hesitate, taking off like lightning toward his little brother as I clutch his phone to my ear tighter. "We're coming, Linc," I promise him, hating how quiet he's gotten. "Just hold on. We're coming."

I hear the noises around him, his gurgling voice, his strained gasps, and it terrifies me. I hear Noah calling out. "LINC," he screams, only the sound isn't coming from somewhere in front of me, it's coming through the phone. "NO. No, Linc. Please. FUCK."

I push myself faster, racing around the bend when I see them up ahead. A black car is stopped in the street, the driver has his hands buried in his hair as he stumbles around on the road, but Linc is lying motionless in someone's yard. Blood is everywhere, and as I hold the phone to my ear, I don't know whose terror-filled gasps I'm hearing— mine, Noah's, or Linc's.

"No, no, no," Noah cries, gripping his brother's limp body against his chest. "Don't close your eyes, Linc. Fuck. Stay with me. Please, stay with me."

I crash into Noah's side, my knees dropping heavily to the ground as I scramble for Lincoln's hand, squeezing it with everything I have. "It's going to be alright, Linc," I promise him as my fingers furiously press the buttons on the phone, calling for help. Only as Noah holds his brother and an unfamiliar voice answers my call, I know he's already gone.

My chest heaves with shock, devastation racing through my veins as I struggle to catch my breath. Linc can't be gone. I have to be wrong, but as Noah's wide, glassy eyes lift to mine, I know it's true.

Linc is gone.

One minute he was right there, wanting to play football with his big brother, and the next . . . *gone.*

A heavy sob tears from deep in my chest, and I fall forward, throwing my arms around Linc's body as if I could protect him from the driver's prying eyes or the unforgiving asphalt beneath him. I hold on to him, the deepest pain I've ever felt filling my veins.

I'm distantly aware of Noah screaming, and the raw agony in his tone is something I don't ever want to hear again. I gently release Linc's body and scramble toward Noah, my chest slamming against his. His big arms close around me as I bury my face into his shoulder. My tears instantly stain his shirt, but he doesn't let me go, not when the police and paramedics show up, not when his mom's car careens around the corner, not even when my dad tries to pull me away.

He holds on to me, and as the grief eats us both alive, I realize that our lives are never going to be the same.

From here on out, everything changes.

Chapter 21

NOAH

Walking out of Mrs. Thompson's office, I tick off counseling for another day. It's my fifth session since being at East View, and so far, I'm surprised that it doesn't entirely suck. It was supposed to be biweekly, but I find myself knocking on her door a little more frequently.

Mrs. Thompson is patient. She allows me to work through what I'm feeling in my own time and explains how not processing things keeps me from moving forward. And yeah, I suppose she's right.

My first session was fucked up. I was angry, but what's new? I'm always fucking angry. Only, today, I've just been broken, and I know it has everything to do with the conversation I had with Zoey last night. Finding out about her leukemia as a child and learning how fucking oblivious I was has put a lot of things into perspective.

Zoey has already been through so much, and all I've done is add to her pain.

I'm sure that I probably broke some kind of trust with Zoey by sharing, but the second I sat down in Mrs. Thompson's office, I told her all about it, and yet, she didn't seem surprised. I was left wondering just how much of Zoey's past the school knows about. Though I suppose that's not exactly any of my business. I've lost the right to know those things about her, and that's on me, it doesn't change the fact that I feel like a piece of shit for not knowing all this time.

The only thing I didn't share with the school counselor was that kiss. It felt too private, like it was just ours, and I don't exactly feel like sharing that with the whole world. Besides, while it was incredible and everything I knew it would be, news like that would spread like wildfire around here, and I can't see people like Shannan Holter taking it well. She's already making Zoey's life a living hell due to my actions, and this would only make that worse.

Making my way through the student office, I find it just a little easier to breathe. It's the same weightless feeling I have when Zoey is in my arms, and I know it has everything to do with Mrs. Thompson forcing me to talk about Linc. She doesn't ask me about his death, how it happened, or what the days following were like, but she asks me about his life. What kind of music he listened to, what sports he was into, and what fond memories I have that I'm willing to share. And honestly, it felt fucking amazing to talk about him like that, to not have to focus on the worst moment of my life.

I'm finally starting to move forward, and I don't feel like breaking every second of the day, and it has everything to do with this place, with Zoey.

"Mr. Ryan," I hear my voice called from across the student office.

My hand pauses on the door, and I let out a heavy sigh as I mentally go over everything that's happened over the past few days. Usually, when the school principal uses a tone like that, it's because I've done something to fuck up my enrollment.

My hand falls away from the door, and I slowly turn to find Principal Daniels taking up too much space in the student office. "Can I help you?" I ask, confusion booming through my chest. I've been on my best behavior, attended every last class, and haven't even smoked on school property. At least nowhere he'd be able to see me.

"Why don't you come into my office."

Ah, shit.

Daniels turns on his heel and stalks deeper into the student office, passes a few rooms with closed doors, and stops in front of the one at the end of the hallway. He pulls the door open for me. "Make yourself comfortable."

Letting out a heavy breath, I stride into Daniels' office and quickly glance around. It's a nice office, definitely not as nice as the one I burned down a few weeks ago. In hindsight, that was probably the most fucked-up thing I've done, but my mistakes are what brought me here. Brought me back to life.

"I take it you don't have any current plans to burn down my office?" Daniels says, a smug-as-fuck smirk across his face as he strides around his mahogany desk and takes a seat, leaning back in his chair and crossing his arms over his chest.

"Not currently."

"Good," he says. "I'm fond of this office."

"Glad to hear it."

The room falls into silence, and Daniels just stares forward, trying to intimidate me, but honestly, the only person in this world who has the power to affect me by stare alone is Zoey fucking James.

"I've had some disturbing reports," he starts.

I quickly cut him off, saving us both time and effort. "Whatever it was, I had nothing to do with it."

Daniels arches a brow. "So, the black Camaro that was stolen out of the student parking lot and left two thick lines of rubber down the street wasn't yours?"

I nod toward the window that has the perfect view of the student parking lot. "Don't know what you're talking about," I tell him. "My car is right there, clearly not stolen."

"I'm not in the mood for games, Noah," he says. "Give me a name."

And dump Zoey in a world of shit? Like hell I'm ever going to do that. Besides, it was my property that was stolen, and I got it back . . . and more.

No harm, no foul. There's nothing more to it.

Stealing my car was Zoey's way of sending a message. It's our business and nobody else's, especially not Principal Daniels'. "Like I said," I reiterate. "I don't know what to tell you. My car is right where it belongs, not a scratch on it. Besides, I was at football training when it happened, and I don't know if you've noticed, but my window tint is just about as dark as the law will allow. I didn't see shit."

His stare only hardens, and it's clear he doesn't believe me, but I'll go down on this hill if it means protecting Zoey. Besides, it's not as though he's ever going to suspect her. She's the most polite, well-mannered girl in the whole fucking school. He'll somehow find a way to accuse me of being the one behind the wheel, despite the many witnesses.

Let's be honest. I'd rather go down for this than ever allowing eyes to fall on Zoey. I've protected her since the day she was born, and I've failed her in so many ways over the past three years. It's time to start making up for that.

"Whether you like it or not, this is a school incident. Your car was stolen on school property, and the suspect drove recklessly, endangering the lives of the students of East View."

Laying it on thick, I see.

"With all due respect, sir, you couldn't be more wrong," I say, ready and willing to say whatever is needed to keep this from coming down on Zoey. "My car wasn't stolen. A friend needed a ride after school, and I willingly gave up the keys. And as for the reckless driving, were you there? Because I saw the whole thing. My car was well off school property before the burnout started, which you can clearly see from the marks left on the road. The school has nothing to be concerned with."

Principal Daniels narrows his stare at me, drumming his fingers on his desk. "Who are you trying to protect, Noah?"

I scoff, more than happy to pull out my usual attitude that I keep reserved solely for authority. "Do I strike you as the type of kid who's looking out for anyone but himself?"

"No," he says, almost sounding disappointed. "Not even a little bit."

There's a slight pause, and I'm about to haul ass out of here when he goes on, keeping me pinned in my chair. "Okay, here's what's going to happen," he says. "You and I both know that I'm not buying your bullshit. You're either going to give me a name, or you're going to spend every lunch period for the next week right here in my office. But be warned, a week's worth of detention puts a mark on your record. Earn a second one and that's grounds for suspension."

I arch a brow, not exactly pleased with my options. Protect Zoey or risk my enrollment? What a stupid fucking question. Where Zoey is concerned, there's not a damn thing I wouldn't do to protect her, even if it means giving up my future. "Then I guess I'll see you at lunch," I tell him, not even a hint of hesitation in my tone.

"Very well," Principal Daniels says, watching me with suspicion. He holds my stare a moment longer before taking a deep breath.

"You've barely been here a week, Noah. I don't want to see you getting in trouble. I've had nothing but good reports from your teachers, and even Coach Martin seems to be impressed by you. That's no easy feat. You've stuck to your counseling sessions, and as far as I'm aware, you have had full attendance to every class. I'm not foolish enough to believe that this will last, but I am hopeful that it will. I don't want to see you fall behind. You could be a great addition to this school, a role model to the younger students, and your football endeavors could put this school on the map. However, I stand by what I said; one fuck up, Noah, and you're out on your own. I understand you are protecting someone, and as noble as that is, I will not allow it to pass again. You said you're the kind to look out for only yourself, and while I am no longer sure that is entirely true, I want to see you put your money where your mouth is. I want to see you look out for yourself. Look out for your future and stop selling yourself short."

Fuck, why does his judgment seem to sting so badly? It's almost as bad as the judgment I saw in Zoey's eyes when I first saw her in the halls of this very office.

"I've got it under control," I tell him, needing to look away. I haven't had a damn thing under control in three long years.

Daniels lets out a sigh, watching me through a narrowed stare before pressing his lips into a hard line and finally nodding. "Alright, Noah. Get to class," he says, waving toward his office door. "Let's hope I don't need to call you into my office again."

"Let's hope," I repeat, and with that, I throw myself out of the chair and back through his door, more than ready to get my ass out of here.

Chapter 22

ZOEY

This week has sucked.

It's the first Friday night football game of the season, and the whole school is buzzing with excitement—Tarni being the most excited of them all after Noah accidentally bumped into her in the hall and caught her by the waist so she wouldn't break her nose against a locker. She's been crushing on him since the moment he arrived at East View High, but these past few days have been intolerable. If only she knew that he had me up against the wall of my closet with his tongue down my throat and his body pressed so tightly against mine that I couldn't tell where he ended and I began.

Yeah, I think I'll keep that little adventure to myself.

I can only imagine how the cheerleaders of East View will react if that snippet of information accidentally ends up in the wrong hands. They'll turn that beautiful, passionate moment between me and Noah into something filthy, and I refuse to allow that to happen.

It's been four long days since our kiss, and not a damn thing has changed. Well, I suppose that's not entirely correct. While Noah has continued to watch over me from afar, it's no longer done with hostility in his eyes. He doesn't openly try to despise me, but he's certainly still keeping his distance. I can only hope that this is the start of his walls beginning to crumble.

He's starting to come back to me, and I'm terrified of the hope that surges through my chest every time I think about it, knowing that if he pulls back now and shuts me out, this time it'll be for good. At least I'm prepared now. If he tries to shut me out, I'm going to hold on until he's able to see that he's right where he belongs, just like he would have done for me.

We haven't said a word to each other since he slipped out of my bedroom window on Monday night. I knew things wouldn't go back to normal so easily, but I didn't expect my body to react to him every time he's around. I've always wanted him, always knew how it felt to be in his arms, but now that we're older, the way he held me was different, felt different.

The way he kissed me, the way his hunger burned in his dark eyes. Things have shifted. We're not little kids playing dress-up anymore. It's real now, and I just hope our relationship can get back to where it was always supposed to go.

My gaze flicks to the clock on my living room wall as I fidget with my phone on the armrest of the couch, flipping it over before flipping it right back.

I'm not going to his game. Not in a million years. Buuuuuut hypothetically, if I were to leave now, I'd be there with just enough time to get the best seats in the grandstand. Besides, if I did go, it would only be to show support for the school, which is really just the appropriate thing to do, right? It would have absolutely nothing to do with the fact that I've dreamed of being able to cheer Noah on from the sidelines like I used to. And it certainly has nothing to do with the overwhelming need to watch him race up and down the field with a sheer layer of sweat coating his tan skin, or watching the way his strong muscles flex as he launches the ball clear across the field.

God, no. It definitely has nothing to do with that.

But like I said—not in a million years. I'm going to park my ass right here all night with a bowl of popcorn and watch a movie. Perhaps I'll watch a thriller, something to get my heart racing and my mind off the sweaty football player who will no doubt have the crowd chanting his name.

Ughhhh. I'm in so much trouble here.

Kissing Noah Ryan was the biggest mistake of my life. He's destroyed me, and not in the *tore my heart out and trampled all over it for three long years* kind of way. No, he's made me want something I can't have. He made me crave him in a way I never have before, and that is the most terrifying thing I've ever experienced.

God, I want him to kiss me again. I need it like my next breath.

Nope. No. I can't think like that. I need to knock these traitorous thoughts out of my head. I need to calm myself. Perhaps a little meditation is in the cards for tonight, not that I have any idea how to do that. But what could it hurt? I'll give it a try.

After pulling my legs up and crossing them on the couch, I try to force my feet up to rest on top of my knees before taking slow, deep breaths just like they do in the movies. Closing my eyes, I hold my hands out to my sides and try to clear my mind. I imagine the way each intrusive thought falls away, leaving my head fresh and clear. I slowly count to ten and back down again while focusing on my breathing. When I get back to zero, I open my eyes only to scream like a freaking banshee, finding Hazel standing right in front of me with a ridiculous grin on her face.

"WHAT IN THE EVER-LOVING DONUTS ARE YOU DOING?" I screech, my heart racing out of my chest.

"You like?" she questions, indicating down her body before doing a spin, making my jaw fall right to the floor as I take in the Mambas' football jersey with the name RYAN across the back, so similar to the ones I have stashed in a box, hidden deep within my closet, never to see the light of day again.

"Where the hell did you get that?"

"Where do you think?" Hazel says, her grin widening. "Noah came by yesterday after school and left it for me."

A pang of jealousy blasts through me, poisoning my veins and leaving me feeling heavy, and I realize that this is the second time I've been jealous of Hazel and Noah's friendship in less than a week. I've got to get a grip. "Okaaaay," I say slowly, trying to give myself a second to push the ugly feelings away. "And why are you wearing it?"

"Because you're taking me to Noah's game."

"Yeah," I laugh. "That's not going to happen."

"He said you'd say that," she tells me, her eyes sparkling with silent laughter.

"Oh really?" I question. "Dare I ask what else he said?"

She raises her chin, as smug as anything. "He said you were too chicken to show up to his game and that you'd sit right here on this couch watching some stupid movie you're not even interested in like a stubborn ass all night."

Well, crap. No one ever claimed that he didn't know me, but that was far too close for my liking.

I arch my brow, gaping at my little sister. "He did not say that I was too chicken to go."

"He sure did," she challenges. "So, what's it going to be? Shall I put some popcorn in the microwave so you can prove him right, or are we going to go and watch his game?"

Oh, hell no! I fly to my feet, scooping my phone up as I go. "Get your crap, Hazel. We're going to the game."

"YES!" she squeals, racing out of the living room and straight up the stairs, her feet thumping against the floor like a herd of elephants. "FOR THE RECORD," she calls down the stairs. "HE SAID THAT CALLING YOU A CHICKEN WOULD WORK LIKE A CHARM."

Ah, crap. I should have seen that one coming. If I stay home and watch movies all night, I'm proving him right. But if I take his bait and go to the game because I refuse to be called a chicken, I'm also proving him right.

Well played, Noah Ryan. Well played.

Fifteen minutes later, we're pulling into the overflowing parking lot of East View High and Hazel is bouncing in her seat, barely able to contain her excitement. After having to circle the lot twice, we finally find a parking space, and before I know it, Hazel's dragging me toward the stands.

"ZOEY!" I hear my name called from the stands. My head whips up, finding Tarni waving her hands around with Abby and Cora beside her. "Up here."

Hazel grins before practically pulling me up the stairs, and before I know it, we're settled in beside Tarni and the girls as Hazel stares out at the field, watching in awe as people flood through the gates. They are all here to see Noah Ryan's first game of the season.

It's the kind of turnout one would expect for the championship game, and I can't help the pride that resides in my chest. The cheerleaders' pre-show hasn't even started, and the crowd is already cheering wildly.

The stands are a sea of maroon and black to represent the

Mambas, but there's only one who's special enough to wear Noah's name on her back. Spotlights shine down on the field, bright enough to be seen from space, and music pounds through the speakers.

The only time I've ever really had an interest in football was . . . before, but this right here, it's clear to see why people love it so much. You know, apart from the actual game. The atmosphere and overall mood of the night is such a vibe, it's incredible. I even catch myself cheering as the anticipation of the game drums through my veins.

Before I know it, my mood plummets as the cheerleaders decide to grace us with an ass-shaking number, and while there's no denying that they're an incredible team, after the way they dumped their drinks all over me last Friday night and called me trash for almost two weeks straight, I can't appreciate their moves down on the field.

They're just wrapping up their routine when both teams bound out of the locker rooms, and the way the crowd throws themselves to their feet is simply incredible. Tarni grabs my hand and forces it into the sky as she screams out for Noah, cheering him on and deafening me in the process.

Hazel stands on her chair to get a better look and I find Noah immediately as a rush of nostalgia brutally slams right into my chest. I feel like I've taken a massive step back in time to being that little girl hovering at the sidelines, cheering so loud for Noah that her throat was raw by the end of the game.

He walks across the field with his helmet tucked under his arm, and as his gaze lifts to the stands, I almost drop to the dirty ground, knowing without even trying that his eyes will come directly to mine. And that's exactly what happens, as if he'd followed that pull from the invisible string between us.

Noah's gaze holds mine, and just like every other time he's looked at me, I'm captivated. I can see the smugness in his eyes, knowing that

I played right into the palm of his hand. He used Hazel to manipulate me into being here tonight, and I don't doubt that Hazel knew exactly what she was doing. Their plan worked like a charm.

Chapter 23

ZOEY

Noah holds my stare for a moment, and as a small smile begins kicking up the corner of his lips, he smothers it before dropping his gaze to Hazel at my side. Taking in the jersey he got her, he grins wide—that boyish one I used to love so much—and as Hazel beams beside me, Noah makes a face.

I roll my eyes, trying and failing to pretend that I don't love their interactions, when Tarni's hand falls away from mine. She leans into me, talking right into my ear to be heard over the roar of the crowd. "What the hell was that?" she demands, nodding toward Noah out on the field as the team huddles around Coach Martin.

"What was what?" I question, unease slowly pulsing through my veins.

"Noah," she insists, a spark of jealousy and anger flashing in her blue eyes. "Why was he looking at you like that?"

"He wasn't looking at me like anything," I say, my back stiffening. "He was looking at Hazel. They were hanging out the other day and he invited her to his game. He gave her a jersey and everything."

Tarni's brows furrow, and she looks around me as if only just noticing my little sister beside me. "Oh," she says with a bite in her tone before staring back toward the field, her eyes glued to Noah's ass. "I didn't realize he was so chummy with your family again."

What in the fresh hell is her problem?

"He's not," I say, unsure why I feel the need to defend this—to her of all people. She's the one person who should understand without an explanation. "His mom forced him over for dinner the other night, and he hid out in Hazel's room to avoid having to talk to anyone."

Her brows furrow, and her head whips right back toward me, gaping at me as though I'm a stranger. "What the hell, Zoey?" she snaps. "He was at your place, and you didn't say anything? You could have invited me over. You know how much I like him."

"It was a *family* dinner," I argue. "Besides, Mom only told me they were coming like two seconds before they walked through the door."

Tarni rolls her eyes and looks back toward the field, inching a step away before leaning toward Abby on her other side and whispering something in her ear that makes my blood run cold. Cora leans in to find out whatever's being said, and as the three of them talk shit between themselves, I try not to think the worst, but that doesn't stop me from scanning the already packed stands to see if there's anywhere better that Hazel and I could watch the game from.

Having no luck, I focus on the field, watching as the two teams go through a few warm-ups, and before I know it, the game has started, and Hazel is going apeshit beside me. I don't think I've ever heard her cheer so loudly for anyone in my life.

Noah dominates the field, and as I watch him, the rest of the world fades away. He's incredible out there. No wonder all of East View showed up to support him. Even Principal Daniels is watching him from the sidelines, trying to hide the fact that he's secretly impressed while reveling in the fact that the one student he didn't want is going to be responsible for putting this school on the map.

Coach Martin screams at his team from the sidelines as the cheerleaders shake their pom-poms, really getting into the whole school spirit.

The Mambas are up against the Scheyville High Titans, and so far, the game is evenly matched. Only, the Titans don't have Noah Ryan.

Hazel cheers non-stop beside me, but the moment Noah gets the ball, her shrill shrieks become deafening. Her excitement is contagious, and I find myself cheering right along with her. Every second of this feels so damn right.

When the Mambas get through their opponent's defenses and score a game-changing touchdown, Noah looks up at us, and I can't find it within me to tear the smile off my face.

He's not even the one who scored the touchdown, but that doesn't change a thing. He's just ecstatic that we're here, supporting him just like we used to. His smile is dazzling, and seeing that undeniable happiness shining in his eyes makes me so damn proud. I would give anything to be able to run down the stairs of the grandstand and throw myself into his arms. God, I wish things could be the way they used to be before Linc . . .

Noah Ryan is going places, and as soon as he learns how to navigate the darkness swirling within him, he's going to fly. I just hope that when he does, I get to be right there watching from the sidelines.

As the game swings back into action and Noah's gaze falls back to the field, I see Tarni from the corner of my eye, her curious gaze lingering on me, but I pretend I don't see her. I'm not in the mood to give her the attention she wants. I don't even know how to answer whatever bullshit questions she's going to throw at me. Instead, I hold

Hazel's hand and cheer for the Mambas, more than intent on enjoying this moment with my sister.

We're about ten minutes from halftime, and my throat aches from screaming and laughing with Hazel. That's when I catch sight of Shannan at the bottom of the stairs. She looks up and waves, and judging by the movement from the row behind us, I can only assume we're sitting directly in front of her friends.

Lucky us.

I ignore her, my gaze shifting back to the game, only when Shannan breaks away from the group of cheerleaders at the bottom and races up the stairs, my stomach sinks.

Shit. There's no way I'm going to get away from this without something happening in front of Hazel. I wanted to shield her from all of Shannan's taunts, but I suppose I just ran out of luck.

I keep my gaze locked on the field, watching Noah as he expertly catches the ball and scans the array of players, looking at them like toy soldiers he can manipulate to do his bidding. As Shannan scooches along to the row behind me to reach her friends, I stop cheering. I don't want to draw any unwanted attention to myself, but I don't dare tell Hazel to stop. It's not fair to ruin her fun just because the nasty cow behind me has forced the fear of humiliation into my soul.

The girls behind us squeal and laugh, and I hear a lot of *OMG's* and *like totally's*, but I zone them out. Only when a disgusted scoff fills the air, my back stiffens. "Look at this bitch wearing Noah's jersey like a desperate whore."

No fucking way did she just say that about my sister. An eleven-year-old girl. An innocent little girl who's only here to support someone she's always looked up to.

Hazel's hand tightens in mine, and she stands as still as a statue, clearly having heard Shannan, but I squeeze her hand. "Ignore her," I urge. "She'll go away soon."

Glancing at Hazel, I see the way she clenches her jaw, and her eyes fill with tears. I don't doubt that she's had her fair share of bullies, every girl has, but I can guarantee that at eleven years old, she's never had a senior high school cheerleader call her a desperate whore.

God. I'm so fucking angry.

"Oh my god. It all makes sense," Shannan says. "The whore is with the trash. Why am I not surprised to find them together? Both of them pining over what they can't have. God, that's so embarrassing."

I close my eyes, trying to count to ten, waiting for the bullshit to fade away. Hazel is tall, and I'm sure if Shannan knew it was a child she was currently calling a whore, she'd be horrified by herself, but that's absolutely no excuse.

The bullshit keeps coming, and the snickering at Hazel's back makes her tears overflow and streak down her cheeks. She hastily wipes at her eyes, and my heart breaks for her. She should never have been exposed to this. She's too young.

The insults keep coming, one after another, and when Hazel's bottom lip wobbles, I clench my jaw. I've had more than enough. It's one thing for this bitch to call me trash, but bringing my sister into it? She's got another thing coming.

I whip around, and the explosive anger in my chest threatens to cripple me. I'm more than aware of just how quiet Tarni is beside me. A smirk settles over Shannan's face, clearly seeing how she's affected me. "What the hell is your problem?" I spit. "Are you so desperate for Noah that you have to tear down everyone who might possibly stand in your way?"

Shannan scoffs. "Are you implying that you think you could ever be standing in my way when it comes to Noah Ryan? Look at you, Zoey. You're a joke. Fucking pathetic. You don't stand a fucking chance with him, so take yourself and your little slutty friend and get the hell out of here. No one wants you here."

I gape at her, unable to comprehend how she could possibly be so vile. "That little *slutty friend* you're talking about, the one you've been calling a desperate whore for the last ten minutes is—"

Hazel whips around, her head held so damn high I almost don't recognize her. "Noah's eleven-year-old sister," she finishes for me, slightly changing how the end of my sentence was supposed to go.

Shannan's face falls. "Wait you're—"

"*A child?* Yeah," Hazel spits. "Now, I don't know about you, but my brother probably isn't going to be too happy when he learns about this. I can only imagine what he's going to say. You know, he's very protective of me."

Shannan blanches and even goes as far as to look at me for confirmation, but there's no way in hell I'm about to clear this one up. Besides, growing up, Noah was always like a brother to Hazel anyway, so I suppose there's some level of truth to it . . . kind of.

"Wow," I say, blowing my cheeks out, exaggerating my response. "You're fucked."

Shannan looks back at Hazel. "I'm sorry, okay," she says, clearly having no concept of a heartfelt apology. "I didn't realize you were a kid."

"Oh, so if I wasn't a kid, that would have made it okay?"

"I . . ." Shannan trails off, and a smugness tears through me, filling my body with the sweetest kind of elation. I don't think I've ever seen Shannan lost for words. "Look, please just keep your mouth shut about it. I was having a little fun with you. It was just a joke."

"Right. Fun. That's what we call sexualizing children."

Shannan blanches again, and I gape at Hazel, wondering where the hell she learned that, but my questions will have to wait until Shannan decides she's had enough and takes off.

The second she turns and sprints down the stairs, Hazel and I turn back around, and when we do, she lets go of the fear, and the tears burst from her green eyes, sailing down her cheeks like rivers. I throw my arms around her, pulling her into my chest. "Welcome to high school," I tell her, running my fingers through her hair. "It's okay. You just took down the queen of the school. Most people can only dream of doing something like that."

"I never want to be like her."

"You never will be. Your heart is too pure. It's not possible."

Hazel wipes her eyes and pulls out of my arms to focus on the game, but I can tell she's no longer interested. She pulls at Noah's jersey as though she's never been so uncomfortable in her life. The idea that someone could think something so un-pure of her simply for wanting to show support to someone she's looked up to her whole life makes her second guess herself.

My heart breaks for her, and I nudge her with my elbow. "You don't have to wear it," I tell her. "He'll understand."

As if desperately needing that approval, she shrugs the offending jersey over her head, and I take it from her, bunching it up in my hands. The clock counts down the final few seconds before halftime, and when the crowd roars for the Mambas, who are now decently ahead, Hazel glances up at me. "Is this the end?" she whispers, a hopeful tone in her voice.

"No," I tell her. "It's only halftime, but we don't have to stay. If you want to go, we can."

"Oh." Hazel spares a glance toward the field to where Noah stands huddled with his team, his eyes glued on us, and his brows furrowed. "Do you think . . . Will he be sad if we go home?"

"Of course not," I tell her. "But you know Noah. He's going

to demand answers. As soon as he's done here, I guarantee he'll be knocking down your door wanting to know what happened. So as long as you're good with that and feel confident in talking with him about it, then we're good to go. Otherwise, we're going to have to stay and play the part. But just between you and me, he's already watching us, and judging by the look on his face, he knows something's up."

Hazel's gaze snaps up, her eyes widening, and seeing the concern in Noah's curious stare, she gasps. "Oh no. Do you think we can get out of here before he notices we're gone?"

"No chance in hell," I laugh, thinking of the way he's able to find me in an overcrowded room as though I had screamed his name. "But considering Coach Martin's tendency to give really long pep talks, we might be able to make a break for it while Coach is demanding his undivided attention."

Hazel nods, determination flashing in her eyes. "Deal."

With that, we make a break for it, squeezing our way past the other people in our row before clutching each other's hands and bounding down the stairs. I feel Noah's gaze on us every step of the way, and for a moment, I wonder if we can blend in with the other people taking toilet breaks during halftime, but he saw the look in my eyes. He knows we're leaving.

We hit the ground and hurry through the throng of bodies, and just when we approach the student parking lot and think we're home free, that deep tone that haunts my every moment cuts through the night. "Where the hell are you going?"

Hazel and I stop to glance back, and as I take in Noah with his helmet braced against his hip, I can't help but see the hurt flashing in his eyes. But he doesn't get to hurt. If it weren't for him, Hazel wouldn't have been exposed to that ugliness. Though, I suppose that's not fair. He's not responsible for how Shannan behaved, but he was certainly responsible for putting her in that position in the first place.

"I'm taking her home, Noah," I say, glancing back toward the field where Coach Martin is looking this way, and judging by the look on his face, Noah certainly didn't receive approval to come over here. "Go back to your team before you get in trouble."

His gaze flicks to Hazel, scanning over her face, not giving a single care for the team back on the field. "What happened?"

"What happened is that you gave Hazel a jersey with your name on it and painted a big red target on her back the same way you did me," I say, taking the scrunched-up jersey from my hand and throwing it into his chest, unsure why I feel so angry with him when all he did was invite an adoring fan to his first game of the season. "It's one thing for your harem of cheerleading skanks to attack me and call me trash just for knowing you, but for that same bullshit to be aimed at Hazel? That's not okay."

Understanding dawns, and horror flashes in his eyes as he quickly closes the distance between us, grabbing Hazel and pulling her against his chest, his arm circling around her body. She tries to hold herself together, but it's clear that Shannan's words are still hitting hard.

Noah drops a kiss to her temple as though she's the most precious little girl in the world. "I'll fix it," he says, ignoring Coach Martin's demand that he get his ass back to the field.

"Fix it?" I scoff, anger lacing my veins and filling me with ugliness. "How the hell are you going to do that? She's already been exposed to it. No amount of fixing can change that."

Noah curses under his breath before letting out a pained sigh and holding my gaze. "Zoey, I . . . Fuck. I know I've done nothing but let you down, but I'm asking you to have faith in me. I'm going to fix this."

I hold his stare for a moment when Coach Martin's bellowing cuts through the silence, and we all glance back to find him a shitload closer than he was before, his face red with anger. "Noah Ryan, you get your goddamn ass back on my field right this fucking minute, otherwise, you'll be warming the bench for the whole damn season."

"Shit," Noah mutters, releasing his hold on Hazel and glancing back over his shoulder to see his coach, and as I glance back in the same direction, I can't help but notice two sets of eyes locked on us— Tarni looking as though she wants to murder me, and Shannan looking as though her whole world just came crumbling down.

Noah still hovers, and I step closer, giving him a little shove, hating the zap of electricity that burns between us as my fingers skim across his skin. "Go, Noah," I tell him. "Hazel will be fine. We'll stop for chocolate sundaes on the way home."

He meets my stare, and the reluctance in his eyes tells me there's still so much he wants to say, things that he's left unsaid for years. But now isn't the time.

"Go," I urge.

Pain flashes in his eyes, and he quickly glances away, looking down at Hazel and ruffling his hand over her hair, the same way he used to do to Linc. Hazel laughs and swats him away, then before he can convince himself to say something he's probably not ready to say, he shoves the jersey back into Hazel's hands and takes off at a jog back to the field.

Slinging my arm over Hazel's shoulder, we make our way back to my Range Rover, then just as I go to reach for the door, I stop, pulling Hazel to a halt at my side. "Remember how Noah and Linc would have gone to the ends of the earth to protect us?"

Hazel nods, her brows furrowed as she looks up at me.

"Wanna bet Noah still will?"

With that, we turn back to the field just in time to see Noah stride straight past his bellowing coach and the other exhausted football players, and the rigid way he holds his shoulders tells me shit is about to go down.

Shannan sees him coming a mile away, and I listen to Hazel's sharp gasp as she realizes what's happening. Then in front of the entire school, Principal Daniels, and the opposing team, Noah strides right into Shannan and backs her up against the boards of the grandstand until she's trapped there.

The terror in her eyes is visible from here, and I watch as he leans into her and says something in her ear, not laying a single finger on her as the color drains from her face. And with that, he's done with her. He pushes away and walks back toward his teammates while Shannan drops to the ground, shaking against the boards, her arms locking around her knees as tears stream down her face.

Chapter 24

NOAH

The game has barely finished when I race back to the locker room, whipping my helmet off and throwing it down into my pile of shit. I tear off my uniform before having the quickest shower known to man. I'm just stepping out to get dressed when the rest of the team pours in through the doors, booming about our epic win, but honestly, I'm not feeling the celebration tonight.

I haven't been on a team that's lost a game since middle school, and we only lost because most of us had been severely hit with a bout of food poisoning and couldn't run more than ten minutes without almost shitting ourselves. It's not exactly a night I think fondly of, but Linc never let me live it down. The thought brings a smile to my face.

"Yo," Liam says, striding over to me, clapping me hard on the back. "Did you see that? We fucking thrashed 'em, bro."

I don't bother responding because he's already gone, talking shit with the next guy he sees as I quickly get dressed and grab my phone, wallet, and keys from my locker. Before Coach Martin can even get in here to give us the after-game talk, I'm already heading for the door.

"Where the fuck are you going?" Lucas Maxwell says at my back, gaining the attention of nearly every fucker in the room.

I glance back, not bothering to slow down. "Got shit to do."

"Wait," Liam says, looking at me as though I just grew a second dick right in the center of my forehead. "You're bailing? What gives? We just won the first game of the season. Don't you want to celebrate? We're throwing a party at Landry's place."

I shake my head. "Like I said, I've got shit to do."

Liam grunts. "This doesn't have anything to do with that bitch . . . What's her name?" he questions, clicking his fingers as he tries to figure it out. "Ummm. Zoey. We all saw you skipping out on the halftime game prep to talk to her, man. Trust me, she's not worth it. Landry's been trying to score with that for months. She's a frigid bitch. I thought I told you that."

My jaw clenches, and as I meet his stare, he backs up a step, knowing damn well he just crossed a line. I don't even need to tell him to keep Zoey's name out of his fucking mouth. He just knows. "It's got nothing to do with Zoey," I grunt, my hands balling into fists at my side. "It's about—You know, it's none of your fucking business."

"Alright, whatever," he says, throwing his hands up in surrender, knowing when to back down before he gets his ass handed to him. "Just hit me up when you're done doing whatever it is you gotta do. We'll have a few shots. Maybe get a little fucked up and take some girls to bed."

Yeah. Unlikely.

I give him a nod, knowing damn well he's not going to stop until I've given him some indication that he gets to be my special little guy, which is one of the many problems with having to move schools so often. Everyone wants to be my best friend, everyone wants my attention, and most of the time, not a single one of them can take a hint.

Finally having no one at my back, I race out the door and to the parking lot before throwing myself into the driver's seat of my car and tossing my shit on the seat next to me. I could hardly focus on the second half of the game after seeing the accusation in Zoey's eyes.

She didn't blame me. I know her too well to know that she was just trying to let off steam. She was angry, and rightfully so. Hazel was hurt because of the bullshit I allowed to happen, but what it comes down to is that Zoey was right. I unintentionally painted a target on Hazel's back. I should have known better than to give her a jersey with my name on it, especially considering how hard the cheerleaders have been going for Zoey's throat just for being seen with me.

I have to know that Hazel is okay and make things right with her, but on top of that, I need to know that Zoey doesn't hate me for this. She can take a lot of shit when it's between just me and her, but where her little sister is concerned, she's not taking any chances.

When I saw her up in those stands with the widest smile on her face as she looked down at me, cheering for me like she used to . . . fuck. Her eyes were so full of happiness that it almost brought me to my knees.

Hitting the gas, I peel out of the still-packed parking lot, and floor it all the way to Zoey's place. Only unlike last time when I barged my way through here, I head straight for the door and knock like a normal human being.

I wait only a second before Henry answers the door, and it seems our little family dinner earlier in the week did nothing to lessen his apprehension about me. "Not tonight, Noah," he mutters, pressing his lips into a hard line. "Whatever you did has put her in a mood. She doesn't want to see you."

I ignore the way his comments sting but refuse to walk away. "I'm not here for her. I wanted to check on Hazel, make sure she's okay."

He studies me for a moment, watching me closely as if trying to work out what kind of angle I'm working, but he won't find one, not tonight. The moment seems to drag on forever when he finally steps aside and waves me in. "She's in her room."

Thank fuck.

Walking in, I turn directly to the right and make my way straight up the stairs, my whole body twitching as I pass Zoey's room, knowing the other half of my soul is right on the other side of that door. I try to respect her privacy. Her dad said she didn't want to deal with me, so be it.

Music blasts from her room, and I hear her singing something about it being a cruel summer before screaming at the top of her lungs about some dude looking up grinning like a devil. It takes everything within me to keep walking down the hall, and when I reach Hazel's door, I lean against the frame, much like I had after our disastrous dinner.

Hazel is curled up on her bed, scrolling on her phone, and she notices me almost immediately. "I was wondering when your big head was going to show up in my doorway," she mutters, but the insult doesn't land as her bottom lip juts out.

"Wanna talk about it?"

Hazel refuses to look up, and even without seeing her eyes, I feel the sadness radiating off her, and I can only imagine what kind of nasty bullshit she had to endure. "Are you going to be mad at me?"

"What?" I grunt, pushing off the door frame and striding into her room, bypassing her desk chair piled high with clothes and taking a seat on the end of her bed. "Why the hell would I be mad?"

"Well . . . When the cheerleader was saying those mean things," she says with a cringe before finally glancing up and meeting my stare. "I lied about you to make her scared."

My brows furrow, wondering what the hell she could have possibly lied about and hoping that whatever it is doesn't somehow affect Zoey when she's at school. "Out with it, kid. What did you say?"

Hazel winces and drops her gaze again. "Well, she called me a desperate whore and a slut because I was wearing your jersey, and so I told her I was your little sister and maybe implied that you were going to be really mad when you found out what she said to me."

My blood boils beneath the surface, knowing damn well that when I cornered Shannan against the boards of the grandstand, I wasn't nearly vile enough, but I keep my expression calm and offer Hazel a small smile. "Okay, but where's the lie in that?"

Her gaze snaps right back to mine, her eyes widening as the sadness seems to evaporate. "I told her you were my brother," she confirms, just in case I somehow missed that part.

I hold her stare, a challenge in my tone. "Aren't I?"

She bounds up onto her knees, excitement brimming in her eyes—eyes that are so much like her sister's. "Really? I mean, like I've always thought so. Both you and Linc. But then . . . you know, and we didn't see you for a really long time, but I thought just because you were mad at Zoey, that maybe you weren't mad at me. And like . . . ewwwww," she pauses, horror stretching across her face. "You have the hots for your sister."

"What?"

"Zoey! I know you're totally crushing on her. It's so obvious. Me, Mom, and your mom talk about it all the time. We have bets on when you'll finally figure out that you can't live without each other. But like, just so you know, you can't say that you're a brother to me and also want to put your tongue down my sister's throat. Isn't that like . . .

incest?"

"I, uh . . . I don't even know how to respond to that," I say, my face scrunched as I try to dig myself out of this hole. "But look, you and me, brother and sister. Me and Zoey . . . definitely *not* brother and sister."

A slow grin spreads across her face, and when she meets my eyes, I know exactly what's about to fly out of her mouth. "Is it because you're in luuuuurrrrvvvvveeeee with her?"

I grab one of the stuffed bears off the end of her bed and launch it at her, unable to wipe the smile off my face. "I am not having this conversation with you."

"Ewwwwww," she laughs, throwing herself off her bed just so she has more space to point while she's laughing. "You want to kiss her." She makes a fake gagging sound, pretending to shove her fingers down her throat. "Smooch her and do all icky things with her."

"Dare I ask what icky things you think I want to do with her?"

Her whole face turns bright red as though she's about to burst from the seams. "You want to touch her boobies."

Ahhhh, fuck. I just had to go and ask.

I shake my head, springing to my feet, more than ready to hightail it out of here. "Okay," I say, needing to get the image out of my head. "I take it you're not upset anymore?"

"Oh, no," she says. "I haven't been upset since after my chocolate sundae. I heard you coming up the stairs and faked it. Zoey tried to teach me how to fake cry on the way home and said something about getting you right where it hurts. But I couldn't make the tears come, not even after pinching myself."

"She said that, did she?"

"Uh-huh."

I can't help but laugh as I make my way back to her door, only she calls out to me, forcing me to a stop. "Noah?"

I pause in her doorway and glance back. "What's up?"

"I'm really glad you're not mad at us anymore."

I give her a tight smile and let out a heavy breath, feeling the weight of her words slamming right against my chest, threatening to bury me right here where I stand. "I was never mad at you, Hazel. At any of you. I never could be. I was just . . . mad at myself."

Her brows furrow, clearly not liking that. "Sooooo . . . Now that you're back, does that mean you're all good now? You and Zoey can go back to how it used to be?"

"Honestly, Hazel," I say, really having to think about it. "I don't know. I think there's some shit that needs to be figured out before that could even be considered."

She gives me a sad smile, and as she drops back down on her bed, I walk out of her room, giving her some peace and quiet to get back to doing whatever the hell she was doing before I barged in here.

As I make my way back down the hall, I find myself pausing in front of Zoey's door, my hand twitching at my side.

Don't do it, Noah. Keep walking. Don't be that asshole. Give her space.

Damn it.

I reach for her door.

It swings wide, and I hover in her doorway just like I'd done with Hazel. Only, unlike her sister, Zoey is lost in her music, gently swaying her hips as she stands in her full-length mirror, putting her long hair up.

She spots me almost immediately, her gaze meeting mine through the mirror, the loud music fading around us. Her eyes widen for just a moment before hurt flashes within those green depths. It tears at my chest. I hate that I keep hurting her, whether it's intentional or not.

Zoey holds my stare through the mirror, her hands falling from her hair, watching as I slowly step into her room and nudge the door closed with my foot.

Just like after the dinner, the room fills with undeniable tension and it's as though that tether between us is tightening, physically pulling us together.

I take a step, and she shakes her head, not daring to take her eyes off mine through the mirror, but I don't stop. How could I?

I keep going until I'm standing right behind her with my chest pressed against her back. I see the rapid thrum of her pulse at the base of her neck and notice how her chest rises and falls with heavy breaths.

She visibly swallows, and as her hands tremble, I skim my fingers down the length of her arm, leaving a trail of goosebumps across her skin until my hand closes around hers. "Noah," she breathes, her fingers clutching on to mine like a lifeline.

God. This feels so right.

Zoey slowly turns in my arms, and as she stands right before me, I press my fingers to her chin and lift until her sweet gaze is locked on mine. There's a reluctance in her eyes that kills me, but it's deserved. I've done nothing but hurt her, and in those times when she needed me the most, I wasn't there.

"You shouldn't be here," she whispers, a crack of pain in her tone. "You should leave."

I shake my head, both of us knowing that it would be impossible for me to walk away now. "I can't do that."

Zoey whimpers as though my admission physically pains her, and all I can do is curl my arm around her waist, holding her to me as though that could somehow dull the ache I've put in her heart. She braces one hand against my chest, and just when I expect her to push me away, her fingers bunch into the fabric of my shirt.

Zoey tugs me closer, and I can't wait a second longer, dipping my head and closing the gap between us. My lips press against hers, and I feel her body weaken in my hold, melting against me as though she needs this just as much as I do.

A soft moan slips from between her lips as they move against mine, and when her other hand slips around the back of my neck, she deepens our kiss, taking exactly what she needs from me. Her tongue moves against mine, our lips perfectly in sync. It's nothing like the hungry, desperate kiss from Monday night. This one is different. This one holds nothing but pure pain between us as we try to navigate our way around it, desperately clawing to find our way back to each other.

My fingers tighten on her waist, and as if having a bucket of ice water tipped over her head, Zoey stiffens in my arms. She pulls away and violently shoves against my chest, forcing me back a step as she stares at me in horror, her fingers pressed against her swollen lips.

Her chest heaves as my brows furrow, confusion sweeping through me. "What's wrong?" I question, inching toward her. Did I hurt her? Push her too far?

"No," she says, holding up a hand and halting my progression, fury flashing in her eyes. "Not like this."

"Like what?"

She scoffs, and I watch as she tries to figure out the overwhelming emotions coursing through her body. "After everything," she breathes, the fury morphing into sadness. "After all the hurt you caused over the past three years, you think you get to just walk in here and kiss me as though I still belong to you? You can't keep doing this to me. You either want me or you don't, but you can't have both."

"Zo," I say, trying to step toward her again, only she holds up her hand to deny me.

"The next time you kiss me," she says, her hands shaking again. "It better be because you're mine and I'm yours."

I stare at her, horror blasting through me at the idea of her pushing me away. "I've always been yours, Zoey."

"No, you haven't been mine in a long time. You're barely a figment of my imagination." I see the exact moment her heart falls out of her chest and shatters on the ground between us. "I want something real with you, not this *almost there* bullshit. I'm not doing this sneaking around thing where you get to push me away and then have me when it's convenient. You're either all in or all out."

"Zo—"

"Don't," she tells me, pulling out of my reach, tears spilling from her eyes and tormenting my already shattered soul. "I don't want to hear how you can't, how you're hurting and drowning in a sea of guilt and darkness, because *I am too.* I've been hurting since the day Linc died, and I needed you. You were the one person who could have eased that ache inside me, and you weren't there. You made me suffer alone, Noah. You broke me, and now you want to waltz back into my life, thinking you can slide right back into place. That's not how this works."

She pauses, tears pouring from her eyes as she holds my stare, unaware of just how deeply I'm crumbling inside. "I want you to come back to me, Noah. I want it more than anything, but only when you're ready to really let me in."

Unable to keep the distance, I step into her, pulling her straight back into my arms as she buries her face against my chest. I hold her there, my hand knotted into her hair as she falls apart. "I promise, Zozo," I whisper, closing my eyes as the agony claims me. "I want to give you everything you deserve, and I have a lot to make up for. I know you feel like I'm not yours anymore, and that's on me, but you have to know that I've never stopped belonging to you. It's always been you, Zo."

"It hurts," she whispers against my chest.

I hold her tighter, my hand roaming up and down her back. "Give me your pain, Zo," I murmur, hating myself for everything I've put her through and vowing that I will never make her feel this way again. "Let me take it away."

Chapter 25

NOAH

THREE YEARS AGO

Zoey's hand clutches mine so damn tight her knuckles turn white, but I don't dare let go. I can't because, at the front of the church, my little brother's body lies broken beyond repair in the black casket my mom spent the last three days agonizing over.

The past week has been a blur. Mom and Dad have fought. Random people I don't know have knocked on our door, offering their bullshit condolences. The police. The funeral home director. Tears. Hazel. But all I've seen is darkness.

It's like a cloud hovering over me, bearing down on my shoulders, getting heavier every day, and I've tried to hold it back, tried to push it away, but it's too fucking hard. Everybody is relying on me to be strong. Mom keeps looking at me as though I can somehow make her pain go away, and Dad? Dad has been nothing but an ass these last few days. But Zoey needs me the most, and I'm trying to be strong for her, but I'm slipping. I can't take it anymore.

The guilt, the anger, and the darkness are eating me alive. It's agony.

I killed my fucking brother. He's lying there in that casket because *I* sent him away.

This is all my fault.

Zoey was right. I should have told him that Mom was planning a movie date for him and Hazel, and he never would have tried following me to the park. He never would have been out on that road. I wasn't even nice to him.

Some old asshole stands at the front of the church, talking about how much Linc will be missed, and Zoey's head falls against my shoulder as silent tears roll down her face. Keeping my eyes on the old asshole, I grit my teeth, anger burning through my veins as I reach up and wipe the tears from Zoey's cheeks.

This dickhead never even met Lincoln. How dare he stand there and tell everyone how much he'll be missed. He doesn't know that. He doesn't know what kind of kid he was, what he liked, what he didn't. Doesn't know he was probably going to grow up to be East View's biggest menace, and he sure as fuck doesn't know that over the next few years, he would have eventually figured out that Hazel James was going to be his whole world, the same way Zoey is mine.

With each passing second of Linc's funeral, the numbness takes over, and when it finally comes to a close, I break away from Zoey and storm down the long aisle, barely able to breathe. I break out into the hot Arizona afternoon, gasping for air with my hands braced against my knees.

I can't do this anymore.

Everybody needs me to be something, to hold them up, but how the hell am I supposed to do that when I can barely get through the day? I always thought I was strong. I thought I was everything that Zoey would ever need, but I'm fucking pathetic. I killed my little brother, and soon enough, she's going to see it. She'll know that I'm just a worthless fraud and realize I'm not good enough for her, not anymore. How can I be what she needs?

The cloud of darkness grows heavier, the guilt weighing down on me, pulling me further and further until I'm drowning in my own grief, and as I drop to my knees outside the church, I can't fend it off a second longer.

I fucking break.

It claims me, filling my veins and pulsing right into my soul, staining it with its ugliness, infecting me with nothing but guilt and anger. Where there used to be hope, love, and a beaming excitement for my future, there's nothing but charred ruins.

I can't be the person they need me to be. I can't be anything.

Not anymore.

I'm drowning, and anyone caught in my orbit is going to be dragged down with me and there's not a goddamn thing I can do to stop it.

Zoey James is the epitome of goodness, and I'm her exact opposite. I'm cruel and unforgiving, and when pushed enough, there's no line I won't cross. But what the hell does that say about me? How long before I aim that cruelty toward Zoey? How long until I'm sending *her* away and history repeats itself?

If I lose Zoey like I lost Linc . . . fuck. I won't just be drowning in grief, I won't just be struggling to breathe, I won't fucking survive it. She's my whole world, but this darkness that clouds over me . . . I can't let it destroy her too.

"Noah?" I hear that sweet, angelic voice say, and as my head snaps up, I see Zoey standing at the top of the church's grand entrance, that

SHERIDAN ANNE

chestnut hair sweeping back over her shoulder in the breeze. Her eyes are glued to mine, trying to read me just like she's always been able to, but I shut her out, needing to sever that connection between us.

I'm a killer. Linc's blood is on my hands, and I refuse to stain them with Zoey's too. I won't do it to her. I can't allow her to be dragged down by me. She won't survive it. She'll crumble under the pressure, and in her need to stand by my side, she'll willingly allow me to destroy her.

I won't do it.

I can't.

I have to distance myself from her. It's her only hope, her only chance to survive me.

"Noah?" she questions again, inching toward me as other funeral guests pour out of the church around her, but she doesn't dare take her eyes off mine, and I see the moment she reads it in my eyes.

Zoey sucks in a slight breath, her brows furrowing as a deep pain flashes in her bright green eyes, and when she tries to inch toward me for answers, I shake my head, refusing to let her get any closer. "Don't," I say, my voice catching on the lump in my throat.

She clenches her jaw as my mother appears on the step beside her, both of them staring at me. "Noah, honey?" my mom says slowly as if recognizing that this person standing before her is no longer the son she once knew. "It's going to be okay."

She inches toward me, just as Zoey had, but I shake my head, knowing that this life I once had, the easy, happy world I thrived in is no longer mine. I'm a shell, a killer with a black heart, and the sooner I get away from them, the sooner they learn that I'm no good for them.

They're strong, and Zoey has Hazel. They'll be okay.

As for me, there's nothing left to do but run.

Without a backward glance, I take off as my soul shatters into

248

a million irreparable pieces. Zoey James can't be anything but an agonizing memory, one I will bury with the body of the brother I killed.

Chapter 26

ZOEY

"Zoey," Ms. Lennon, my biology teacher, says from her desk, and my head snaps up to find her signaling me to come to the front of the class.

My brows furrow as I make my way through the single-spaced desks, trying to go over everything that could have possibly resulted in me getting called out in class, but I come up blank. Apart from being a little behind on homework for a few weeks, I've been a perfect student.

As I reach her, I see a smirk resting on her lips, clearly knowing where my mind has gone, but she quickly puts me at ease when she hands me a slip of paper. "Chill out," she laughs. "I just need you to dash down to the student office and ask for twenty copies of this worksheet."

"Oh," I say, letting out a heavy breath, trying to ease my racing heart. "I thought I was in trouble."

Ms. Lennon's brow arches. "Is there something you should be in trouble for?"

I let out an unladylike scoff. "Only my taste in the opposite sex," I mutter, my mind instantly going to Noah. It's been almost two weeks since he stood before me in my bedroom, promising that he's always been mine, and since then, I've been a wreck. He's tried to talk to me a few times, but for once, I'm the one keeping him at arm's length. He knows that I'm just waiting for him to tell me what he wants, but he's not ready, and I'm not going to allow him to rush into this. That wouldn't be fair for either of us.

We're both very different people than we were three years ago. So much has happened, and so much has changed. Our hearts are no longer the same, and there's a lot we need to figure out before we can come together.

With the worksheet in my hand, I turn on my heel and hightail it out of the classroom before Ms. Lennon gets a chance to question me on my comment. She's not exactly the nosey type, but if there's something she feels she can help a student with, she's always more than willing to give advice. Most of the time, it's welcomed, but where Noah Ryan is concerned, the only advice I want to follow is the one coming from deep inside my chest.

The school corridors are deserted with most of the students locked away in their classrooms, and it's one of the most peaceful times I've had walking these halls. The bullshit I get from Shannan has died down since the football game, but that doesn't mean there haven't been lingering effects. She sneers at me at every opportunity, and while others haven't got the memo and continue to chant *trash* at me, I try to keep my frustrations hidden from Noah. He's struggling enough as it is.

Making my way into the student office, I pause, my heart coming to an abrupt stop as I spy Noah sitting in the chair outside the counselor's office. He leans forward, his elbows braced against his knees as his head hangs low between his shoulders. From the look of it, he's just finished his session, and I can only assume that Mrs. Thompson touched on some hard topics today.

Everything shatters within me, and I war with myself, wondering if I should go to him or leave him alone with his thoughts. Walking over to Dorris, the student office admin, I hand her the worksheet and explain what Ms. Lennon wants, expecting Noah's head to whip up at the sound of my voice, but he doesn't even flinch. It's as though he's so lost inside his own torment, he can't escape.

Dorris shuffles off to make the copies, and I hesitate, but when it comes down to it, if Noah needs me, I'll always be there.

Making my way toward him, my heart races, but I don't stop until I'm stepping right into him, settling myself between his knees as my fingers brush through his hair. "Are you alr—"

I don't even get to finish my question before his arms are around me, pulling me into him as he presses his head against my torso, taking deep, shaky breaths. I wrap my arm around the back of his head as the other hangs over his shoulder and down into the center of his back. My fingers roam over his back, giving him the time he needs to make the pain go away.

We stay there for minutes, or it could be hours, I don't know. I hear Dorris calling for me, saying she's got Ms. Lennon's worksheets ready, but I don't move. I can't.

At some point Principal Daniels strides out of his office, and after a brief chat with Dorris and a lingering glance toward us, he takes the worksheets down to Ms. Lennon's classroom himself.

My hand never stops moving across Noah's back, needing this moment almost as much as he does. Then all too soon, his breathing evens out and he drops his hands to my hips before pulling back, putting just a little bit of space between us.

Noah lifts his gaze, meeting my stare, and the pain hidden beneath the surface almost drops me to my knees. I haven't seen him like this since Linc's funeral, since the moment right before I lost him.

Reaching out, I brush my fingers across the top of his brow and down the side of his face until I feel the roughness of his stubbled jaw. "Are you okay?" I whisper, not wanting Dorris to overhear our conversation.

Noah silently shakes his head, but as he gives me a small, broken smile, I take that as my cue to give him privacy. "Okay," I tell him. "You know where to find me if, you know . . ."

He nods, and I go to walk away, but the second I take a step, he catches my hand and pulls me back. "Don't," he says with such heaviness in his tone. "Don't go."

I move toward the seat beside him, and as I turn to drop down onto it, he pulls me onto his lap instead. I immediately settle in, not willing to question it or tell him no, because honestly, there's nowhere else I'd rather be. My arm loops around his neck as he holds me to him, one hand on my thigh, the other securely around my back.

He's silent for a while, and I just sit here with him, waiting until he's ready.

"I killed him, Zo," he says, that darkness radiating out of his chest and consuming us both. "That day. I sent him away. He was walking down that road because of me."

His pain and guilt feel like a fist closing around my chest and squeezing until I can't breathe, but I simply wrap my arms tighter around him, hating that he's harbored this type of agony for three long years.

Adjusting myself on his lap, I twist to face him, curling my hands around the back of his neck, my thumbs stretching around to rest against his strong jaw. "Linc's death wasn't your fault. You're not responsible for what happened to him. He was hit by a drunk driver—that asshole who willingly got behind the wheel after impairing his senses. He is responsible for this, and he's rotting in a cell just as he should be. He took Linc's life, not you. It was his decision to drive after he'd been drinking, his bad call is what took Linc away from us."

Something breaks in his eyes, and the guilt is almost too much to bear, but I'll bear it for him if it means lessening the pain that suffocates him. "Zo," he breathes, holding my stare. "I. Sent. Him. Away. I told him to fuck off and go home because I wanted to be with you. All he wanted was to toss a fucking ball in the park, and *I sent him away*."

"Yes, you sent him away, told him to get lost, and you have every right to feel guilty for those things. You're allowed to have regrets for how that day panned out and wish you could have done things differently, but what you're not going to do is shoulder the blame for someone else's actions," I tell him, holding his gaze and waiting for those words to sink in before continuing. "Linc loved you so much. He thought the whole world shone out of your ass, and I can guarantee that the whole time he was making his way back home, he would have been muttering to himself about how much of an asshole you were and planning some ridiculous revenge prank. But you and I both know that he wouldn't have blamed you, and I'm sure that if he could, he'd be haunting your ass and kicking you in the shin every time those intrusive thoughts plagued your mind."

Noah scoffs, a small smile kicking up the corner of his mouth, and I lean in, gently brushing a soft kiss to his lips. "You're going to be okay, Noah. I know it hurts," I tell him, pushing my fingers back through his hair. "The second you realize that you don't need to hold on to all of this guilt, I'll be right here, ready to celebrate your brother's memory with you the way he deserves."

He nods and curls his hand around the back of my neck, pulling me in until my forehead rests against his. "He'd like that, wouldn't he?" he mutters, his tone much lighter now. "He always loved when people bragged about him."

A wide grin stretches across my face, remembering it so clearly. "He really did."

A door opens behind us, and I glance back to find the school counselor, Mrs. Thompson, stepping out of her office and doing a double take when she finds Noah still here. She pauses, watching us through a narrowed stare, her brow arching as Noah lets out a heavy sigh. "Don't think for one second that you can ask me about this at our next session."

"Mmm-hmm," she says, clearly making a mental note to do just that.

"What's the matter?" I tease, nudging Noah. "You don't want to talk about me?"

Noah scoffs. "Baby, I talk about you every fucking chance I get."

My cheeks flame, and as Noah's hand squeezes my thigh, I drop my gaze, unable to handle the look in his eyes, and the way he called me *baby* circles my mind on repeat. He's called me every name under the sun, but something about that just felt so . . . intimate.

Seeing me scramble for words, Mrs. Thompson cuts in. "I haven't seen you in my office for a while, Zoey. How are you doing?"

I give her a smile that quickly turns into a wicked grin. "I haven't attempted to burn down any schools recently, so I must be doing alright."

Noah groans, tipping his head back against the wall as Mrs. Thompson smiles back at me, her eyes dancing with a professional kind of laughter. "That's the spirit," she says, her gaze flicking toward Noah. "I've already got one arsonist to deal with. I don't need another."

She gives us each a warm smile before offering a slight nod and then walking away, giving us space to continue whatever this is, but honestly, I think we're done.

Noah squeezes my thigh again, drawing my attention back to him. "So," he says, his brows arched in question, but the way his eyes sparkle puts me on edge, knowing something's coming. "Wanna skip fourth period and go make out in my car?"

My cheeks flame again when another voice cuts through the office. "Gee, Noah. Thanks for the offer," Principal Daniels says, not even bothering to glance our way as he strides through the student office. "But I don't think my wife would be down with me taking on a boy toy right now. I'll take the consolation prize of getting your asses to class though."

"Fucking hell," Noah mutters under his breath, shaking his head as Principal Daniels disappears down the hallway, probably heading to his office.

"NOW!" his voice rumbles over his shoulder.

My constant need for approval has me springing to my feet, my eyes wide with the mere idea of getting in trouble, and I grab Noah's hand, pulling him up behind me. "Shit," I breathe, glancing up at the clock and realizing I've been gone from class for far too long. "Ms. Lennon's going to eat me alive."

"Bullshit," Noah murmurs, his hand low on my back as we make our way out of the student office. "Every single teacher in this school has their heads so far up your ass, they wouldn't dream of getting you in trouble."

I smile because he's right, and as he meets my eye, all I can do is grin up at him. "Pays not to be an asshole," I tell him. "You should try it sometime."

"I'll pass," he says, walking me back down the hall despite the fact his economics class is in the opposite direction. "Besides, I have it on good authority that you like bad boys."

I gape up at him. "Who the hell told you that?"

"Who do you think?"

I shake my head, not bothering to respond.

It seems I need to have a little chat with my sister when I get home.

Chapter 27

NOAH

Hobbling through the door of my home, I drop my shit and stride through the house. Training was a fucking killer this afternoon. Liam decided he wanted to talk back to Coach, and as a consequence, we all paid the price.

My hand slips into my pocket, pulling out my phone, and before I even know what I'm doing, I'm typing out a number I've tried so hard to forget.

Noah: That offer to make out in the back of my car still stands.

Zoey: Who's this?

I shake my head, a shit-eating grin tearing across my lips as something squeezes inside my chest.

Noah: You know damn well who it is.

Zoey: Ahhhhh, the resident asshole. How could I have missed that?

Noah: You better not be changing my name to that in your phone.

Zoey: Too late!

Noah: So…back of my car?

Zoey: You need to work on your pick-up game. This is terrible! It's a mystery how you have so many girls desperate for your attention.

Noah: A mystery? Have you seen my face? I'm fucking gorgeous.

Zoey: *Poop emoji*

I laugh as I slip my phone back into my pocket, knowing she has to have the last word. Otherwise, we'll end up going back and forth until our phones die, and I'm not above sitting by my charger. Actually, neither is she.

My hand hovers at my bedroom door when I find myself turning around and taking the few steps back to the one door I haven't pushed through in three years.

Linc's bedroom.

Nerves settle within me. I don't know what Mom has done in here. She may have emptied it out already, or I might be about to walk into a time capsule that makes me feel as though he's still here. For three years, I've avoided this room as if it stopped existing at the same moment that Linc did. I've never found the strength to open the door and walk in, but over these past few weeks, especially after sitting with Zoey outside Mrs. Thompson's office today, something clicked into place.

I don't want to grieve for him anymore. I want to celebrate him.

I still feel an overwhelming amount of guilt for Linc's death, and despite how Zoey feels about it, I will always shoulder the blame for what happened that day. I was his older brother. He was my responsibility, and in my own selfishness, I sent him away. That will always remain my greatest regret. Yet, Zoey's faith in me and her ability to see who I am through the darkness has somehow managed to breathe life back into me. For the first time in so long, I feel as though I'm ready to face everything that happened that day and accept it for what it was—a tragic accident.

Sucking in a deep breath, I curl my fingers around the cool handle, and as I exhale, my hands shake. I slowly nudge the door open, and my eyes timidly shift around the room.

It's so unbelievably Linc.

Everything is right where it was. His clothes. His messy desk. His empty glass sitting on his bedside table. And instead of feeling that crushing agony I always assumed would come, I feel peace. Happy almost.

I smell him in here, even after three years. I feel his presence, the good times and the bad. The divots in the wall from when our play flighting turned a little too serious. I can still see us racing in here, Linc screaming as I barreled in behind him, intent on whooping his ass after he talked shit about Zoey for the first and only time. He sure as fuck learned that lesson quickly.

Making my way deeper into his room, I scan over the crap on his desk, the things he'd been scrawling into his notebook. He was a bit of an artist, but not the good kind. He liked street art and was just shy of stealing a few cans of spray paint and tagging his name across the living room wall. He didn't have the balls to actually graffiti a wall outside of our home, but I don't doubt that it was coming. He would have taken Hazel to be his lookout, and the two of them would have thought it was great.

Among all the chaos of his desk, I see a photo half hidden under the notebook, and I pull it out to see the four of us. Me, Zoey, Linc, and Hazel. It must have been taken maybe six months before he died, and seeing the cheesy grin on his face now has a matching one spreading across mine.

I've gone out of my way not to look at photos of him, but seeing his face now . . . fuck.

I fall back onto his bed, clutching the photo like a lifeline as I sit at the end, my gaze locked on his face. God, I miss him so much. The hell we would have raised together, with Zoey and Hazel too. The four of us would have been the best kind of trouble. Then I never would have pushed her away, and things never would have had to change.

I hear someone at the door and glance up to find Mom leaning against Linc's doorframe, looking in and watching me as though I'm about to break. "I don't think I've seen you in here since—"

"I haven't," I admit, not forcing her to finish that sentence. "It's not what I expected. I thought it would feel different."

Mom strides into the room, moving in beside me and peering over the photo in my hand. "He loved that photo," she tells me. "He used to call you guys the four musketeers."

My brows furrow. "Really? I don't think I ever knew that."

"Yeah," she laughs. "He only said it around me. He didn't want to risk not sounding cool in front of his big brother."

A fond smile pulls at my lips, and I clutch the photo just a little bit tighter, loving that even after death, I'm still learning new things about my little brother. But he was right, had I known he'd called us that, I would have teased him relentlessly. Then he would have told Zoey, and she would have put me right in my place before forcing me to apologize. She was the glue that kept us all together—kept *me* together.

"Sounds about right," I tell her before letting out a heavy sigh. "I wish I was better to him. He always wanted to hang out, and I always told him to go away. If I'd known, I never would have—"

"I know, my love," Mom says, squeezing my shoulder. "But while you may have regrets, just know that Lincoln was the happiest little guy I've ever known. Even when you were busy with Zoey, he was still living life to the fullest. He had Hazel, and they got up to even more mischief than you and Zoey ever could."

A barking scoff tears from the back of my throat. "Okay. Now I know you're lying."

"Say what you want, but right after that photo was taken," she tells me, glancing down at the picture of the four of us in my hand, "Linc talked Hazel into shoplifting for the first time."

I gape at her, not sure which part of that to pick apart. The fact that they shoplifted together, or the fact that she said that was their *first* time, implying it happened more than once. "How the hell didn't I know that?"

"Ha," she laughs. "Like I was about to put that idea into your head. Knowing you and Zoey, the two of you would have tried to outdo them and would have come home with a whole jewelry store and a convoy of police cars behind you."

A stupid grin stretches across my face. She's probably right.

"Oh, God," she says with a heavy sigh, her gaze lingering on the photo. "I do miss the four of you together."

My gaze sails over Zoey, taking in the wide smile she has for the camera, but when I glance at myself, all I'm smiling at is her. "I, um . . . I was wondering if we were going to head out for our usual Friday night dinner with Zoey's family?" I ask, getting up and striding back over to Linc's desk, sliding the image back under the notebook exactly where I found it.

"Huh?" Mom grunts, her face scrunched up as she watches me, a deep suspicion flashing in her eyes. "Why? I ask you to come with me all the time, and I get the same big whopping 'No' every single time. Besides, you're well into the football season now. You usually head out to some ridiculous party on a Friday night."

"Yeah," I mutter, making my way to the door. "You're right. Forget I asked."

"Noah Ryan, you get your stubborn ass back here and tell me what the hell is going on," she says, making me pause in the doorway and turn back. Then as I meet her curious stare, she prods a little further. "Why do you want to go to dinner all of a sudden?"

I shrug my shoulders and give her a stupid grin. One I know she can see right through. "Because Erica makes a kickass lasagna."

Her eyes start to sparkle as if she's figured something out. "Erica's lasagna tastes like the cardboard box it came out of, and you know it," she says, her gaze narrowing. "Unless there's another reason you'd like to go."

I press my lips into a hard line, trying to keep the smile from stretching across my face. "Don't know what you're talking about."

"OH, NOAH!" she squeals before throwing herself at me, her arms flying around my neck and squeezing me so tight I think I might pass out. "About damn time."

"Ugh," I groan, rolling my eyes, but I can't manage to wipe the smile from my face. "Come on, Mom. Be cool."

"Oh, honey. I can't," she beams. "If you were raising a hellhound like yourself, you'd understand how good it feels to find out he's finally falling for the one girl that can keep him grounded and out of trouble."

"Laying it on thick, don't you think?" I say, the laughter rich in my tone. "Besides, Zoey isn't the same girl she was at thirteen. Maybe I'll just drag her down with me."

Mom is horrified as she pulls out of my arms and swats my chest, but the look in her eyes tells me she's never been so happy. "You wouldn't dare," she tells me. "You've always loved that pure innocence about her."

She's right, I have.

She lets out a heavy breath before moving out of Linc's room and closing the door behind her. "Come and sit down," she says in a serious tone.

My brows furrow, and I follow her into the kitchen where she pulls out one of the stools at the island counter and demands I take a seat. I do so without hesitation, knowing I'd have hell to pay if I didn't. After all, you don't raise two boys without learning how to keep them in line.

Glancing up at Mom, I watch as she makes her way around the other side of the counter before pressing her hands against the marble and fixing me with a heavy stare. "I haven't been the best mother to you over the past few years, and while I'm under no impression that you're as innocent as I hope you to be, I think it's time that we have this talk."

My face scrunches, confusion quickly pulsing through my body. "What the hell are you talking about?"

She blows her cheeks out as though she's never been so uncomfortable in her life. "When you're with Zoey, you're going to start having some urges—"

"Ugh, Mom," I say, cutting her off, horror filling my veins. "Tell me you're not about to have the sex talk with me. You should know I'm well aware of how it works."

"Shut up and listen," she tells me. "This is important. Zoey isn't like the girls you're used to dealing with. She's not going to throw herself at you and ask for the things you're all too happy to give. She's a good girl, Noah, and I want to make sure that when that time comes, you're mature enough to know the difference between *wanting* something and being *ready* for it."

"I . . . I would never hurt her," I say, reading exactly where she's coming from.

"I know you would like to be the man she needs, but the truth is, while I know you've never hurt her physically, you have already shattered her heart once before and left her in a lot of pain. For women, sex is . . . very different than what it is for men. It's an emotional connection. So, I just want to make sure that when you cross that line with her, you're doing it for the right reasons."

I nod, hearing every word, but honestly, when I think of being with Zoey, while I could only imagine how good being with her physically would be, it's her heart I'm after. Anything more she's willing to offer is a bonus that I will protect with my life. "I don't want to break her like that again," I tell her, feeling more vulnerable than I ever have before. "I hate myself for what I've put her through."

"I know you do, honey," she says. "But this is your chance to make amends, earn her forgiveness, and show her that she can trust you again."

Mom turns and reaches for the top cupboard, grabbing a bottle of champagne as though this is some huge celebration, and as she looks back at me, her eyes are sparkling with undeniable happiness. "Oh, Noah," she sighs, popping the cork. "You know how much that girl means to me, so if you're going to do this, then you're going to treat her like a queen. She's already been through so much in her short life. She deserves nothing less."

"I got it handled," I tell her, saying each word like a solemn vow.

She finds a glass and fills it with a few ice cubes, muttering something about wishing she had some warning so that she could have chilled her champagne first. "You know," she says, pausing and glancing up at me. "Why wait until Friday? It's still early. Perhaps we could make dinner at Erica's tonight."

"Don't jump the gun," I tell her, flying up to halt her movements as she searches for her phone. If we're not careful, Erica and Mom will have a whole wedding ceremony planned out. "Nothing's official just yet. We're just taking it slow, I guess. She's still hurting after everything I did, and I have a lot to make up for before she can allow me back in like that."

"Okay," she says, a hint of disappointment in her voice as she gets back to filling her glass. "I suppose that's fair enough."

She takes a sip, and as I move around the kitchen trying to figure out what the hell we're going to make for dinner, I catch Mom watching me a little too closely. "You're staring," I mutter into the fridge.

She lets out a happy sigh, and I brace myself for whatever bullshit is about to fly my way, but instead of professing her undying love, she crashes into me and flings her arms around me for the second time tonight. "It's good to see the real Noah again," she tells me. "I've missed you like you wouldn't believe."

My heart shatters for the hell I've put my mother through, and I realize that Zoey isn't the only one I need to earn forgiveness from. Then wrapping my arms around her, I squeeze tightly. "I'm sorry, Mom. I didn't mean to cause you so much hell over these past three years. I've just been—"

"Lost," she offers, and honestly, there's no better way to describe it.

"Yeah," I say, holding her a moment longer than necessary. Only she doesn't let go, she just holds on as though she'll never know when she might be able to do it again. "Ahhh, Mom," I mutter, gripping her shoulders and trying to peel her off me, but she holds on tighter. "You can let go now."

"Shut up, and love me, Noah," she demands. "You're not going anywhere until I'm done with you. Now wrap your arms around me and settle in for the long haul. It's gonna be a long night."

Well, shit.

Chapter 28

ZOEY

Noah's message comes through almost the second after he steps off the field. It's their third game of the season, and I'm not surprised to find that the Mambas are still undefeated. I overheard Tarni talking to the girls at lunch recently about her thorough research on Noah and his flawless winning streak since freshman year. Apparently, no one else thought her super-stalker mode was creepy.

Resident Asshole: You saw that right? I dominated that game.

A smirk settles across my face as I grab Hazel's hand and lead her down the grandstand while trying not to trip and fall. And because I'm just so nice, I do what I can to keep Noah's ego in check.

Zoey: Wait. What did I miss? I was too busy watching the hottie on the other team. You know, the one who nearly took you

out. Did you see the arms on that guy?

Resident Asshole: You're an ass. Just tell me how great I was.

Zoey: You were a dazzling shining star. I'm sure if your game were a ballet, you'd be showered with hundreds of bouquets of the most stunning roses this world has to offer.

Resident Asshole: …

Resident Asshole: I don't know what to make of that.

Zoey: Just tell me how great I am.

Resident Asshole: Touché, Zoey James. Touché.

I laugh to myself for a job well done before focusing on getting the rest of the way down the grandstand, pleased that Hazel and I managed to make it through a whole football game without either of us being shamelessly tormented.

We make our way back across the field to the lot, and I listen to Hazel's recap of the game from start to finish as though I didn't just watch the whole thing right by her side. I unlock the car, and we're just getting in when my phone buzzes again.

Resident Asshole: Soooo…There's a party tonight, and I know I told my mom that I'd come to dinner at your place. But do you wanna bail with me and party instead?

Zoey: Wow! Is that your way of asking a girl out because it kinda sucks! But also…I don't know. Me and parties don't really mix. You remember what happened at the last one, right?

Resident Asshole: Shannan knows what'll happen to her if she goes anywhere near you again. Let your hair down, Zozo. Have a little fun. Besides, think of all the things we could do at a party that we can't do at your dining table.

Resident Asshole: Also, for the record, you'll fucking know

when I'm asking you out.

Butterflies swarm through the pit of my stomach as Hazel groans. "Are we just going to sit here all night or are you actually going to turn on the engine and drive us home? I don't know about you, but I'm hungry, and watching you grin at your phone isn't helping me get fed."

I roll my eyes and groan before tossing my phone down into my bag and getting us out of here. The drive home is filled with music and Hazel's mindless chatter about how cool Noah was, and I find myself zoning out, wondering exactly what it would mean to go to a party with Noah Ryan.

Though, would I actually be going with him, or will I just happen to be in the same place at the same time while both of us watch each other from opposite ends of the room like we've been doing ever since he got to East View? It's not like I get to complain about that. I was the one who put limitations on us. I told him not to kiss me again until he was mine, and now I'm regretting that decision. I want to feel his lips on mine, even if he's not quite ready to emerge from the hell he's been living through these past few years.

The reality is, high-school girls are mean, and when it comes to Noah Ryan, they're absolutely brutal. I don't want to be caught doing anything with him, not even having a simple conversation, until I know it's endgame. Well, I already know he's endgame for me. It's been that way since before I can remember, but there's still a lot we need to work through until we can get there. Not to mention, he's trying really freaking hard to break down my walls. It's like something clicked into place for him, and he's somehow managed to let go of some of his pain.

He's coming home to me. He's so damn close. I just have to be patient a little while longer.

Then there's the issue of Tarni. With every passing day, her ridiculous crush on Noah gets worse. Not that I pay much attention to it. These past couple of weeks, I've practically been a ghost sitting next to her. Our friends don't even try to include me in conversations anymore, and I sure as hell don't force it. To be completely honest, I don't even think they've noticed the wedge between us, and it breaks my heart. Tarni has been one of my closest friends for so long, but lately, she's felt like a stranger.

Pulling my Range Rover into the driveway, I barely get the engine shut off before Hazel flies out the door and slams it closed behind her. I roll my eyes at her performance before grabbing my bag and following her inside, only I get all of two steps through the door when an excited gasp fills the air.

My gaze swings around to the living room to find Mom and Aunt Maya lounging on the couch, each with a glass of wine in their hands and their sharp, knowing gazes locked on me. Mom looks like she's about to start crying, while Aunt Maya beams at me and springs to her feet. "Oh, my little warrior," she says, clearly a few glasses deep as she strides across the living room. She reaches me in no time and throws her arms around me, pinning me to her chest and squeezing me tight. "I always knew this time would come."

What in the fresh hell is she talking about?

She holds me for a second too long before gripping my upper arms and pushing me back, tears of happiness in her eyes. She looks at me like her whole world finally makes sense. Then it hits me.

Noah.

That big asshole.

He said something.

"Okay," I say slowly, inching away from Maya. If I stay for dinner, my whole night is going to look like this. Only at some point, they're going to pry for details, and I really have no idea what to tell them. For some reason, I think mentioning the whole unbelievably hot make-out session up against the wall of my walk-in closet isn't exactly an appropriate dinner conversation, especially in front of Hazel and my dad. "So, um . . . There's a party tonight, and I was kinda hoping that—"

"Fine," Mom says with a heavy sigh. "Just don't do anything stupid. And no drinking. Oh, and certainly no walking home in the middle of the night by yourself."

"I wasn't by myself," I argue. "Noah walked me home."

"Oh? He did? That's so sweet. What a gentleman," Aunt Maya says with hearts in her eyes as she turns back to my mom. "See, I knew under all that grunting assholery that he's really a romantic at heart."

I scoff, debating whether I should burst her bubble and tell her there was absolutely nothing romantic about it, but then I decide that I'll leave that one for Noah to deal with. After all, that's the least he deserves after allowing me to walk into this without so much as a warning.

Leaving Mom and Aunt Maya to their swooning, I turn on my heel and make my way upstairs, pulling my phone out as I go and pressing a few buttons.

Tarni's voice comes through barely a second later. "Hey, what's up?"

"Are you guys going to that party at—" I pause, realizing I actually have no idea where tonight's party is.

"Well duh, we're going," she says. "Liam cornered Abby outside her car after the game and begged her to come. Apparently, he misses her after like . . . four weeks of dead silence, and he mentioned that Noah was actually going to show up to this one. So like, you can guarantee that every girl in East View is going to be there tonight."

"Oh, okay," I say, trying to not let her hear the edge in my tone as

I push into my room and immediately scan through my clothes. "Are you leaving soon? Do you think you could swing by and get me? I'm gonna go."

"WHAT!" she screeches, feigning a gasp. "Did I hear you right or am I having a stroke? Zoey James is voluntarily coming to a party? It's a miracle."

I roll my eyes but can't help the smirk that pulls at my lips. "Yes," I groan. "Can you pick me up or not?"

"Of course, girl," she sings. "We're leaving in ten. Cora's driving, but fair warning, Abby and I already had a few shots, so you're going to have to play catch up."

Unlikely. "Sure."

"I'll text when we're outside." Tarni doesn't wait for a goodbye or even a confirmation that I heard her before ending the call, but that's nothing new. She's been like that since the moment she got her first phone.

Realizing just how little time I have, I rush to get ready, opting for a black cropped tank with a high-waisted miniskirt and a pair of black suede thigh-high boots that make me feel like a sexy goddess.

I style my hair into a half-up half-down look and put a little makeup on, trying to replicate the look Hazel created for the last party I went to, and if I had the time, I probably would have begged her to do it for me. Happy with how I look, I dash downstairs and spend my last few minutes shoveling food down my throat before Tarni texts that they're outside.

Saying a quick goodbye to Mom and Aunt Maya, I hurry outside to find Cora's Lexus waiting in my driveway. I dart across the lawn before scrambling into the backseat to a chorus of whoops and applause, each of them putting on a performance of how shocked they are to see me.

Rolling my eyes, I settle into my seat before pulling out my phone.

Zoey: YOU TOLD YOUR MOM!!!!!!!! What the hell is wrong with you? They're both crying into their wine.

Resident Asshole: Ah shit. I knew I forgot to tell you something.

Zoey: Wait. What exactly did you tell her? Because I don't even know what this is let alone how to tell someone else about it.

Resident Asshole: Come to think of it, I didn't really say anything. Mom just kinda worked it out then made her own assumptions.

Zoey: Great. Just what I need!

Resident Asshole: My offer still stands. We could bail on dinner. I'll swing by and pick you up…you know, assuming you have enough self-control to keep your hands off me.

Zoey: I bailed on dinner ages ago. I'm already on my way.

Zoey: And for the record, keeping my hands off you is going to be a breeze. It's you I'm worried about, Mr. Follow Me Into My Closet And Throw Me Up Against The Wall.

Resident Asshole: I'm shocked, Zoey James. Were you even going to tell me or were you hoping I'd show up to dinner and have to sit through it by myself?

Resident Asshole: You think I can't control myself?

Zoey: I know you can't!

Resident Asshole: Challenge accepted. May the best player win.

Zoey: I intend to.

Pulling up at the party, my stomach swirls with butterflies at the idea of getting to see him again, though it's ridiculous. It's not as though I'm actually going to spend time with him. It'll be another night of stolen glances across the room, pretending my stomach doesn't do all kinds of flip-flops whenever he looks my way.

I don't know what he was thinking by offering to pick me up. Was he planning to kick me out halfway down the street and then pretend we didn't arrive together? I wouldn't have argued if he wanted to just skip the party altogether and just keep driving.

Abby slips her arm through mine as we make our way up to the party, dodging the people lingering out front. "Whose place is this?" I ask, looking up at the massive home, which is definitely far too big for any of the students at East View. "I don't think I've been here before."

"Lucas Maxwell's," Abby beams as a crack of thunder booms through the sky, making us all jump and then immediately break into laughter at the way it frightened us. "His dad is loaded, and he's never here, so Lucas throws parties all the time. How did you not know that?"

I shrug my shoulders, but Tarni throws a response in before I get a chance. "Probably because Zoey is allergic to fun," she laughs, grabbing my hand and pulling me toward the front door as the first few drops of rain fall. "Come on, we've gotta get you drunk before you realize what's happening and decide to leave."

Rolling my eyes, I let her drag me in through the door, but I have no desire to get drunk. I'm definitely okay to have one or two, but I drank so much at the last party that I couldn't even fight off the asshole who thought it was okay to get handsy with me. If Noah hadn't been there . . . I don't want to think about it.

We make our way through the foyer, and I'm gaping before we even reach the living room. It's insane. This place is huge, but it makes me wonder why the hell Lucas isn't enrolled in some fancy private school.

Tarni drags me through the house as if knowing exactly where to go, and considering they've partied here a million times before, I shouldn't be surprised. Within minutes, there's a drink in my hand, and I make a show of taking tiny sips to keep the girls off my back. We all sink into the music, and I start swaying my hips, feeling the mood of the night sweep through me.

For the first time in weeks, I feel comfortable with the girls, like I'm not an outcast, and it's more than I could have asked for. Tarni quickly annihilates her first drink and is coming back with more when I notice the way she's scanning the people around us, her brows furrowed. "What's up?" I call over the music.

"Have you seen Noah yet?" she asks, having to lean in and shout right into my ear. "I don't think he's here."

He's not. I would have felt it the second he walked through the door.

I shrug my shoulders, feigning indifference. "Don't think so," I say. "I haven't seen him."

"His car wasn't outside," Cora shouts toward us.

I glance at Tarni. "Why? What does it matter?"

She presses her lips into a hard line before glancing at the girls as if she wants to say whatever she's thinking, but when she looks back at me, she forces a smile across her face. "Okay, so like . . . don't get weird about this," she starts, immediately putting me on edge. "But tonight is the night. I'm going to screw Noah."

I try not to blanch, but I am only able to cover my discomfort because I know that's never going to happen. Noah would never. He couldn't stand her when we were kids. He hated her from the second she showed up in my life, and he has gone out of his way to pretend that he doesn't have a clue who she is since coming to East View. She doesn't stand a chance in hell, but the idea of her throwing herself at him . . . I don't know. It makes me feel sick.

"Oh," I say, trying to force an encouraging smile. "Good luck, but are you sure? I thought he was all over Shannan."

"Wait. You haven't heard? Have you been living under a rock?" Tarni blanches. "Whatever you said to him at that first football game has forced Shannan into hiding."

"What did you say to him?" Abby asks. "The whole school has been dying to find out."

"Nothing," I say, shrugging my shoulders. "You know how much he cares about Hazel, and she was upset after what Shannan said to her in the stands. Noah promised her that he'd fix it, and I guess he did."

"Oh, is that it?" Tarni questions as if she were looking for something juicy to be able to spread around the school, but that's when I feel it. *Feel him.* "Oh shit," Tarni squawks, gaping toward the foyer over my shoulder. "He's here."

My heart pounds, and I slowly turn back, peering through the party guests as the world seems to fade around me. His eyes are already on me, those dark pits of history holding so many of our cherished secrets.

It's like an electrical storm, lightning blasting right through my chest and filling my veins with the most intense power. His gaze lingers as people crowd around him, but it's as though he doesn't even see them. Only me.

A smile pulls at my lips, and as the most beautiful one graces his, Tarni grips my arm in a death hold, her nails digging into my skin and making me gasp. "HOLY SHIT!" she screeches, stealing my attention away. "Did you see that? Noah Ryan just smiled right at me!"

Abby and Cora squeal right along with her, and I bite my tongue harder than I ever have before, angry that she's stolen this moment away from me, making it all about her as usual.

"Oh, crap," she starts to panic, lifting her drink to her lips and swallowing everything that's left inside it. "He's coming over here."

"What?" I grunt, my eyes bugging out of my head.

"Be fucking cool," she says, slathering a seductive smile across her face as I glance back to see those intense eyes locked right on mine. "I can't believe this is actually happening. Holy fuck. I'm going to pass out."

Noah continues making his way through the overcrowded room, only shifting his eyes off mine when it becomes far too obvious who has his attention. His gaze is somewhere behind me, but he's all too aware of me, just as I am of him, and then he moves right into me, his hands discreetly brushing across my waist, his body right up against mine as he passes behind me. He's so close that I feel his breath across my skin, and good God, it's everything.

His hands fall away as he takes a step past me, but Tarni shoots around us, forcing herself right in front of Noah, bringing him to a stop. She all but thrusts herself at him, and as he backs up to put space between them, he steps right into me again, his fingers discreetly clutching mine behind his back.

"Get the fuck off me," Noah growls in disgust, using his other hand to shove her back.

Tarni gapes at him, her brows furrowed. "But I thought . . . you were looking at me."

Noah scoffs, and I have to really concentrate on keeping my face neutral. "You thought I was looking at *you*?" he questions as though it's the funniest thing he's ever heard, the rich laughter in his tone speaking right to my soul, while the other part—a really small part—hurts for Tarni. She really thought this was happening, but she's truly a moron if she thought she stood a chance with him. Especially considering how much he's always despised her. It's not like he ever made it a secret. "Fuck off, Tarni. Go and whore yourself out to someone else. You and I are never gonna happen."

He goes to step around her, having to release my hand, but she's a real sucker for punishment and steps into him again. "Hold up a second," she says. "We've known each other forever. I thought eventually we'd just come together."

"No, I've known Zoey forever," he says, making me wince as Tarni's gaze briefly flickers to me. "And as for you, you were a leech who wouldn't fuck off. I tolerated you because, for some fucking reason that never made sense to me, Zoey liked you, so don't mistake that for anything else."

Ah, shit.

Noah shoves her aside like trash under his foot and walks away, leaving Tarni gasping for air.

"Shit, girl," Abby says, stepping into her, putting her hand on Tarni's back and pushing her into the middle of our circle as if to hide her when she falls apart. "Are you okay? That was kinda rough."

"Right," Cora agrees. "I'd heard he had a bit of a mean streak, but I didn't realize he was that cold and cruel."

"I just . . . I don't understand," Tarni says, discreetly wiping her tears. "I thought he was interested. He's been watching me all week."

She looks at me as though I can offer her some insight, and I just shrug my shoulders. "I don't know what to tell you," I say. "I don't know him anymore. He's different from the kid I used to know. Perhaps he's just going through something."

Tarni snatches the almost full drink out of my hand and throws it back before muttering under her breath. "That's a bullshit excuse and you know it."

Forcing a smile across my face, I take the empty cup from her hand, trying to figure out how the hell to salvage our night before she reads too far into it and sees everything I've been trying to keep hidden. "I say we go get you really drunk," I tell her. "And then we'll see just how good your table dancing skills have gotten."

A stupid grin spreads across her face, and she throws herself into my arms, squeezing me tight. "See? And that's exactly why you're my best friend."

Without wasting a single second, the girls down shot after shot while I throw mine right over my shoulder. Tarni and the girls laugh like hyenas, and I can't wipe the grin off my face. Within moments, I'm dragged back to the dance floor.

I try to keep up with them, but it's not possible, and I quickly find myself out of breath. "Oh my god," Tarni groans, clutching my hand and tugging me with her. "I need to pee."

I follow behind her as she weaves her way through the bodies, and as we pass by the billiards room, something has me glancing in, and a shy smile cuts across my lips when I find Noah chilling with most of the guys on the football team. I feel that familiar tug on the invisible string between us, and he glances up, those mesmerizing eyes coming right to mine.

He smirks, and my cheeks flush, but Tarni keeps pulling my hand, and all too soon, he fades from view. "Shit. Shit. Shit," Tarni chants. "I'm gonna wet my pants if I don't find a toilet soon."

"I thought you'd been here a million times before."

"I have," she whines, leading me down a long hallway. "But everything seems backwards and my head is kinda spinning."

She laughs to herself, and when she finally finds the bathroom, I've never been so relieved. I wait outside as she pees, making sure she comes out alive, and the second she's done, we trade places. I quickly pee and wash my hands before fixing my hair in the mirror and wiping the smudged eyeliner from below my eyes.

Once I'm certain that I don't look like a train wreck, I come out of the bathroom to grab Tarni, but she's nowhere to be found. "Tarni?" I call, positive that she wouldn't have just walked away and left me to navigate this mansion by myself.

I make my way further up the hallway, stopping at each door and pushing them open to check inside, coming up empty every time.

"You good?" a deep voice rumbles behind me, making goosebumps spread across my skin.

Despite being worried for Tarni, I can't help but smile as I close the door I just checked behind and turn to lean against it, finding Noah way too close to be innocent. "I lost Tarni," I tell him.

"She bailed on you," he says, nodding back down the hall. "She's currently offering to suck Liam's dick."

"Shit," I sigh, realizing just how much that's going to hurt Abby when she finds out. "She really is a shitty friend, huh?"

He nods, his gaze dropping from my eyes to my lips. "I've been telling you that for years," he murmurs, skimming his hand across my waist.

"Noah," I warn, unable to keep the smile off my face. "You're standing awfully close for someone who's supposed to be controlling himself."

"Now why the hell would I want to go and do something stupid like that?" he questions, and with that, he reaches around me and opens the door at my back, stepping into me and pushing us into the room. The door closes, and before I can even remember why this is a bad idea, his lips are against mine.

I instantly melt into him, my knees weakening as his strong arms curl around my back, holding me against his chest as he backs me into the wall, just like he had in my closet. His whole body is up against mine, and I still can't get enough. My every thought fades away and leaves nothing but me and him and the feel of his lips moving against mine.

The electricity burns between us, and I groan as his hand trails down my body, over my hip, and down to the sliver of thigh between the hem of my skirt and my boots. His big hand curls around it, and I instinctively bring my knee up, hooking it around his hip as he presses harder against me. I pull back just an inch, gasping for air, and he doesn't hesitate, dropping his lips to the base of my throat as my arms lock around his neck, holding him so damn close.

It's everything I always knew it would be with Noah, like fireworks on the Fourth of July, absolutely breathtaking.

Needing more, I place my hand on his jaw, bringing him back to my lips as fierce hunger throbs through my veins. Then as his hand slips beneath the hem of my cropped tank, the door tears open and a familiar gasp sails through the room.

Ah, fuck.

Noah pulls back, and my head whips around, finding Tarni standing in the doorway, staring at me like a stranger. She whimpers as though she has been physically slapped across the face, her eyes burning with betrayal. "How could you?" she breathes, her voice cracking. "You're dead to me."

And with that, she's gone.

"Shit," I curse, pulling out of Noah's arms and heading for the door, only he catches my hand.

"Don't go after her," he says, his hand so warm in mine. "She's been a fucking terrible friend to you. She's not worth it."

"I just . . ." I cringe, pulling my hand free. "I have to. I know she's . . . well, Tarni. But without her, I have no one."

Hurt flashes in his dark eyes, and he steps closer, his hand falling to my waist. "You have me."

I shake my head, look up, and meet those eyes I've loved all my life. "But I don't," I tell him, letting him see the pain in my gaze as the lingering distance between us becomes that much more noticeable. "You are right though. She's been a terrible friend for way too long, but if I didn't have her every day at school, I'd be alone, and as much as I wish I could break away from her. I owe her too much."

"You don't owe her shit," he says, but all I can offer is a sad smile. With that, I turn my back and hurry out of the room, desperate to find the one person who stood by me through my three years of agony, the one who somehow managed to pull me out of the darkness.

I feel Noah at my back, following me out, my name on his lips drowned out by the loud music pounding through the house. I look everywhere, checking the drinks table, the billiards room, and even the dance floor to realize that Abby and Cora aren't here either.

I hurry outside into the pouring rain. They couldn't have gotten that far.

The rain showers over me as I run out into the street, seeing the red taillights of Cora's Lexus shining against the rain-soaked pavement as they disappear down the road.

"Shit," I mutter, coming to a stop in the middle of the street, my face falling into my hands, feeling the tears stinging my eyes.

"Zo," Noah says, striding up the street behind me. I turn, taking in the way the rain makes his dark, unruly hair stick to his face, and his dark clothes somehow look even darker. "What are you doing? She's not worth it. She's thrown herself at me countless times over the past few weeks, knowing damn well how it would hurt you. She doesn't give a shit about you, Zo, and for the life of me, I can't figure out why the hell you should give a damn about her."

"Noah," I cry, my voice breaking as he reaches me and pulls me into the warmth of his arms. I bury my face against his chest, and his chin rests against the top of my head. "She was there for me when I needed her," I tell him, letting him hear the depth of my despair. "She was the one who held me up when I couldn't run to you. Without her . . . I was in a really dark place. I owe her my life."

He remains silent, but I know he understands what I'm saying, and a part of me wonders if he went through the exact same thing. Only, he didn't have someone holding him up. He had to break through the darkness all on his own.

Wiping the tears from my eyes, I pull back and look up at him, not daring to tell him just how much my heart is breaking. "Will you take me home?"

"Yeah, Zozo," he says, pulling me right into his side and nodding up the street. "Come on." And with that, we make our way through the pouring rain, the sound of the party roaring behind us as the thunder claps loudly through the Arizona sky.

Chapter 29

NOAH

Liam talks shit beside me, but I don't hear a word he says. My mind is locked on Zoey. Every last bastard at Lucas's party on Friday night saw me race out of his house after Zoey, saw me in the street pulling her into my arms and holding her like I'd never let her go, and all day, I've been questioned about it. And I know Zoey has too.

The shit I've heard people say, making comments about her not being good enough for me, comments that she's just trying to ride my dick until she can claim a payday when I reach the NFL, that she's nothing but *trash*. Fuck, every last thing I have heard has had me ready to fucking snap.

All of this shit has come down on her shoulders simply because I can't seem to keep away from her at school. If I were any other guy, Zoey would be free to talk to me. We'd have a chance at a real relationship, and nobody would give a shit, but because I come with a reputation, people suddenly think they get to have an opinion. And most of them are based solely on jealousy. Not to mention the shit Tarni has been saying about her all day. Add that to the bullshit Shannan started at the beginning of the semester, and things haven't been looking great for Zoey.

She deserves better. At the start of all this drama, she fought back, but now she's tired of fighting and allowing it to slowly kill her, and the more I watch her walking around the school with her head down, the more I want to break.

Zoey James was not meant to hide, she was born to fucking shine, and I'll be damned if the assholes at this school try to dull that glow a second longer.

Liam is saying something, and when he nudges my arm, it's clear he asked a question, but my attention is across the room as Zoey strides into the cafeteria. Her gaze sweeps toward me, just as it always does when she walks into a room, and I give her an encouraging smile, more than happy to get out of here if she wants to eat somewhere else, but her gaze flickers back to her usual table.

She pauses by the door as if trying to gather the courage to walk across the room, and when she looks at me again, I give her an encouraging nod, letting her know that she's got this despite my thoughts on the situation. If I had my way, she would have gotten rid of her years ago, but Zoey wants this, so I'll give her whatever support she needs.

I watch as Zoey pulls her shoulders back and lifts her chin before letting out a heavy breath, her cheeks blowing out, a sign that she's nervous. Then before she gets a chance to change her mind, she strides across the cafeteria to her usual table.

I'm too far away to hear what she's saying, but I keep watching anyway, trying to make out what little bits I can. Zoey must ask Tarni to talk, and I grit my teeth as Tarni scoffs and looks away from her, as though she's somehow beneath her, but anyone with half a brain can see that Zoey has always been a million miles above anything Tarni could ever be. Zoey is a goddess, and Tarni . . . She's the vermin who tears people apart, who smiles at your face and then plots against you, and that's exactly what she's done to Zoey since we were kids, time and time again. When her wicked scheming would break Zoey, she would fall apart in my arms, and I would put her back together every damn time.

Zoey inches forward, her gaze shifting to the other two girls at the table, girls whose names I haven't bothered to learn, and as she seeks their attention, they both look away.

Despite the distance, I can still hear Zoey's sharp demand. "Are you guys serious right now?" she says, her back as stiff as a rod as she takes a retreating step as if preparing to run.

Tarni lifts up her water bottle and takes a long sip, acting as though Zoey isn't standing right in front of her. Knowing Zoey, she probably went into this prepared to grovel and apologize, but my girl is stubborn to the bone. There'll be no apology now.

Slowly, Tarni turns her putrid gaze on Zoey, and I watch as she flinches, my whole body vibrating with rage. "You're making a fucking scene," she says too loudly, gaining the attention of the room, all eyes falling on Zoey.

"What the hell are you doing?" Zoey seethes, her voice now flowing effortlessly through the room as everyone shuts up to hear what's going on.

"Shannan was right," Tarni says, getting up from the table, clutching her drink bottle a little too hard as though it could help center her anger. "You are trash. Hell, I don't know how I haven't seen it, but now that I do, it's glaring right at me. It's always been *poor sad Zoey, be nice to Zoey, she had such a hard life,* but I'm done. You're pathetic."

"I'm pathetic?" Zoey fires back at her. "Look at yourself, Tarni. I came over here to try and make things right, but you would rather put on a performance. Wasn't the performance you put on for everyone on Friday night humiliating enough?"

The eager spectators laugh, and while I want nothing more than to applaud Zoey, the embarrassment only fires Tarni up. "You want to talk performances?" she spits. "You're a fucking man-stealing whore. All I wanted was one thing—one fucking thing, Zoey—but nooooooo, poor fucking Zoey couldn't handle not being her precious Noah's one and only. You just had to take what wasn't yours. Newsflash, whore. He's not into you. Anyone with two fucking eyes can see that."

Oh fuck no.

"I'm the whore?" Zoey demands. "You've spread your legs for nearly every guy in the school. Oh, wait, not Liam, though. But that didn't stop you from trying on Friday night, did it? Tell me, what were you offering to suck?"

"What?" One of Tarni's little bitch friends demands, her eyes going wide as she gapes at Tarni. "Tell me she's lying. You didn't. You wouldn't do that to me. You know how I feel about him."

Tarni gapes at her friend, looking at her like a deer in headlights, but the moment quickly passes, and she turns her anger back on Zoey. In a flash, she tosses the contents of her water bottle right at my girl, drenching her from head to toe. "You're such a fucking liar," Tarni seethes as Zoey's gasp tears straight through to my soul. "As if I would go anywhere near that STD-riddled asshole."

I spring from my chair as the laughter of the cafeteria rumbles through the room like an endless loop of torment, every last bit of it aimed at Zoey. And as if that's not bad enough, the chants start, this time with Tarni leading the pack.

"Trash. Trash. Trash."

Zoey wipes the water off her face, focusing her stare on Tarni as people crowd around her, chanting and tormenting her. "Call me what you want," she says. "But I've been in love with the same guy since I was six years old. It's only ever been him for me. I've never even dreamed of touching another guy, and if that makes me a whore, then so be it. But at least I can hold my head up high and say that I have respect for myself. I bet you can't do that."

Tarni just stares at her as I push people out of my way, desperate to get to Zoey, but as the chanting crowd grows around her, she starts to panic. She looks around, her green eyes so damn wide, searching for a way out, but she won't find one, not this time.

Zoey finds me through the throng of people, and as her terrified gaze rests on mine, her chest rises and falls rapidly. I move faster, forcing people aside.

"Trash. Trash. Trash."

I force my way through the circle, shouldering past the assholes who think they can talk shit about my girl, putting a few of them right on their asses, and then finally she's in my arms. I pull her in, my hand cradling the back of her head as I hold her to my chest, my lips brushing over her temple. "You're okay," I murmur for only her to hear as shocked gasps sound from the crowd, their chants quickly fading away as they realize how much fucking trouble they are about to be in. "They can't hurt you."

Zoey glances up, those beautiful, teary eyes meeting mine. She doesn't say a word, but she doesn't need to, everything she wants to say is right there in her eyes, and before she can argue with me, I drop my lips to hers, kissing her deeply as I hold her against me.

Finally claiming what has always been mine feels so right. None of these assholes will hurt Zoey now. I should have done it right from the start and saved her the torment of the last month. I'll always regret how long it took me to get here, but hopefully, she will give me the chance to make it up to her.

I don't stop kissing her until her body finally relaxes in my arms and her knees go weak as she blocks out the people around us. It's only me and her existing at this moment. Then when I pull back, I hold her chin, keeping her gaze locked on mine. "So, you're still in love with me, huh?"

Zoey's cheeks flush, and it's the most breathtaking thing I have ever seen. "Nah, I made it up," she teases. "Haven't you heard? I'm a liar now."

I grin down at her. "You always were a shitty liar," I tell her, dropping another swift kiss to her lips before pulling back again and curling her into my side, keeping a hand on her at all times. My gaze slowly makes its way around the circle, studiously taking in the faces of every single person who willingly took part in tearing down my girl, but I don't stop until my gaze rests on Tarni's.

Her eyes are wide, filled with fear, and I revel in it, hoping it fucking cripples her, just as she's done to Zoey. "From here on out," I announce to every last bastard in the room, my gaze remaining locked on Tarni. "Tarni Luca does not exist. Anyone who wishes to object to that will see the same fate."

Tarni's eyes go wide, and I watch as her two friends inch away from her. "Let me get one thing straight," I tell the crowd, shifting my stare away and focusing on the people around us, all too aware of the way Tarni sinks back into the crowd and disappears without a word, suddenly no longer in the mood to fight. "Zoey James is my fucking girl. An attack on her is a direct attack on me. You fuck with her, you fuck with me. If I hear even a whisper of the word *trash* within the walls of this school, every last one of you will pay the price for the hell you've put her through."

Murmurs immediately fill the cafeteria as people scramble to get away from me, scurrying like a thousand little rodents, but I tune them out, focusing all my attention on Zoey's wide eyes. Reaching up, I wipe the tears off her cheeks before pulling her right back into me. "You're okay," I tell her.

"Why did you do that?" she whispers, her eyes darting between mine. "There's no going back now."

A small smile pulls at the corners of my mouth as everything softens within me. The rage of seeing her targeted fades to a distant hum, leaving me with nothing but this overwhelming need to adore her. "Because it's time," I declare. "I should have done it the second I walked through the door of the student office the first fucking day. Hell, I should have done it three years ago and never let you go."

More tears fall, and she leans in, dropping her forehead against my chest. "I never wanted you to see me like this."

I smile and pull her into my side as I lead her out of the cafeteria. "Zoey, I've seen you suffer through the worst parts of a gastro bug. If that didn't scare me off, then a few high-school bitches aren't going to do it. Besides," I add, "I didn't see any weakness. I saw you hold your head high and fight with dignity. You approached her to apologize, despite the fact she didn't deserve it, and she decided to take the low road. You're the bigger person here. Plus, watching you put her in her place after all these years was so fucking hot."

Zoey rolls her eyes, her hand slipping into mine between us. "I outed her for trying to get with Liam."

"It's not like it was a secret. She did it in front of the whole football team. Word was going to spread sooner or later."

"I suppose," she says, clearly not liking it. "I just don't usually like to play dirty."

I scoff. "You forget who you're talking to," I remind her, thinking of the countless times when she has more than played dirty to get a win. After all, I was usually the one who got duped in the process.

We walk out into the afternoon sun, and I lead her right down to the football field, weaving through the pillars beneath the stands until we're out of view from the school and able to have just a little privacy.

"Come here," I say, dropping into the grass and leaning up against one of the pillars, pulling her down on me.

Zoey straddles my lap, her knees on either side of my thighs, and she leans her body into mine with her head against my shoulder. "You never said goodbye," she whispers, her words slicing right through me and getting straight to the core of one of my greatest regrets.

I let out a heavy sigh, my hand roaming up and down her back. "I know," I tell her. "I think about that every fucking day."

She pulls back to meet my eyes, her brows furrowed. "You do?"

I nod, the back of my knuckles brushing down the side of her face as she leans into my touch. "You have no idea how much I hate myself for doing that to you or how many times I found myself standing at your door, ready to fall to my knees and beg for your forgiveness, but I couldn't. I was drowning in grief and didn't know how to process it. I was hurting everyone around me, pushing them away until they couldn't fucking stand to be near me, and I couldn't do that to you. I knew if I stayed, I would have hurt you the most. I was a ticking time bomb, and it would have taken only the slightest nudge to explode. So I pulled away, but in doing that, I still hurt you anyway."

"I would have been okay," she tells me. "If you'd stayed."

I shake my head. "No, Zoey. You wouldn't have," I tell her honestly. "I don't regret pushing you away because the alternative . . . I wouldn't have been able to live with myself if I had hurt you like that. The way I behaved hurt the people I loved . . . It was so bad that only six months after Linc died, despite how much Mom needed him, my dad left. My own fucking father couldn't stand to be around me. He decided that breaking Mom's heart and leaving her alone to deal with the grief of losing her youngest son was easier than putting up with me. I wasn't going to do that to you, Zo. I know you were hurting, and I know I was causing you undeniable amounts of pain, and I will spend the rest of my life trying to earn your forgiveness for that, but trust me when I tell you that despite how much it hurt, it was better this way."

"Noah," she breathes, her heart on her sleeve.

"I was so angry, Zo. The guilt was tearing me apart, and I know, right down to the core, that you would have sacrificed your own heart to heal mine. I hate myself for it, but I would have eventually turned that anger on you just to make you stop."

"I hate that you were going through all of that alone," she tells me, leaning back in and wrapping her arms around me, holding me close as her fingers knot into the back of my hair. "I feel like I've missed so much of your life. I was your biggest cheerleader for so long, and when you left, I felt like the other half of my soul had gone away." She pauses, and I wait to respond, knowing she's not done. "I spent countless nights wondering what I'd done wrong until I'd convinced myself that I just wasn't enough anymore, that you didn't love me. It hurt so bad. I've never been broken like that before. I couldn't breathe without you."

My head falls into the curve of her neck as her words crush the remaining fragments of my soul. "I'm so sorry, Zozo," I say, my voice breaking with the agony of what I've put her through. "I love you so fucking much. I knew when we were only kids that you were my whole world, my everything. The sun and sky started and finished with you, but when Linc died, that gut-wrenching pain and grief . . . I never wanted to feel it again. But I knew . . . I fucking knew that if I were to lose you in the same way, I never would have survived. I know it was selfish of me, but every day when I fell to my knees and hated myself for what I did to you, I told myself that I was doing myself a favor just to keep me from running back into your arms."

"You have no idea how much I wish you did," she tells me. "I would have accepted you right back. I wouldn't have cared about the pain or how much time had passed, just as long as I had you."

"You have me back. I'm home, Zoey. I'm not going anywhere."

A soft smile hits her lips as she pulls back again, resting on my thighs. Her heated gaze blazes a trail across my chest, over my shoulders, and down my arms. Her hands tremble as they graze the bare skin above my collar, and she trails her fingers over the same path her eyes have carved across my body. "You're so different now," she tells me, her fingers lingering on my skin, grazing over the defined muscle from years of training. "In my head, you were always frozen in time."

A smirk pulls at the corner of my lips. "You're one to talk," I say, purposefully dropping my gaze to her chest as my hands fall to her thighs.

"Noah!" she flushes, swatting my chest before dropping her face into her hands as though she's embarrassed, but I quickly pull them away and tug her back into me, pressing a quick kiss to her lips.

"You're fucking gorgeous, Zoey. Don't be embarrassed by that. Trust me, every guy in this school is fantasizing about you and has a bruised ego because you won't give them the time of day."

"You're lying."

"Wanna bet?"

She rolls her eyes and straightens again, pressing her lips into a hard line. "You know, after the whole leukemia thing, I figured the world kinda owed me a little kindness during puberty."

"Zoey," I say, my voice dropping to a low, pained groan. "If you had any idea how hard it's been for me to keep my hands off you, you wouldn't dare question how perfect you are."

Her face flushes again, and her fingers drop to my waist, fidgeting with the material of my shirt. "What does this mean for you and me?"

My hand falls on top of hers, stilling her fingers and bringing her gaze back to mine. "What do you mean?"

"You practically slapped a *property of Noah Ryan* stamp across my ass in front of the whole school," she reminds me as though I somehow forgot that I claimed her right in the middle of the cafeteria.

A smile pulls at my lips, liking the idea of stamping those words across her ass more than I'll ever admit. "It means, Zoey," I say, annunciating every word, making sure she truly hears me. "*That I'm home*, and that I'm going to start making up for all the hurt I've caused you over the past three years. I'm not going anywhere, and I'm sure as hell not about to let you go again. I want to put your heart back together."

Her eyes glisten with unshed tears as she lifts her hand right over my chest, feeling the rapid beat of my heart below. "Do you love me, Noah Ryan?"

I nod, lacing my fingers through hers over my heart. "I've never been so in love with you."

"Then you've already put me back together."

Chapter 30
NOAH

The playground looks empty as I pull to a stop and cut the engine. I gaze out over the steering wheel, finding Zoey perched on one of the swings like she used to when we were kids. She doesn't glance up, and as I watch her, it's clear she's lost in thought. She grips the chains on either side with one foot planted on the ground as she slowly rocks back and forth.

I've caught her like this a few times this week, and every time it always comes down to the same thing—Tarni Luca.

It's been almost a week since their fallout in the school cafeteria, and while Tarni has been silent and kept her distance as the school's newest outcast, she clearly hasn't been cut up about it. But Zoey hasn't stopped hurting. Her heart is too big for her own good.

Making my way to the playground, I slip around the back of the swings and come up behind her, my hands coming down on her shoulders. "Stop thinki—"

Zoey screams, leaping from the swing, her eyes wide as she whips around with her fists up, ready to take me out. All I can do is laugh as she realizes it's just me. "Holy shit, Noah," she breathes, bracing her hands against her thighs and taking slow, deep breaths. "Are you trying to give me a heart attack?"

I arch a brow, standing back and watching as she tries to get control of her breathing. "Were you going to punch me?"

"Damn straight," she says. "Your ass was about to get laid out. You're just lucky I saw you before I started swinging." She cuts through the swings and steps right into me, pushing up onto her tippy toes to kiss me as my arms circle her waist. "You know, only a man with a death wish sneaks up on a girl like that."

"I figured you heard me coming," I tell her. "My car isn't exactly quiet."

She pulls a face, almost embarrassed because she knows I'm right. "How'd you know where to find me, anyway?"

"Lucky guess," I say with a shrug.

"Try again," she says, pulling out of my arms and arching a brow, knowing damn well I'm lying.

"Okay fine," I say with a groan, not surprised to see just how well she's able to read me. "I swung by your place and your dad said you'd gone out, and seeing as though Hazel was still at home, your car was in the driveway, and you kinda don't have any friends, it narrowed down the options."

She lets out a heavy sigh, her bottom lip jutting out, and I know it has everything to do with my comment about her friends. "She really hates me."

I step back into her, pulling her into my arms again and dropping a kiss to her temple. "She does," I say, not bothering to sugarcoat it. "But that's because she's a spiteful bitch who can't see past her own wants and needs to the people around her. She doesn't deserve your tears, Zo. You've given her ten years of friendship, and she's going to throw it away over jealousy."

She lets out a heavy breath, not willing to let it go just yet, so I go on, more than ready to drive my point home. "She was there, Zo. She saw us as kids. She watched from the sidelines as we fell head over heels in love with each other. She knows how happy you are when we're together. If she's the kind of person who wants to stand in the way of your happiness, then she was never a good friend to you," I tell her. "She's never had your best interests at heart. I saw it the very first day I met her, and I just hate that it's taken this long for her to show you her true colors."

"It just . . . It hurts," she whispers, letting out a heavy sigh.

"I know it does," I say, my hands rubbing up and down her arms. "But soon it'll fade, and you'll realize you never needed her."

"Let me guess," she says, her chin tilting up to meet my stare. "Because I have everything I need right here?"

"Wow," I tease. "Whoever said you weren't a fast learner?"

She rolls her eyes, but I grab her hand, pulling her back toward my car. "Come on," I say, "I want you to come somewhere with me."

Her brows furrow, but she allows me to pull her along, stepping into my side as we make our way back to my car. "Where are we going?" she asks as I open the door for her, knowing how my mom would clip me over the back of the head if I wasn't the perfect gentleman.

"Linc's grave," I tell her, watching for her response. "I haven't been since the funeral."

Her eyes widen. "You haven't?"

My lips press into a hard line, and I shake my head, almost embarrassed by my admission. "I've never known what to do if I went or what to say. I've had this fucked-up vision stuck in my head that he'd claw out of there like some shitty zombie movie and try to drag me back down with him."

Zo gives me a blank stare. "You know, he probably would just to screw with you."

"I'm more than aware."

Zoey laughs and settles into her seat as I close the door and make my way around to the driver's side. I'm kicking over the engine when a smirk stretches across Zoey's lips, and she swivels in her seat to look at me. "Okay, so you should probably know that Hazel leaves letters for him all the time, and I, umm . . ." She cringes, and I raise my brow, waiting to hear what's about to fly out of her mouth. "I kinda respond to them as Linc, so she's convinced he's actually coming back from the dead to write her letters."

I gape at her in shock, but I'm also a little impressed she's been able to keep this going for three years without Hazel being the least bit suspicious. "You have to tell her."

"Hell no, I don't. It'll crush her."

"Zoey Erica James."

"Noah McFunPolice Ryan."

I let out a sigh, knowing a lost cause when it's staring me in the face. "What are you writing to her?"

"Nothing that will get me in trouble," she admits. "It started out innocent. I went to his grave a few days after Mom and Hazel had been, and I saw the letter and couldn't help reading it. Then I was sitting there for a while and thought maybe it was a good idea to leave him a message too, so I flipped her letter over and wrote *I miss you* on the back, and next thing I knew I was walking in the door after school and Hazel was running up to me saying that Linc had responded. I didn't have the heart to tell her it was me. Then it just got a little out of control from there."

"How out of control?"

"Like, almost once a week," she says sheepishly. "But I always keep it short and sweet. Like when she needs someone to tell her that she's doing okay or when she needs guidance. Though I may have used it to my advantage when she was crushing on this asshole kid at school by suggesting that Linc thought he was a piece of shit."

A wide grin stretches across my face, and I reach over the center console to take her hand, feeling more at peace every day. Talking about Linc used to be so fucking hard that I would crumble, and now . . . I find myself welcoming it. Even *needing* it.

"Soooo . . . If I have to be on trial, then so do you," Zoey says.

I narrow my stare on her, glancing at her for a moment before looking back at the road. "Yes?" I question, unsure why I feel so nervous.

"Okay, I've been dying to know, but I didn't want to seem like the gossipy type, but if you don't tell me, I think I might go insane," she starts, pausing for a second and watching me as if still debating if she's going to ask or not. "The other week at your first game of the season, what the hell did you say to Shannan that got her to fade out of existence?"

I laugh. "Really? That's the big question that's been plaguing your pretty little mind?"

"Uh . . . yeah."

"Who would have known that Zoey James was so nosey?"

"You, Noah," she says bluntly. "You knew that."

I grin. Yeah, I did.

"Okay, fine," I finally say, sparing her a quick glance. "So, despite the semester only just starting, Shannan was already failing a few classes and had been skipping enough to get the principal's attention. Then during my week of lunchtime detentions with Daniels, I overheard that she'd been offering some of her teachers sexual favors for better grades."

Her mouth drops, and I have to force myself to keep my eyes on the road. "You're lying," she gasps, her eyes widening. "Tell me you're lying."

"I don't lie," I tell her.

Zoey scoffs. "I have literally sat with you and helped you come up with lies before."

I smirk. "Okay, fine. I lie occasionally, but I'm not lying now."

"Holy crap," she breathes. "That is some juicy gossip."

"Zo," I warn.

"I know. My lips are sealed, but I'm not going to lie, it's nice knowing I have that little bit of information in my back pocket to save for a rainy day," she says before fixing me with a hard stare. "Now, are we going to pretend you didn't just gloss over the week of lunchtime detentions? Care to share?"

I laugh and shake my head. "I can't tell you all my secrets now, can I?"

Zoey rolls her eyes but falls silent as I pull into the main entrance of East View Cemetery. My hands start to shake on the wheel as a lump forms in my throat, and I try to hide how hard it is to breathe. Undeniable guilt washes over me for not having been here since Linc's funeral, but if I didn't have Zoey here with me, I wouldn't have the strength to go further than the front gates.

"It's okay," she tells me. "You can do this."

I hold her stare for a moment before letting out a deep breath and hitting the gas.

East View Cemetery is huge, and since I haven't been here for so long, Zoey has to give me directions. Then all too soon, she's telling me to pull over. My hands never stop shaking, not when I get out of the car, and not when Zoey falls into my side and takes my hand in hers.

We walk through the manicured grass, and a part of me is glad to see how well this cemetery has been looked after. Every single tombstone is sparkling, and despite the many trees lining the rows of graves, there's not a single fallen leaf lingering on the ground.

Zoey leads me through the rows of graves, going the long way around to be respectful and not cut across any of them. When she slows, her gaze bounces up to meet mine. "He's just over here," she murmurs before pointing to the familiar grave a few places down.

My gaze locks on to it, reading over the words on his tombstone.

IN LOVING MEMORY
LINCOLN ALEXANDER RYAN
05/31/2011–07/19/2021
BELOVED SON, BROTHER & BEST FRIEND

"Fucking hell," I mutter, blowing out a shaky breath as I drag my hand down my face. Reading those words hurts so bad.

Unable to focus on the tombstone a second longer, I drop my gaze to the handful of things scattered at the bottom. There's a plastic folder that's almost overflowing with papers, and I can only assume they're the letters Hazel writes to Linc. There's a photo of the four of us—my family—Mom, Dad, me, and Linc. I don't think I've ever seen that photo, but I remember the day it was taken. It feels like a lifetime ago. There's a second frame holding the same photo that lingers on Linc's desk in his room. Me, Zoey, Hazel, and Linc, only the words the *four musketeers* are etched into the frame, and it brings a smile to my lips.

Fresh flowers rest on his grave next to a football and his jersey from middle school with his name and number on the back—a jersey he earned during tryouts but never got the chance to use. Pride swirls through my chest. This is exactly how he would have wanted it.

"Who brought all this stuff?" I ask Zoey as she gazes down at Linc's grave, a fondness shining in her tear-filled eyes.

"Everybody," she tells me. "Your mom brings fresh flowers every week, and I've seen your dad here a few times. I'm not sure how often he comes by, but I'm pretty sure he was the one who left the football and jersey."

"And the pictures?"

"Me and Hazel," she tells me. "She wanted to leave the one of the four of us and wrote about us being the four musketeers, but I never really understood that. And I left your family photo because—"

She trails off, and I inch closer, tugging on her hand and pulling her into my side. "Because?" I prompt.

Her hand comes up, and she discreetly wipes her eyes. "Because I knew you weren't visiting him, and I wanted Linc to remember how much you loved him, and if for some reason he wasn't able to look over you, then he'd be able to remember your face here."

My heart shatters, and I drop my lips to her temple, pressing a lingering kiss, not willing to pull away so soon. "God, Zo. I don't deserve you."

She lets out a breath and presses her hand to my chest, her chin tilting up to meet my stare. "Did you want to talk to him?"

"I . . ." I pause, caught off guard. "I don't know what I would even say."

"Just tell him about your life. How you've been doing, how much you miss him and wish he were here. Tell him about the guilt you've felt and the struggles you've had trying to navigate the darkness. Tell him you're sorry that you haven't been the man you wanted to be over the past three years. He'll want to know that you're trying to do better, and when in doubt, tell him about your shenanigans with Hazel or how football has been going."

The pressure drops down on my shoulders, and the nerves become almost unbearable when Zoey steps out of my arms and walks right up to the edge of his grave. She bends down and grabs the plastic folder filled with Hazel's letters before clutching it to her chest. "I'll be over at the car," she tells me. "Unless you want me to stay."

I give it thought, warring back and forth with my options before giving a slight shake of my head. "I'll be alright," I tell her, needing to find the strength to face this, to be the brother Linc always thought I was.

Zoey gives me a small smile before slipping away, and before I know it, I'm down on the grass in front of his grave, my gaze locked on the inscription written on the granite tombstone. I sit for a few minutes, having no idea where to start, but the second I do, the words seem to flow.

"Shit, Linc. You'd be so fucking ashamed of me," I tell him. "I think the day you died, I died right along with you. Only I was stuck here, living like a fucking ghost, barely going through the motions. I fucked up everything. Hurt everybody just to try and escape the guilt, but nothing ever helped. I miss you, bro. I fucking miss you so bad, it hurts. Every. Fucking. Day. I should never have told you to go home that day. If I knew . . . I never would—" I stop abruptly, unable to say the words out loud, not to him at least. "I should have been a better brother, Linc. All you ever did was want to spend time with me, and I was so fucking selfish. I should have given you the time you needed or threw the fucking ball with you more. I always told you that I'd teach you how to ride a dirt bike, and we never got to do that. There are so many things I never got to teach you, and I hate myself for letting you down like that."

I let out a breath, needing a second before I continue. "It's been three years already, and I'm so ashamed of myself for not visiting you until now. I wasn't strong enough, but Zoey is bringing me back to life. She's breathing oxygen into my veins and keeping me going, and while I finally feel as though I can see a way out of the darkness, it also makes me feel guilty. How fucking dare I be happy and have love when you—fuck. You'll never get to have those things, and I know you would have had them all. You and Hazel would have been just like me and Zoey, and maybe if you were still here, you would have already realized that she was it for you. Or maybe it would have taken you another few years. She's only eleven, a few months older than you were when you—" I pause again.

"Hazel misses you. It's different for her than it is for me and Zo. You were her best friend. There wasn't a single thing that happened in her life that she didn't run to tell you about. And even though I pushed Zo away for the last three years, I've leaned hard on the dream that I'd be good enough for her again one day—because nothing is as final as death. Hazel . . . When she lost you, she didn't just lose her best friend, she lost every possibility of the life you two may have had, and I know she feels that loss every single day. I'm trying to be there for her, trying to be that friend she needs, but it's not the same.

"I really hope you're up there somewhere, watching over us all," I continue. "Mom puts on a brave face, but I've put her through the worst kind of hell, and most days, I think she's on the brink of falling apart. She holds herself together for me though, and for a while, I think I needed that, but now it's time for me to be the man she needs me to be. I won't let her down anymore, Linc. I'll carry the burden on my shoulders. I promise, I won't put her through it anymore, but she could really use a sign from you, anything just to let her know you're still here."

My elbows brace against my knees, and I tip my face into my hands, needing a moment to calm myself and find control. "That day

. . . finding you like that on the ground. You have no idea how much I wished you would just move, just get up and walk it off like you always would. Hell, we used to play rough all the fucking time. I used to put your head through walls, and you'd just shake it off, but not this time. I'll never get the image out of my head, Linc. It haunts me. Every time I close my eyes, I see you just lying there, staring lifelessly, and it makes me wish I could trade places with you. I would have done anything to be able to save you from that. I would have laid my life down for you, Linc. You had so much to live for."

My voice cracks on that last one, and I let my words fade away, just sitting there as the shadow from Linc's tombstone slowly moves from one side to the other. I've never once allowed myself to cry, to feel the overwhelming grief break me like that. Not the day he died, not even at his funeral. I always needed to be strong for Mom and Zoey, they were counting on me, but here, sitting with him now, just me and my brother, the tears finally come.

I let the guilt fade from my veins and blow away into the sunny Arizona sky, leaving me feeling refreshed and at ease for the first time since racing down that road and finding his lifeless body.

Then when Zoey starts walking back toward me after sitting and waiting in my car for what must have been hours, I let out a breath and get back to my feet. "I love you, Linc. I promise I won't be a stranger."

Zoey reaches me a moment later, lays the plastic folder of letters back where she found it, and steps right into my arms. "Are you okay?"

"Yeah," I tell her, glancing back at the photo of the four musketeers one last time, my chest filling with a bittersweet joy. "I'm okay."

Chapter 31

ZOEY

Having Noah back in my life has restored my faith in love and everything good. It's been a few weeks, and every moment of it has been magical as we've rediscovered each other and learned all the little things we've missed over the past few years. It's as though he's slid straight back into position, right where he always belonged, and while it's so easy and natural and feels like absolutely nothing has changed, it also feels as though everything has.

I think this is just our new normal, and every time something happens, or Noah wins another game, we're always going to be filled with happiness that will be clouded by the pain of not being able to share that moment with Linc. It's a pain that we'll live with for the rest of our lives, but we're not going to stop living or making memories because that's the only way Linc would have wanted it.

We're at the end of the football season, and tonight, the Mambas are killing it just like I knew they would. They're playing for the championship trophy, and the buzz in the air is electrifying. It's everything. I've never been so proud of him.

It's an away game, but I'm not surprised that my whole family has come out to cheer him on. Aunt Maya sits between Mom and Hazel, and I swear, she'll no longer possess a voice box after this game.

It's a close game, and we're well into the final minutes of the game. Noah told me on the way here that their opposition is known for playing dirty when they've got their backs up against the wall, and right now, they couldn't possibly be more cornered.

The Mambas push themselves to their limit, giving it their all. They've never won a championship before, but with Noah on the team this season, they've pushed themselves during every training session, determined to make something of this, and they're so close. Their hard work is finally going to pay off.

There are two minutes left in the game, and every last person is on their feet in anticipation. Principal Daniels and Coach Martin look as though they're about to throw themselves onto the field and join in. The cheerleaders can't seem to remember their routine because they're all glued to the game.

It's insane.

I've been to a few of Noah's championship games when we were younger, but they were nothing like this. The stakes are higher, and a lot of these players have college riding on their performance, something they might not have been able to reach if it weren't for the extra push they've received from Noah.

The Mambas have the ball, pushing through the other team's defense, and I hold my breath, certain they're about to get one more touchdown in for the night. The fans go insane, and the stands vibrate under the intense weight of the anxious crowd.

My ears ache from the constant screaming, but I don't dare stop, both Hazel and I are about ready to lose our minds. Cameron Landry has the ball and I watch with wild anticipation as he breaks through and makes a run for it, cradling the ball like it's the most precious cargo in the world.

He sprints toward the end zone and the whole crowd seems to hold their breath in unison as the other team quickly gains on him. "GO. GO. GO," Hazel roars beside me, sounding possessed.

The Mambas run after Cameron, trying to help him, but he's too far out, so he's on his own. Three guys are there, and he manages to dodge one, but the other two aren't having it. He's so close to the end zone. He only has to hold on a little while longer, push a little harder, but they fly at him with the force of a freight train. With so little time left on the clock, the other team is determined to keep the Mambas from scoring.

They finally reach him and Cameron goes down hard under their weight. The whole crowd gasps at the impact, and when both players get off him, Cameron is left motionless on the ground. There's a horrified silence that settles over both sides of the stadium as we wait for him to recover, and then just like that, he's back on his feet.

"Holy crap," Aunt Maya says. "I thought he was in trouble there."

"This is terrifying," my mom says to Aunt Maya. "I don't know how you deal with this. If my girls were getting taken down like that, I'd be a wreck."

"Tequila," Aunt Maya says with a smirk. "A lot of tequila."

The crowd roars and my heart has never raced faster.

Okay, that's not true. The very first day when I saw Noah in the student office and he walked right into me, that overwhelming delicious scent wrapping around me, that's the fastest my heart has ever pounded. This is a close second though.

Noah shouts orders as the Mambas line up for another play, and despite already having the upper hand, I can guarantee that Noah wants another touchdown. The ball is snapped and delivered right into Noah's waiting hands as the other team forge ahead, determined to get the ball back in their possession.

Noah side steps, hesitating for just a moment when I realize his receivers are blocked and in a flash of breathtaking awe, Noah dodges and weaves the opposition before taking off at a deadly sprint.

"Holy shit," I breathe, realizing he's taking the run.

He runs for all he's worth as I scream so loud I taste blood in the back of my throat. My gaze flicks between Noah and the clock. Only a few seconds left. He can make it. I know he can. He's too good.

He pushes himself out in front of the other team's defenses with ease as my voice box permanently fades out of existence. "GO NOAH!" I scream, jumping up and down, clutching Hazel's hand in a death grip, probably yanking her arm right out of its socket in the process.

He runs like his life depends on it, his feet pounding against the earth, and propelling him closer to the end zone. Then in a moment of absolute perfection, he throws himself toward the ground, the ball slamming down in the end zone as his momentum has him skidding across the field. The clock stops and the ref blows the whistle just as the crowd roars for their new champions.

"YES!" I scream as Noah launches himself to his feet, throwing the ball up in the air as his teammates barrel into him, and before his gaze can even shoot toward the stands, I'm already running.

I barge through the overfilled stands, shoulder past all the people, and hit the stairs running. When my feet strike the pavement at the bottom, I propel myself toward the field as Noah shoves past his teammates.

A horde of people push onto the field behind me, but they aren't nearly as fast as me. I bound toward him, and he barely has time to unclip his helmet and yank it off his head before I leap into his strong arms, thread my fingers through his dark hair, and kiss him deeply.

He pants in exhaustion, and despite struggling to breathe, he gives me everything he's got.

"You were amazing," I tell him, grinning uncontrollably and forcing myself back. His shoulder pads aren't exactly comfortable to squish up against, but I'll take him any way I can get him.

"Get a room," Liam shouts from somewhere behind Noah, but Noah just grins and brings his mouth right back to mine.

All too soon, my family and Aunt Maya crowd around us, and Noah reluctantly puts me back on my feet as they each give him their congratulations. In a matter of seconds, his teammates steal him away, and before I know it, I'm watching men in suits line up to shake his hand.

The Mambas are awarded their championship trophy, and that's when the real celebration starts. After a while, our parents take off with Hazel, and the crowd quickly dissipates, leaving only the overexcited high-school students ready to party.

I hover by Noah's car, but I don't have to wait long before he's right here with me, barreling into me, his strong arms weaving around my waist. He pulls me in tight against him and kisses me deeply before walking me right around to the passenger side of his car and opening the door for me. "I hope you're ready for a big night," he warns me. "We're going to a bonfire down by the lake."

A wide grin stretches across my face. I haven't been to a lake party in ages. The last time I went to one, I'm pretty sure I was with Noah when I was thirteen, maybe a week or two before we lost Linc. "Can't wait."

Noah smiles right back at me before closing the door between us and all but skipping around to the driver's side. He climbs in and hits the gas in seconds as the other players pull out around us.

"I can't believe how incredible that was," I tell him, my voice hoarse from the constant screaming.

"The guys were on fire," he agrees, sparing me a quick glance. "But I have to tell you something."

I watch him as he drives, one hand on the steering wheel, the other casually resting on the gearshift, and damn it, he looks so good. "Does it happen to have something to do with all those guys in suits who just had to shake your hand after the game?" I question, knowing damn well this is about the million colleges across the country who are desperate to recruit him.

"Maybe," he tells me with a slow grin.

My eyes widen, excitement drumming through my veins. "You got an offer?"

"A few actually," he says. "Georgia. Michigan. Ohio State. But I also got the Wildcats."

"Wait," I say, sitting up straighter in my seat, my gaze locked on his as he flicks his attention between me and the road. "The Wildcats are in Arizona, right? They're only like . . . I don't know, maybe two hours from here."

"It was a no-brainer, Zo," he tells me, abandoning the gearshift to take my hand. "I accepted."

My eyes fill with tears of overwhelming happiness, knowing that his dream of playing college football is only a breath away, and not only that, but he's still going to be close enough that we can see each other all the time. For a year at least. I'll be filling out my application for the University of Arizona the second I can.

"Holy shit, Noah," I say through my tears. "That's so incredible. I'm so proud of you."

"I wouldn't have been able to get this far without you, Zo."

"No, you did this one all on your own," I tell him. "I'm not letting you give up any of the credit for that. You're the one who put in all the hours during training and in the gym. You're the one who impressed all the scouts and had people flying in from all over the country just to see you. But are you really sure that Arizona is what you want? You have so many amazing teams that would kill for you."

"It means nothing to me if I have to leave you, Zo. Arizona has always been my goal. I can come home on the weekends and see Mom, and it's not too far for you to come to my games. I wouldn't have it any other way."

The tears stream down my face, and the quicker I wipe them away, the sooner they're replaced with more. "We can manage two hours," I say, trying to sound confident about it, but in reality, two hours is still two hours away, and when I'm missing him and not getting to see his face every single day, those two hours are going to feel like two light-years.

"Yeah, we can," he tells me, moving his hand to my thigh and giving a firm squeeze. "If we can make it through three years of radio silence, then we can do college. It'll be one year, and then you'll be right there with me."

I nod because I can picture it perfectly. Where Noah goes, I go. If the roles were reversed, I know without a doubt that he would follow me blindly.

Sitting back in my seat, I watch him drive, my heart so full and happy. The guy I'm looking at now is the real Noah, and so many times over the years I was worried I would never get to see him like this again. He's come so far, and I'm amazed by the man he is today, but from the first day I met him, I knew he'd be incredible.

Since pushing away the pain and guilt, he's been able to reclaim a part of himself, and he's soared ever since. He's no longer drowning or sick with internal agony. Don't get me wrong, there are days when his grief cripples him, just as it does me, but he no longer pushes me away. On those days, we spend a few hours down at East View Cemetery, and when we leave, it's just a little bit easier to breathe.

It's a long road, and he still has miles to travel—we both do, but we're heading in the right direction, and I can't wait to see where it leads us.

It's a short trip back into East View, and before I know it, we're pulling up at the lake. A crowd falls in around Noah's Camaro before he's even able to cut the engine. He squeezes my thigh again, and in this very moment, the world has never been so perfect. "Are you ready?" he questions, turning that all-too-charming smile on me and knocking the breath right out of my lungs.

"I've never been so ready."

Chapter 32

ZOEY

Christmas and New Year's Eve came and went in the blink of an eye, and before I know it, I'm waking up on my seventeenth birthday to the sound of pebbles striking my bedroom window. A warm smile spreads across my face, and I stretch with a groan as I open my eyes.

Another pebble hits my window, and I can't wipe the grin off my face. It's not hard to guess who's standing outside my window. Throwing my blanket back, I get out of bed and trudge across my room to open the blinds and peer out into the front yard, immediately laughing.

Noah stands in the middle of the lawn with an old boom box resting on his shoulder. In one hand, he clutches a stack of papers, and the boom box wobbles as he reaches down to grab another pebble from the pile at his feet. I open the window, more than ready to throw myself right out of it and drop straight into his arms, but I'll settle for hearing whatever it is he's come to say.

Only, he doesn't say a word as he reaches up to the boom box and presses a button, filling the whole street with the sweet sounds of *My Neck, My Back* by Khia.

My cheeks flame with embarrassment, and my gaze quickly darts up and down the street, hoping no one decides to come out and see what the hell all that noise is. "NOAH!" I hiss, reconsidering the whole jumping out the window thing, only it wouldn't be to drop into his strong arms, it'd be to kill him.

Noah doesn't say a word, just simply smiles as he holds up the papers in his hand with big bold letters scrawled across the first one.

HAPPY BIRTHDAY, 2020

The first page falls away, and I suddenly don't care about his choice of music as I read his second message.

I AM EMBARRASSINGLY IN LOVE WITH YOU

A wide smile pulls across my face, and the next paper falls away.

SO IN LOVE WITH YOU THAT I FEEL IT'S MY RESPONSIBILITY TO TELL YOU...

I wait on bated breath, the anticipation burning through my veins. But then he drops the next piece of paper, and that wide smile vanishes as though it never even existed.

YOU'RE REALLY FUCKING LATE FOR SCHOOL

"WHAT?" I screech, my head whipping back toward my bedside table to look at the clock, seeing that I'm not just really late, I'm *it's just about lunchtime* kind of late. "Oh shit."

I grab the window and yank it down, Khia's demands to lick her all over now muffled through the closed window, but it does nothing to muffle the barking laughter that quickly follows. Rolling my eyes, I ignore him and quickly scramble around my room, searching for something to wear before dashing into the bathroom and throwing my hair into a ponytail. I don't bother with any makeup, and before I know it, I'm grabbing my things and hurrying downstairs.

Noah sits at the island counter, helping himself to the muffin Mom left out for me this morning, and I pluck it out of his hand before shoving it into my mouth and giving him a muffin-filled kiss. "You're an ass," I say around my muffin.

"Bullshit," he says, taking my things out of my arms and leading me to the door. "You can't honestly tell me that you've had a better wake-up call than that."

"Maybe I have," I challenge, knowing damn well he's right.

Noah scoffs as we reach the door, and he grips my elbow before pulling me to a stop and turning me to look up into those dark eyes I love so much. He pauses just a moment, his gaze sailing over my face before gently brushing his fingers across my forehead and fixing my unruly hair. "Happy birthday, Zo," he murmurs, his deep tone sending butterflies soaring through the pit of my stomach.

A soft smile spreads across my lips, and I press up on my tippy toes to give him a proper kiss. His arms curl around my waist and hold me to him, and my knees grow weak as I melt into him. My eyes flutter, and before I lose all sense of control, I pull back just an inch, meeting his dark gaze. "Thank you."

"Come on, let me get your ass to school."

I laugh and he drags me out of the house, knowing just how I feel about being late for things, and today, I really outdid myself. We get into his car, and before I know it, we're pulling into the student parking lot of East View High. There are students everywhere, telling me that the lunch break has already started, and as Noah insists that I wait so he can open the door for me, I find myself gazing at him, my heart pounding in a way it never has before.

He's so undeniably amazing. Every inch of him is chiseled from stone and sculpted to perfection, and for God knows what reason, he's decided to love me.

He opens the door, holding out his hand for me to take, and as I lay mine into his, a jolt of electricity fires through me, only this is supercharged, and I quickly realize what this is. I'm ready to take our relationship to the next level, ready to open myself to him and truly be together.

I'm ready for sex.

The mere knowledge of that revelation has butterflies soaring through my stomach again, and as Noah leads me away from the car, I find myself blurting it out. "Noah," I say, his gaze coming to mine. "I'm ready."

His brows furrow, and a flash of confusion flickers in his dark eyes. "For what?" he asks. "Lunch?"

"No," I groan, realizing I'm going to have to spell it out for him. Why now though? Every other time I have anything to say, he seems to pluck the words right out of my head. But he chooses this time not to be able to read my thoughts. "I'm ready . . . for *it.*"

"It?" he questions, confused before a flash of understanding dawns on him and his eyes widen. "Oooh, *it.*"

I nod, not really sure what I'm supposed to say now. Sex isn't really something we've ever discussed. Things certainly get heated between us, but he's never gone to make a move further than anything I haven't already initiated, and I love that about him. Because up until now, we've been so clearly on the same page that sex hasn't needed to be discussed. But this is uncharted waters for me, and I'm going to need him to take the lead.

"Shit, Zo. Way to catch a man off guard," he says as we stop in the middle of the student parking lot, neither of us willing to have this conversation in front of anyone else. He steps right into me, his fingers lifting my chin. "Are you sure? Because my mom—"

I blink, trying to keep the smirk off my face but failing miserably. "Let me get this straight," I say, cutting him off. "I tell you that I'm ready to get naked with you, and the first thing you think about is your mom? Wow! I was expecting a lot of things to come from this, but certainly not that."

Noah gives me a blank stare. "Are you done?"

I smile innocently then let out a heavy breath and nod. "Yes," I say. "It's out of my system. Go on. What were you going to say?"

"That my mom has already had this conversation with me."

"Eh?"

"Yeah, trust me, it was even more uncomfortable than it sounds," he tells me. "But what she was saying is that she wanted me to really make sure that you were ready and not just wanting something that you think you should have because everyone else is doing it or because you think it would make me happy."

My heart swells in my chest, and I push up to kiss him again. "Thank you for caring that much about me," I tell him. "But you know that I'm not the type of girl to do something because of peer pressure or because everyone else is doing something. As for what I think would make you happy. I'd be a fool to assume that you didn't want to, but I would also be a fool if I thought that you would ever sleep with me without being certain that I was ready. You've always had my best interests at heart, and you've always protected me from everything, even when it was myself I needed protecting from."

"So, you're sure?"

I nod, a shy smile gracing my lips. "I'm ready, Noah. I want to be with you."

He leans in and kisses me as his hand falls to my waist, slowly curling around my back and pulling me in against him. "You don't mean right now, do you?"

"Yes, right now," I tell him without skipping a beat. "I want to strip down and get with you right here in the middle of the student parking lot." He gives me a firm stare, clearly not appreciating my teasing, and I try to smother my smile before getting serious. "No," I finally say. "I don't mean right now, or that it has to be today. Just when it feels right."

"I can work with that," he says before his gaze lingers on mine, those dark eyes filled with curiosity. "I don't want to screw this up, Zo. It'll be your first time, and I want it to be just the way you've always imagined."

"I don't really know how I imagined it," I tell him. "I don't want anything special or some big grand, scheduled event because that's going to make me feel awkward and pressured, and the last thing I want is to be awkward about it. I just . . . I don't know. I want it to be spontaneous and in the moment."

His gaze softens, and he drops his forehead against mine, his fingers tightening on my waist. "Anything for you, Zozo."

My hand rests against his chest, feeling the steady thumping of his heart, a beat that isn't wild or anxious, but sure and confident. "I trust you with everything I am," I tell him. "You'll take care of me, and just because it's you and me, it's going to be even more perfect than I could have ever imagined."

His lips come down on mine, kissing me softly. "I love you, Zo," he tells me, his tone unwavering. "But now that you've told me that, there's no way I want to share you with the rest of the school. Let me take you out. We'll spend your birthday just you and me."

My gaze shifts up toward the school, and the second I take in the overcrowded hallways and immature boys screwing around to impress one another, I glance back at Noah. "Nothing would make me happier," I tell him. "Let's get out of here."

Hazel screeches beside me at the dinner table, her eyes widening in pain as she reaches down and grips her leg. "Owwww," she groans, glaring at Noah. "What the hell was that for?"

"Ahhhh, shit, sorry," he says, trying to muffle his laugh but failing. "I was aiming for Zoey and didn't expect to find your shin. What the hell is it doing over here anyway? Did your legs grow ten inches overnight?"

"My shin doesn't accept your apology," she throws back at him, fixing him with a glare that could bring the most vicious armies to their knees.

I hold back a grin as I meet Noah's stare across the table, his dark eyes shimmering with laughter, and that's all my control can handle before I burst out laughing right along with him. Hazel huffs and puffs and crosses her arms over her chest.

We get side-eyed from the parents, my dad's eyes lingering on us the longest. I hold his concerned stare, narrowing my gaze to let him know that I've caught him, but he doesn't look away.

I know what he's thinking. His little girl is growing up, and she's putting herself in a position to get her heart broken again. Or maybe he's just realized that we've been together for a while now and perhaps that's when things might start progressing.

I shake the thought from my head. I can't think about the idea that my dad might be concerned his daughter is ready to have sex. The thought sends an uncomfortable shiver sailing down my spine. But then, if I was right in my first thought, that maybe he's just worried that I could get my heart broken, then he needs to know that's not going to happen. Noah isn't about to take off again. He's right where he belongs, and he knows it. The two little matching infinity tattoos we got today are proof of that. Not that my parents need to know about them. Nonetheless, to have this small symbol of what Noah and I share marked on my body for all eternity is more than I could have asked for.

My tattoo is across my ribs, barely the size of a grape, while Noah's is directly over his heart. I told him it was cheesy to get it there, but he didn't care. He told me that maybe he's just a cheesy kinda guy, then he kissed me before telling me to sit down and shut up so he could get it over and done with.

Noah's never been one for needles. He didn't exactly have a panic attack or turn into a blubbering mess, but he went out of his comfort zone to share something with me.

I carry on with my birthday dinner but don't really eat much. My appetite just hasn't been great today, and after all the effort Mom and Dad have put into making tonight special, I immediately feel guilty.

I've heard the phrase, *How many times will our precious girl turn seventeen* a million times already, but it was expected. They go all out for my and Hazel's birthdays, celebrating every single one of them to the fullest extent because they know what it feels like to wonder if their baby girl will ever see another birthday.

I force as much dinner down my throat as I can, ignoring the way Noah watches me through a suspicious, narrowed stare. "So," Mom says, glancing our way and forcing the heat of Noah's stare off my face. "Are you getting excited for college? Not long to go now."

Noah nods. "Yeah. Just need to get through a few more months of classes until graduation."

Aunt Maya sends a smirk his way. "How on earth are you two going to survive being apart from each other like that?" she teases.

"We'll be fine," I say, rolling my eyes, but honestly, the closer we get to the end of the school term, the more anxious I become about it. I've tried to be confident and hide my worries. After everything Noah has been through already, I refuse to make him feel bad for having to go away, but the cracks in my resolve are starting to show.

The rest of dinner passes slowly, and even though my mood plummets, I force a smile across my face as Mom and Dad insist on singing "Happy Birthday" to me over a big cake. But all I can think about is the distance.

Two hours. Two light-years away.

It's the mantra that's been on repeat in my head ever since Noah's championship game, and every single time, it darkens my soul just a little bit more. In the grand scheme of things, it's only a year, and I'll still see him as often as I can, but over the past six months, he's stormed back into my life in such an intense way that I no longer know how to breathe without him.

We sit in the den watching *The Notebook* on Dad's prized flat-screen TV. It's way too big to be considered normal, but he couldn't resist getting one. Though, part of me wonders if he only bought it because a guy at his work got one and wouldn't stop boasting about it.

The movie plays, but as I watch the characters' hearts break, I don't take any of it in.

"What was that?" Noah asks, pulling me into his side, his lips brushing over my temple.

"Huh?"

"At dinner. One mention of college and you disappeared."

"It's nothing," I say, looking up and forcing a smile. "I'm fine."

"Out with it, Zo," he says. "You don't think I've noticed how anxious you've been getting and the bullshit 'We'll be fine' responses you keep giving everyone who asks? What's going on in that pretty little head of yours?"

"Don't," I say, having to look away to hide my tears.

"No way," he says, grabbing my chin and forcing my gaze back to his, his brows furrowing as he sees my glassy eyes. "This is fucking killing me. Let me in, Zo. Do you not think we'll be okay?"

"No," I say, throwing myself off the couch and hastily wiping my eyes, immediately pacing through the den as he watches me silently. I start feeling lightheaded, but I ignore it, needing to share this with him. "It's nothing like that. Of course we'll be fine. It's just . . . I'm scared, okay? I'm terrified of how much it's going to hurt while you're away."

"Zo," he murmurs, inching toward the edge of the couch as though he's about to reach out and pull me back into his arms, but I move further away, needing just a bit of space. Otherwise, I'll never get the words out.

My head spins, and an instant headache booms in my skull. "Don't try to give me a pep talk now," I tell him, sensing it coming. "I know we'll be fine, and in a year when I'm there with you, this whole conversation will feel ridiculous. Despite knowing that you'll call me every day, and I'll still be part of your world, I know what it feels like to be away from you, how bad it hurts when I can't just reach out and hold you when I'm having a shit day."

My head really pounds, and I stop pacing, swaying a little on my feet.

"Zo?" he questions.

I reach up to wipe the fresh tears off my face, but the swaying gets worse, and before I know it, the ground is coming up fast.

"ZOEY!"

Noah throws himself off the couch, his arms scooping under me just as I hit the ground, and he immediately pulls me into his chest as I go limp in his arms. "Zo," he says, gently shaking me as my eyes flutter open, looking up into his terror-filled ones. "Zo, baby. Are you okay?"

I close my eyes again, groaning as my head pounds. "I don't feel good."

"Shit," he says, reaching up and feeling my forehead. "I think you're getting sick. You've gone pale."

My bottom lip pouts, and I let out a heavy sigh. "This isn't how I wanted to spend the rest of my birthday."

"I know," he says, sitting me up just a little, the movement making my head spin worse. "When was the last time you had water? Can you get up?"

"Okay, Mom," I mutter, forcing myself up, despite the way I wobble on my feet. "I had two glasses of water with my dinner. I'm fine. I'm probably just coming down with something. You know, half the school has had the flu this week."

His face scrunches with distaste. He's not a fan of sharing germs when other people are sick, but he hasn't dared to take his hands off me. His arm curls around my waist, and as I wobble my way out of the den, Noah decides he can't handle it, and he scoops me into his strong arms.

I curl into his chest as he walks through my house, murmuring something to my mom about a headache. She promises to bring me some painkillers and a glass of water, and before I know it, I'm tucked into my bed, curled into Noah's side.

"You sure you're okay?" he questions, his fingers brushing through my hair.

"I'm already starting to feel better," I tell him honestly. "Maybe I just got too worked up over the whole college thing."

"Ya think?" he scoffs, a smile in his rich tone.

I yawn, despite it barely being eight in the evening. "I got you something," he tells me as he digs into his pocket and pulls out a little velvet box.

He hands it to me, and I gape at him. "You've been carrying that around all day?"

Noah laughs. "Maybe."

I roll my eyes and take it from him, a strange mix of excitement and anticipation burning through my body. I hold my breath, my fingers braced against the little box, and as I open it, it takes my breath away.

A beautiful gold necklace stares back at me—a dainty, subtle chain that drops down to a gorgeous pendant, the letters Z and N wrapped in a heart and making my own flutter. I glance up at him, wonder shining in my eyes. "You had this made for me?"

"Of course I did," he says as though any other option simply doesn't exist to him.

"Thank you," I tell him, tilting my chin and giving him a small kiss, a wide smile spreading across my lips. "It's incredible. I love it." Then gazing down at the way the Z and N so perfectly fit together, I pull it out of the box and hand it to him. "Will you put it on me?"

"You're about to go to bed."

"And?" I question. "I'm never taking it off."

Knowing a losing fight when he sees one, he takes the necklace from my fingers and we each sit up as I brush my hair over my shoulder. He loops the stunning gold chain around my neck, brushing his fingers over my skin as he fastens it at the back. His lips drop to my shoulder, and he gently kisses me there as I glance back to meet his warm gaze.

"It's perfect," he tells me, my cheeks flushing, knowing he's not talking about the chain.

"I love you," I tell him. "With everything that I am. You're my *bestest friend*."

He pulls me back into his arms, scooching us down in bed as he pulls me into his chest, and as my fingers run over the beautiful pendant hanging from my neck, his lips press against my temple. "You're my whole world, Zoey James," he tells me. "I don't know how I would ever survive without you."

Chapter 33

ZOEY

March, April, and May passed in a blur, and I don't know how it happened, but one second, we had months up our sleeve, and the next, Noah is close to graduation, and all we have left is the upcoming summer.

It's been a long day and an even longer final period. My gaze drifts up to the clock above the whiteboard, watching the last few seconds of the school week countdown with heavy eyes. I've been so tired lately. I even slept right through my alarm this morning, and it has everything to do with the constant worrying about what this next year is going to bring, that and Noah calling me every night. It's always a short call, intended just to say goodnight, and somehow, we end up talking for ages. Sometimes hours go by before I realize what time it is.

The second hand makes its way right to the top, and on cue, the bell sounds through the school. My classmates quickly pack their things and file out of the room, all of them buzzing with excitement over the weekend and a woods party tonight. I'm not surprised to find I'm one of the last ones through the door. I just don't have the energy or the enthusiasm over the epic party everyone can't stop talking about. It sounds like a disaster waiting to happen. How many horror films have started with a party in the woods? I'll pass.

Making my way to my locker, I stop to get my things when a big body falls in beside me, his familiar scent hitting me first. Noah grabs me, pulls me away from my open locker, and presses me into the next one. As his body pins me there, his arms cage me in, and before I can even smile up at him, his lips are on mine.

He kisses me deeply before his lips trail down my neck. "You ready to get out of here?" he murmurs between kisses.

"Mm-hmm," I groan.

His lips come back to mine, kissing me once more before allowing me a second to finish getting my things and closing my locker. Noah immediately takes my books out of my arms, holding them for me as he slings his other arm over my shoulder, pulling me right into his side.

As we head toward the student parking lot, we pass Tarni, who glances up at the last moment and glares. I look away, not letting her hate affect the rest of my afternoon. As Noah always reminds me, I've already spent too many hours broken over her, and she sure as hell doesn't deserve any more of my time. Besides, it's been at least eight months. It's time for her to move on.

We get into Noah's car, and as he's reversing out of his spot, he glances at me. "What do you wanna do?" he questions. "Hungry?"

"Ummmm—"

"Park? Lake?" he says, throwing around options. "We could take Hazel to see that movie she keeps bugging you about."

"Nah, I think she said something about having a sleepover at a friend's place tonight, so I doubt we'll see her all weekend," I tell him before letting out a heavy sigh. "I'm kinda tired though. Some guy wouldn't quit talking my ear off all night."

"Some guy, huh? Do I have something to worry about?"

"Oh, yeah. This guy is . . ." I hold my hand up, mimicking a chef's kiss. "Little rough around the edges, hot as sin, and definitely has a mean streak, but I have it on good authority that when he really kisses a girl, she crumbles in his arms."

"Hmmm," he says, a smirk playing on his delicious lips. "Sounds like a loser."

"Massive loser," I tease.

Noah rolls his eyes and glances across at me, his hand bypassing the gearshift and dropping to my thigh, giving a gentle squeeze just as he always does. "You wanna just chill at my place?"

"Yeah, unless you wanna eat," I say. "I could sit at a table and pretend not to fall asleep while you scarf your food down like a pig."

"I don't scarf my food like a pig."

"No, you're right," I say. "You just inhale it."

Noah grins. He knows I'm right, but nonetheless, he takes the turn to head back toward his place. He hands me his phone to give me full control of the music, and before I know it, he's pulling to a stop outside his home.

I go to grab my things and reach for my door when I glance back and realize he's not making a move to leave. He hasn't even cut the engine, and I settle back into my seat. "What's wrong?" I ask, watching how his usual carefree expression becomes almost fearful.

"I, umm . . ." he looks back at me, taking a deep breath and reconsidering. He nods toward his home. "Come on, we'll talk inside."

My brows furrow, and I go through the motions of getting out of the car and walking up the path toward the front door. He holds my hand, but this Noah isn't the one I was with at the end of school, this one is unsure, and I've never known him to be that way.

"Is something wrong?" I ask in a small tone, my mind running wild with endless possibilities that could potentially destroy my world.

"Stop," he murmurs, squeezing my hand as he unlocks the front door and leads me inside. "You're overthinking it."

"What else was I supposed to do?" I mutter. "You look at me like you're about to be sick and then say *we'll talk inside.* The end of the world is literally happening inside my head. If this is the big *I'm going to college soon and want to explore my options* talk, you could have at least told me at my place so I could have kicked you out, but now I'm gonna be stranded here and forced to ask for a ride home in the middle of my sob fest."

Noah groans and stops in the hallway before turning back to me and pressing a kiss to my forehead. "You're insufferable. You know that, right?"

I roll my eyes, and he drags me down the hall, past Linc's bedroom and into his. He drops onto his bed with his back against the headboard and reaches for me, pulling me straight onto his lap until I'm straddled over him. "I'm not breaking up with you, Zo," he says as I fidget with the material of his shirt, a nervous habit we've both become accustomed to. "I'm not sure if you've been around these past eight months, but I'm shamelessly in love with you."

"Then what is it?" I ask, needing to be put out of my misery. "Hit me with it. Have you been recruited for some secret mission that requires you to fly to space for the next ten years? Only ten years in space is going to be like . . . a million here, and when you get back, you'll be more interested in my great, great, great, great granddaughter."

His mouth pops open, feigning offense. "Hold up a second," he says. "You mean to tell me that if I got sent to space for some highly dangerous mission, which I'm sure would have something to do with saving the whole human race, you'd be down here, shacking up with some guy and having babies?"

"I mean, it depends. Was this space mission optional? Did they come to you like, we think you'd be good for this job, but if you're too busy, the dude down the street has some time, or were they holding a knife to your throat, threatening that if you don't go, they'll destroy everything you love?"

"Definitely option two."

A smile pulls at my lips, and I lean into him, bracing my hand against his chest and feeling the heavy thump of his heart. "Then you already know I'd be right here waiting for you."

Noah kisses me and curls his arm around my waist, but as he pulls back, he lets out a heavy breath, and I prepare for the worst. "Zo, I . . . shit," he says, not knowing how to break this news to me. "I know you have this whole plan for the summer to make the most of every second, but I received an email today—"

"What email?" I rush out, my heart racing.

"From the coaching staff at UA," he says. "They want to get a head start on training, and the whole team needs to be there a week earlier."

Horror blasts through my chest, and I feel our time together slipping away. "A whole week?" I breathe. "But that . . . So we only have . . . I don't know. I can't math right now."

"Ten weeks," he tells me as though he's already sat down and painfully counted what little time we have left together. "It's going to be alright. I'll be home every weekend and blowing up your phone during the week. You'll be so fucking sick of me, you'll have to come up with new ways to tell me to fuck off."

I swat his chest, gasping in outrage. "I would never do that."

"You're right," he says, a smirk lifting the corner of his lips. "You'll pretend your phone is broken and avoid my calls until I'm busting down the door, demanding an explanation."

"Noah Ryan, you are more trouble than I can handle."

He grins wide and the way those dark eyes sparkle has my heart racing a million miles an hour. His arm tightens around my waist, and he pulls me in, crushing my lips to his as we continue to make up for the three long years spent without each other.

His hands work their way under the material of my shirt and as his fingers skim across the bare skin of my back, he sets me on fire. But I need more. I need him to touch me everywhere.

Reaching down I grip the hem of my tank and work it up over my head, feeling him freeze beneath me, his lips pausing against mine. His gaze shoots to mine as his hands roam over my bare back. "Zo?" he says in a questioning tone, but all I can do is smile back at him.

"Shut up and kiss me," I tell him.

A low growl tears through the back of his throat, and he slams his lips to mine, kissing me deeply as he explores the way my body feels. Then, not wanting to be the only half-naked person in the room, I reach down and grab his shirt, and he's all too eager to tear it over his head.

My heart races, but I can't stop or calm myself down. I've never needed him like this before, and I can't possibly get enough.

Butterflies swarm through the pit of my stomach, and as Noah pulls me right back in, the electricity between us ignites.

My hands roam over his body, feeling the tight ridges of his muscled chest and abs, my fingers digging in and needing more. He keeps kissing me, allowing me to set the pace and take my time with whatever I want to come from this, ready to give me anything I ask for, no matter how big or small.

I pull back, needing to catch my breath as his lips drop to the base of my throat. "Noah," I whisper with a moan, the butterflies now swarming at full speed.

His hand trails right up my spine, curling around my neck as he pulls back to meet my stare. "I don't want you to stop," I tell him.

Noah holds my gaze for a moment, searching my eyes for any sign that I don't really want this, but he won't find any. I've never been so sure in my life. I'm ready.

"Are you sure?" he murmurs, his eyes so full of love.

A small, shy smile slowly spreads across my lips, and I nod as I reach behind me and unhook the clasp of my bra, letting it fall from my arms.

Noah's gaze sails over my body, his chest rising and falling with rapid movement. "Fuck me," he breathes in wonder. "Do you have any idea what you do to me?"

My smile widens as he leans back in to kiss me deeper, his hands roaming all over me, trailing right down to my ass and back up until they lock around my waist. Then in a flash, I'm on my back, and my hair fans out over his pillow as he hovers over me, his hips settled between my thighs.

His gaze is so dark, darker than I've ever seen it, and the desire flashing within those eyes makes me feel more like a woman than ever before. His fingers start in my hair, slowly trailing down the side of my face and to my shoulder, and my gaze locks on his movements.

I swallow hard, a shiver trailing across my skin as he works his way down, over the curve of my breast, and to my waist. The butterflies in my belly have erupted into chaos, but it's the best kind of chaos I've ever felt. I need so much more.

My heart hammers as he leans in close again, his lips pressing down on my collarbone. "I love you so fucking much, Zoey," he tells me, not just repeated, meaningless words, but a declaration of what's inside his heart.

My eyes flutter as his fingers continue working over my sensitive skin. His warm lips work their way down over the curve of my breast until they're closing over my pebbled nipple. My back arches off the bed, and I gasp, never having imagined that it could feel so good.

His hands move further down until they're at the button of my shorts, but I don't dare stop him. Nothing has ever felt so right in my life. I thought I would be a nervous wreck. I imagined my hands would shake and I wouldn't know what to do, but it's the exact opposite, and I realize we were right to wait.

Noah pops the button before slowly dragging the zipper down, and as his thumb hooks into the waistband of my shorts, he pauses again, his gaze lifting back to mine. "If you want me to stop, just say the word," he tells me, his lips hovering above mine.

I tilt my chin, capturing his lips in mine, kissing him slowly. "Don't you dare stop," I whisper. "I've never been so ready. I want this with you more than anything."

A soft groan rumbles through his chest, and he deepens our kiss as he works my shorts and underwear over my hips and down my legs. I kick them off my feet, and as his hands trail further south, my eyes flutter with anticipation.

Reaching between us, I work his belt buckle open and pop the button on his jeans. He helps me push them down, and then I feel him there, and I suck in a breath as the nerves finally begin to creep in. I've never done this before, but I'm more than ready to learn how.

Noah takes his time with me, worshiping every inch of my body as I hook my thigh over his hip. My fingers tangle in his hair, and just when I think it can't get any better, I feel his fingers at my core. He watches me as he works my body, making sure I'm okay, but I've never been so good in my life.

I gasp, sucking in a deep breath as a moan slips from between my lips, and I can't wait a second longer to reach down between us and curl my fingers around him. Slowly working my hand up and down, I get a feel for what I'm doing, and as his head falls to my shoulder, a low groan rumbles through the room, and I can only assume I'm doing something right.

He keeps working me, making me feel things I never thought possible, until his eyes come back to mine. "Zo?" he asks, those dark eyes still searching mine. "Are you ready?"

I nod, holding his stare, the electricity pulsing between us so raw and intense.

His lips come down to mine again, and I feel him reach across the bed to his bedside drawer. There's a crinkle of a wrapper and then his hands are down between us, and I feel him right there at my entrance. "I don't want to hurt you," he tells me, visibly swallowing as if he's nervous. "I'll go slow."

All I can do is nod again, the anticipation burning through me as his palm finds mine, and he laces our fingers together, squeezing gently. Finally, he closes the gap between us, slowly bringing us together as he inches inside of me.

It burns in a way I wasn't expecting, but he takes his time, allowing me to adjust and get used to the alien feel of his delicious intrusion. As I take a shaky breath, his lips come down on mine, his other hand brushing over my hip and down between us to that sensitive bundle of nerves.

He gently rubs, and as my eyes roll with undeniable pleasure, my body finally starts to relax. He smiles against my lips, and with that, he starts to move, blowing my mind and showing me just how good it can be.

Chapter 34

NOAH

Sitting on the edge of Zoey's bed, my head falls in my hands. We have one more night together, less than twenty-four hours before I'm packing my bags and heading to college, and despite the smile that she forces across her face, I know she's breaking inside.

I try to tell her that it's only two hours away and remind her just how often I'll be home. I don't mind driving back every night if she needs me. Nothing is going to change, but it doesn't keep her from reliving the hurt she felt when I forced the distance between us after Linc's death. And I'm not going to lie, despite the easy-going murmurs of confidence I give her, I'm feeling it too.

As a kid, I hated being away from her, and I hated going on family vacations unless I was able to bring her with me. A few times, I flat-out refused until Zoey had her bags packed. The three years without her almost killed me, and now? Fuck. It's going to be hard, but we'll be alright. This is the exact reason why I didn't select another city to play in, otherwise, I would have been a fucking wreck. She would have had to come with me and complete her senior year wherever I ended up, even if her parents said no.

Zoey is my everything, my whole fucking world, and one day, once college is over and I'm signed to the NFL, we'll finally start our lives together. I can see it so perfectly. Zoey is the type to want dog babies before we even think about real ones. Probably a cat or two as well, maybe a bird or a bunny. It'll be a zoo, but it'll be our zoo. Just the thought of starting a family with her gives me chills.

She strides out of her closet, ready for tonight's party, and as I sit up, she climbs straight into my lap and straddles me. It blows me away. Ever since we took our relationship to the next level and slept together, her confidence has shone like the fucking sun. She was never exactly shy with me, but I've since realized just how much she held back, but not anymore.

"What are you thinking about?" she asks, her arms looping around my neck.

"Wouldn't you like to know," I say, gripping her by the ass and lifting us. Her legs immediately lock around my waist, and I walk her straight back into her closet, kicking the door closed behind her as my lips come down on hers.

She laughs and mutters something about ruining her hair and makeup that she just spent far too long on, but she does absolutely nothing to push me away. Instead, she's the one to pull me closer. Then just like the first time I really kissed her in this very closet, I press her up against the wall. The need I have for her is simply never sated.

My lips drop to the base of her neck as she reaches down between us, freeing me from my pants as I reach beneath her short skirt to remove her panties. "Condom?" she pants, bringing my lips back to hers.

I fish one out of my back pocket, and she takes it from me, tearing it open with her teeth before rolling it into place. Then finally, I'm there, pushing into her as she holds on to me, both of us panting with a deep hunger until we're exploding with intense pleasure.

Once she's settled back on her feet, her underwear fixed in place, she steps into me, pressing up on her toes to kiss me. "Are you ready to go?"

"We could just stay here," I suggest, not really in the mood to party tonight, but that's exactly what summer is for, and with Zoey by my side, it's been the best summer of my life.

"You leave tomorrow," she says. "And as much as I'd love to stay right here and do that all over again, you have to go. It's the last time you'll see most of these guys. Besides, it's not like we have to stay all night. Just a quick stop to show your face, and then . . . just you and me."

I groan, pulling her in hard against me. "What the hell happened to you? You're usually the first person to suggest skipping these things, and now you're dying to go?"

Zoey scoffs as she pulls out of my arms and strides across the room to grab her phone off her desk, shutting off the music. "Trust me, I'm definitely not dying to go to this thing," she tells me. "Maybe you've forgotten that apart from you, I literally had no one to talk to at school, so going tonight is only going to remind me just how many friends I don't have. Buuuuut, you have about a billion of them, and they're all desperate to see you one last time."

"I don't give a shit what they want."

"I know," she says with a heavy sigh. "But you're still going, and you're going to have a great time, and when we get home, you're going to spend every last minute loving me." She rolls her tongue over her bottom lip, hunger flashing in her eyes. "You're gonna love me in the back of your car. In my bed. Up against the wall. And maybe if you're lucky, I might even let you love me right here on the floor."

I groan. Her words only make me want to stay home with her more. "Okay, fine," I finally tell her, taking her hand and pulling her into me before leading her out of her room. "But we're staying for an hour, tops. I don't want to waste what's left of tonight on them when I could be with you."

A soft smile spreads across her lips as we make our way downstairs, and as usual, she gets a lecture from her mom about underage drinking while Hazel goes out of her way to offer me a plate of food that looks far too suspicious to be innocent.

Once Zoey's convinced her mom she's not about to turn into a sloppy drunk, we get going, and she remains silent the whole drive out to the lake. "You good?" I ask as I park and get out of the car. I walk around the front and meet her there, taking her hand and leading her toward the party.

"Yeah, fine," she finally says, glancing around. "Just want to get this over and done with so that I don't have to share you."

I give her a tight smile, about to tell her that we'll leave right now, when I see the guys from the football team bounding across the shore of the lake to tackle me away from Zoey. As they pull me away, I glance back, and she gives me a small smile that doesn't reach her eyes. "I'll be fine," she tells me. "Go have fun."

I hold her stare a little while longer, not wanting to leave her alone, but she trails off to get herself a drink and smiles at a few girls. They seem to welcome her in, and when she starts laughing with them, my chest eases, and I allow the guys to drag me away.

They're talking shit and having a few drinks, but I don't touch the drinks table. I'm not willing to put myself in a position where I have to drive drunk and potentially ruin another family's world the same way mine was.

Girls throw themselves at the guys, and Liam goes as far as allowing some chick to suck his dick right here in front of everyone while saying something about how college is going to be amazing. I shove a few girls off me, each of them suggesting they could give me something Zoey never could, but they have no fucking idea just how much she gives me. Shit, without her, I simply couldn't breathe.

People race into the lake, squealing as they splash water at everyone, while some couples take to the nearby woods for some alone time. Not that a few trees in front of them conceal them from the party.

Music blasts across the lake, and as I glance back to check on Zoey, I find her with a cup in her hand, only it doesn't look like she's actually drinking anything. A girl stands in front of her, and there's something eerily familiar about her, but I can't put my finger on it. "Yo," I say to Liam when he's finished with the girl on her knees. "Who's that girl talking to Zo?"

Liam's brows furrow, and he looks out across the lake, scanning the faces before finally finding them. "Oh, I'd recognize that ass anywhere," he says, a smirk stretching across his face. "That's Shannan. You know, the cheerleader you all but condemned to hell."

I scoff, sneering at the girl's back, remembering the fresh hell she put Zoey through. "Okay, but what the fuck is she doing talking to Zoey?"

"Who knows," he says, shrugging his shoulders. "Probably staking her claim for when school goes back."

"What the fuck is that supposed to mean?"

Liam gapes at me. "Shit, man," he laughs. "Are you so fucking wrapped up in your girl you haven't heard what happened? Are you living under a fucking rock?" I give him a blank stare, and he visibly swallows before finally telling me what I need to hear. "Shannan flunked out. She didn't graduate and will be repeating her senior year."

My stomach sinks, and I turn back to the girls, finding horror flashing in Zoey's eyes. I'm sure she's just learned the same thing.

This isn't good. The hell Shannan put Zoey through at the beginning of her junior year is going to look like child's play compared to whatever bullshit she'll rain down over her, and what's worse, I'm not going to be there to put a stop to it.

"SHIT!"

I make my way toward them, ready to put this shit to rest before it even starts, when Liam captures my elbow, pulling me back. "Don't get in the middle of it," he warns me. "That's only going to fuel Shannan. Besides, you're not going to be there this time. Zoey needs to figure out how to do this on her own. Stepping in for her is only going to hinder her more."

Fuck. I hate it when this asshole is right. It's rare, but occasionally it does happen.

"She's going to tear Zoey to shreds."

"Mm-hmm," Liam agrees, but I keep my eyes on Zo, watching as she glances over Shannan's shoulder to find me, and I don't know what she sees in my eyes, but whatever it is prompts her to throw the contents of her cup all over Shannan.

I hear Shannan's scream right across the lake, and as people turn and start laughing, she quickly runs away, leaving the few girls she was talking to fawning all over her. Zoey glances back at me, and I arch a brow, silently asking if she's alright. She shrugs her shoulders before a ridiculous grin stretches across her face. I can just imagine how good that felt. She's been waiting for that moment for almost a year, and it came at the perfect time.

Someone rushes over with a new drink for her, and she gingerly accepts it, but only to be polite. She won't drink anything at a party unless she is the one to make it.

Realizing she's going to be just fine, I drop back into my chair, chilling with the guys just a little while longer, promising myself that I'll give it only another thirty minutes before getting my girl and taking off.

Lucas and Cameron fall in beside me. Lucas sits back with a beer in hand, watching the bikini-clad girls in the water, while Cameron gazes back at the party with one of the cheerleaders in his lap.

"Fuck, man," Liam says to my right. "Senior year was epic. We fucking ruled that school."

"Damn straight we did," Lucas agrees, holding up his beer toward me. "Wouldn't have been the same without you."

"Yeah," I scoff. "None of you assholes would have scholarships or a fucking championship trophy."

Liam scoffs. "Fuck off. We would have been alright."

"Sure you would," I agree, unable to keep the grin off my face as the boys shake their heads. They know I'm right, and up until now, I've been mostly humble about it, but who cares at this point? We all know it's true. No point in pretending it's a secret.

Liam rolls his eyes, and his gaze shifts toward something behind my shoulder before turning his gaze back to the girls in the water. "What do you say, man? Ditch the girlfriend and we'll fuck those bitches out by the woods, just like old times. We can make it a party. Come one, come all."

My face scrunches up in disgust. "The fuck is wrong with you? It almost happened once. Let it go. I'm not about to start fucking girls with you for team sports. You wanna get with them, then get to it. Take these assholes with you, but I'm out."

Liam scoffs. "The fuck is wrong with you, bro? Zoey's got you by the balls. Live a little. You're going to college, and not only that, but you'll be going in with a reputation. You'll be at the top of the fucking food chain. Hoes will be throwing themselves at you, and not just the boring missionary types like Zoey, you'll have the girls who are willing to do anything you want. These are supposed to be the years you let loose and enjoy yourself. This is when you're supposed to fuck around and make stupid mistakes, but you went and got yourself attached."

I shake my head. I've never bothered to explain to these guys the depth of our relationship. I don't even think they realize that Zoey and I knew each other before I came to East View. But whether they know about us or not, Liam knows better than to talk about my girl. I've had to knock him out a few times over the past year, and unfortunately, this seems to be a lesson he refuses to learn. "Alright, I'm out of here," I say, getting up.

I don't bother to say goodbye as I walk away, and when Liam whines at my back, calling me a little bitch, I just keep moving. He doesn't matter to me. After tonight, I'll never have to see him again. I'll never have to put up with him unless I just happen to face him on the field, but it's unlikely. He won't make it through the first season, and if he somehow does, he sure as hell won't make it on the field. He'll be a reserve if he's lucky.

Letting out a heavy breath, I walk toward the group of girls Zoey was hanging out with and come up short, not seeing her familiar wave of chestnut hair. My brows furrow, and I scan the party, looking over the faces and checking the drinks table. I even turn back to the lake, making sure she didn't feel the need to go for a midnight swim.

Not finding her, I pull my phone out and quickly pull up her name before hitting call, only it rings out and my heart starts to race. I try again, but this time, the ringing cuts off as though she rejected the call.

"What the fuck?" I mutter to myself, still searching the faces. Perhaps she snuck away to pee.

I write out a text, needing to know she's alright.

Noah: You good? Can't find you.
Zoey: Do me a favor and leave me alone. I'm going home.

What in the actual fuck?

I try calling her again, and she rejects it almost immediately, forcing me into a sprint toward my car, determined to find her. I swear, if she's left this party and is walking home alone after midnight, I'm going to lose my shit.

Noah: What's wrong? Where are you? I'll come get you.
Zoey: What do you say, man? Ditch the girlfriend and we'll fuck those bitches out by the woods, just like old times. We can make it a party. Come one, come all.

Fuck. I can almost hear Liam's tone in her text, and it has me just about ready to turn around and put the fucker out, but if it weren't for the idea that Zoey is out there somewhere, possibly alone on the side of the street, I probably would have. I saw the way he glanced over my shoulder before saying that. He must have seen her and decided he knew what was best for our relationship.

Noah: You know I don't think like that. Liam is an asshole. That's no secret. The only person I want is you.
Zoey: I know.

There's a short pause before her next text comes through.

Zoey: I just need a little space. Clear my head.
Noah: At least let me take you home. I don't want you

walking home like this. Your dad will kill me.

    Zoey: It's fine. I got a lift from Abby and Cora. I'm safe.

    Noah: Babe, it's our last night.

    Zoey: I know…

Hitting the gas, I peel out of the parking lot, determined to get back to her, hitting call on her number again, only this time it goes straight to voicemail, and I realize she's turned her phone off. Panic tears at my chest, not wanting to spend what little time we have left together like this, but if she needs time, I'm not going to force it.

Then just to make sure she's really alright, I drive by her house, slowing to a stop and looking up at her bedroom window, watching as she makes her way around her room. Then as if hearing the rumble of my engine outside, she strides across to her window and just stands there a moment, her gaze lingering on mine. My heart races, waiting for her to pick up the phone and tell me it's alright to come in, only she makes a show of locking her window before pulling her blinds closed.

A moment later, her room falls into darkness and with my heart crumbling in my chest, I drive away, knowing this is so much more than what Liam said. She's terrified of what tomorrow signifies, terrified that I'm going to slip away and that a newfound distance is going to force its way between us, but I'm not going to let that happen, and I know damn well that she won't either.

But if she needs tonight, then I'll give her that, and in the morning . . . fuck. In the morning, I'll hold her for as long as she needs as we say goodbye.

Chapter 35

NOAH

I've been pacing back and forth in my room since five this morning, and as seven rolls around, I can't wait another damn second. My car roars to life, and I'm speeding down the road toward Zoey's place.

After leaving her place last night, I sat in my car at the park, staring out at the empty swing set where we used to share all our wild secrets. By the time I got home, I was about ready to turn back around and crawl straight into her bed, desperately needing to hold her. Instead, I stayed up and packed my bags, a job I'd put off for weeks simply because I didn't want it to feel this real. But now, there's only three hours left.

Three hours before I drive away, and I'll be damned if I leave without saying goodbye. I've made that mistake once before, and I'll never do it again.

I think I slept all of two hours before flying out of bed to get to my girl.

Last night sucked, but I don't think she's angry with me. If she heard our conversation, then she knows I told Liam to fuck off, so that's not the problem. I think she's angry and frustrated with the whole situation, and I can't blame her. She hates that I'm going away, hates the thought of putting this distance between us again, and hates that she can't just reach out and hold me.

Shit. I hate it too.

But it's only a year. At least, that's what I keep telling myself. No amount of repeating that is ever going to make it an easier pill to swallow.

A whole fucking year.

I don't know how the hell I made it through three.

Two hours. Two fucking light-years.

Pulling up at her place, I cut the engine and make my way toward the side of the fence, more than ready to take the shortcut straight up to her room, but the front door opens, and Zoey's dad appears before me, his lips pressed into a tight line.

Shit. I guess I'll be going through the front door after all.

"I don't know what happened between you two last night," he says, "but she's not here."

I stop in the middle of the lawn, my gaze pointedly shifting to her Range Rover still parked in the driveway. "Really? She's not here," I question, letting him hear the doubt in my tone, more than happy to call him on his bullshit if it means making things right with Zoey.

Henry gives me a blank stare, and I inch closer to the front door. "Please. I just need to see her," I beg. "I'm leaving today, and I—" I let out a heavy sigh, "I can't leave without telling her goodbye."

"I don't know what to tell you, Noah. She's really not here," he says. "She took off about an hour ago."

"Fuck." I turn and start pacing across the lawn, just as I'd done this morning, my jaw clenching. If she's not here, that means she's still upset, still falling apart. I should have left ages ago. I could have made things right by now and taken the pain and fear out of her heart.

It takes all of two seconds to figure out where she's gone, especially considering that her car is still here. There's only one place she ever goes to be alone.

Just as I turn away, Henry calls out to me. "Noah," he says, stopping me in my tracks. I glance back, my hands balling into fists at my side. "Don't break her heart this time."

"That's the last thing I'll ever do," I tell him. "She's just anxious about me going to college, but I'm not going anywhere. This isn't like last time."

"I hope not," he says. "It's been a long time since I've had to sit up at night listening to my daughter cry herself to sleep."

Jesus Christ. It's like a rusty blade right through the heart.

"Like I told you last fall, Zoey and I are two halves of the same whole. She won't be able to get rid of me, even if she tries. I'm in this for the long haul," I tell him. "I don't know if you've noticed, but I'm in love with your daughter, sir. I plan on having a whole life with her. Marriage, children, a whole fucking zoo if she wants it, and I'll be right by her side until fate comes to take me out of this world. We only have a year of distance to get through and then we'll be done. She's strong, she's going to be okay, and in those times she's not, I'll be straight in the car, flying down the highway to get to her. This year is going to be hard and sometimes she's going to hate me for being so far away, but we're going to get through it."

He just watches me through a curious gaze as though he still hasn't worked out if he wants to forgive me for the three long years of hell I put Zoey through, and honestly, he shouldn't. Those years caused his daughter irreparable hurt and left scars all over her heart—ones I've been desperately trying to heal, but scars never fully go away. Once you've been hurt, the memory will always linger, terrified it could happen again.

"Okay, Noah," he finally says with a slight nod. "Go get our girl."

I nod, breathing a sigh of relief as I storm back to my Camaro and kick it over before the door even slams behind me. I hit the gas, performing a U-turn right in front of Zoey's house and doubling back the way I came, kicking myself for not having checked the park first.

Pulling up a few minutes later, I spy Zoey on a swing like always. When she hears the roar of my engine, she glances back over her shoulder and meets my stare through my windshield, offering me a small smile that doesn't meet her eyes.

She's broken, and it has everything to do with me.

My gut twists into knots as I step out of my car, and as Zoey turns her attention back to the ground in front of her, I walk across the park, the Arizona sun already bearing down on us.

I walk around the swing and plant myself in front of her, my knees dropping into the sand as my hands reach out, gently gripping her calves. There's a deep sadness rooted in her eyes as she looks up, and it's clear by the puffy redness that she's spent the night in tears. "I was wondering how long it would take before you showed up here."

"I would have been here earlier, but I convinced myself to wait for the sun to rise first," I tell her. "I've been up since five."

"Packing?" she questions, a hesitant tone in her voice.

"Yes," I say, "But that's not why I was up. I couldn't sleep, not after leaving things like that."

Her gaze falls away, the sadness radiating out of her and crushing me. "Zo," I whisper, reaching up and stroking my thumb across her cheek, wiping away the fresh tears. "I hate that you're hurting like this and there's nothing I can do to take it away."

"I'm sorry," she whispers. "I ruined our last night together. That wasn't how I pictured last night, but when I heard Liam talking about the kind of life you're going to have in college, it just became all too real."

I shake my head, taking her hand in mine. "Liam was wrong," I tell her. "What he said . . . That's not my life or one that I want to have. That's his idea of the perfect college lifestyle, but for me, all I want to do is focus on training, games, classes, and you. I don't give a shit about the girls or the parties or the booze. All I'm focusing on is training and games until I get to have you there with me."

"Are you sure?" she whispers, her bottom lip wobbling. "Because if you need to take this year to go be wild, sleep with every girl who looks at you, or go crazy at every single frat party that pops up, then do it. Rip it off like a Band-Aid, but don't string me along. I'll understand, really. I'll hate it, and I'll be devastated, but it's better than being lied to. That's what college is for, right? We're so young to be in a committed relationship. It's a lot. I get that, but I just don't want to get five or ten years down the track and come home to you saying that you resent me for not having those years to go crazy."

I shake my head, unable to believe what the hell I'm hearing. "Zoey," I breathe, my hands sliding back down to her calves and gently squeezing. "Where the hell is this coming from?"

She shrugs her shoulders, wiping away more tears. "I just—"

"No," I say, cutting her off. "Have I ever given you the impression that I give a shit about that kind of stuff?"

"No, but—"

"Have I ever led you to believe that I want to be with anyone but you?"

She swallows hard, her throat bobbing. "No."

"Then stop working yourself up over this," I beg, giving her a tug until she's falling off the edge of the swing and down into my lap. I wrap her in my arms, and she buries her face into my chest, wiping her tears on my shirt. "I don't want to spend these last few hours with you hurting."

"I'm sorry," she murmurs into my chest. "I'm just . . . I'm so terrified of watching you leave again. It hurts so much, but I know deep down that we're going to be perfectly fine. You're going to come home as much as you can, and I'll come visit. But no matter how much either of us tries to convince ourselves that nothing is going to change, we both know that the second you get in your car, everything changes."

"Fuck, Zo," I murmur, my voice breaking as something grabs ahold of my heart and squeezes. "I don't know what I can say to you to make this better or how to make the hurt go away, but just know that with every single beat of your heart, I'll love you even more."

My hand runs over her hair, feeling her finally start to calm against me. "We're not going into this blind, Zo. We know this next year is going to be hard, and you're right, we can pretend all we want and try to convince ourselves that everything is going to stay exactly the same, but it's not. You're not going to be right there when I need you, and I'm not going to be there to hold you when you've had a shitty day, but I promise you that every chance I get, I will be there for you. All you need to do is call, and I will drop everything to get to you. Whether we're in the middle of a tornado or you just want someone to hold you because life is shit. I will come. Do you hear me, Zo? I. Will. Come."

She nods against my chest before finally lifting her head, her red, swollen eyes lingering on mine. A moment of silence passes between us when she drops her forehead against mine, closing her eyes and simply breathing me in. "I'm terrified of how much it's going to hurt to miss you, and Noah," she whispers, "I'm going to miss you every second of every day."

My heart shatters, and I crush her to me, holding on as though I'll never let her go. "I love you so fucking much, Zoey," I murmur into her hair. "The thought of leaving you behind, of not getting to touch you every day, to see the way your eyes light up when you smile at me or feel that pull between us when you walk into a room. It's killing me. I don't want you to learn how to not need me."

"I will never not need you," she vows.

We remain in each other's arms, and I lay back against the sandy ground of the park, refusing to let go. She silently cries into my chest, her tears soaking my shirt as she sniffles, and each time she does, I tighten my hold around her, my fingers slowly brushing back and forth over her skin.

Almost an hour passes before she lets out a shaky breath. "When do you have to leave?" she asks. "Ten," I tell her. "But I can push it out to eleven."

"What's the time now?"

"I don't know. Maybe eight-thirty. Nine."

"Shit," she mutters, pulling herself up off my chest and hastily wiping her eyes on the back of her arms.

"Do you want to get breakfast?" I ask, determined to make every minute of this time count. "I can take you back to my place to get my stuff. Then drop you home and say goodbye to Hazel and your parents."

I specifically don't mention saying goodbye to her, knowing what those words will do to her. Instead, I just watch her, waiting to see what she wants to do. "I don't think I could eat," she tells me. "But I don't want you to go without me."

"Okay," I tell her, getting to my feet and offering my hand to help her up beside me. "Then it's back to my place."

Zoey steps right into my side, and I take her hand before looping my arm right over her shoulder. "We're going to be okay," I promise her. "We haven't come this far and fought this hard just for something like a year of college to screw it up for us. I stand by what I said, Zo. You're gonna be so fucking sick of me blowing up your phone, you're gonna be begging me to leave you alone."

A smile pulls at her lips, and it breathes life right back into me. "You and I both know that's never going to happen," she tells me, her smile stretching just a little bit wider before we reach my car, and with that, she drops down inside as I try to figure out how the hell I'm supposed to say goodbye to my whole damn world.

Chapter 36

ZOEY

Despite the summer sun blazing high in the sky, the world has never felt so dull. My heart aches in a way that I wasn't prepared for, and with every passing second, it only gets worse.

Noah pulls up outside my house, and despite knowing he's coming in to say goodbye to my family, we just sit here, neither of us wanting to go in. Because once we do, we're one step closer to goodbye, and we both know just what that goodbye is going to do to me.

I've never ached like this, and a part of me knows just how ridiculous it is. I'll see him every night on FaceTime and probably almost every weekend, but something feels so final about it. His life is going to change over the next year. He's going to become the star of the Wildcats and every person in the state is going to want something from him, whether they want to be his best friend or want to see just how well he can put it down.

Women are going to throw themselves at him, and the crazy life of partying will try to lure him in, but I trust him. I trust what he said this morning, that none of it matters to him. He's spent the past few years in a downward spiral, and I don't think he wants to go back there anytime soon. But it still hurts.

I was a fool to allow Liam's bullshit words to affect me, to ruin our last night together. I could have spent hours wrapped in his arms, but instead, I spent what little time we had left uncontrollably sobbing in bed. I feel like such an idiot, and what's worse, my inability to see past my own selfish emotions means that Noah had a shit night too.

The clock ticks dangerously close to eleven, and my heart races, not wanting to face the fact that this is about to happen. But hiding from reality isn't going to make it any less true.

Noah lets out a heavy, broken sigh before reaching over and squeezing my thigh. "Come on," he murmurs. "If we sit out here any longer, your dad's probably going to kick my ass."

A small smile pulls at the corners of my lips. My dad has his hang-ups about my relationship with Noah and hasn't quite been able to forgive him as quickly as I have. Though there's no denying how happy Noah makes me, and that's the only thing that keeps my father from trying to step in.

"Okay," I say with a heavy breath as my fingers curl around the door handle and quickly open it before I change my mind.

We slowly walk up the path together, hand in hand, taking advantage of every last second, and then before I can even reach for the door, it flies open, and my little sister stands before us, looking up at Noah as though she's just as broken.

Hazel stumbles out to the porch with her arms wide, and as she crashes into Noah, she holds him tight, pinning his arms to his side. "Do you really have to go?" she questions, sounding almost as broken as I feel. "You have to call every day. Oh, and when you get there, FaceTime me. I wanna see what a college dorm looks like, and . . .

Maybe me and Zo could come for a campus tour because I've never been there before, and we all know Zoey isn't going to say no to that."

Her string of comments falls out of her mouth like word vomit. It's like she has far too much to say that she can't think straight or decide which comment is more important than the other.

"You know I'm only two hours down the road, right?" Noah laughs, wrestling his arms free so that he can give her a proper hug. "Plus, I'll be home on the weekends."

Hazel scoffs and pulls out of Noah's arms, a skill I clearly haven't mastered that well. "I don't care about that," she says. "I just wanna know all about college life. You know, I wasn't born for this whole middle school thing. It's kinda dull. But college, I'm going to dominate at college."

I shake my head, and just as I go to remind her just how long it will be before she can live her dominating life, my parents move into the open doorway. Mom's lips press into a tight line as if trying to keep herself from being emotional. "Oh Noah," she says, walking right into him and pulling him into a tight hug. "How are you already off to college? It feels like just yesterday I was watching you and Zoey stuffing your faces full of candy and then whining about stomach aches."

My father mutters under his breath. "They still do that."

Noah laughs as my mom moves back to give him space. "It's gone faster than I care to admit," he says, sparing a quick glance at me.

"Well, that happens when you disappear for three years," Hazel chimes in with a smirk, but damn, doesn't she know how the reminder of that time tends to slice me wide open?

"You're not wrong," Noah tells her, trying to keep the mood light.

"You have everything you need?" Dad questions.

Noah glances at my father and gives him a firm nod. "Yep, all good, sir."

"Good, then don't be a stranger," my father responds, a strange emotion flashing in his eyes, one I'm not really sure I can decode. "I don't need any more reasons to want to kick your ass."

My eyes widen in horror, and my jaw practically falls to the ground. "Dad!" I hiss. I've never heard him so forward with Noah before, but Noah seems to take it in stride. He doesn't even flinch at the comment.

Mom and Dad step outside onto the porch with us, and before I know it, we're all huddled by Noah's Camaro as Mom and Hazel give Noah another round of hugs. But all I can do is stare at his car, contemplating if I could somehow get away with slicing all four of his tires before any of them can stop me.

I zone out trying to shield my heart from the words of my mother's teary goodbye, and then all too soon, my family slips away to give us space.

This is it.

This is the moment I've been dreading since he first told me about his acceptance.

My hands shake as Noah steps into me, and his hand curls into mine to hold it steady. His dark eyes lock on to mine. "Are you okay?" he asks hesitantly.

I nod, not trusting the way the words will come out if I say them aloud.

He stands right in front of me, his chest so close to mine but not quite touching as though he's trying to be respectful of my family watching. He takes my other hand as well, lacing our fingers as he tilts his head toward me. "You're strong, Zo," he tells me because God knows, I feel as though I've forgotten. "You kicked leukemia's ass and got through a year of hell during your junior year. And on top of that, you survived through the grief of losing Linc when I wasn't here to hold you up. This is nothing compared to all of that."

"That doesn't mean it's going to suck any less."

"I know," he tells me. "Nothing I can say or do is going to lessen the sting of having to be away from you, Zo. And though it feels like our whole world is crumbling, we're gonna be fine. You'll see. It's nothing more than a stepping stone that will lead us to the life we'll eventually be living together."

A small smile pulls at the corners of my lips, but I can't help the silent tears that track down my face. "I like the way that sounds."

His eyes sparkle with warmth. "I thought you might."

I let out a shaky breath. "You really have to go now?"

"Yeah," he says before releasing my hands and brushing his thumbs over my cheeks, wiping away the constant flow of tears. He pulls me into his chest, his strong arms curling around me. One clutches my back, and the other knots into my hair as he holds me tighter than ever before. "Fuck, I knew this was going to be hard, but I didn't think it would kill me like this."

"Don't, Noah," I warn, my voice shaky. "If you fall apart, I'll be a wreck."

"I love you more than anything in this world, Zo. Just one word from you, and I'll be right back here."

I nod against his chest, wiping my eyes on his shirt. "I love you too," I tell him when I feel his fingers at my chin, lifting my face until those dark, dreamy eyes are locked securely on mine.

"Not goodbye, Zo. Just see you later."

"*Not goodbye*," I repeat, and then his lips are on mine, kissing me deeply as I fall apart in his arms. He holds me up, not daring to let me fall, and when he pulls away, I feel my mother's hand on my shoulder.

She tugs me back into her gently, and I shake my head, watching as Noah strides to his car. "No," I breathe, my heart shattering inside my chest as my mother hugs me from behind, pressing a kiss to my temple.

Noah pauses by his car door and glances back at me, and the look in his eyes makes me falter. He was putting on a show for me, being brave so that I wouldn't break quite so bad, but damn it, he's just as shattered as I am. Then before he convinces himself to run back into my arms, he gets into his car, and the loud engine rumbles through the quiet street.

I pull out of my mother's arms, my head shaking more violently as desperation pulses through my veins. This can't be it. I take off, racing toward his car. "NOAH!" I cry, but he's gone in a flash, hitting the gas and storming down the street as I feel that tether between us stretching and adapting to this new normal.

A loud sob tears from the back of my throat as I hurry out into the road, every last piece of my soul tearing to shreds, and despite being so far away and unable to see through the flood of tears pouring from my eyes, I know he sees me through the rearview mirror, watching as his whole world gets further and further away.

Then as I watch his car disappear around the bend, what's left of me crumbles, and I fall to my knees on the hard asphalt, the remnants of my soul turning to ash and blowing away with the last of summer.

Chapter 37

ZOEY

A year ago today, Noah blasted back into my world like a soldier on a mission, only at that point, neither of us had any idea what his mission actually was. Now, looking back on everything that came from the past twelve months, I almost can't believe it.

It's been a week since he left for college, and while he's stuck to his word and called me every day, it hasn't been the same. There's nothing I hate more than distance, but if having mere scraps of him is what I need to survive over the next year, then that's exactly what I'll do.

I stare in my mirror.

Senior year.

I always thought that I'd be excited when this time came, but somehow, I just know this is going to be the hardest year of my life. Shannan has already let me know that she plans on rising back to the top this year, and I'm not going to lie, I was kinda hoping the humiliation of having to repeat her senior year would keep her down, but apparently, she's not the type to learn from her mistakes. Or perhaps now that I don't have Noah backing me at school, she will no longer see me as a threat. If that's the case, I'll be her favorite target all over again.

Then there's Tarni.

I've known her too long not to assume that she isn't going to try to work her way back into the spotlight. She likes the attention too much, and if she has to step on me to get in with Shannan and her followers, she will. The only difference is, she doesn't have Abby and Cora backing her up anymore. Truth be told, I was kinda hoping that Abby and Cora might have grown up a little over the summer and wouldn't completely hate it if I hung out with them. They were happy to drive me home from the lake party last week, but I'm almost certain they just felt sorry for me.

Letting out a heavy breath, I finish brushing through my hair and twist it up into a bun before backing up a few steps and dropping down onto the end of my bed. I've been so tired this week, and I keep telling myself that it's just the emotional turmoil of being so far away from Noah, but there's this little nagging feeling in the back of my mind warning me that it's something more.

It's not normal to be this tired, to wake up first thing in the morning feeling lethargic. Most nights this week I've gone to bed early after the dizzy spells hit, and damn it, it makes me so nervous.

I was only six when I was diagnosed with leukemia. I remember the day so clearly. It's the day I forced Noah to fake propose to me in the backyard. Linc was three and running around doing his own thing, and Hazel was still just a baby.

Noah had gotten down on one knee, told me how beautiful I was, and then asked me to marry him. It was everything—until he decided he didn't like my girl kisses. I suppose things really do change because now, it seems that my stupid girl kisses are his most favorite thing in the world.

It was maybe only an hour or so after that when my parents sat me down and told me what was happening to me, and I didn't understand a single thing. They were telling me I was a very sick little girl, but I remember thinking they were wrong. I didn't feel sick. I was fine, but the hell the doctors had in store for me . . .

I don't ever want to go through that again. But this is different. This tiredness, this lack of energy . . . It has to be different, right?

Maybe I'm just imagining the whole thing just to keep myself from having to go to school. Besides, Mom takes me for regular tests, and in six months, I'll hit the ten-year anniversary of being cancer-free.

The thought has my gaze shifting to the framed picture of me in that damn hospital bed. I feel a million miles away from that little girl. She was so strong. She knew exactly what she wanted in life and had the spirit and determination to fight for it. But that's not me. I feel like that little girl is a ghost who lives inside of me now, slowly fading away and screaming to be heard.

Glancing toward the clock, I realize if I don't leave now, I'll end up being late for homeroom, and that's not exactly how I want to start my first day of senior year.

Grabbing my things, I take off down the stairs, finding Hazel striding out of the kitchen with an apple in her hand. "You ready?" I ask.

She nods. "Mm-hmm," she mumbles, clearly not thrilled about going back to school either, and with that, we walk out the door and down to my Range Rover.

I'm just backing out of the driveway when a call comes through Bluetooth, and Noah's name appears on the screen. I press the little accept button on the steering wheel as I continue backing out onto the road. "I knew you'd be late," his voice fills the car.

"I am not late," I argue.

"Bullshit," he mutters. "Hazel?"

"Oh yeah," the little brat says, her eyes sparkling with mirth. "She's definitely late. Had to skip out on breakfast and everything."

"Babe," Noah groans. "You need to eat."

"I will," I grumble, knowing damn well I don't have time to stop and get something. It'll have to wait, but it's fine. It's not like I'm planning on participating in an intense workout over the next few hours. I'll be more than alright.

A nearly inaudible sigh comes through the phone, and I cringe, knowing exactly what's coming. "You're such a liar, Zoey Erica James."

"Don't you dare middle name me, Noah McAssCrack Ryan."

"You did not just call me a McAssCrack."

"Whatcha gonna do about it?" I throw back at him.

He laughs, and the sound wraps around me, thawing me from the inside out and giving me exactly what I need to make it through the day. We chat about boring things, but the second he hears me drop Hazel off at her school, the conversation shifts. "I fucking miss you, Zo," he says, undeniable pain in his tone. "How are you doing?"

"Barely holding on," I admit, being as honest as I can. "Every time I get in this car, I have to convince myself not to drive to you."

"You can, you know," he tells me. "I'll drop everything, even if it's only to hold you for two seconds."

"Don't tempt me," I tell him. "Are you ready for classes to start?"

"I suppose," he mutters, probably not giving a shit about his classes. "You?"

Despite him not being able to see me, I shrug in response. "I just want to make it through the door without being eaten alive."

"Don't let Shannan push you around, Zo. She's a nobody with a bruised ego who has already peaked," he tells me, and while he's definitely right, it doesn't make it any easier, especially considering that I'll be walking in there without a single friend at my back. Shannan on the other hand will probably be trying out for cheer captain again and will inevitably become the most popular girl in school. I just hope that she'll be spending the day more interested in figuring out which football protégé she'll be digging her claws into.

"Yeah, easier said than done," I tell him as I pull into the student parking lot of East View High, wishing I could be anywhere but here.

I sit and stare up at the school as the other students flood through the gates, most of them looking more than excited about being here and seeing all their friends again. "Zo, you got quiet on me," he says. "You're there, aren't you?"

I let out a heavy sigh. "Yeah," I groan. "I better get going."

"Okay," he says, a smirk in his tone. "For the record, I'll still love you if you accidentally clock Shannan right in the face. After all, nothing puts a mean bitch in her place better than a broken nose, but if you're going to punch her, remember your thumb goes on the outside. I can't have you breaking your fingers. I'm gonna need them for when I see you next. Oh, and make sure someone records it because that'll be the perfect addition to my spank-bank."

My mouth drops as my cheeks flush the darkest shade of pink. "Noah!" I shriek.

He laughs. "Get your ass to homeroom, Zo," he tells me. "You're going to be fine, but if you just happen to have a moment where you feel like your world is falling apart, just think about how good it's going to feel when I'm sliding inside of your sweet pu—."

"Holy shit, Noah," I flush. "I'm hanging up."

"Bye, Zo," he says in that deep, sultry tone. Then before I melt into a puddle right here in my car, I press the little red button to end the call, preparing to get out and make my way through the gates of hell.

The bell sounds for lunch, and I quickly hurry out of Ms. Lennon's classroom. While part of me loves that I have her again for my senior year, I hate that I now share this class with Shannan. She's been in three of my classes so far today, which isn't exactly how I wanted to start the day, but for the most part, all she's done is sneer at me. Though I'm not foolish enough to think that's all that's coming my way.

I suppose I could always punch her right in the face—with my thumb on the outside of course—and call it an accident. I've got most of the faculty in my back pocket, especially Principal Daniels. He's got a soft spot for me after Mom told him all about my past. He's always looked out for me and made sure I was doing alright, even going out of his way to put Noah in his place this time last year.

Making my way down the busy corridor, I find my locker and start rifling through it, and by the time I close the door, my anxiety has started to build. I've been dreading this all day.

Checking my phone, I find a text from Noah with a picture attached, and I open it up to find an image of the incredible view of the Wildcats arena from right at the very top of the massive grandstand. A wide grin stretches across my face, knowing just how much he'd love that. This has always been his dream. At least, a very important stepping stone to the ultimate dream of playing for the NFL, which will be a whole new experience in itself, but I have no doubt that he'll make it. He's too good not too.

But the pictures I've been getting from him this week only go to prove that he's in his zone right now. He's exactly where he needs to be, and I need to do what I can to reel in my emotions because I don't want to ruin this for him. I don't want him to feel guilty every time he steps onto the training field. I want him to soak up every moment of college life and absolutely love it because he deserves no less. He put the work in to get where he wants to go, and I want to see him succeed with every part of my soul.

Leaning against my locker, I quickly shoot off a reply.

Zoey: That's incredible! But I'm still waiting for my locker room pic. Preferably when everyone has just had their showers and they're all dripping wet with towels low on their hips. Actually, scrap that, just take the pic with all of you sandwiched in those showers together. You know, I really wanna feel like I'm experiencing it right there by your side.

Resident Asshole: Don't make me come down there, Zoey James. I'm not above bending you over my knee and spanking that bad behavior out of you.

I gape at my phone. He's always been the biggest flirt with me, but he's been on fire today, pushing the boundaries, and I absolutely love it.

Zoey: Noah McWashYourFilthyMouthOut Ryan, stop making me blush at school. You're supposed to be a gentleman.

Resident Asshole: Let's be honest, being a gentleman is boring. You prefer it when I'm throwing you up against a wall and fucking you until you scream.

Hooooooly shit.

Zoey: **skull emoji**
Zoey: I need a cold shower. Maybe two.

Resident Asshole: Yeah…me too.

I laugh and tuck my phone into my pocket before heading down the hallway with my head held a little higher, and it has everything to do with the suspicious timing of Noah's texts. He's been doing it all day, as if knowing exactly when I would need him to give me the strength to keep going. Even miles away, he's still helping me get through the day.

No one ever claimed that Noah Ryan didn't know the exact path to my heart.

Making my way into the cafeteria, I blow out a heavy breath, quickly scanning the room. The game plan—find Abby and Cora and hope for the best. Only I pause by the door when I find them sitting side by side at our old table with Tarni standing before them, easing her way right back in as though she didn't spend the last year ostracized from the world.

Tarni says something else, and the next thing I know, the girls welcome her back in with open arms. She sits down on the opposite side of the table, and I feel myself starting to slip.

Shit.

"You new here?" a voice asks beside me.

My brows furrow as I turn to find an unfamiliar face staring back at me, and I shake my head as I take her in. She's stunning, definitely someone who will have jaws dropping all over the school. She has the kindest smile I've ever seen, immediately putting me at ease. "Nah, just trying to figure out where the hell I'm supposed to fit in all of this," I tell her, feeling as though I can be honest with her.

"Me too," she says, sparing a glance toward the busy cafeteria, looking as though she's about ready to pass out with nerves. "I'm Hope. I just transferred from St. Michael's and don't know a single person."

"Well, now you know me," I tell her with a wide smile, wondering if she knew Noah back when he was a junior at St. Michael's, raising hell all over campus. "Come on, we can be clueless together."

Hope smiles back at me, relief in her eyes as she loops her arm through mine, and we stride across the cafeteria to the one empty table left in the room. We make ourselves comfortable, and as I give her the rundown of the school, I don't miss the curious glances I get from Tarni across the room.

"Okay, so there's probably a few things you need to know about this school before you decide to get too close to me," I say, giving her a fair warning about what it will mean to be my friend. "I um . . . I'm dating last year's quarterback, which kinda put me on the shitlist with the cheerleaders, and well . . . the cheer captain, Shannan. She was supposed to graduate but didn't. So now she's repeating her senior year, and I can guarantee now that Noah's not here to scare her away, she's going to try and make my life a living hell."

"Shit," she says, her brows arching. "She sounds like fun."

"Oh yeah, she's a real treat," I tell her. "I've been mobbed in this very cafeteria too many times than I care to count. Not to mention, she trained the whole student body to chant *trash* every time I walked into a room last year."

"That's um . . . kinda terrifying, but also," she says in a teasing voice, "props to her for having that kind of pull over such a big school. That's certainly impressive."

"I mean, I have other descriptive words for it, but sure, let's go with impressive."

Hope laughs, and her blonde ringlets fall over her shoulder, framing her pretty face. "Seriously though, I'm not into that shitty behavior. I find it embarrassing. People who act like that . . . I don't know, they might as well be holding a sign above their heads saying *I'm*

SHERIDAN ANNE

insecure. It's not cool, and I'm sorry that you were tormented like that over something so silly as being with the person you love. At least, I don't mean to make assumptions that you're in love with this mystery boyfriend of yours, but like, are you?"

I laugh, a wide grin stretching over my face, and before I can even respond, Hope's grinning right back at me. "Oh yeah. You're definitely in love with this guy. What did you say his name was? Noah?"

"Yeah, that's right," I say. "Actually, you might know him. He would have been a senior at St. Michael's last year, but he transferred."

"Quarterback, you said?" I nod and she scrunches her face. "Maybe. But to be completely honest, I'm not into football. Now, those scrawny computer nerds with cute faces who blush every time a girl looks their way—Now that's what I'm into. As for your boyfriend, the name kinda rings a bell, but I couldn't put a face to the name even if I tried."

I smile. The thought of having a friend who isn't in love with my boyfriend eases my fears and makes me want to keep her. "Um . . . Okay. So totally don't judge him on this, but you might know him as the guy who burned down your principal's office."

Hope's jaw drops, and she gapes at me. "No way," she breathes. "Okay, yeah. I know exactly who you're talking about." She laughs and shakes her head, almost unable to believe what she's hearing. "Wow, girl. I have to be honest. You don't strike me as the kind to go after the typical player bad boy."

"Dare I ask what type you think I would go for?" I ask, not bothering to correct her on the *typical player bad boy* comment. She wouldn't understand.

Hope looks at me for a moment, really thinking it through. "I don't know," she says thoughtfully. "You definitely seem like a girl who goes for the athlete type, someone with a sexy body, but not someone high up on the roster who's going to give you a hard time when it comes to other girls. I don't think you're interested in that shit. Maybe like, the typical nice guy, golden-retriever vibe."

I laugh. "In that case, you have me pinned pretty well. That's Noah all over. Only he has a mean streak for anyone who wants to screw with me and doesn't let the outside world see the real him. Ask anyone in this school, and they'd say Noah is the biggest ass they've ever met, but not me. I've known him since we were . . . Well, since I was born really. He was my first friend, and he's been right by my side ever since. He's the only one who's ever truly had my back."

I don't bother to explain those three dark years, that's definitely a conversation for when I know her better. But I already know, without a doubt, that I'll be comfortable opening up about it and telling her all about Linc.

"You know, that is honestly the sweetest thing I've ever heard. Best friends growing up together and slowly falling in love."

"Oh, there was nothing slow about it," I scoff. "I was madly in love with him at thirteen, and it's only ever gotten stronger. He tells people all the time that we're two halves of the same whole."

"Soul mates," she murmurs, her blue eyes shining with fondness.

"Exactly," I tell her. "What about you? What's your story?"

Hope scoffs. "Compared to that, my story is boring. I've never had that big, all-consuming first love or had any issues with nasty girls. I'm just . . . plain Hope. Just hoping to get through high school without any drama—but maybe a handful of parties."

"You know what?" I say, a genuine smile resting across my lips as I meet her kind, icy blue eyes. "Stick with me. You sound like everything I could possibly need."

Chapter 38

ZOEY

My luck has more than run out.

We're four weeks into senior year, and just as I expected, Shannan couldn't wait to play her wicked games. Only it's so much worse than it ever was last year. She's had time to plan and hit me right where it hurts. Rather than public performances to humiliate me, which would leave her vulnerable to witnesses, she keeps it private. Stalking me into bathrooms. Editing my face onto naked selfies to spread through the school. She's even gone as far as hacking into my phone and spreading some of my risqué texts with Noah.

Tarni hasn't been any better either.

Now that she's got her friends back and is no longer the school outcast shamed under Noah's reign, she's moving back up the ranks and taking revenge in the form of snide comments and insults. Though, I know Tarni better than she knows herself. This is only the beginning.

School is about to become my biggest nightmare. The little six-year-old version of me who was fighting cancer would even pity me now. If I didn't have Hope, I'd be lost. She's been my rock over these past few weeks, and despite the little time we've known each other, she's become closer to me than Tarni ever was, and she knows more about my life and who I am as a person. What's more, outside of Noah, she gives me something to be excited for.

Hope isn't shy about her dislike of Shannan, and because of how genuine and kind she is, she naturally draws people in, all of whom stand with her against Shannan when she brings out the claws. So far, it hasn't rattled her. Shannan's used to people not liking her, but Hope makes me feel optimistic that things will be better one day.

As for all of this, I haven't dared to tell Noah.

I've given him a few updates here and there and told him that Shannan's been causing trouble, but I haven't explained the depth of it. If he knew the truth, he'd drop everything to race back here and try to make things better. But I need to learn how to stand on my own two feet. There was a time I thought I had learned how to stand on my own, but it turns out, I was just pretending. I've never felt strong on my own, but I think I'm getting there.

Over the past four weeks, Noah's only been able to come home once, and it's killing him. He feels like he's letting me down, but he's been so incredibly busy adjusting to college life. Staying on top of his schoolwork and meeting the required training schedule for football is a full-time job. He's starting to settle into his new schedule though, and the second he does, I don't doubt that he'll be sneaking in through my bedroom window just like he used to. There's no denying it though, every second he's been gone, my chest has ached for him. The way I miss him . . . It's breaking me.

It's been a big week with too many assignments already building up, but nobody claimed getting through senior year was supposed to be easy. On top of everything else, I still can't seem to find energy, and my world has slowly been spiraling out of control.

I was almost home on Friday afternoon when I got a call from Hazel that she'd missed her bus. I had to turn right around to go get her, and after a silent and broody drive home, she's stomping up the sidewalk in front of our house before I can even put the Range Rover in park. She's not exactly having the best day, and for some reason, I think it has something to do with a boy. It's *always* got something to do with a boy.

Striding through the door that Hazel left wide open, I pull it closed behind me just as my phone chimes with an incoming text.

I glance down to dig it out of my pocket and find a text from Hope. Before I check the message, I haul my ass up the stairs and drop into my bed with a long sigh.

Hope: Sooooooo…I know I demanded that we go to that party at Laura's place, but would I be a total ass if I bailed? My mom may or may not have found a joint hidden in the bottom of my bag, and I may or may not be grounded.

I gape at the phone, unable to believe what I'm reading, but I'm also kinda thrilled about not having to go to a party tonight. I just want to crash.

Zoey: A joint? WTH!!!! And to think…I thought you were a sweet, innocent person when you've really just been waiting for your opportunity to corrupt me!

Hope: I mean, maybe there might have been a small reason why my parents had me transferred out of St. Michael's.

Zoey: I'm flabbergasted!!!!

Hope: So, I take it that you don't want to sneak out and

smoke it in the park tomorrow night?

Zoey: F L A B B E R G A S T E D!!!!!!

Zoey: And also, I'm 100% there! Love a good corruption story! But if that shit makes me puke, you're responsible for everything that happens after that.

Hope: Your big scary boyfriend is gonna kill me.

Zoey: They're the risks you take when you live on the wild side, girl! Get used to it. Besides, he's all kinds of sexy when he's angry and defending my honor. It'll be the best fun I ever had!

Hope sends me back the vomit emoji, and I laugh as I sprawl out over my bed, stretching my arms wide on either side of me as I just stare at the ceiling. Before I know it, I close my eyes and fall into a deep, exhausted sleep.

I hear Mom getting home, and I peel my eyes open, surprised to find my room cloaked in darkness. A loud yawn rips from my chest, and I sit up, feeling like the living dead. I must have napped for a few hours at least, definitely not my usual Friday afternoon activity, but I needed it all the same.

Mom starts fussing around with pots and pans and the sound flows right up the stairs and assaults my ears in the worst way. Then just when I go to get up and trudge downstairs, my phone rings from somewhere on my bed. Feeling certain that it's Noah, I quickly scramble to find it.

Noah's name lights the screen, and a wide smile stretches across my face as I quickly hit accept, scooching up my bed and bringing my blanket right up to my chin. "Well, hey there, stranger."

"Were you sleeping? Did I wake you?"

"No," I grumble before I'm hit with another yawn. "Sorry to disappoint, but Mom had that honor."

"Damn, and to think I didn't get to be the one to ruin your granny nap."

I laugh and snuggle deeper against my pillow, closing my eyes and just listening to the sound of his soothing tone. "What are you doing?" I ask, picturing him as though he were right here in front of me. "Is there some big start of the season party tonight?"

"It's college," he says with a laugh. "Of course there's a big party tonight."

I roll my eyes. I should have seen that one coming. "And?" I prompt.

"And what?"

"Are you going?"

"Maybe," he says, his tone deepening. "But I'd prefer to be in that bed with you."

I scoff, sitting up. "I'm not in bed," I argue, not wanting to sound lazy when I should be living some kind of extravagant life. "Not anymore at least. Hope and I were going to go to a party. Rumor has it, it'll be the best one of the year."

"You're not going to that party," he states.

"Excuse you, resident asshole, but I'll have you know that I can go to any damn party I want," I tell him, as my brows furrow. "Wait," I say, my heart starting to race. "How the hell did you know I was in my bed?"

A gentle knock sounds on my bedroom window, and my head snaps up to find Noah perched outside like some kind of creepy stalker, but the hot kind the girls always fall for. "Like I said," he rumbles. "You're not going anywhere tonight because you're all mine."

I squeal, undeniable happiness surging through my chest as I throw myself out of bed, my phone catching in the blankets and flying across the room. I race to the window with overwhelming emotion pulsating through my body and sending hot tears streaming down my face.

I struggle with the broken lock, and before I know it, the window is open, and Noah tumbles right through it and into my arms. The force of his momentum sends us both tumbling to the ground. His arms lock protectively around me so that I don't get hurt, and before I can even gasp, his lips are on mine.

Noah kisses me as though it were the very last time, savoring every second of it as I do the same. I take in the feel of his muscled body weighing down on mine, the feel of his tongue sweeping into my mouth, the sound of my racing pulse beating so loudly in my ears. My hands shake as I struggle to pull him closer, and damn it, no matter how long I kiss and hold him, it'll never be enough.

His hands roam over my body, each of us desperate for more until I can't take it a second longer and pull his shirt over his head. Noah is more than happy to oblige, and before I know it, I hear the familiar crinkle of the condom wrapper. It all happens at warp speed, and then finally, he's right there, easing the ache I've held for him for way too long.

When we're both exhausted and panting, Noah drops his forehead to mine, his hands so soft against my bare skin. "Fuck, I've missed you, Zo," he tells me.

"If that's how you show a girl you missed her, then you ought to miss me some more," I tease.

He laughs as his lips drop to mine. "Then just wait 'til you see how I show a girl exactly how I make up for missed time," he tells me, sending an electrical thrill shooting through my body and lighting up every inch of me. "As for now, I think I need to get dressed, sneak back out your window, then go down to knock on the door."

I grin wide, knowing damn well that it won't be long before Mom comes up here and knocks on the door to let me know dinner is ready. "I think that's a smart idea. This whole college thing must be knocking some sense into that brain of yours," I tell him, watching as he reluctantly climbs off me and offers me a hand, helping me to my feet. Then just to be the perfect idiot I've always known him to be, his hand comes down in the perfect arc to my ass, the sound like music to my ears and making me jump.

He grins down at me, not daring to move his hand off my ass as he produces my panties in his other hand. "I think you'll be needing these."

I snatch them right out of his hand, and he laughs as he quickly gets dressed. Then all too soon, his lips are on mine, telling me he'll see me soon, and as he slips back outside my bedroom window, I can't possibly wipe the smile off my face, not even if I tried.

With my window closed and locked, I get myself dressed and hurry down to the bathroom, needing to splash some water over my flushed face. As I close the bathroom door behind me, the lack of energy hits me hard, and I sway, falling right into the bathroom vanity. My hip slams into the porcelain sink as I try to catch myself.

I whimper as agony tears through me, and I lower myself to the ground, needing to breathe through it as my head spins.

I close my eyes, trying to find myself, when Mom's voice sails through the house. "ZOEY," she hollers, her tone telling me she's just found Noah at our front door. "Someone's here to see you."

I cringe, knowing she expects me to race down the stairs with the force of a whole army, but there's no way I can pull that off right now. Both Mom and Noah will see right through me. They'll know something is wrong.

"Give me a sec," I call back, hoping they can't hear my voice waver through the closed door.

Mom and Noah are talking downstairs, and a second later, I hear Hazel's heavy thumps outside the bathroom door as she races out of her room and down the stairs, her high-pitched "NOAH!" booming through the house.

I grip the vanity for balance as I pull myself off the ground, and a throbbing pain shoots through my hip. There's no way I'm going to get this one past Noah.

I get control of my spinning head while trying not to think about what this could mean, but it's hard not to fear the absolute worst. Instead, I focus on trying to enjoy having Noah home, even if it's only for a short while.

Creeping out of the bathroom, I make my way to the stairs, following the sound of voices coming from the entryway. As I reach the top of the stairs, his eyes come to mine, and his whole face lights up as though he's never been so happy in his life. Every fearful thought of this constant dizziness and lack of energy fades away, leaving nothing but *him*.

A wide, booming smile breaks across my face, and I want nothing more than to throw myself down the stairs. "Look who the cat dragged in," I tease, inching my foot down the first step, only to come to a startling halt, agony blasting through my hip.

A pained whimper slips through my lips before I get a chance to stop it, and I watch as Noah's brows furrow, his smile fading away, replaced with pure concern. "What's wrong?" he rushes out, already halfway up the stairs as Mom peers around Noah's big frame from the bottom of the stairs.

His hands are on me in seconds, roaming over me as he tries to figure out what the hell could have happened in the last ninety seconds.

"It's nothing," I tell him, catching his hands and bringing them to a stop in front of me before he accidentally touches my hip. "Just a little water on the bathroom floor. I slipped and rammed my hip into the sink, but I'm fine."

The second the word hip comes out of my mouth, he pulls his hands free from mine and grips my shirt, easing it up before slipping his fingers into the waistband of my shorts and pulling down the edge of it. He takes a look, and as I see the way his eyes widen, my heart races, regretting not waiting a second to check it for myself. "How bad is it?"

"Fuck, Zo. You need ice."

"Shit."

When Noah tells you an injury needs ice, that means it's borderline catastrophic. At this point, I should avoid looking down because I probably don't even have a hip left. Noah is usually the type to just shake it off. He thinks Band-Aids are a waste of time and bruises are a trophy of whatever ridiculous thing you did to earn them.

"I leave you alone for two fucking seconds," he mutters under his breath, letting the rest of the sentence trail off. With that, his arm curls around my back, and just when I think he's about to help me hobble all the way to the bottom, he scoops me up against his wide chest, lifting me off the ground.

I loop my arms around his neck, and he walks me right to the bottom, not stopping until he's lowering me on the couch. Then before I can even say thank you, he's in the kitchen, rifling through the freezer for ice.

He gets me sorted out, and it's not long before Mom calls Aunt Maya, deciding that tonight we'll have our own kind of party. Dinner is served, and as Mom and Aunt Maya lose themselves to three bottles of wine, Noah sits with me on the couch, holding me against his chest as Hazel finally explodes and tells us all about this boy at school who is absolutely not worth her time.

The hours pass far too quickly, and when I'm falling asleep on the couch, Noah lets out a sigh and scoops me up. "Mmmmm," I groan.

"What are you doing?"

"Taking you to bed," he tells me as I snuggle in, more than content with staying right here. "I don't need to go back until Sunday afternoon, so I'll be sneaking back through your window first thing in the morning."

"Okay, but just so you know, Hope and I are sneaking out tomorrow night to smoke a joint in the park."

Noah sputters and gapes at me as he makes his way up the stairs, and all I can do is grin. "Tell me you're lying."

"Like you've never done it," I scoff.

"That's beside the point," he says, but as I snuggle back in and close my eyes, he just shakes his head. "Guess it's time that Hope and I have a little chat."

And with that, he lowers me into my bed and presses a gentle kiss to my lips. "Love you, Zo," he murmurs. "Sleep tight."

Chapter 39

ZOEY

Storm clouds roll in early on Monday morning as I sit up in my bed, staring out the window with my hands shaking. Noah didn't end up leaving until after dinner last night, and I'm so grateful that he stayed, but I also hope he doesn't get in trouble for being tired at training today.

As for me, I've never been so tired.

I didn't sleep. Last night wasn't great. I was lethargic again, barely able to keep myself up to really be here in the moment with Noah, but my body just didn't feel right. I needed to lay down, needed to pass out, and when the dizziness returned, I forced myself to yawn and watched with a broken heart as he put me to bed and demanded I get some sleep.

But the problem with lying in bed too early to sleep, your mind starts wandering, and despite knowing the signs and symptoms of leukemia like the back of my hand, I found myself researching it and looking up everything there was to know about the disease I've already beaten.

Maybe I'm just a hypochondriac, convincing myself of something that isn't really there, but what if I'm right? What if the battles I've already won were nothing but a practice run for something bigger?

I've already cheated death once; I'm living on borrowed time. Maybe death is finally knocking on my door, demanding it's time to come home.

Fuck.

My gaze sweeps to the clock. 6:30 a.m.

Mom and Dad will still be sleeping, but if I'm right, they would want me to wake them. Hell, they would be wishing I had mentioned something when I first started feeling off. I just didn't want to believe it, and I didn't want to repeat the most terrifying time of my life.

Figuring that Mom and Dad need to be up soon anyway, I get out of bed and pad toward my desk, scooping up the picture of me as a little girl fighting for her life. I hold it to my chest like a security blanket, and with shaky hands, I walk out of my room and down the hall.

I creep past Hazel's room, not wanting to wake her or have to worry her, especially if this is something else. Perhaps I was right all along, and this is nothing but emotional exhaustion from being apart from the other half of my soul, but I know in my gut that it's not.

It's barely ten steps to my parents' room, but by the time my hand curls into a small fist and gently knocks on their door, the tears are welling in my eyes.

I don't bother waiting for them to tell me to come in, I just push the door open and slip straight in. Hazel and I aren't the type to bother them often when they're in bed, especially so early in the morning, so the second I walk in, Mom pushes up on her elbow, looking at me with furrowed brows.

She watches me for a second, her eyes adjusting to the fresh morning, and as she sees the tears staining my cheeks, she pulls her blankets back, welcoming me in. "Oh, honey," she says, pulling me into her arms as I snuggle into her bed, still gripping the photo frame. "Don't cry. Noah will be back soon."

I swallow over the lump in my throat, my whole body now violently shaking as the tears turn into sobs. "It's . . . It's not that," I tell her, pulling out of her arms, needing to sit up for this. "I . . . I have to . . . to tell you something."

Mom looks up at me as Dad rolls over to face me, looking just as concerned, even more so as they both take note of the photo in my hand. I scramble over Mom, putting myself right between them, and they immediately sit up, sensing that whatever this is needs their undivided attention.

"Honey, what's going on?" Dad murmurs, gently taking the photo out of my hand as though that could be the reason for my tears and wanting to separate me from it.

"I—" I cut myself off, not having the strength to get the words out as my heart shatters into a thousand broken pieces.

"Sweetheart," Mom says, taking my hand and giving it a squeeze. "You're starting to worry me. Is everything okay? Did something happen?"

I shake my head, trying to breathe through the painful sobs as I reach for the photo again. "I . . . I think it's happening again," I say, finally getting the words out.

Mom glances at Dad, and despite not seeing the look in her eyes, I can picture it clearly, and my panicked sobs grow even louder. "What do you mean?" she questions cautiously, a nervous tone in her kind voice.

"Mom," I cry, leaning into her, and she wraps her arms around me, holding me closer than ever before. "I think I'm sick again."

"Oh, honey," she soothes, her hand rubbing over my hair. "Why do you think that? You're perfectly healthy. We go for routine tests every year," she tells me. "If something was wrong, they would have caught it at your last one. Besides, you know that the likelihood of leukemia returning after ten years in remission is slim to none."

"I don't understand where this is coming from," Dad questions. "Are you having trouble at school?"

"Every teenager has trouble at school," I throw back at him, not liking the accusation in his tone. "But I'm not just taking wild guesses at this. I feel it in my gut. I've been having—"

"Been having what?" Mom asks.

I swallow hard and glance away, ashamed to admit the one thing I've been so scared to say out loud. "Symptoms," I murmur, saying the word as though it's poison on my tongue.

"What?" Dad questions, his whole body stiffening. "What do you mean? You've been having symptoms? You're perfectly healthy. What symptoms?"

"I've been lethargic every day," I tell them in a small voice, barely whispering the words, not brave enough to meet either of their horrified stares. "And not just *had a big day* kind of lethargic. I've been heavy, sometimes barely able to even pull myself out of bed. I've been falling asleep all the time and having no energy to do anything. And then there's the dizziness," I add, pain slicing straight through my chest. "I lied the other day . . . about my hip."

"What are you talking about?" Mom whispers, her voice breaking as she clings on to my hand so tight that I fear my fingers will break.

"I didn't slip on water," I admit with a heavy sob, so ashamed of myself. "I fainted. I fell into the vanity and slammed my hip into the sink, and it's not the first time. I fainted on my birthday."

"What?" Dad demands. "Your birthday was back in February."

"I know," I say, my voice a little louder. "I was with Noah, but we just assumed I was getting sick. Everyone at school was coming down with the flu, and maybe that's all it was, but . . . I don't know. What if it wasn't and it's been gradually getting worse since then?"

Mom holds me so damn close, I can barely breathe as Dad gets out of bed, pacing in front of the window. "You're sure about this?" he asks, a strange tone in his voice that I've never heard before. "You really think it's back, that you've . . . relapsed?"

I shrug my shoulders, not really sure what to say. "I think I'm getting sick, and I really hope that I could be wrong, that there's some other explanation for this, but you've always taught me to trust my gut."

Mom silently cries at the thought of me getting sick in the same way, while Dad tries to think rationally about this. "Okay, here's what we're going to do," he finally says, his eyes filling with unshed tears. "We're going to go about our normal day, have a shower, get ready for your day, and after Hazel is dropped at school, your mother and I will take you to see Dr. Sanchez to get some tests done. After all, there's no need to panic or jump to conclusions until we're certain."

I nod, the lump in my throat now so big it's almost impossible to breathe. "Okay," I say, my voice breaking as the tears continue flowing. I glance at Mom, meeting her green eyes that are so identical to mine. "What if—"

"Don't do that, my precious girl," she weeps. "Don't start asking yourself what if until we know. If it comes down to that, then we'll cross that bridge then, okay? For now, positive thoughts."

I nod, and with that, Mom scooches back in her bed, pulling me down with her and into her side before pulling the blankets right up to our chins. Her fingers brush up and down my arm as Dad excuses himself to go to the bathroom, but instead of hearing the shower running, I hear the subtle sound of his broken cries.

Mom and I stay like this until Dad finally emerges from the bathroom, dressed and ready for the day. We hear Hazel down the hall, turning on her music and singing, completely oblivious to the way my whole world feels as though it's about to crumble. "I'll drive her to school," Dad mutters, barely just going through the motions. "Then I'll head back here and pick you up."

Mom and I sit up and nod, and with that, Dad is out the door, putting on the performance of a lifetime as he tells Hazel to hurry her ass up and get out to the truck.

I get up out of my parents' bed, and as I go to walk out of the room, Mom stops me and pulls me back into her arms. "We're going to be okay, Zo," she promises me. "Whatever comes our way, we'll fight it together. You've beaten this beast before, and if it comes down to it, you'll beat it again. You're the strongest person I've ever met, my love. You're a survivor, and whatever this is that has got you not feeling your best, you're going to get past it."

I bury my face into her chest, the tears starting all over again. "I'm scared, Mommy," I cry, clinging to her shirt.

"I'm scared too," she tells me, gently pressing her fingers to my chin and lifting until I meet her eyes. "But the beauty is that we have each other to be scared with, and when you have someone holding your hand, sometimes those scary things really aren't so bad."

She gives me a warm smile, and with that, I make my way out of her room, still clutching the photo, desperately needing it to remind me that even in the face of the impossible, I've beaten all odds, and if I can do it once, then I can sure as hell do it again.

When I was a kid, Dr. Sanchez's office seemed huge, but now, it's nothing more than a regular doctor's office. Perhaps it's because when I was young, looking at the doctor who cured my cancer, I always saw her as larger than life, but as the years went on, I gained a better understanding of my illness, and everything was brought into perspective. And now as I sit in this office, I'm filled with nothing but fear.

My parents sit on either side of me as I hold my hands in my lap, trying to conceal just how frantically they're shaking. We've been here for two hours waiting for a chance for the doctor to squeeze us in. She's highly recommended, and getting an appointment with her can sometimes be impossible, but I've been a frequent flier here for over a decade now. I'm on a first-name basis with most of her staff and nurses, and when I walked through the door, they were more than happy to try and squeeze us in. I just hope that this is all for nothing.

Mom has been quiet all morning, and Dad has done what little he can to keep us both from falling apart, but truth be told, he's right on the edge as well.

Hope has been blowing up my phone all morning, wondering where I am and if I'm alright, and so far, I haven't had the energy to respond, and it makes me feel like a cold-hearted bitch. But as soon as we're out of here and I'm back home, I'm sure I'll be feeling up to it. Right now, the fear of the unknown has my complete, undivided attention.

I've told Hope all about my past with leukemia and spoken about it openly, something I never really did with Tarni. Sure, she knows about it, but it was mentioned almost as an afterthought and then quickly shrugged off as though it didn't matter. Hope though, she asks questions, wonders about that time in my life, wants to know how it all went down, and she makes me feel normal for still feeling the need to cry about it despite being cleared over ten years ago.

The nerves from sitting in this very office are eating me alive, and my knee bounces. I avoided Noah's call this morning, knowing if he heard the sound of my voice or the tremble of fear within it, he would have jumped straight back in his car, leaving training behind. So, I settled for a quick text, letting him know I was running late and that I'd call him after school, making it two people I've let down today.

I'm not that person who hides things. I don't lie to my friends, and I sure as hell don't avoid Noah's calls, especially when I'm in a constant state of missing him. But they will understand. They have to.

Dr. Sanchez's office door opens, and as I look back over my shoulder, Mom places a steadying hand over mine, trying to help calm me.

Dr. Sanchez walks in, and a wide smile immediately spreads across her face. "Oh my, Zoey James," she says fondly. "You seem to grow another whole foot every time I see you."

Despite my nerves, a genuine smile pulls across my face, and we all stand up. Mom goes in first, giving Dr. Sanchez a warm hug before making the usual small talk. *How have you been? It's wonderful to see you again.*

When the doctor walks around her desk and takes a seat, she's looking at me like I'm a personal achievement of hers. "You must be seventeen now, is that right?" she asks, dropping down into her desk chair and flipping open my file.

"Yes, that's right," I say, watching as she scans over my paperwork, her brows furrowing. "We're coming up to the ten-year anniversary of when you declared me cancer-free."

"Indeed we are," she says, a strange note in her tone. "However, according to my paperwork, I'm not scheduled to see you for another two months." Her head snaps up, her honey-brown eyes scanning over my face in a new light. "What's going on, Zoey?"

My gaze drops away in defeat. "I've been having symptoms," I tell her as Mom reaches for my hand again.

"What kind of symptoms?" she pushes.

"I've been lethargic, having dizzy spells, and fainting," I tell her. "No energy and tired all the time."

"Okay," she says, her gaze dropping back to my file as she digs a little deeper. "I see you've been keeping up with all of your scheduled tests. When was your last one?"

"Last December," Mom supplies.

Dr. Sanchez nods before plucking papers from the back of my file and studying them closely, and I can only assume these are a copy of my latest results, though we were told everything was good, no cause for alarm. "Alright, so everything looks as it should on these results, but since you aren't feeling well, I'm happy to bring forward your scheduled test," she tells me. "Though I'm sure you've done your homework and are aware that a relapse after ten years of remission is quite rare, it's not unheard of."

I nod. I spent the whole night reading all about it.

"When did you start noticing these symptoms?" she asks.

I give her the whole rundown, the same way I'd done with Mom and Dad this morning, and she takes in every little detail like a sponge.

"Right, okay," she says. "So, these symptoms could be signs of a number of different things. I think we need to do a complete blood count, just so we can narrow this down a little. In the meantime, we'll get started on your bone marrow aspiration. How does that sound?"

"Terrifying," I tell her honestly.

"I know, but let's get some results back before we start fretting. This could be a simple case of anemia, or it could be something a little more serious."

Mom nods, listening to everything the doctor has to say before spouting a million questions I would never have thought to ask, but I suppose this is what happens when you've already been through this once before.

They chat for a few minutes, and Mom is already asking about plans of action, but Dr. Sanchez is reluctant to go into too much detail before we get my results.

"Alright," Dr. Sanchez finally says. "Let's get you in my exam room and we'll do a thorough check-up, draw some blood, and get moving on your bone marrow aspiration."

With that, we all stand, and as Dad pulls me into his side, holding me tight, we make our way into Dr. Sanchez's exam room, hoping like hell that our lives aren't about to crumble into a million irreparable pieces.

Chapter 40

NOAH

She's acting weird.

I first noticed it last weekend after she hurt her hip. She said she slipped and fell into the bathroom sink, but I know the exact way her voice shifts when she lies and the way she glances away, unable to meet my stare. But I let it pass, figuring she'll tell me when she is ready.

But then she was off the rest of the weekend. Saturday she was mostly alright, but she kept drifting off like something else was holding her attention, and then Sunday rolled around, and she was like a stranger. She was frazzled, unable to concentrate, and couldn't get a sentence out without forgetting what she was trying to say.

Her mind was somewhere else, and when she faked a yawn . . .

I'm still trying to convince myself that she wasn't trying to kick me out. That's not how we've ever done it. If she's tired or wanted some space, she's always been able to tell me. But is that it? Has she gotten so accustomed to me being away that she doesn't need me around like she used to?

I've tried to give her space this week, testing the theory, only calling every now and then, not flooding her with texts, and a few times she's avoided my calls and responded to messages with nothing more than a lousy one-word reply. The times I've actually gotten through and spoken to her on the phone, I've told her about my day while listening with a gaping hole in my chest as she gave me silence in return.

Something is up, and I need to know what.

If she's hurting or something is happening at school, I want to know. Or if she's finally realized that she's too good for me and is ready to call it quits . . . Fuck. It would kill me, but I love her too much to hold on to her if she's not happy. I want her to fly free, to be happy and filled with love, and if I'm hindering that, then I'll let her go, but it'll be the hardest thing I'll ever do.

It's Thursday afternoon, just after lunch, and despite my business class starting in twenty minutes, I find myself flying down the highway to get to her. It's the longest fucking drive of my life, but I make it just in time, pulling into East View High's student parking lot just minutes before the bell sounds.

I pull up right behind Zoey's Range Rover, get out of my Camaro, and lean against the hood as I wait, never having felt this uneasy in my life. Just the thought that she could be done with me is fucking me up.

I knew a lot of things would change when I went to college, but never in a million years did I think this could have been a possibility. If I thought this kind of distance would have pushed her away, I . . . I don't know what I would have done differently. I'm as close as I can possibly be.

By the time the bell sounds, I've more than convinced myself that Zoey is about to tear my heart right out of my fucking chest. Students begin pouring out of the school, and I keep my gaze locked on the doors, waiting more impatiently than ever before.

She walks out a minute later with Hope, both of them talking with their heads down, and the toxic part of me wonders if this change in Zoey is Hope's influence. But Zoey seems to really like her, and I immediately feel like an ass for questioning it, but then . . . It wouldn't be the first time Zoey has been wrong about her choice in friends.

Students gape at me, and it's not long before my name sails across the school grounds. Zoey is halfway to the parking lot when her head snaps up, and just like always, her eyes come right to mine. She pauses, and for just a second, fear flashes in her eyes. It's gone quicker than it appeared, but it's just enough to make that seed of doubt expand until it's turning into a raging storm inside of me.

She clutches her bag, and in a flash, Hope is forgotten as she hurries toward me.

I don't take my eyes off her, barely getting a chance to push off the hood of my Camaro before she barrels into my arms, right where she belongs.

Zo nuzzles her face into my chest, holding on to me so damn tight that I hate myself for having to be away like this. "What are you doing here?" she murmurs, pulling back just enough to meet my stare.

My brows furrow, taking her in. She looks like she hasn't slept all week. Her eyes look sad, devastated almost, and God, I hope like fuck this isn't my doing.

I clench my jaw, nodding back toward my car. "Get in, Zo," I mutter.

She doesn't move, looking at me through a cautious stare. "But . . . my car?" she says. "Don't you have to go back? I'll need it to get back here in the morning."

I shake my head. "I'll stay at Mom's tonight and drive you back here in the morning."

She still doesn't budge. "You have an away game tomorrow," she says, so in tune with my schedule. "I thought you had to leave early to catch a flight."

"It's fine, Zoey. Just . . . fuck." I turn away, walking back to my car door before finally glancing back at her. "Just get in my fucking car, babe. We'll figure it out. But right now, we need to talk."

That same fear I'd seen earlier flashes in her eyes again, and I know without a doubt that she's thinking the worst, but I'm already too fucked up to try easing her fears.

I wait until she starts moving before getting into the car, and when she's finally settled beside me, I hit the gas and get us out of here. I drive and drive, not knowing where the hell I'm going, trying to figure out how the fuck to bring this up. I don't try to reach for her hand or take her thigh like I usually do, and every second of it tears me apart.

We make our way around the streets of East View, and when I pull into the familiar parking area of the park that's become ours over the past seventeen years, I finally ease onto the brakes.

Neither of us move to get out of the car, and I can almost hear her heart racing in her chest, so in sync with mine.

I grip the steering wheel, needing something to do with my hands to keep from reaching for her and pulling her right into my arms, begging her to tell me that this is all in my head.

I feel her questioning stare on me, but I don't dare look her way, knowing the second I meet those eyes, I won't have the balls to ask her what's been coursing through my mind all fucking week. My hand grips tighter on the steering wheel, my knuckles turning white, and as the pain rockets through my chest, I drop my head, unable to bear it for another fucking second. "Are we done?" I ask her in a gravelly tone, my voice breaking as a lump forms in my throat. "Are you breaking up with me?"

Zoey gasps, and within the blink of an eye, she scrambles across the center console and into my lap, straddling me as she wraps her arms around my neck, pulling me into her. "Why the hell would you ask me that?" she questions, a gut-wrenching pain filling her voice.

She sits back, meeting my stare, tears lingering in her beautiful green eyes. "Zo," I say, letting her in and showing her my deepest insecurities, letting her see exactly what I've been feeling this past week: the rejection of her snubbed calls, the hurt of her distant conversation, the agony of her pushing me away.

Then reaching up, I push her hair back off her face, my fingers lingering a second too long. "Do you know that you have exactly four different kinds of cries?"

"What?" she breathes, searching my gaze for some kind of understanding.

"There's the pained whimper when you've hurt yourself, like last weekend when you fucked up your hip," I start, my fingers brushing over the bruise I know still lingers beneath her jeans. "There's the trembling lip cry that you get when you're watching *The Notebook*. They're the two I always hope for when I hear you crying, but sometimes . . . it's different. Sometimes it comes right from the soul, and that's when I know you're heartbroken or when I've done something to hurt you so deeply you can't possibly hold it in any longer. And fuck, Zo, I'm the only one who's ever made you cry like that."

"That's only three," she murmurs, those silent tears tracking down her cheeks as her fingers knot into the front of my shirt—her nervous habit.

"The fourth," I tell her, wiping the tears off her rosy cheeks. "I've only ever heard it once, and it fucking killed me."

She nods, already knowing what I'm referring to. "The day Linc died."

I nod right back. "That cry . . . That one gutted me. That's the cry of someone who's hurting beyond measure, a cry that not even I could have helped."

Her gaze drops away, her bottom lip trembling. "I . . . I don't understand why you're telling me this."

There's a nervousness to her tone, and I'd kill to be inside her mind right now, to know what she's thinking, to know what quick assumptions she's making of this conversation, but I also know her well enough to know that whatever's going through her mind, it's as bad as it gets.

My thumb brushes across her trembling lip, trying to soothe her as I feel myself starting to fall to pieces. "Because I've spoken to you every day this week," I explain, barely in a whisper as I hold her saddened stare, "And while you've pretended to be interested in whatever mindless bullshit I was talking about, you sat on the other end, silently crying. Every damn time."

Her eyes widen, and my lips pull into a soft smile, trying to let her know that I'm not mad. "You thought that you were being discreet," I murmur, my hands falling to her waist, desperately needing to hold her, "but I can tell just by the change in your breath that you were crying."

A deep shame flashes in her eyes before her gaze falls away, and I hate every second of it. She should never have to feel shame for something like that, all I want is for her to let me in. "This cry, Zo . . . This one is different," I tell her, gripping her waist a little tighter as though she might just disappear. "It makes me uneasy because it means I either don't know you as well as I thought, or that you're hurting so fucking bad that you can't even find the strength to share it with me."

"Noah," she cries, gripping my shirt tighter and falling into me, plastering herself against my body.

I reach up, my hand gently stroking the back of her hair because even in my own pain, I can't stand the thought of hers. "You're my whole world, Zo. If I didn't have you, I don't know what I would do," I tell her. "I can't stand the thought that there's a part of you that you're not able to open up to me about. Did something happen? Did I do something wrong that makes you feel you can't confide in me anymore?"

"I'm sorry," she whispers, her lips moving against my neck. "I never intended to make you feel like that. You've always been everything to me, Noah. The only person I've ever truly needed. You know how much I love you."

"So why the hell does it feel like you're pulling away from me?"

She shakes her head. "It's just been a really hard week, and hearing your voice just made everything feel so much easier. I didn't realize you could hear me. It's just . . . You're my peace, Noah. Talking to you, even on my worst days . . . You make me feel as though nothing else matters, that no matter what, I'm always going to be okay."

My lips press against her temple, and I breathe her in, my chest aching in a different way. She still needs me, more than ever, but she's holding back, not able to open up and share whatever it is that's been plaguing her all week. "Zo, please. What's going on?" I beg. "If something is hurting you or bringing you down, I want to know. I want to help you. I can't stand that I don't know what's going on with you right now."

She pulls back, her hand still knotting into my shirt. Her eyes are wary, as though she's deep in thought, warring with herself about something. "It's . . ." she says hesitantly, pausing as her lips press into a tight line, and then I see the exact moment she decides that she's not ready to let me in, and it fucking destroys me more than the thought of her possibly being done with me. "I just . . . It's been a shitty week. I haven't been sleeping well, and on top of missing you, school's been . . . hard."

There's a level of truth in her tone, and I don't doubt anything that she's saying. It's clear from the exhaustion in her eyes that she hasn't been sleeping, but whatever this is, it's so much bigger than whatever is happening at school, but I'm not about to push her on that. All I can do is hope that when she's ready, she'll be able to let me in. "What's happening at school?" I ask. "Is it Shannan?"

She nods, glancing down at her fingers in my shirt. "Yeah, she's been . . . it's bad."

"What do you mean *bad*? I thought she was leaving you alone." Zoey winces as though my comment physically pains her, and I realize that for the past few weeks, she's been sugarcoating everything that's been going down at school to avoid worrying me. "Fuck, Zo. What's she doing?"

She glances away again, that same shame seeping into her gaze. "I think the better question is what *isn't* she doing?"

I curse under my breath, my jaw clenching as my arms tighten around her. "Zo," I prompt, my patience quickly wearing thin.

She lets out a heavy breath before reaching across the center console and grabbing her phone from her bag. She unlocks the screen before pulling up a picture and turning it around to show me. My blood instantly turns cold at the photoshopped image of Zoey taking up the screen. She's on her hands and knees, ass high in the sky as she looks back over her shoulder while touching herself. "This is only the beginning of it," she tells me. "It gets worse from there."

"Worse?" I grunt. "How the fuck does it get worse than this?"

"She had someone hack my phone, or I don't know, maybe they stole it from my locker and put it back before I realized. But they took screenshots of our messages—the ones that are . . . you know, more than just flirting."

"Fucking hell, Zoey. Why didn't you tell me any of this?"

"Because you're in college now. You have so much more to be focusing on," she argues. "You shouldn't be spending every minute of the day trying to figure out how to save me when you should be focused on training and classes. Besides, what does that say about me? That I can't handle this on my own and need my scary boyfriend to come and protect me every time someone even looks at me wrong?"

"Look at yourself, Zo. You're fucking miserable," I growl. "I don't want you to live like this. If something happens, you need to tell me. You need to let me fix it."

"Noah—"

"No," I cut her off. "You're my whole fucking world. You are the other half of my soul, Zo. If someone is fucking with you, they're fucking with me."

Zoey leans into me, her forehead dropping against mine. "Please, Noah. For me, just let this go. You're not there every day to make sure she stays down. If you step in, it's only going to make it worse in the long run. I'm not responding to her, and eventually, she's going to get bored and move on to her next victim."

I don't respond, and she holds my stare. "Please, Noah. For me."

I shake my head. The thought of letting this slide goes against everything I stand for, but how the hell can I tell her no when she's the one who's at that school every day dealing with the fallout? "I don't like this, Zo."

"You don't have to," she tells me. "You just have to accept that I know what I'm doing and be there to hold me when it all goes to hell."

"It's the *going to hell* part that's fucking me up."

"I know," she murmurs, snuggling into my chest. "I'm sorry. If I knew I was going to have you doubting us, I would have tried harder. I never want you to feel like that because when it comes to you and me . . . there's no question, Noah. I want to grow old with you and have a bunch of babies. These seventeen years haven't been nearly enough. But for what it's worth, having you here now with your arms around me makes me feel like everything is going to be alright, that all that shit at school doesn't even matter because, at the end of the day, I have so much to look forward to with you."

"Ten more months, Zo. Ten more months and you'll be at UA with me."

She nods, and after having her in my arms for the last hour, her lips finally come down on mine, and with that single kiss, every last of my fears fade away. No matter what, at the end of the day, she has me, and I have her. And with something so fucking powerful, how could anything ever tear us apart?

Chapter 41

ZOEY

It's exactly 4:38 p.m. when Mom's phone rings on the kitchen counter. Both Mom and I freeze for a moment as our gazes collide over the kitchen sink.

It's been a little over a week since my appointment at Dr. Sanchez's office, and every moment since has been nothing but pure torture. I've been through this a million times, waiting for the results of my blood tests and bone marrow aspirations, but none of them have had me in a chokehold the way this one has.

Every time the phone rang over the past week, a piece of me died. The anticipation and anxiety have been like nothing I've ever experienced in my life.

The kitchen is silent apart from the sound of Mom's phone ringing, and I watch as she glances down and sucks in a breath. "It's Dr. Sanchez," she murmurs, her gaze flicking back to mine.

My knees shake, and I grip the side of the counter as the pulse in my ears quickens, thumping so loudly, it's deafening. Mom's hand moves toward the phone, and I watch her like a hawk as my dad moves in behind me, his hand gently resting on my back for support.

Mom glances at Dad over my shoulder, and as one, we all seem to take a collective breath as Mom accepts the call and lifts the phone to her ear. "Hello," she says, her voice shaking.

"Erica, hi. It's Nicole," Dr. Sanchez's voice seems to boom through the phone, despite the call not being on speakerphone. "I'm sorry to have kept you waiting. I can't imagine what must have been running through your mind over this past week. However, I've just received Zoey's results. I think it's best you come down to the office tomorrow."

"No," I breathe, my tone barely audible.

If it was good news, she would have just said I was clear. She would have put us out of our misery. She's a highly sought-after oncologist with many patients going through the worst kind of hell. Her time is too important. She wouldn't be careless with it or waste an appointment like that.

"Of course, we'll clear our schedules," my mother says, her voice breaking as she holds Dad's stare, both of them utterly terrified. "But with all due respect, Doctor, we're all here right now. None of us are going to get a wink of sleep until we know. Please," she begs. "We need to know now."

There's a short silence, and as Dr. Sanchez lets out a pained sigh, Mom's unshed tears spill down her cheeks.

"Okay," Dr. Sanchez says soothingly, prompting Mom to put the call on speakerphone. She walks around the kitchen counter, pulling me into her arms and holding on tighter than ever before. "I prefer not to give this kind of diagnosis over the phone, but considering your circumstances, I'm happy to make an allowance."

Dr. Sanchez pauses for a second, and by the time she goes on, my whole body is violently shaking, the tears already streaking down my face. "Zoey, honey, are you there?"

"Yes," I say, my voice breaking.

"I'm sorry, but your suspicions were correct," she tells me, sounding just as broken as I feel. "Your blood tests and bone marrow aspiration are showing an overwhelming amount of leukemic white cells in your system."

I suck in a shaky breath, so loud it cuts her off, and I crumble in my mother's arms as Dad grabs my waist to keep me on my feet. "No," I cry, the tears coming so rapidly that my vision blurs as Mom's heartbroken whimpers sound through the kitchen. "No, I can't do this again."

"I'm sorry, Zoey. I know this isn't easy news to hear," Dr. Sanchez tells me, her soothing voice doing nothing to ease the terror blasting through my chest. "It's fairly aggressive. However, I will need to run more tests to determine just how advanced your case is and to determine if these cancerous cells have spread and how far. From there, we'll be able to work out a treatment plan."

The sobs break from the back of my throat until Mom and Dad can no longer hold me up, their own grief claiming them as we crumble to the kitchen tiles together.

My face falls into my hands, the tears pooling in my palms.

Mom and Dad pull me into their arms as Dr. Sanchez continues, saying words that don't register to my ears as her earlier words play on repeat in my head.

Your suspicions were correct.

Overwhelming amount of leukemic white cells in your system.

Fairly aggressive.

Run more tests to determine just how advanced your case is.

If these cancerous cells have spread and how far.

It hits me like a fucking train.

I have cancer.

Again.

And this time, it's aggressive.

Mom and Dad wrap up the conversation with Dr. Sanchez from where we sit on the kitchen floor, and neither of them can form proper sentences. Then with a promise to show up tomorrow, Mom's phone drops to the ground beside us, shattering the screen.

"Oh, Zoey," she sobs, burying her face into the curve of my neck, her tears dropping to my collarbone as I just sit and cry, feeling broken and empty, my whole world crumbling around me. This isn't how my senior year was supposed to go. I was supposed to make memories, go to parties, and wait with bated breath for Noah to come home to me.

But now . . .

The devastation squeezes me like a vise until I can no longer breathe, and as my parents fall apart, preparing for a war that I don't know if I'm strong enough to win, I find myself racing out the door with keys in my hand.

I'm a mess as I peel out of the driveway, sitting in absolute silence as I push the Range Rover to its limits. The sun quickly falls from the sky, dipping low beyond the horizon as my phone goes crazy with calls and messages from Mom and Dad. But there's only one place I want to be right now, one place I *need* to be to ease the overwhelming panic and fear coursing through my cancer-riddled body.

I need my home. *My heart.* I need him to hold me and tell me that it's going to be okay, that I'm going to survive this, that no matter what kind of mountain we have to face, we'll climb it together and find ourselves back over the other side with our whole lives ahead of us.

It's after 7:30 p.m. when I pull into one of the many campus parking lots at UA, just outside the football stadium and closest to Noah's dorm. There are people everywhere, and I quickly try to pull myself together, but it's no use. No amount of wiping my eyes is going to mask the devastation pouring through me.

Glancing out through the windshield, I find a bunch of guys, and when I recognize one of them as Noah's teammate, I search through the crowd a little closer, finally finding Noah among them.

They look like they're on their way out, maybe to have dinner or a study session. All that matters is crumbling into Noah's arms and hoping like fuck he can somehow dull the ache inside of me. To tell me that everything is going to be okay, that he'll be right here holding my hand, and that I don't need to be scared.

Desperation courses through my veins, and I grip the handle, pushing the door wide. As I tumble out onto the asphalt, my gaze snaps up again, seeking him out. Fresh tears stream down my face as I find him in the middle of the group of football players. They're crossing the road, heading toward some kind of hall, and as he talks to the guy beside him, a brilliant smile stretches across his face, and I find myself pausing.

He talks animatedly, and as I watch his movements, I smile. He only ever talks this animatedly when he's talking about me or Linc, and I realize just how much he's opened himself up to his life here. It's not easy for him to open up or talk about the things that matter most, and the fact that he's able to do that with these new people speaks volumes about how far he's come from the distraught boy he was a year ago.

His world is only just getting back on track, and that darkness that clouded him for so long has just finished clearing, but now? How can I do this to him? How can I tell him about my diagnosis and set alight the progress he's made?

I'm going to have to tell him. It's not something I can keep hidden from him because I want to be selfish. I have to have him by my side through all of this because I simply won't survive it without him. But I don't have to tell him tonight. I don't have to blurt it out in the middle of the street around all of his new friends. There won't be much I can control over the next few years of my life, but this . . . I can.

I'll wait until I've wrapped my head around it and worked out the best way to break the news to him, but I can't wait long. Dr. Sanchez is going to put a rush on these tests, and I'll be back in that same old treatment center, hooked up to who knows what, receiving the most intense form of chemotherapy, and I'm going to need him right at my side. But more so, if I go through any portion of this without him, spouting the same old bullshit about trying to protect him from this, he'll never forgive me. It will hurt him so deeply that he won't know how to come back from it.

The thought has a whimper pulling from deep in my chest, and I find myself inching back to my car, settling into my seat, and closing the door behind me, unable to take my eyes off him.

Sooner or later, I'm going to have to break his heart, and he's going to crumble like he's never crumbled before. Hearing my diagnosis is going to destroy him, and despite not knowing many details about the severity of my cancer yet, I know he's going to think the worst.

Pressing the push start button, I prepare to back out of my spot before my hands fall into my lap, and I find myself just watching him. He's almost at the entrance of the hall, and I can't help but wonder if this is what my life with him would have looked like next year. Only . . . I suppose I'll be trading class rooms for clinical rooms. I still remember all the poking and prodding with needles, the intense chemotherapy that made me violently ill, but it's so much worse now that I understand what's truly at stake.

Noah's group disappears into the hall, only he hangs back, pulling his phone out of his pocket, and a moment later, his name is in block letters across the dashboard of my car, the soft sound of his call ringing through Bluetooth.

He stands under the lights of the building, and I see him so perfectly, just taking him in that I almost miss the call, but I can't bring myself to let it ring out. "Hey," I say, forcing a smile across my face as the tears continue tracking down my cheeks.

"You good?" he asks, his whole body stiffening, reminding me of what he said in his car last week, how he's able to tell I'm crying by nothing more than the sounds of my uneven breathing.

"I will be," I tell him, not wanting to lie, not about this. "When do I get to see you next?"

"Babe," he says, his tone shifting. "That was the worst subject change I've ever heard. It wasn't even a little subtle."

"Hey, I never claimed to be subtle."

He laughs, but the sound is forced. "Zo?" he prompts.

"It's been a rough night," I admit. "But I'm going to be okay. I don't want you worrying about it."

"Right, because that's possible."

"Really," I insist. "I'm on my way to Hope's place. We're going to have a movie night with popcorn and ice cream. Who knows, I might even find a bong hidden under her bed."

"Don't even joke about that," he tells me, digging his hand deep into his pocket as he leans back against the wall of the massive building. "I let the whole joint thing slide last weekend, but that's it. After I had to carry your ass the whole way home while you sang Taylor Swift at the top of your lungs, I'm calling it on your little experimental phase. Can't you disappoint your parents some other way?"

I shrug my shoulders, despite knowing he can't see. "I mean, Mom found that box of condoms in my side drawer."

I watch as his face falls. "You're lying. Tell me you're fucking lying."

"Would I lie about the practice of safe sex?"

"Fuck," he mutters. "Your father's going to eat me alive."

I laugh, wiping my face and realizing the steady stream of tears has finally begun to ease. "What are you doing tonight?"

"Just heading out to dinner with the team. It was supposed to be just me and a few of the guys, but Coach thinks we need to bond a little more, so it turned into a mandatory team dinner," he explains. "I wouldn't be surprised if he quizzes us on our knowledge of each other right in the middle of our meals."

"In that case, maybe I need to start texting all of your most embarrassing secrets to all of your teammates."

"You wouldn't dare," he says as a brilliant smile crosses his face, one he reserves only for me.

"Wanna bet?"

Noah scoffs, knowing damn well that every secret we've ever shared is safe between us. "Hey, listen," he says. "I have a game on Friday night here in our stadium, and I was thinking, if you don't have too much schoolwork, you'd wanna come? Kickoff isn't 'til seven, so you'd have plenty of time to get here after school."

"Noah McLoveOfMyLife Ryan, why do you sound like a thirteen-year-old kid asking a girl out for the first time?"

"Just tell me you're coming to my game."

I laugh, a smile stretching right over my face, realizing that for the first time since leaving my place, it's so much easier to breathe. "I'd love to."

"Good, saves me from having to come home and drag your ass back here kicking and screaming."

"You wouldn't dare," I challenge.

He scoffs. "Wanna bet?" he says, mimicking my earlier comment, and damn it, I know he would. There's nothing he loves more than having me up in the stands watching him play, and honestly, there's nothing I love more than being there.

Someone comes out of the hall, catching Noah's eyes and indicating for him to hurry up. "Shit. I have to go, but Zoey," Noah mutters, not sounding very pleased about it. "You know I fucking love you, right? No matter what."

I nod even though he can't see me. "No matter what," I repeat. "I'll talk to you later."

"Alright, no bongs, okay? I mean it."

"Yes, sir."

"That's more like it." He pauses for a moment, and I watch as he pushes off the side of the building, not wanting to end the call. He takes a deep breath, and a sad smile pulls at his lips, leaving me wondering if he knows I'm holding back from him again. "Bye, Zo."

"Bye, Noah," I whisper, sending out a silent vow that I won't make him wait long before finally telling him the one thing that could potentially destroy him.

Chapter 42

NOAH

The whistle sounds and the crowd roars as they spring to their feet after watching the most thrilling final few minutes of our game. I immediately look up at Zoey in the VIP section of the stands, her hands around her mouth as she screams out.

Fuck, she looks so happy.

There's nothing better than having her eyes on me while I play. It's such a fucking rush, and what's better, I get to look forward to this for the rest of my life.

The pride shining through her beautiful eyes is enough to make me momentarily forget how distant she's been over the past two weeks, but after driving home on Wednesday night, I trust her to come to me when she's ready. I just hope it's soon because I can't handle her pushing me out.

She jumps up and down, cheering so loud that I can hear her sweet tone sailing across the frenzied crowd. And even though this isn't a championship game, I know that this very moment will be one

I treasure until my dying days.

Our coach calls us in, and after the usual post-game bullshit, we're sent back to our lockers to get cleaned up. I rush through a shower, more than ready to get out of here and find Zoey. I hope she's okay in this crowd. It can be daunting, especially when you're alone and new to the area.

Knox Parker, possibly the greatest wide receiver I've ever met, steps in beside me as we make our way out of the stadium, both our gazes locked on Zoey across the lot. He takes in her wide, cheesy grin and the way her eyes light up like Christmas morning. "Yo, is that your girl?" he asks, his gaze eating her up like a meal.

"Sure fucking is," I tell him, watching as she breaks into a sprint toward me. "Keep your grubby hands off."

Knox just laughs, more than prepared to spend the rest of the night screwing with me over it. "Ohh, protective of this one," he comments. "She's gorgeous. There's no telling what I could do with a girl like that."

"Even think about it, and I'll put you in the ground," I tell him letting him hear the edge in my tone, that despite his teasing, I'm dead serious.

I can't take my eyes off Zoey, my grin mirroring hers as she darts through the crowd. I pick up my pace, Knox long forgotten even though I can hear the echo of his laughter through the bodies behind me. When she finally reaches me, she throws herself right into my arms and her legs lock around my waist.

Zoey's lips crash down on mine, kissing me deeply as her arms snake around the back of my neck, holding on to me as though she'll never let me go, and fuck, these kinds of embraces are my favorite. When she holds me as though I'm her whole world, like she can't breathe without me, it feels like pure ecstasy pulsing through my veins.

I don't know how I survived those three years without her. What the fuck was I thinking?

Zoey pulls back and buries her face into the curve of my neck, breathing me in as I simply hold her, hating that I can't do this every minute of every day. "Do you have any idea how good it feels to be up in those stands, watching you play?" she asks, her fingers tangling in my hair as she pulls back to meet my stare.

"Probably about as good as it feels to be on that field knowing that you're right there watching me." She grins back at me, and I walk back toward her car before placing her on the hood. "What do you wanna do?" I ask. "Have you eaten? We could grab dinner and then head out to celebrate with the boys."

Zoey's grin widens. "Oh, I'm hungry," she murmurs. "But not for food."

"Goddamn, Zo," I groan, my fingers digging into her thighs. "I can't wait for you to be here with me next year."

She smiles, but as she does, the fire and passion fade from her eyes until she's left looking empty. "Yeah," she says, glancing away, unable to meet my stare.

My brows furrow, and I take her chin, lifting it and bringing her blazing green gaze back to mine. "What's the matter?" I ask, desperately searching her eyes.

"It's nothing," she says, trying to give me an encouraging smile, only the longer she forces it, the easier it is to see through, and fuck, the guilt radiating out of her puts me on edge. "It's nothing. I'm just . . . I'm just being weird."

She looks away again, but I don't stop watching her, feeling in my gut that something's not right, but why would she feel guilty over a simple comment about looking forward to being here together next year? Why would she get so torn up about something like that? Unless . . .

Fuck.

"You're not planning on coming here, are you?"

Her eyes shoot back to mine, and the guilt flooding them almost knocks me back. "I . . . I'm sorry, I just—"

"Fuck, Zo," I say, stepping away, everything breaking within me. "I thought you wanted this. Coming here was our plan."

"Noah, please," she says, jumping down from the hood and walking straight into me, taking my wrists in her hands and forcing me to meet her stare. "It's not that simple. Of course I want to be here with you. I would follow you anywhere, and you know that. I just . . . shit."

She pulls away from me, her eyes filling with tears as I try to figure out what the fuck could have changed her mind. "Tonight was supposed to be about you," she finally says. "This isn't how this was supposed to go."

"What the fuck are you talking about?" I demand, moving back toward her. "Isn't how what was supposed to go?"

"Everything," she says, the tears only getting worse. She shakes her head, heartbreak and regret flashing in her beautiful eyes. "Please, Noah. Can we not do this tonight? Let's just go to that party and have a good time, and then tomorrow, I swear, I'll explain everything."

I scoff, gaping at her. "You're fucking kidding me, right? You tell me you're not coming here next year and expect me to just forget I heard anything and go to a party? What the fuck, Zo? You've been a stranger for the past two weeks, and I'm trying to give you whatever space you need to figure yourself out, but the more you shut me out, the more it fucking kills me."

"Okay," she says, those big green eyes filled with tears. She steps right back into me, tilts her head down until her forehead is pressed firmly against my chest, and I wrap my arms around her, not knowing how to help her right now.

Zoey takes a few calming breaths before her soft tone fills the emptying parking lot. "I'll tell you everything," she promises me. "Just not here, okay? Somewhere private. It's not something I can just blurt out."

"Anything," I tell her before nodding back to her Range Rover. "Come on. I'll drive."

She lets out a shaky breath, and I walk with her to the passenger side, opening the door and watching her with a sharp eye as she climbs in, her gaze locked on her hands. But the fear I see in her eyes scares the shit out of me.

After closing the door, I make my way around the car and get in beside her before starting the engine and backing out. The car is silent, apart from the soft whimpering of Zoey's subtle cries, and I reach across the center console and take her hand. "I promise you, Zo," I murmur as I pull out of the parking lot and onto the road. "Whatever this is, we'll be okay."

She gives me a small smile, but it doesn't reach her eyes, and it's clear from the way her gaze falls back to her lap, she doesn't believe me. She doesn't think we stand a chance of pulling through this.

Not knowing what to say or how to make the tension in the car fade away, I just drive, every possible worst-case scenario going through my mind. I don't even know where I'm driving, just that my foot is on the gas, and I can't seem to find anywhere to pull over because the second I do, she's going to tell me something that I know is going to tear me to shreds, and I'm not ready. I don't want to burst this perfect bubble we live in.

I drive and drive, gripping the steering wheel until my knuckles turn white. The tension in the car becomes so thick that I can barely breathe. Dark clouds form above us, and a soft sprinkle falls against the windshield before quickly morphing into a raging storm. Rumbles of deep thunder sound in the distance, and I can't help but think how it matches so perfectly to the storm raging inside my chest.

The fear of the unknown becomes too much, and I find myself skidding to a stop in the middle of the deserted road, unable to take it a second longer. "Zoey," I beg her, needing her to put me out of my misery. "Please. I can't take this anymore. I need to know."

She looks back at me, those thick tears streaming down her cheeks, each one of them tearing at my soul. "Noah, I—this isn't how I wanted to tell you."

"Tell me what?" I ask, the desperation clawing at me, but all I can do is watch as her face falls into her hands, the tears quickly turning into heaving sobs. "Fuck, Zo," I mutter, reaching for her and dragging her across the center console until she's in my arms. "What's going on? Please, let me in. I can't stand seeing you like this."

Zoey swallows hard, her chest rapidly rising and falling as she takes gasping breaths to calm down. She adjusts herself on my lap, straddling me and leaning right in with her forehead pressed against mine, and it's clear that whatever this is, whatever she needs to say, is the hardest thing she's ever had to say in her life.

Her hand rests against my chest, and even through my shirt, I feel the way she shakes. Reaching up, I wrap my hand around hers, squeezing tight and hoping like fuck I'm somehow able to take her fear. Then as she closes her eyes, she lets out one final shaky breath. "Noah," she murmurs, her voice flowing right through to my soul as she finally opens her eyes again, her broken gaze meeting mine. "Do you remember the day I forced you to propose to me, and I gave you a hard time because it had to be perfect? I think we were six and seven."

I nod, the day permanently etched into my brain for so many different reasons. "Of course, I do."

"That day," she says, her voice so shaky. "Do you remember after that, my parents came into my room because they needed to talk to me?"

"They were crying," I say, able to picture it so clearly. "That's when they told you that you were sick. But what's that got to do with anything?"

Zoey sits back a little, wiping her eyes on the back of her hands before her fingers fall to my shirt, playing in the fabric as she tries to find the strength to keep going. "Leading up to my diagnosis, I'd been really tired. I don't really remember much of it, but it was enough to get Mom and Dad to take me in for tests."

I search her face, shaking my head as I reach up and brush the backs of my knuckles across her tear-stained cheek. "Zo, I don't understand why you're telling me all of this."

"Noah," she whispers, a fresh tear rolling down her cheek, her voice barely audible over the sound of rain pelting the car. "I'm telling you this because . . . because it's happening again."

My brows furrow, and I shake my head a little harder. My fingers clutch her waist as my heart races. "What?" I whisper, my blood running cold as my world stops spinning. "What do you mean it's happening again?"

Zoey forces a smile, trying to ease me into this and help me understand. "For the past few weeks," she says, her bright eyes filled with the deepest kind of agony. "I've been really tired with no energy. At first, I thought maybe I was just emotionally exhausted, but it kept getting worse. I've been lethargic and heavy and falling asleep at the drop of a hat." She looks down, not meeting my gaze. "Then that Friday night when you were at my place, and I hurt my hip—"

"You lied," I supply, remembering the exact moment she told me she slipped and how it didn't sit right with me, but I didn't push her on it.

She swallows hard and nods, more tears appearing in her eyes. "I didn't slip on water," she admits. "I was lightheaded and collapsed. I just . . . I'm sorry. It wasn't my intention to be dishonest with you, but I didn't want to worry you. I knew that both you and Mom would have started fussing about me if I told you the truth, and I just wanted to enjoy my night with you. But then, I started really thinking about it, about why I was feeling so tired all the time and getting so dizzy to the point I was passing out, and it terrified me because that's only ever happened once in my life."

"When you had leukemia," I finish for her, my words breaking as I put all the pieces together, fear closing around my chest and squeezing like a fucking vise.

I can't fucking breathe.

Zoey nods, her lips wobbling as she tries to hold herself together. "I asked Mom and Dad to take me for testing with Dr. Sanchez," she tells me in a small voice. "It could have been a number of things, but something in my gut . . . I don't know. I was almost due for tests anyway, so we asked for them to be brought forward—"

Her out-of-control tears swallow her words again. "What are you saying, Zo?" I question, tears now welling in my eyes, already knowing what she's about to tell me, but I need to hear it from her lips to confirm the worst.

"I relapsed, Noah," she says, her voice breaking on a sob and crumbling into me as my world fades back to darkness. "I got my test results back on Wednesday night. My leukemia is back."

"No," I breathe, gripping her tightly with quivering hands. I can't seem to wrap my head around the magnitude of this, the idea of Zoey being sick again, having to go through all that pain and suffering when she's already had to fight this battle once before. "No. No. There has to be a mistake. You're perfect, Zo. There has to be another reason for this. You can't be sick again. I can't fucking lose you."

"We've spent the last two days running tests," she finally says, her hands framing my face as she holds my gaze. Hot tears fall from her jaw and soak into the front of my shirt. "I'm sure, Noah. We've ruled everything else out."

Fuck.

I hold on to her, not knowing what to say as everything good in my life crumbles. She's only seventeen. She's not supposed to have cancer. She's supposed to fly. She's supposed to graduate high school and prepare to take on the whole fucking world, not spend her days in agony as her body attempts to kill her from the inside out.

"I'm sorry I couldn't tell you. I didn't want to worry you unless I was positive."

I shake my head, hearing her words but unable to take any of it in. *She relapsed.*

My heart races and my chest heaves as I gasp for air, but I can't seem to take a proper breath. My mind whirls with what this means for her. *For us.*

Chemotherapy. Tests. Pain. Hospitals.

Zoey searches my face, terror in her eyes. "Noah, are you—"

I take her hips and lift her off me before falling out of the car into the pouring rain. Panic surges through me like fire, and when the cold rain hits my skin, my thoughts explode. How could this be happening to her again? How the hell is this fair? Is this punishment for the three years of hell I put her through? Is this the universe's cruel way of trying to take her away from me?

"Noah," I hear Zoey calling behind me, but I race out in front of the car, into the glow of the headlights, and drop to my knees at the mere thought of the hell she's about to endure.

Fuck. I can't lose her. *I can't fucking lose her.*

I crumble against the road, banging my fists against the asphalt, barely able to keep myself up as I scream out, the agony tearing at my chest, tears falling from my eyes and mixing with the rain that pours over me.

"Noah," Zoey calls as I hear the sound of the car door closing, and then she's there, dropping to her knees before me and pushing me up. She barrels into me, throwing her arms around me and holding me with everything she's got. "We're going to be okay," she vows as I lock my arms around her and pull her into my lap, burying my face into the curve of her neck, terrified to let go.

"I can't fucking lose you," I tell her, the despair eating me alive. "I don't know how to be without you, Zo. I can't breathe when you're not with me."

"You're not losing me," she promises, her fingers knotting into my hair. "I'm not going anywhere. I've beaten this before. I can do it again."

"Zo," I breathe, not knowing what else I can say. I haven't felt this helpless since the day my brother died in my arms in the middle of the street. Images of his pallid face and the blood pooling in the corners of his mouth swim before me, and I have to keep telling myself that Zo isn't Linc. The feeling of her trembling body against mine is as real as the cold rain soaking through my clothes and the bite of the asphalt beneath my knees. I repeat in my mind over and over again, *She's here. She's alive*, as I hold her tighter.

"We're going to be alright," she promises as we kneel in the deserted road. "We're going to get through this and start the rest of our lives together. It's nothing but a stepping stone. I've got you right here holding my hand, and because of that, I know I can make it through this. Nothing's going to keep me from starting a life with you.

We've already fought through hell to get here. We can do it one more time."

I nod, pulling back to meet her eyes, taking in every inch of her in the glow of my headlights and committing this moment to memory. "I've got you, Zo," I vow. "Whatever you need, I've got you."

Chapter 43

NOAH

The drive back to East View is agonizing. I thought nothing could ever be as bad as the day Linc died. Losing my brother broke me in a way I'll never fully recover from, but knowing there's a chance I may lose the love of my life feels like the cruelest turn my life could take.

What Zoey is up against . . . fuck. It'll be slow and torturous. Some days she won't be able to get out of bed, some days she'll want to find a gun and put a bullet between her eyes just to make all the suffering stop. But she promised me she'll fight, and I'm trusting her to stand by her word because a world without Zoey isn't a world I want to live in. How could I? She's the other half of my soul. We're two halves of the same whole.

Without her, my life will no longer hold value to me.

She holds my hand, clutching it like it's her only lifeline as I drive, barely able to focus on the road ahead. "So, you've been dealing with this for two weeks?" I ask her, needing to keep my mind occupied before the devastation eats me alive.

"Yeah," she says in a small voice. "It's mainly just been an anxious waiting game, hoping I was wrong or that it was something minor."

"Two fucking weeks," I mutter, not knowing if I'm talking to myself or to Zoey. "You've been a fucking ghost for two weeks, dealing with this, probably terrified, while I thought you were pulling away from me."

"I'm sorry," she whispers. "I didn't want to worry you before I knew for sure. It could have been nothing, and that waiting game would have killed you. Having you not know and be the one person in my life not looking at me like I was about to drop dead is exactly what I needed."

"I get that," I tell her. "I understand why you didn't want to tell me sooner, but how many nights did you cry yourself to sleep? Having me be normal with you might have been what you *wanted,* but it's not what you *needed.* I could have been there, Zo. Every fucking night, I could have helped you."

She swallows hard and nods. "I wanted to protect you from hurting the way I was," she says. "But the second I found out, I was going to tell you. I don't think I am capable of doing this without you, even if that makes me selfish."

"It doesn't make you selfish for needing me, Zo."

"But your games, your life at college. You have so much going on right now, and I'm terrified that I'm going to be a distraction. I know you, Noah. You're going to be at home every chance you get, being here with me through all of my treatments, even if it means risking everything you've got going on at college. I don't want you to lose that, but I also can't stand the thought of having you anywhere else."

"College and football doesn't fucking matter to me, Zoey. You do. If you need me here, then I'll be here, every fucking second of every fucking day. I'm not going anywhere. Nothing is more important than this," I tell her. "There will always be football, another time, another team, but there's only one of you, and if being here to hold your hand makes you stronger and gives you what you need to fight this, then that's my priority."

Zoey wipes her face on the back of her hand, tears streaming down her face as we sit in the heat, both of us drenched from the raging storm outside. "I'm scared," she finally says.

"I know, Zozo," I say, swallowing over the lump in my throat. "I am too. I'm fucking terrified, but I'm not about to let you give up."

"Dr. Sanchez says the chemo is going to be intense, worse than when I was a kid," she says. "It's aggressive, like it's been lying dormant in my system for the last ten years, and now it's come back with a vengeance."

"Fucking hell," I mutter, needing to pull off to the side of the road and stop the car again. My head falls into my hands, and I let out a shaky breath.

"I'm sorry. I didn't mean to scare you," she tells me, reaching for my hand again. "I just wanted to be honest with you. I don't want to sugarcoat this, not with you."

"I know," I tell her, finally able to lift my head back up. I take a moment, trying to remember what she told me over a year ago when I first realized her sickness had been leukemia. "Is it the same as before? Three rounds of chemo over eighteen months and then you should be in the clear?"

"Best case scenario, yes. That's what we're hoping for, but when I was a kid, my leukemia wasn't nearly as advanced. This is going to be more intense, and there's a good chance that my body doesn't respond to the chemo."

"Then what?"

"Then we look into other treatments like radiation therapy or a stem cell transplant and hope like hell I'll still be strong enough to fight it."

"You will be," I promise her. "I know you, Zo. You're going to kick this thing's ass."

She gives me a sad smile and squeezes my hand. The determination in her eyes is enough to ease the fear inside my chest, if only a little, making it easier to breathe. Hitting the gas, I get back onto the highway, hating the thought of having to leave her alone in her bed tonight. "How are your parents taking it?"

"They're not," she admits. "They're barely holding on. Every time Mom looks at me, she crumbles, and Dad . . . He thinks he's being strong for all of us, but I hear him crying at night when he thinks everyone is asleep."

"Shit," I grunt, blowing my cheeks out as I try to hold myself together, reminding myself to check in on Mom. "And Hazel?"

Another tear rolls down her cheek, and she looks away, needing a second to compose herself. "We told her last night," she murmurs. "She's terrified. She thinks this is Linc trying to take me away from her. She thinks she's being punished."

My jaw clenches as every last part of me shatters, but I do what I can to hold myself together, knowing the second I break, Zoey will too. But I need her to know that she can lean on me when this gets hard.

"I have to go in on Monday morning to get my subcutaneous port implanted in my chest," she tells me. "It's only a small procedure and doesn't take long, but for some reason, it's terrifying me more than everything else."

"Subcutaneous port?"

"It's like a permanent catheter. It'll deliver the chemo directly into my veins. Saves me from having to get poked and prodded each time I go in. It'll come out once my treatments are done."

"Will it hurt being in there?"

Zoey scrunches her face and shrugs her shoulders. "I don't actually remember," she says. "I'm assuming it will be uncomfortable for a while, and probably hurt like a bitch if I accidentally bump it, but in the grand scheme of things, I think it's the least of what I need to worry about."

I've never heard a truer statement in my life.

"It's going to be alright, Zo. You don't need to be scared. I'm going to be right there holding your hand the whole time. I'm not going to let you fall."

"I know," she whispers, squeezing my hand.

The rest of the drive home, she tells me about the past two days, how she's been at Dr. Sanchez's office getting every test under the sun to determine just how far her cancer has spread. She tells me about her fear of losing Hope when she tells her about her diagnosis and about her concern for Hazel and me in all of this.

When we finally make it back to her place, it's after midnight and she's exhausted.

I get out of the car and make my way around to her side, opening the door for her, and as she climbs out and takes my hand, I see her exhaustion. I can't help but wonder if this is normal because it's so late or if this is an effect of the leukemia coursing through her veins.

Taking her inside, I expect to find the house asleep, only there's a single lamp on in the living room. Zoey's mom sits alone with a glass of wine, tears staining her cheeks, and hearing us walk in, she turns our way. From the looks of it, she's more than made her way through a whole bottle, but who can blame her? I wouldn't mind a stiff drink right about now.

"Oh, honey. I didn't realize you were coming home tonight," Erica says, giving me a tight smile as she gets up from the couch. "I thought you'd be staying."

Zoey glances down, not able to handle the overwhelming sadness in her mother's eyes. "Yeah, I was," she admits. "But then Noah and I . . . talked, and we just sort of ended up back here."

Erica's gaze shifts to me, and realizing that I know, her tears flow harder. She reaches out and places her hand on my shoulder, giving a gentle squeeze. "That couldn't have been an easy conversation," she says.

"It wasn't," I agree. "But if you don't mind, Zo is exhausted. She needs to get to bed."

"Of course," she says with a nod.

Zoey and I turn toward the stairs when I stop and glance back at Erica. "With all due respect," I tell her. "I know how you feel about me sleeping over now that we're . . . grown, but I can't leave her. Not tonight."

Erica nods, and I breathe out a sigh of relief. "I thought that might be the case," she tells me. "Head on up to bed, and in the morning, you can give me some ideas on how I can break the news to your mom."

"Shit."

"My thoughts exactly," she says.

Zoey squeezes my hand as we make our way up the stairs, and I press my hand to her lower back, not liking the way she sways on the stairs. Pushing through her door, Zoey heads straight for her bed, not even having the energy to stop by the bathroom to wash off her makeup.

She kicks her shoes off and drops down onto her bed as I shrug out of my shirt and let my jeans fall to the ground. I climb in beside her, knowing I won't be getting even a single wink of sleep tonight, but that doesn't matter to me. She scooches in right beside me, and I pull her into me, her head resting against my chest as her legs become tangled with mine.

"I'm sorry," she murmurs into the darkness as we listen to the softening rain hitting the roof. "This wasn't the plan I had for us."

I feel her tears against my chest, and I hold her tighter, every second of this breaking my heart. "Plans change all the time, Zoey, but that doesn't mean we have to go through this blindly. It just means that we have a chance to make an even better plan. But for now, my only plan is to see you smile every day of the rest of our lives."

"I think I can manage that," she tells me.

"Damn straight, you can, Zozo. You're a fighter, and I'm not nearly done with you yet."

Chapter 44

ZOEY

Five days after Noah's football game, I climb out of my bedroom window and sit on the roof, watching the sun peek over the horizon. Today, my life will change, and for the next few months, I'm not going to know if it will be for better or for worse.

My hands shake in my lap as I try to hold myself together. Noah hasn't left me for even a second since I told him my cancer returned on Friday night, even risking my father's wrath to demand that he sleep here. Noah has always had the greatest respect for my parents and their rules, but there's not a single line he won't cross to remain by my side.

The morning rays are almost as bright as my determination used to be, but they give me hope.

Today, I start chemotherapy and the thought alone has me ready to double over.

I'm terrified.

I remember the day I started chemo over ten years ago, and I don't remember feeling this way. I went in with my head held high, ready to fight. Perhaps that's because I was so young. I didn't truly understand what was happening to me. I didn't know what was at risk, but now at seventeen, I know exactly what I want in life, and I'm terrified of slipping away and leaving this world behind before I've even really had a chance to live.

I sit out on the roof until the sun rises above the treetops, and as I turn to make my way back inside, I see Noah standing at the window, watching me with an unbelievable sadness in his eyes. I creep closer toward him, and as I come back inside, he steps into me, propping my ass on the window frame and brushing his fingers down the side of my face as though I were the most precious thing in the world. "Are you ready?" he asks.

I shake my head, trying to hold myself together. "Not even a little bit," I admit.

He moves right in, pulling me into his warm arms. "You've got this, Zo," he tells me. "Don't think of how horrible it's going to be, think of this as the start of the rest of our lives."

My bottom lip pouts out, and I drop my forehead against his chest. "I wish you could stay today," I tell him, hating how the treatment center only allows one person to remain with the patient during chemotherapy, and for today, that will be Mom.

"I know," he tells me, his hand brushing over the back of my hair. "But the second you're done, I'm going to be right there."

I nod. "Are you heading back to college?"

"Yeah, as soon as you're settled in your room, I'll start driving back," he tells me. "I've requested a meeting with Coach Sanderson and the Dean to see if there's any kind of leniency they can give me. Coach isn't going to budge on my training schedule, but he might allow me to log my gym hours in East View. As for my classes, I'm hoping they might allow me to livestream my lectures or take online classes so

I can be here more often."

I lift my head off his chest and meet his soft gaze. "I don't want to put a strain on your schoolwork and training like that, especially if it's going to get you in trouble."

"I know, but that's exactly what this meeting is about. I need to see where they draw the line, so I know not to cross it."

A smirk pulls at the corner of my lips. "Just get right up close and personal with it, then?"

His grin is dazzling, making butterflies swarm through the pit of my stomach. "Exactly."

I roll my eyes and let out a heavy breath when I see Mom appear in my doorway, her gaze coming straight to mine. "Are you ready, honey? We need to leave in fifteen minutes."

Nerves pulse through my veins as I nod and glance toward the bags that are packed and waiting by the end of my bed. It's going to be a five-week stay in the treatment center—five weeks of complete hell—but I'll have a private room and get to make it my own during that time.

Mom contacted the school on Friday to let them know what was going on, so during the times when I feel alright, I'll have plenty of schoolwork to do. Only in the big scheme of things, working out math equations barely seems like a priority.

I've always prided myself on being a straight-A student. My work is generally done on time, and I put a lot of effort into studying, only with the time I'll be here in the treatment center, plus my next round of chemo in a few months, I don't see how graduating is going to be an option. I'll fall too far behind . . . That's assuming I make it out the other end of this, of course.

Mom gives me an encouraging smile, but I see the pain behind her eyes. She walks away, and Noah takes my waist, helping me down off the window frame. I grab a pair of sweatpants and a tank before making my way to the bathroom, passing Hazel's bedroom and peering in to find her sitting up in bed, hugging a teddy bear to her chest—the one that used to be mine.

Fresh tears well in my eyes, but I force them back. I need to be strong for her. She already thinks I'm dying.

I continue to the bathroom and get dressed, my gaze lingering on the port beneath my skin. I was right. It's uncomfortable as fuck, but it's going to help save my life, so I'm going to learn to love it.

After brushing my hair and teeth, I shove my hairbrush and toothbrush into my small toiletry bag and head back down the hall, stopping in Hazel's room and sitting with her for a minute. Neither of us says a word, both just sitting with our thoughts and pain as she curls into my side. And then all too soon, it's time to leave.

It's a forty-minute drive to the treatment center, and my hands shake the whole way. By the time Dad's bringing the car to a stop in the parking lot, I'm a mess.

Noah carries my bags in one hand and holds me in his other as the five of us make our way into the clinical foyer. I swallow hard, twisting my hands in the hem of my shirt.

An intake nurse leads me straight to my private room and quickly admits me, and before I know it, it's time for Dad, Hazel, and Noah to leave. The panic really starts to set in, and Dad steps forward, pulling me into his strong arms. He presses a kiss to my temple and tells me how much he loves me before Hazel steps in and crushes herself against me, wiping her tears on my tank.

Dad pulls her away and then there's Noah.

His gaze lingers on mine, neither of us wanting to make a move because, once we do, it brings us one step closer to saying goodbye.

I watch as he swallows hard, undeniable pain in his eyes.

Leaving me today goes against everything he is, and damn it, I'm selfish enough to beg on my knees for him to stay, but I know he can't, at least not today. After my first few sessions, I'm sure there will be a point where Mom will happily allow him to take her place. Until then, I'll see him in the afternoons, once visiting hours have opened up, and I'm sure he'll be the first one through the door.

He finally steps into me, wrapping me into the warmth of his loving arms, his lips immediately coming to mine. His kiss is soft and full of passion as he cradles my face with one hand, his other wrapped right around me and holding me against his body.

When he reluctantly pulls back, he drops his forehead against mine, each of us breathing one another in as though we may never get this moment again. "I love you so fucking much," he tells me, his voice breaking. "You know you can call me at any time, and I'll answer, even if you don't have anything to say."

I nod, tears welling in my eyes. "I'm going to be okay," I promise him.

"I know you will. You're stronger than anyone I know," he tells me, before slipping his hand into his pocket and pulling out an old phone. He hands it to me. "I want you to take this."

My brows furrow as I glance up at him, meeting his stare. "What's this?"

"Just something that got me through the really bad times after Linc died," he tells me. "It kept me from drowning in grief, and if it can offer me just a little bit of peace, then hopefully it might do the same for you."

I nod, pushing up on my tippy toes and brushing my lips over his. "Thank you."

A knock sounds at the door, and I reluctantly steal my gaze away from Noah's and turn toward the sound, finding Dr. Sanchez with a clipboard under her arm and a strained smile across her face. "Ah, you made it," she says, striding into the room, her gaze shifting to mine. "How's my patient today? Feeling good?"

I arch a brow and scoff. "I feel like I've been superglued to the middle of the road with bull ants biting my ass. There's a semi heading toward me with failed brakes, and I'm just waiting for the collision."

Dr. Sanchez nods and spares a quick glance toward my parents, probably concerned about my mental health. "That was, uh . . . oddly descriptive."

"I'll say," Noah agrees with a grunt.

Dr. Sanchez glances toward him and holds his stare a second longer than necessary, watching him with a fierce curiosity as if trying to remember something. "You seem familiar," she tells him before her eyes widen and she glances at me, then to my parents. "This isn't little Noah, is it? The same kid who used to kick and scream outside Zoey's door until I let him in."

Mom grins wide. "The one and only."

"My goodness," Dr. Sanchez says. "Time really does fly. It's good to see you two have stuck it out all these years and are still best friends."

A smile pulls at my lips, and I don't bother to correct her. I'm sure we'll have plenty of time to catch up on the drama that's been mine and Noah's lives over the next five weeks. Hell, over the next few years.

A nurse comes in, ready to prep me for the day, and as if on cue, Dr. Sanchez glances at my parents and starts going through everything that's going to happen today. As she explains the things we need to look out for, the nurse ushers me over to my bed.

I climb in, and before she can hook me up to machines, Noah walks over to my side and leans down, pressing a kiss to my lips as I clutch his old phone in my hand. "I'll see you soon, okay?"

I nod, trying to be brave for him, knowing if he sees me break, he's going to spend his whole day sitting outside my door, kicking and screaming until someone lets him in, just like when we were little. "I'll call you as soon as I'm done."

With that, he strides out of my room, stopping by the door to glance back at me. A million messages pass between us, but with Dad and Hazel walking out, he has to keep moving.

The nurse starts documenting my vital signs and doing all of her checks as Dr. Sanchez stays with us, going over everything that's going to happen today and giving us the rundown of any reactions I may have to the drugs.

She explains how we'll start by drawing blood and running some tests. The second those results are back, and everything looks good, I'll receive some anti-nausea medication and be hooked up to a chemotherapy cocktail that will take me right through the afternoon and toward dinner time. Following that, my IV will be flushed with saline, and I'll be free to spend the rest of my night how I'd like . . . within the safety of my room of course.

"Now," she continues after all the nitty-gritty stuff is out of the way. "We have our treatment room, and there are a few other girls your age who will be receiving their treatment in there today. You're more than welcome to go in there, or you can opt to remain in your room."

I glance at Mom, who's made herself comfortable in the chair beside my bed, knitting needles, magazines, a book, and her laptop protruding from the top of her bag. She just stares right back at me, leaving this completely up to me. "I, um . . . I think I'll stay in here," I tell her. "At least until I know how my body is going to react. I don't want to be hurling all over everyone in there."

"That's perfectly fine," she says before nodding toward the nurse. "Once Nurse Kelly is done drawing your blood, we'll get it tested and hopefully have you started within a few hours. Do you have any questions?"

I shake my head, somehow feeling the kind of questions running through my head right now aren't exactly appropriate, and considering what I'm about to go through, I should try to avoid being scolded by my mother.

Dr. Sanchez gives me a smile before stepping right up beside my bed and showing me the small remote. "If you need anything or have any questions, just press this button and someone will come," she tells me. "All your meals will be delivered right to your room. Now I know food is going to be the last thing you'll want, but it's important that you eat, even if it's only a little here and there. Keep yourself hydrated as well."

I nod, knowing Mom will shove it down my throat if it might help me get better. "I can do that."

"Wonderful," she says, giving my foot a gentle squeeze. "I'll come check on you later, but remember, I'm just one button away if you need me."

I give her a real smile, liking how she makes me feel so at ease about something so terrifying. She gets on her way, probably to check on another patient, and before I know it, two hours have passed, and I'm all set up with my medicine hanging from my IV stand and slowly making its way into my body.

The nerves are like nothing I've ever experienced, and it's not long before I feel queasy. I can only imagine how bad it would have been had I refused the anti-nausea medication. I get a constant flow of texts from Noah, Dad, and Hazel, and I do what I can to respond to them all, but I feel so heavy, and the sleepiness quickly overwhelms me.

I close my teary eyes as Mom holds my hand, her thumb brushing back and forth over my knuckles. She's done what she can to try and stay positive, to comfort me through the worst of it, but it's so damn hard.

I fade in and out of sleep before having to haul myself up in bed, scrambling for my little blue vomit bag, and damn it, I've never felt so sick in my life. Mom pats my back as I throw up. "Good girl," she soothes, sounding as though she's about to burst into tears. "Try and get it all out."

"I can't do this," I cry. It's only day one, and it's already too much.

"You can do this," she tells me, glancing at the clock on the wall. "You're nearly halfway through your first dose. You just need to power through it, and it'll be over for the day, and you can relax."

Resentment pulses through my cancer-riddled veins. Easy for her to say. She's not the one with leukemia. She's not the one who has drugs pumping into her body that make her want to die.

Lying back on my pillow, I try to get comfortable, snuggling up on my side as tears roll down my cheeks. When my lunch is delivered, the smell of it instantly makes me queasy again, and as I take deep, calming breaths, I spy Noah's old phone on the small table beside my bed.

Quickly grabbing it, I unlock the screen, grinning to myself when I find it has the same passcode as his locker combination at school last year—my birthday.

A smile pulls across my lips finding an old picture of the two of us as the wallpaper. I was nine or ten, and Noah was just a year older. His arm is around me, both of us grinning like idiots at the camera, completely unaware of the hell we had waiting for us.

I search through the phone, wondering why he gave it to me. It's practically empty. No texts. No emails. Not even a few boring games to keep me busy, but when I open the gallery and find my and Noah's whole life together, documented in pictures and videos, I finally get it.

My heart swells, and I scroll all the way to the bottom, passing years of images before finally reaching the ones from right after I was born. The first time Noah ever met me. He's peering over the edge of my bassinet, his big eyes so wide.

I scroll to the next and then the next, each one filling me with such joy that I forget the way the potent chemo pumps through my body. One after another, I follow the journey of our lives, loving the videos the most.

Hours pass, and I watch as we grow, watch the way Noah's friendly gaze shifts into something more, something I never really understood until we were older. There's a video of the day I forced Noah to propose to me out in the yard, our moms were sitting out on the deck watching us, both of them crying, and I realize that must have been when Mom first told Aunt Maya about my leukemia.

It goes on and on, all of our weekends spent together, all of the times we got into mischief, and the times he pulled me into his arms and held me so tight when he thought no one was watching.

It's everything. Our whole world is right here in this little phone, and the fact he held on to it, that he needed it in those dark years after Linc died, speaks volumes. Noah has always been my whole world, but seeing the way I've been his only makes me want to fight harder.

I want that future with him, I want a life, I want to build a home and have a family with a million little Noahs running around because nothing else would make me happier.

Before I know it, there's only two hours left of my first treatment, and I find myself sitting up in bed with a new inspiration. "What are you doing, honey?" Mom asks, looking up from her book as I pull out my laptop.

A stupid smile pulls at the corners of my mouth as I open a blank document. Warmth spreads through my chest, making me realize that no matter what, I'm going to be okay because I have Noah by my side. "Nothing," I murmur, almost feeling shy about it. "Just wanted to write something down."

"Okay," she says, her gaze dropping back to her book.

Only it's not enough for me, I can't just move on without saying something, and I find myself handing over Noah's old phone. "Have a look at this."

Mom takes the phone from my hand, and as she gazes down at the screen, seeing all the incredible memories from my childhood, a fond smile stretches across her face. "Oh my. I never knew he held on to all of these," she murmurs, scrolling through the pictures one after another, laughing and sighing at all the right times. "You were always so precious to him—the sun in his whole sky. He's never stopped looking at you like that."

"I know," I say, my cheeks flushing.

"He's going to marry you one day," she tells me as though it's already set in stone.

My smile widens, and not knowing how to respond to that, I focus my attention on the blank document before me and start writing.

"Zoey Erica James," he says, not daring to take his eyes off mine as the soft spring breeze catches in my hair, blowing my chestnut locks around my face. "Will you marry me?"

Chapter 45

ZOEY

My gaze shifts down to my phone, reading over Hope's text for the millionth time, not knowing how to respond.

Hope: Earth to the living dead? Are you still alive? Where have you been? I'm starting to worry about you. People are talking, wondering why you're not here, and trust me, it's not pretty!

It's been over a week since I last showed my face at school, and so far, I've been a terrible friend to Hope. I haven't said a word about my diagnosis or given any kind of explanation about why I haven't been at school. Not to mention the week and a half before my diagnosis where I was nothing but a ghost wandering the school. She's messaged me a few times during the week, checking if I was going to turn up, and I haven't responded to a single one. I don't know what to say, but my silence makes me feel like a shitty person.

It's Friday afternoon, and I've been locked up in this clinical prison for two and a half days. Apart from when I'm actually having my chemo, it's not been so bad. I've been tired and sick and sleeping on and off.

Dr. Sanchez has assured me it's all effects of the drugs, but I wish there were some way to really know. I shouldn't expect a miracle after only one round.

Hazel has been here since the second she got out of school. My four walls are dull and boring, but she's made it her life's mission to make my room welcoming. She's brought things from home and is busy setting them up around my room, and I have to admit, her little touches are really helping. It feels less like a prison and more like a home away from home.

It would be better if I had a friend to message when things got bad. Someone who would understand and not push me when I needed time to breathe. Of course, I have Noah and my family, but having a friend would be different.

Bringing Hope into all this though . . . We're still new friends, and this is a lot to ask of her. She didn't sign up to be the sick girl's friend. All she wants is to get through senior year without being someone's chew toy. But on the other hand, even after I told her everything that went down during junior year, she stood by me, not caring if that made her an outcast as well.

She was a good friend to me when I needed it most, so what kind of person would I be if I cut and ran when it got hard? I owe her an explanation, and then I suppose from there, she can be the one to decide if she's down for this. It's not like I'm asking her to be here twenty-four-seven or to be my support system. I just need a friend who'll make me smile when this gets hard.

Already knowing my answer, I quickly hash out a response and hit send before I give myself a chance to change my mind.

> **Zoey: Can you meet me this afternoon? I'll tell you everything.**
> **Hope: Well that was vague…**
> **Hope: But I suppose so. Your place?**
> **Zoey: No, actually. The cancer treatment center.**

I send her a link with the address, and the second I hit send, my hands start to shake.

> **Hope: WHAT THE ACTUAL FUCK???? Why am I meeting you in a cancer treatment center? Has this got something to do with when you had cancer as a kid? Cause like…fuuuuuuuck!**
> **Zoey: Will you come?**
> **Hope: Yeah. Be there in an hour.**

The next hour passes in a blur of emotions: fear, nervousness, anxiety, and the overwhelming need to constantly pee. Why is it that whenever I'm nervous, I suddenly need to pee all the time? It's ridiculous.

Nurse Kelly makes her way around my room, oohing and ahhing with Hazel over the way she's decorating my room before going over my vitals and making sure I'm doing okay. "How are you feeling this afternoon?" she asks, jotting something down on my chart.

"Just tired," I tell her, no difference from the other million times she's asked over the past few days.

"That's to be expected," she tells me. "Try and get lots of rest though. You're scheduled for your next dose on Monday morning."

I groan. I knew it was coming, yet knowing I have to go through all of that again makes my stomach churn. But I'm not going to lie, spending those last few hours immersed in Noah's old phone and my laptop really helped. It's all I've done over the past few days. Mom had to force me to open a textbook or two just to keep me on top of my schoolwork, but the second I'm done, I'm back to my laptop, writing down every little thing I remember, documenting our story— the good, the bad, and the ugly.

"Where's that broody boyfriend of yours this afternoon?" she questions as Hazel smothers a laugh at Kelly's perfect description of Noah. "He's usually scaring off the nurses by now, isn't he?"

I laugh as I adjust myself in bed, lowering the screen of my laptop, not liking when others can see what I'm working on. "Usually," I tell her. "But he has a big game tonight. He needs to be there, but I'm sure he'll force his way through the doors after visiting hours tonight or early in the morning."

"You know what?" Kelly says as she prepares to draw more blood. "I've been doing this job for a while, and I've never quite met a family member or partner quite as persistent as your Noah. It's impressive and kinda terrifying at the same time."

Hazel laughs. "You should have been there when my dad tried to tell him he couldn't have a sleepover the day after he found out her leukemia was back. It was crazy. I think Dad even shook a little."

I bury my face in my hands, hiding the wicked smirk across my face. I shouldn't be so fond of that particular moment, but seeing the way Noah goes above and beyond for me will always make me melt. Even if it means turning that temper of his on my father.

"I can only imagine," Kelly says just as a knock sounds at the door.

My head whips around to find Hope hovering in my doorway, her arms filled to the brim with grocery bags. She takes one look at me then takes in the needle currently sticking out of my arm, the machines, and the room filled with flowers and get-well-soon cards made by the other kids on the ward who wanted to make me feel welcome.

I expect her to yell at me, scream or cry, but she just gapes and holds up the grocery bags. "I bought snacks."

Hope stumbles into my room, dumping the bags on the end of the bed before climbing right up and crossing her legs so we sit face to face. Then before she says a word, she starts unpacking the snacks and hands me a full tub of ice cream and a spoon before her eyes go wide. She pulls it back again. "Wait. Are you allowed this?"

"Yes," I laugh, snatching the ice cream right back. "But don't be surprised if I throw it right back up."

"Ugh, gross," she mutters under her breath.

Kelly gives me a warm smile, and I roll my eyes. She was only just saying this morning that she noticed I hadn't had any visitors apart from my family and Noah, and Aunt Maya, of course. She didn't specifically say that she thought I should open up and allow people in, but her message was loud and clear. I'm starting to realize that Kelly is the type of person who's more than happy to shove her nose into someone else's business, but only for the right reasons, and I'm finding that she's really starting to grow on me.

"I hope you brought a second tub," Kelly tells Hope. "The drugs Zoey has been on are very potent, so no sharing. Be sure to use the guest bathrooms located out in the foyer and wash your hands regularly. Chemotherapy is no joke. You both need to be careful."

"Yes, ma'am," Hope says with a nod, though I'm sure she would have already received this warning from the nurses at the reception desk.

With that, Kelly excuses herself, and I'm left with Hope's saddened gaze on mine. "Chemotherapy, huh?" she asks, her shoulders slumped forward as Hazel putters around the room, straightening the photo frames while pretending she's not listening. "Does that mean you relapsed? Your leukemia is back?"

"Yeah, we found out last Wednesday and everything just moved really quickly from there," I tell her. "Sorry I didn't say anything. I was still processing, and then I was here to start treatment before I knew it."

"Shit," she mutters, her bottom lip jutting out. "I don't know if I'm allowed to give you a hug."

"Of course you can," I tell her. "But an intense make-out session is strictly out of the question."

Hope laughs and scrambles across my bed, throwing her arms around me while being as careful as possible, more than aware of all the machines. I scoot over, and she settles in beside me, dragging the bag of snacks onto her lap and showing me all the yummy goodness that I haven't had an appetite for in nearly three whole days.

"Sucks to be Noah," she mutters darkly, a smirk on her lips. "I bet he didn't take that well."

"Not even a little bit," I say, remembering the look on his face when he realized he wasn't allowed to kiss me until after I was released from the treatment center in five weeks.

"So, what does this mean?" Hope asks, almost using the snacks as a distraction to keep her tears at bay. "You stay here for a little while, have chemotherapy, and then you'll be better?"

"That's the general idea," I tell her. "Only the chemo—considering it works of course—will be delivered in three stages, and between each stage, I should be able to have somewhat of a normal life. I'll go to school when I can, and then hopefully, I'll be cleared and can forget about all of this."

"How long will that take?"

I shrug my shoulders. "That's not exactly the easiest question to answer," I admit. "It all depends on how my body reacts to the chemo."

"Assuming everything goes according to plan?"

"Two, maybe three years until I'm completely in the clear."

Hope gasps, her eyes going wide. "Shit! That long? Holy crap. You're going to be like . . . twenty before this is gone."

"Mm-hmm," I say, more than aware of just how long I'm going to be living with this.

Hope is quiet for a little while, deep in thought. "Does . . . does it hurt?"

I glance down, not able to handle the emotions burning through her blue gaze, and I don't miss the way Hazel freezes across the room, waiting for my response. "No," I whisper. "It doesn't hurt. It just makes me really tired, like I'm lethargic all the time with no energy. Sometimes I get really dizzy to the point I pass out. But if I keep hydrated and make sure I'm eating enough, I can avoid that."

"And the chemo?" she asks. "Is it as bad as they say it is in the movies?"

I nod while offering a small smile, not wanting her to be sad for me. "I'm having quite an intense round of chemo," I explain. "My leukemia is . . . It's bad. It's advanced so we're going hard on the chemo just to be on the safe side."

Hope lets out a heavy breath and leans back against my pillow. "I'm sorry, Zo," she murmurs. "I wish there was something I could do to make this easier."

"Being the bringer of the snacks is more than enough," I tell her. "I already have everyone fussing over me, so just being yourself would help."

"You mean like, coming to you with all the drama from school. Because girl, you've been missing out this week. The shit has hit the fan."

"What do you mean?" I ask, my tone lowering as I gape at her.

"What happened?"

"Tarni and Shannan are what happened," she says, a smirk on her lips as her eyes sparkle with silent laughter.

"Noooooo," I breathe. "Spill."

"Well," she starts. "Without you there to take up all of their attention, Tarni's been trying to claw her way to the top and Shannan caught wind of it. They've been at each other's throats all week. It's the funniest thing. It's like watching a train wreck in slow motion."

Digging my spoon into the half-melted ice cream, I shovel it into my mouth, groaning as the sweet chocolate chip hits my tongue. "That's insane."

"Right," she says, before glancing at me, her lips scrunching with curiosity. "Speaking of school. I'm assuming you want this kept on the down-low?"

"Yeah, I don't need their fake pity," I say. "Mom spoke to Principal Daniels, and he shared it with my teachers so they will email me the work I've been missing, not that I've really been able to get it done. But as for the students . . . I don't know. I feel like Shannan is petty enough to tell people that I'm faking it just to get attention, and I don't want to have to deal with that right now."

"You've got my word," Hope says, making a show of zipping her lips and throwing away the key.

"Thank you," I tell her with a small smile. "Now, quit holding back on me. I want to know exactly what Tarni and Shannan have been doing to each other."

Hope laughs as a wicked grin stretches across her lips. "Girl, you're not even going to believe me." And with that, she dishes on all the dirt until we're both laughing so hard it hurts.

She sits with me until the night staff comes in with my dinner, and she's just about to gather her things when Noah FaceTimes me, only my brows furrow, checking the time. He's supposed to be walking out to the field for tonight's game. What the hell is he doing?

Quickly accepting the call, a beaming smile cuts across my face, finding Noah staring back at me from the sidelines of one of the biggest fields I've ever seen. "Hey Zozo," he says, that deep purr in his tone making me miss him more.

"Aren't you supposed to be warming up?"

"Baby, you know I can't play without your eyes on me," he says, earning a few elbows to the ribs from his teammates and a gag from Hazel.

I laugh and turn the camera around, letting him see Hazel and Hope in the room before turning the camera back to me. "I told her," I tell him, knowing he'd want to know.

"I'm proud of you, Zo," he says. "Now tell me you're going to sit in your bed like a good girl and watch me kick these guys' asses."

I grin right back at him as he sets the phone up on a tripod at the edge of the field, moving it as far back as possible so that I can see the whole field all at once. "Nothing would make me happier," I tell him. "But I swear, you better make it a good one. Otherwise, I'm telling Kelly that you've been sneaking back in after visiting hours."

He gapes at me. "You wouldn't."

"Then give me a good game, and we won't have to find out."

Coach Sanderson hollers at the boys, and Noah cringes, glancing back at his team. "Shit, Zo. I have to go," he tells me. "Don't even think about going anywhere."

"Wouldn't dream of it," I tell him. "Go whoop their asses."

"Love you, Zozo."

"Love you, too."

And with that, he's gone, taking off at a jog to meet with his team as Hope appears beside me, scooching onto my bed, her gaze locked on my phone. "I've never seen a football game before," she admits.

"Are you kidding me?" I ask just as Kelly strides in, her gaze falling to the screen as well, her eyes widening with interest—my only warning that my room is about to turn into the best party this treatment center has ever seen. "Then get comfortable. You're about to witness something incredible."

Chapter 46

NOAH

Zoey is fast asleep in my arms as we wait for Dr. Sanchez to return with the results of her final blood test. It's been an exhausting five weeks, and if it was that shitty for me, I can't even begin to imagine how hard it's been for Zo. But she's held it together, keeping a smile on her face despite wanting to cry.

She's been telling me she feels like she's getting stronger, but I know she's lying. She's exhausted—emotionally, physically, and mentally—but she's not ready to give up. I think she's been trying to manifest good results, willing it into existence, but we've all seen Nurse Kelly's grim expressions. There should have been a change by now, some kind of indication that the chemotherapy has been working, but so far . . . nothing.

Zoey is getting weaker, and the dizziness is coming more frequently, but the chemo . . . fuck. We thought that the first dose would be the hardest to get through, but with each new dose, it kills her just a little bit more. She cried and sobbed while throwing up, and then she just slept. She's been so tired, and at this point, I don't know if it's the drugs or the leukemia.

Either way, she's suffering, and I don't fucking like it.

When she first arrived at the cancer center, she spent hours on her laptop, typing away. She won't share what she's working on, but it's been keeping her mind busy, which is a good thing. On chemo days, she doesn't have much energy, so she usually puts her computer away after a few hours of work.

On her rest days though, she's been living on her laptop like it's going out of fashion. She'll do whatever it is she's doing with my old phone resting on her lap while I sit in the chair beside her bed, trying to listen to my college lectures.

My world has been put into perspective since Zoey got her diagnosis. College and football don't mean anything to me right now. Though, I still push through it because Zoey wants me to. If I lost my position on the team because I was missing too many classes or training sessions to be here, she would be devastated, but being here to hold her hand through all of this is the only thing that matters to me. Like I told her at the start, there will always be another football team or another college, but there will never be another Zoey Erica James.

She's my everything, my heart, my love, and I will burn my world to ashes if it means getting to hold her through her darkest days. There will be time for college and football later—after Zoey is well again.

Hazel moves around the room, packing up all of Zoey's things, but it won't be for long. These things will be right back here in a few weeks when she starts her next round of chemotherapy. And fuck, I need it to work.

I don't know how to breathe without her. If chemo doesn't work and she has to leave this world, my life wouldn't be worth living.

With Dr. Sanchez due to come back soon, Zoey's parents make

their way back into Zoey's room. They've been working around the clock, trying to be here every chance they get while also doing everything possible to hold on to their jobs. But truth be told, at this point, I don't think they give a shit about their jobs anymore. They just want to be here for their daughter, and I want that for them too, but without their jobs, they'll lose the insurance to cover all of Zoey's medical expenses. It's a fucking brutal world we live in.

"How's she doing?" Henry asks, his gaze lingering on his little girl.

"Pretending it's not as bad as it really is," I tell him, not wanting to sugarcoat anything.

"I know," he says with a heavy breath. "She's trying not to worry us."

"It's stupid. She should be focusing on herself, not how we're coping with it. We'll be fine as long as she's getting the help and medicine she needs."

Erica scoffs, moving Zoey's bag off the seat beside the bed and getting comfortable. "Try telling her that," she says, glancing my way. "I swear, Zoey is as stubborn as they come. She learned that from you, you know?"

I smirk. I'm all too aware of all the bad habits I taught her growing up.

"So," I say, pulling Zoey in even tighter against my chest. "Any idea what she's been doing on that laptop?"

Erica laughs. "Oh, I have my suspicions, but she'll kill me if I share them with you. So until she decides she's ready to let you in on the big secret, I'll be keeping my mouth shut."

Damn it. "It was worth a try."

Zoey's dad starts helping Hazel with the cleanup, and as he scoops up my old phone and slides it into her bag, he pauses, a heaviness in his eyes. "Noah, I . . ." his words trail off as if unable to find the right ones. "I don't think I've ever thanked you for all that you're doing for my little girl. Without you here, giving her the strength to keep fighting—"

"I wouldn't be anywhere else, sir," I tell him. "From the day I first met her, I knew I was going to walk my life right beside her. If she's happy, I'm happy, and if she's suffering, then I'm suffering too. We're two halves of the same whole, and I know I've told you that before, but it doesn't make it any less true. She's my world, and if being here every day to hold her hand is what she needs, then that's exactly what I'm going to do."

He nods, that heaviness still right there in his eyes—eyes that look so similar to his daughter's. "Either way, I appreciate you," he tells me. "I know I haven't made life easy for you over the last year, but there's no denying how happy you've made her."

"That's all I've ever wanted for her," I say just as Zoey begins to stir in my arms. She yawns, and the soft, pained groan that follows shatters me.

"Mmmmm," she moans, opening her eyes and peering into the brightness of her room before glancing up at the clock. "Shit. I didn't mean to sleep that long."

"You're fine, Zo," I tell her, brushing my fingers over her waist, terrified of the thought I might never get to hold her again.

She looks around her room, taking in the empty walls and lack of flowers. "Has Dr. Sanchez been in yet? Is it time to go?"

"Not yet," Erica says, leaning forward in her chair to grab Zoey's hand and give it a gentle squeeze. "She should be here any minute with your results for the first phase of your chemo, then we'll be able to take you home and figure out our next steps."

Zoey nods and presses against my chest for leverage to help herself up, and I can't help but notice just how weak she is in her movements.

She rubs her eyes as I reach for her bottle of water and press it into her hands, despite not being asked for it. She's not the best at remembering to have water, so whoever is closest is on water patrol. Every twenty minutes, force her to have at least a few sips, even if it means getting your head bitten off. Same goes for food, though that task has been a little more challenging, especially on chemo days.

Zoey is just finishing her small sips of water and handing me back the bottle when Dr. Sanchez walks in, and she immediately grips my hand like it's her only lifeline. Her eyes go wide and hopeful, though I see the doubt swimming deep within them.

We already know how this is going to go.

"Please tell me there's good news," Zoey begs, her voice already breaking.

Dr. Sanchez looks at Zoey, and the heartbreak in her eyes tells us exactly what we need to know. Zoey whimpers before the doctor says a word and we watch as she takes a seat at the end of Zoey's bed, gently squeezing her foot. "I'm sorry, Zoey," she tells her in a pained tone. "The results of your blood tests have confirmed that this round of chemotherapy hasn't been successful. There are still high counts of leukemia cells in your bone marrow, which, unfortunately, means that you are not yet in remission."

Zoey cries and turns into me, crushing her face into my chest as I hold her, fearing the worst as the doctor's words play on repeat in my head.

The chemo didn't work. She's not getting any better.

Erica cries, sobbing into her hands as Hazel rushes into her father's arms, crying as though she's already lost her.

"Where do we go from here?" I ask, being the only one among us who has the strength to voice the one question that's circling each of our minds.

Dr. Sanchez gives me a warm smile, but it doesn't reach her eyes. "First and foremost, we need to allow Zoey's body some time to rest. There's only so much chemotherapy one's body can handle at a time. She'll get a few weeks to recover, then we'll get her back in to start a second round of chemotherapy at a higher dosage."

"A higher dosage? Does that mean it will be more intense?" Erica questions with fear in her eyes, knowing how much suffering Zoey has been through this first round, but to be *more intense*? Fuck! I don't know if Zoey has the strength to push through. This round tore her to shreds.

"Yes," Dr. Sanchez says with a regretful nod. "It will be more intense. Her leukemia is very aggressive, and over the past five weeks, it has shown that it's not going to give up without a fight. The leukemic cells are developing quicker than anticipated, so we need to be prepared for that. There's also a good chance that in these next few weeks of her recovery phase, the cancerous cells will begin to spread. So we'll require Zoey to come in for regular testing. It's important that we keep a close eye on any progression her cancer may have so we can make adjustments to her treatment plan as necessary."

"What happens if that fails?" Zoey asks, her voice muffled by my shirt.

"Then we start looking into alternate options," Dr. Sanchez says.

Zoey's father shakes his head as if unable to comprehend what's being said. "But . . . If she were to fail her next round of chemo and her cancer continues to spread, will she have the time or strength to even attempt those alternate treatments?" he asks, a gut-wrenching fear in his tone. "The chemo clearly didn't work this time around. So why not try those alternate routes now?"

Fuck. I don't even want to think about what it could mean if this next round were to fail.

Dr. Sanchez shakes her head. "At this point, chemotherapy is still Zoey's best chance of fighting this. I know this is a lot to take in, and it is a devastating setback. However, we're still confident in Zoey's treatment plan. It's just going to be a slightly longer road we need to travel."

My gut twists with unease, but I hold myself together as I clutch Zoey tightly in my arms, my hand roaming up and down her arm.

A heavy silence fills the room as we all digest exactly what's been said and what this means for Zoey. Dr. Sanchez stands, clutching her clipboard to her chest. "For now, Zoey, you're free to go home and get some well-needed rest. I'll be contacting your parents sometime tomorrow with an updated treatment schedule, and in the meantime, you know I'm only one call away. If you have any questions, worries, or doubts, don't hesitate to contact me. Whether it's a quick call or you need to drop in for an appointment."

Zoey nods, devastation clouding her soft green eyes. "Thank you," she murmurs.

Dr. Sanchez steps forward, squeezing her foot again. "I know this is disheartening, Zoey, but I need you to hold on to that fighting spirit. Take the next few days to be sad, get it all out of your system, then remind yourself just how strong you are. You've already survived this once before and made it through your first round. When you return in a few weeks, you'll be ready and in the right mindset to beat this thing. I know you can do this, Zoey."

She forces a small smile, but the heartbreak wins out and she crumbles again. "I'll be ready," Zoey promises her.

With that, Dr. Sanchez quickly speaks with Zoey's parents as Kelly pops in to say goodbye, though it won't be long until we see her again. Erica helps Zoey out of her bed, and her father quickly rushes to her side, curling his arm around her waist to help take her weight, and the fiercest jealousy cuts through me. I promised her that I would always be the man to catch her when she fell.

Instead, I grab her bags, and before I know it, she's back in her parents' car, heading back to East View. It's a long fucking day filled with overwhelming sadness, grief, and helplessness, and by the time night has fallen and Zoey is asleep in my arms, tucked into her bed, I can barely breathe.

After making sure she has everything she needs, I slip out from beneath her before pulling the blanket right up to her chin, keeping her warm and watching the way she snuggles into her pillow. When she's asleep like this, so at peace, it's hard to comprehend how the cancer is pulsing through her body and poisoning her from the inside out.

Feeling myself starting to break, I silently move across Zoey's room and slip out into the hall, pulling the door closed behind me before dashing down the stairs and heading straight out the backdoor. I barely get a step out into the night before I fall to my knees, gasping for air as my eyes grow watery.

She's not getting any better. The chemo was supposed to work. It was supposed to breathe new life into her and give her a fighting chance, but now we're back to step one. Only this time, the leukemia has had a chance to grow and spread through her precious body.

That round of chemo tore her to shreds. How the hell is she supposed to endure another, more intense round?

Fuck. I've never ached like this in my life. I'm trying to hold myself together for her, to be the fucking hero she needs, but seeing her like this is killing me. I'd give anything to take away her pain, to put myself in her place. I would endure it all if it meant saving her from this hell.

Finally catching my breath, I fall to my ass with my back up against the wall of the house. Then despite not touching a single cigarette since Zoey showed me how to find peace, I pull one out of my pocket and light it up, desperately breathing it in.

My hands shake as my world slowly crumbles around me. I feel like I'm screaming out for help, but no one is coming because Zoey is my salvation. *She's my savior,* and now she needs me to be hers, but I don't know what I can do to make her pain go away. She needs me to save her, and all I can do is stand back and watch her leukemia spread, slowly pulling her away from me, no matter how hard I hold on.

I've been sitting outside for over an hour when I hear the backdoor open. Lifting my head from my knees, I find Zoey looking down at me, and as I go to get up, she walks right into me and steps over my legs, dropping straight down into my lap.

Her arms wrap around my neck as I hold on to her, so damn terrified to let go.

"We're going to be okay," she promises me, leaning right in and resting her head against my shoulder. "I love you too much to leave this world yet. I'm not going anywhere, Noah. You're my *bestest friend,* and there is still so much I want to experience with you. You'll see, you still have a million more years to drive me crazy. I'm not nearly done loving you yet."

My hand brushes over her hair and down her cheek, feeling the wetness of her tears. I should be the one comforting her, not the other way around. "Nothing would make me happier," I tell her. "We're going to have it all, Zo. Just you and me until the end of time."

Chapter 47

ZOEY

Well, this is shit.

I stare up through the gates of hell—East View High—and suddenly I don't feel so brave. I don't know what the hell I was thinking about coming back here. Maybe I was seeking some semblance of normalcy during these few recovery weeks, but I clearly wasn't thinking straight. Perhaps the leukemia has spread to my brain and is screwing with my thought process.

Crap. That was dark, even for me. I shouldn't joke like that.

I've already missed almost two months of school and am drastically behind in all my classes, though not a single teacher has pushed me to hand in schoolwork. At this point, I think it's safe to say I won't be graduating. It's not like my attendance is going to get any better over the next few months when I'm in and out of the treatment center. But I figured, why not try and experience life like a normal teenager before it's all stripped away again? Sitting in my room day in and day out, recovering from my first round of chemo, is doing my head in. Don't get me wrong, I've been more than occupied with the story I'm writing on my laptop, but it doesn't keep me from going stir-crazy.

The football season finished a few weeks ago, and without Noah's crazy training schedule, he's been able to spend more time with me, taking his classes online and only going in for exams, which seem to be all the time. I can't complain though, I'll take him any way I can get him. I'm just grateful his campus is so close. If he'd taken any other offer for college, this would be so much harder.

There's only a week before Christmas and New Year's break, then I'll be starting my second round of chemo straight away. And God, it makes me anxious. I know what to expect, how it's going to make me want to claw the flesh right off my body, how my insides are going to tremble as the drugs are slowly forced through my veins. All I can hope for is that I have the mental strength to keep pushing through it.

But if this doesn't work . . . shit. I can't allow myself to go there.

It has to work. There's no other choice. This is my final shot.

I know Dr. Sanchez said there's a plan B, that I have other options if the second round of chemo fails, but at the rate the leukemia cells are spreading through my body and how quickly I've been declining, it doesn't take a genius to figure out that I won't have the strength to keep fighting. Especially considering how weak I'll be following the chemo.

Like I said, I have no other choice. *This has to work.*

My phone chimes in my hand, and I glance down as I wait for Hope, too chicken to walk through the gates by myself.

Resident Asshole: You good? Just got back to campus.
Zoey: I think I've finally lost my mind!

I hit send before holding my phone up and taking a photo of the school gates, letting him know my plans for the day. I quickly attach that to a new text and wait for his onslaught to follow.

Zoey: *Multimedia Message*

Resident Asshole: What the fuck is wrong with you? Why would you want to torture yourself like that? No one expects you to be there.

Zoey: I was listening to hardcore rap from the early 2000s and something just came over me, and I remembered that I'm actually a terrifying badass and none of these preppy bitches can touch me.

Resident Asshole: Zo—I say this from the very bottom of my heart—you're the furthest thing from being a terrifying badass. You're a good girl with a kind heart that shatters like flimsy glass the second someone even looks at you wrong.

Zoey: *Middle finger emoji*

Zoey: I can handle this. It's just school.

Resident Asshole: School is torture.

Resident Asshole: I want a list of names of anyone who even tries to get at you.

Zoey: So you can beat up a bunch of high school kids?

Resident Asshole: Damn straight. It'll give me a chance to let off some steam.

Zoey: I know a way you can let off a little steam. Though I can guarantee it's going to get you all kinds of worked up first.

Resident Asshole: Don't fucking tempt me, Zo.

Zoey: Go and learn some smart people shit. I have a school to dominate.

I grin to myself, picturing the way he would be rolling his eyes and typing out a million different responses before deleting them all. He knows damn well I'm screwing with him. I have absolutely no intention of trying to dominate this school. What's the point? It's not like I'll be spending much more time here. My only goal is to make it through the day and hand in a few of the assignments I've managed to get through over the past few weeks.

"Well, well," I hear Hope saying from behind me. "Look who decided to show up."

A stupid grin stretches across my face as she steps into my side, trying to be discreet in the way she takes my bag off my shoulder and slips her arm through mine. To anyone else, it looks as innocent as two girls walking arm in arm, but I see it for what it is—offering me a crutch if I need her.

"I figured I hadn't endured enough torture, so why not add a little more by coming to school?"

"Not gonna lie," Hope says. "When I read your text this morning, I thought maybe you'd fallen and bumped your head. No one voluntarily goes to school, especially when they've already been given the choice to complete their schooling from the comfort of their own bed."

"I know," I say with a heavy sigh as we make our way through the gates of East View High. "Do you think anyone knows?"

"Nah, no way," she says, pausing to find her phone when a text comes through. "They would have bombarded me with questions if they had even an inkling about why you've been away. Though, I can't guarantee the teachers aren't going to give it away. I think your mom might have mentioned that I know because they've been giving me weird looks lately, and I know they're just dying to ask me how you're doing."

"Great," I mutter to myself as she checks her phone. "That's exactly what I need."

Hope barks an unladylike laugh before shoving her phone toward me. "Your bodyguard is coming for me if you have a bad day."

"Huh?" I grunt, taking her phone and grinning like an idiot as I read over her latest text.

Zoey's Douche Canoe Boyfriend: Watch her like a fucking hawk.

"Really?" I laugh. "Zoey's douche canoe boyfriend?"

"What?" she says, shrugging her shoulders. "He forced me to add his number to my phone right after we got high in the park. Personally, I think it suits him perfectly, but just so you know, next time we smoke a joint, we're hotboxing his car."

I laugh and roll my eyes. "Do I even want to know what that means?"

"Oh, my sweet little innocent child," she says, looping her arm back through mine. "Just imagine all the fun-tastic ways I could corrupt you."

We make our way inside, and I find myself discreetly watching the people around me, making sure there are no lingering eyes filled with pity. Realizing that Hope is right, and my secret is safe, I let out a relieved sigh and find my way to my locker.

"Miss James."

Ah, shit.

I turn and plaster a smile across my face as I find Principal Daniels creeping in beside me, practically radiating pity.

"Good morning, sir."

"Good morning, indeed," he says, his gaze shifting to Hope over my shoulder. "I, uh . . . just wanted to welcome you back. I wasn't expecting to see you roaming around the halls quite so soon."

"Thank you," I say, appreciating how he's being a shitload more discreet than Hope is. "I hope that's okay. I know my teachers have been putting a lot of effort into offering my classes online, but I'm going a little crazy at home and thought I could use a change."

"Of course," he says. "You're always welcome here. However, I take it that means you're feeling much better?"

My gaze falls away, a heaviness resting on my chest. "I, um . . . no. I'm not."

"I see," he says with a nod before letting out a heavy breath, clearly understanding that my treatments haven't worked.

"I'll be going in for another round just after New Year's."

"Another few months, I take it?"

I press my lips into a hard line, hoping he can't see the fear in my eyes that appears every time the topic of my second round of chemo is brought up. "Yes, sir."

"I'm sorry it hasn't gone as planned, Zoey," he tells me with the utmost sincerity. "If there's anything you need, just let me know. There's absolutely no pressure, and I'm sure if you need extra time on your schoolwork, your teachers will be happy to allow extensions until you're feeling better. We could definitely work something out to ensure you still graduate with the rest of your classmates."

"Thank you," I say, not bothering to tell him that the likelihood of me graduating in the spring is slim to none.

"Alright, I'll leave you to it," he tells me. "You know where the nurse's office is if you need some time to recoup or just a little peace from the madness. And I'll be sure to let the faculty know that you're here today."

Principal Daniels gives me a tight smile before continuing down the hall, and the second he's far enough away, I turn back to Hope and let out a heavy breath.

"Well, shit. If I knew being sick was the way to go about getting extensions on my assignments, I would have faked appendicitis for my history paper last week," Hope teases before looping her arm through mine just as the bell sounds for homeroom. "Come on. Let's get you to class before everyone else starts moving around so you don't get trampled."

I give her a tight, grateful smile and allow her to pull me through the halls, only as I look up to see through the crowded bodies, I almost run right into Tarni.

I come to a startled stop and quickly back up a step as Hope pulls me around her, and as I glance back over my shoulder at the girl I grew up with, the girl who once held my hand through these very same treatments, I see nothing but a stranger.

Her eyes linger on mine with vile hatred, and it cuts me right to the core, just as Noah knew it would. I really am the furthest thing from a terrifying badass. I'm a good girl who shatters like glass, but the thing about glass is with the right amount of heat, I can mold myself back together. And Noah, he's all the heat I'll ever need.

Turning my gaze away, I continue down the hallway, putting Tarni to the back of my mind. She's the last thing I need to focus on right now. And with that, Hope walks me straight into homeroom, lays my books down on my desk, and promises to meet me right back here to walk me to my first class of the day. As she leaves, I can't help but smile at her retreating form. She's reminded me what it truly means to have an amazing friend who will always have my back.

Chapter 48

NOAH

Christmas and New Year's Eve flew by, and all too soon, Zoey is back at the treatment center, going through the worst hell of her life. She's three weeks in, and every day just gets harder. I hate seeing her like this. I hate seeing how the light in her eyes dulls a little more each time I see her.

She's seventeen, almost eighteen in a few weeks. This isn't how she's supposed to be living. She's supposed to have the world at her feet with college right around the corner. She's supposed to be learning how to fly, not crumbling under the weight of her disease.

I know she's strong enough to pull through this. She has to be. But it's going to be the biggest fight of her life. She just needs to hold on, endure the worst so we can get to the best days of our lives.

I pull up at the treatment center, letting out a heavy breath, terrified of what I'm about to walk into. Some days she's good. They're generally the rest days between doses, but then some days, I see the pain in her eyes, and I know she's dying inside, silently screaming for me to take her away from this place.

She's never once told me how badly she's suffering. She's trying to protect me from it, doesn't want me hurting for her, but she should know better by now. I can see right through her. Those dazzling green eyes are like a window right into her soul, and when hers is so entwined with mine, I read her perfectly.

Desperate to get in there and see how she's doing, I jam my pockets full of supplies and then glance down at the floor space of my passenger side, wondering how the hell I'm going to get her gift into her room without getting kicked out. I could always sneak through her window, but then I have to scale the high fences, and carrying this with me is going to turn it into a chore.

"Shit," I mutter, realizing I'm going to have to shove it down my shirt.

Reaching into the backseat, I grab my jacket and pull it on before zipping it up, giving myself a little extra padding to conceal Zoey's gift while hoping like fuck I don't get sprung before I get to give this to her. She's going to be so excited. She's always begged her parents for one, but luckily for her, they can't exactly say no right now.

Reaching down, I grab her present and place it onto my lap before making sure I have my phone and keys. Then I grab the single tulip off my dashboard before wrestling her present beneath my shirt and deciding this will have to do.

I make quick work of getting out of my car and hurrying across the lot, knowing my luck is bound to run out at some point. Then almost in a sweat, I sign in at the reception desk, hoping like fuck this thing stays quiet. After a weird look from the nurse behind the desk, I race down the hall to get to Zoey's room.

Barging through her door a moment later, a stupid grin stretches across my face as I spy her sitting up in bed with her laptop open, busily typing away. I can't help but notice how much weight she's been losing or the dark circles beneath her beautiful eyes, but I would never point it out.

The second Zoey glances up and takes me in, her gaze narrows. "You look shady as hell, Noah Ryan," she tells me, suspicion thick in her tone. "Spill it. What are you hiding?"

"Nothing," I say slowly, kicking the door shut behind me as I creep across her room.

She watches me like an assassin, never taking her eyes off her mark. "Your pockets are bulging like crazy, and you're wearing the jacket you put in the back of your car that you never use. Plus, whatever you've got hidden under there is making you look like you've been hitting the gym way too hard and suddenly sprouted ridiculous-sized pecs. Or you got a botched boob job, and if that's the case, you should be asking for your money back."

"Ha. Ha," I say, rolling my eyes as she closes her laptop, offering me her undivided attention. "I'm glad to see the chemo hasn't burned that sarcasm out of your system."

"Great news, isn't it?" she says, her gaze falling back to my torso with a deep curiosity, but when I don't go to show her, she loses her patience. "Just give it to me already. You're killing me. You know I can't handle surprises."

I laugh and make my way around her bed before propping my ass on the side. "You need to be aware that having this here is definitely going to get us in trouble," I warn her before handing her the tulip between my fingers, something I've started doing every single day to the point her room is flooded with them. "But I couldn't resist."

Her brows furrow, her gaze shifting back to mine, as she holds the tulip in her lap, and with that, I loosen my hold around my jacket and pull open the neckline of my shirt before peering down and taking in the big eyes staring back at me. "Come on," I say, a wide smile stretching across my face as Zoey's brand-new ragdoll kitten walks right up my chest and pops her head out through the neckline.

Zoey gasps, her eyes going wide as her kitten looks back at her, the two of them meeting each other's stare. The second they do, it's like the planets align, and the kitten jumps right out of my shirt and scrambles across the bed, not stopping until she's purring in Zoey's lap.

"Holy shit," Zoey breathes, scooping the tiny thing up into her arms, tears welling in her beautiful green eyes. "How did you know? I've always wanted a ragdoll."

"Zo," I laugh, giving her a pointed stare. "I know everything there is to know about you. I've been there on at least ten different occasions where you've begged your parents for one and then had to deal with the fallout when they said no."

She grins, knowing exactly what I'm talking about, but it quickly fades away as she glances back down at the kitten. "Thank you," she says. "I love her, but . . . maybe my parents were right to say no. What if I don't . . . You know, who will . . ."

"I don't want you worrying about that," I tell her. "I've already cleared it with your parents, and I talked to Hazel. She says *if* that were to happen, and that's a big *if* because it's not going to happen, then she will look after her."

"Really?" she asks with wide eyes. "I really get to be a kitten momma?"

"Yeah, Zo. You're a kitten momma."

The beaming excitement that shines through her eyes is the best thing I've ever seen, and with her kitten wrapped in her arms, she leans forward and presses her lips to mine in a hungry kiss, and I don't dare hesitate to kiss her back. Only her eyes widen, and she quickly pulls away. "Oh, shit. I'm not supposed to kiss you," she panics, her hand coming up and wiping over my lips, but I shake my head, lowering her hand.

"You really think a little bit of chemo is going to stop me from kissing my girl?" I ask, pulling her right back in and giving her exactly what she's been wanting. Fuck the chemo. If it makes me sick, I'll deal with it, but nothing is going to keep me from showing my girl how much I love her. I resisted during her first round, but seeing her like this has only gone to show just how short life can be, and I want to live it to the fullest.

She holds up the little kitten before bringing her right to her face, unconditional love already shining in her wet eyes. "Don't cry, baby," I beg her.

"I can't help it," she tells me. "Apart from when I'm with you, I don't think I've ever been this happy in my life."

I smile back at her, absolutely loving seeing her like this. Then trying to keep myself from getting overly emotional and wondering just how many chances I might get to make her this happy again, I stand up and start pulling all the cat supplies out of my pockets.

The kitten watches me like a hawk, eyeing the toys I put down on the bed, more than ready to start chasing them around Zoey's room. I add treats and a portable food and water bowl to the pile, surprised with just how much crap I was able to squeeze into my pockets.

"Holy shit," Zoey says, eyeing it all. "Where am I supposed to hide all of this?"

"Your call, Zo," I tell her. "I can take her home with me tonight and bring her back in the morning or—"

"Hell no," she says, her brows furrowed, looking appalled at my suggestion. "What kind of momma would I be if I let you take my baby away every night? She'll stay here with me."

"You sure, babe? I know you don't like breaking the rules and having pets in a place like this is definitely against the rules. Dr. Sanchez isn't going to be down with this."

Zoey smirks. "Maybe not for you, but when I push the whole *therapy kitty* angle and tell her how happy she would make all of her patients, she won't be able to resist. Besides, it's not like I'm going to advertise that she's here. I'll keep her hidden for as long as I can."

"So, she's going to sleep under the blankets with you?" I ask, a little jealous.

"Uh-huh," Zoey smirks. "But don't be surprised if you get a call in the middle of the night to come and get our cat."

"*Our* cat?"

"Mm-hmm," Zoey murmurs, her gaze so heavily focused on the tiny bundle of fluff in her lap, adoration shining in her beautiful green eyes. "You're my person, Noah. So if this little sweet thing is my baby, that means by default, you're her daddy."

"Ah, shit."

Zoey laughs and holds up the kitten, looking over her with deep consideration. "Hmmm, I think I'll call you Allie."

My brows furrow, having no idea where she pulled that name from. "Allie?" I question.

Zoey grins wide. "From *The Notebook*," she tells me as though I should have already figured it out. "Noah and Allie. I've already got my Noah, but I need an Allie to complete the set."

I shake my head, letting out a heavy breath as I scooch in beside Zoey on her bed, reaching over to put her laptop somewhere safe before pulling her into my arms as she holds tightly on to little Allie. "How are you feeling today?"

"Better now," she admits. "It was mostly a shit day. I got a new neighbor, and the walls are paper thin. All I've been able to hear all day is how easy she thought her chemo treatment was. I'm about ready to march in there and shove my foot right up her ass."

"That bad, huh?"

"Worse," she mutters. "She also likes scrolling through TikTok with the volume all the way up."

"You only need to get through two more weeks, and then you're out of here," I remind her, knowing my words are doing absolutely nothing to make her feel better about her situation.

Zoey lets out a heavy sigh before reaching up and pushing her hair back off her face, only when her hand falls away, she gasps with horror, her eyes widening. My head snaps toward her, trying to figure out what's wrong when I glance down and find long strands of chestnut hair tangled between her slim fingers.

"No, no, no, no," she chants as my heart breaks for her. She reaches up again, grabbing at her hair as if she can't believe what she's seeing, and sure enough, more clumps of hair come free in her hands.

Fat tears roll down her cheeks, and I take her face, forcing her to look at me as she starts to panic. "It's okay, Zo. We knew this could happen. It's just hair. It will grow back."

She shoves at me, her face falling into her hands. "You're a guy. You don't get it."

"Try me."

"It's . . . It's my hair," she cries. "To a girl, her hair is part of her identity. Without it . . . it's just another part of myself I'm losing to this stupid disease."

She scrambles off her bed before allowing me a chance to argue, and I watch as she presses a hand to the wall, steadying herself as she makes her way into the private bathroom. The door only closes halfway, leaving it cracked just enough for me to see as she stands in front of the mirror with tears rolling down her sunken cheeks.

She pulls at her hair, and thick chunks fall into the basin. When she can't take it any longer, she collapses against the sink.

Striding into the bathroom, I step in behind her before taking her hips and gently turning her until she crumbles against my chest. My arms lock around her, holding her tight as she cries, the devastation pouring through both of us for two very different reasons.

My hand roams up and down her back, and I hold her there as Allie cries from the bed, wondering what's wrong with her new momma, too small to risk jumping down on her own.

We stand here for almost an hour as she cries it out, and when she finally pulls out of my arms and wipes her eyes, she turns around, facing the mirror once more. Reaching up to the overhead cabinet above the sink, her hand curls around a box containing hair clippers, and she pulls it down before briefly meeting my questioning gaze through the mirror. "I found it here during my first round of chemo," she tells me. "I just didn't think I'd ever have to use it."

She turns back to me and presses it into my hand, but I take her chin, raising it until she meets my stare. "Are you sure? We don't have to do this today. You can sit with it until you're ready."

"So I can get around looking like Angelica's doll from *Rugrats*? No thanks. I'd prefer to just get it over and done with."

"Okay," I tell her, placing the shaver down on the edge of the sink. "I'll get you a chair."

She nods and turns back to the mirror, those watery eyes tearing me to shreds. Walking out of the bathroom, I grab the chair from beside her bed before stopping and scooping up Allie in my other hand and making my way back.

I find Zoey in the middle of plugging the cable into the outlet and trying to figure out how the shaver works, and I set the chair behind her. She doesn't hesitate to drop into the seat, and a part of me wonders if it's because she's already been on her feet for so long.

She takes Allie and snuggles her in her lap as I take the shaver and switch it on, only I pause as my hand hovers by the top of her head. I meet her gaze through the mirror. "Are you sure you're ready for this?"

She shakes her head. "Not even a little bit, but just do it," she says, a brokenness dulling her green eyes.

My thumb stretches around the shaver to switch it on, and with a heavy breath, I push it back over her scalp, her long chestnut locks falling to the ground at my feet. Zoey cries, holding Allie up to her face and breathing her in as though the tiny little kitten is somehow able to give her the strength that I can't.

I do it quickly, not wanting her to have to endure this for long, and when I'm done, I lift the shaver to my own head, pushing it through my dark hair before she gets a chance to stop me. Her eyes widen as her jaw slackens. "NOAH!" she screeches. "What the hell are you doing?"

"If you get to be a sexy little baldie, then why the hell can't I?" I say, really driving home the point that it's just hair. She's still fucking gorgeous to me whether her hair is on her head or covering the bathroom floor. It's not a big deal. Once she's better and her body has a chance to recover from the chemotherapy, her hair will grow back, and when it does, I'm sure it's going to be just as beautiful as it once was.

She watches me as I shave my head, and I meet her gaze through the mirror. "You think I could pull off a mohawk?"

A smirk pulls at her lips, and she rolls her eyes. "Don't even think about it," she tells me, that smirk only widening, then watching as I go to every effort to shave my whole head except for the strip right down the center, she starts to laugh. "Noah! Stop making me laugh. I'm trying to be sad."

"Don't you think you've been sad enough?" I ask her. "You've cried more tears over the past few months than you have in your whole life, and each one of them has killed me. You've already been through so much, and I know the fear of the unknown is terrifying, but that doesn't mean you don't deserve to be happy. So whether you like it or not, I'm not going to stop trying to make you laugh because when you do laugh and your eyes light up like Christmas morning, it makes me so fucking happy I could die."

"That happy, huh?"

"Yep," I say, nodding as our gazes collide through the mirror. "That fucking happy."

Zoey just smiles, and I lift my chin just the slightest. "Come here," I tell her, holding out the shaver. "Finish this for me so I don't walk out of here looking like a troll."

Zo laughs and scrambles around, handing me the kitten as she stands on the chair and takes the shaver. I brace my other hand against her hip, keeping her steady in case she falls, and with that, she turns the shaver back on and takes away any hopes I might have had of a killer mohawk.

Chapter 49

ZOEY

These have been the hardest five weeks of my life. Every day has been a challenge, but without Noah, my family, Hope, and of course, Allie, I know without a doubt that I wouldn't have had the strength to get through it.

My body aches. I'm weak and have spent every day of the past five weeks throwing up, and what's worse is that despite the side effects and the torture of having to endure the chemotherapy, I know I've failed. Dr. Sanchez hasn't officially confirmed it yet, but I feel it in my gut. Feel it in the way my body continues to weaken, feel it in the way the nurses look at me with such sorrow. It's as though I'm already dead.

I've failed.

My body is giving up, and it's no longer a question of *if* I will die, it's *when*.

I'm on all kinds of medication, including something for the pain. My kidneys didn't appreciate the high dosage of chemotherapy, and neither did the rest of my body.

Dr. Sanchez said that there are other options for me, radiation therapy or stem cell transplant considering we can find a suitable donor. But she also said that the chemo was my best option for survival, and now that that's failed, it doesn't leave me with great odds. The only question is, when it comes time to start those alternate treatment plans, will I be strong enough to endure them?

My knee bounces on my bed as I hold a sleeping Allie to my chest, the anticipation of these test results making me want to be sick. I'll be discharged as soon as Dr. Sanchez gives us the final results of my chemotherapy, then I'll be sent home to try and put my life back together or figure out my next steps.

Don't get me wrong, of course I'm desperately hoping for good news. I would love to know that the pain and torture of the past five weeks wasn't all for nothing, that I'm going to miraculously recover from this a second time, but I'm also not willing to lie to myself either.

The small ray of hope I had that I could survive this has quickly dwindled and burned out, and now I'm just waiting on pins and needles for someone to tell me what I already know—I'm not getting any better.

Noah paces my room as I clutch Allie. She's been my little sidekick for the past two weeks. She hasn't left my side for a moment, even after Nurse Kelly found her hidden beneath my blankets. Where I go, she goes. Even if it's just to have a shower. She'll curl up on the floor mat and wait patiently as if knowing just how much I need her.

Allie has become my best friend, my sweet little baby, and getting to be her momma gave me everything I needed to get through the chemotherapy. I've been starting to wonder if perhaps that's why Noah gave her to me in the first place. If maybe he knew how badly I needed something more to help push me through this. He's always been so in tune with me, always knew what I needed before I did.

Hazel climbs up on my bed beside me. She's been such a good sister through all of this. I know the days she spends here with me are long and boring for her, but she hasn't whined or complained even once. She's always here for me right when I need her. Plus, apart from Noah, she comes fully loaded with the best hugs imaginable, and the fact that she always smells like strawberry shampoo makes it that much better.

She helps straighten my bandana, and I give her a weak smile, thanking her as my eyes grow watery. I never wanted her to see me like this. She was so young when I was sick last time, but I don't remember it ever being this bad, and I'm sure she doesn't have any memories from that time. She just knows what she's seen in pictures or from the brief stories Mom and Dad have shared with her. But this, seeing me this way . . . I hate it. On the other hand, I'm also not willing to pull away because every day I open my eyes, I'm left wondering just how much time I have left with the people I love.

A soft knock sounds at the door, and the second Noah glances up and sees Dr. Sanchez striding in, he crosses to my other side. His grip on my hand is so tight that it hurts, but I don't dare tell him that, not wanting him to let go.

His hair has already started growing back, and I know he did it for me, but damn it, the buzz-cut look is really working for him. But then, everything always works for him, whether his hair is long or short, he's always been so undeniably gorgeous.

Just like last time, Dr. Sanchez takes a seat at the end of my bed, her gaze dropping to Allie pulled up against my chest. She gives me a fond smile, and I see it right there in her eyes, the same look she gave me after my last round of chemo.

It failed.

"How are you feeling today, Zoey?"

"Like you're about to give me the news we've all been dreading," I murmur, not having the patience to do the whole small talk thing. Put me out of my misery. Rip it off like a Band-Aid and get it over and done with so I can figure out my next step and work out how much time I have left on this earth. "It didn't work, did it?"

Dr. Sanchez presses her lips into a hard line, regret shining bright in her eyes. "I'm sorry," she says. "It's time to start looking into alternate forms of treatment."

Noah crumbles beside me, his knees failing as he drops to the ground. His face falls into our joined hands as Hazel breaks out in a gutted sob, crushing herself into my arms, and squishing Allie between us. My parents cry, but I already feel so broken that I don't shed a single tear. I'm just empty now.

"Am I . . . am I going to die?"

"Zoey!" my mom gasps in horror before breaking into even harder sobs, struggling for air.

"No, Zoey," Dr. Sanchez says, squeezing my foot as she always does. "You still have a shot at beating this. We'll arrange an appointment in a few days to go through your options, but I don't want you getting yourself down. I know it's getting harder, but I need you to keep your spirits up. You can still fight this."

I nod, not believing her for even a second, and when she asks my parents to go out into the hallway with her and have a private conversation, I realize she was just sugarcoating it for me or Hazel.

I watch them through the small window and whatever Dr. Sanchez is telling them has Mom crumbling into Dad's side, heaving sobs tearing from deep within her. "It's okay, Zo," Noah promises me, lying through his teeth. "I'm not going to lose you."

Noah grabs my chin, forcing me to hold his stare, and I see nothing but pure desperation shining in his dark eyes. "Tell me," he grits through a clenched jaw. "Tell me you're going to keep fighting this."

"I will," I promise him. "I'm not ready to give up yet."

"Good," he says, letting out a shaky breath with fear in his eyes. "Then we take you home to rest and give you whatever you need to get stronger. Then we come back and finish this. We do whatever we need to do to keep you breathing. You hear me, Zozo? I'm not fucking losing you."

I lean in and drop my lips to his, hating that one day I might have to break my promise, that one day it'll become too much, and I won't be able to fight anymore. "I swear," I tell him. "I'm going to be right here by your side until we're old and gray. I'm not going anywhere just yet."

Chapter 50

ZOEY

My whole life, I've looked forward to my eighteenth birthday. I've always seen it as a rite of passage into adulthood, that I'll suddenly have all the answers to life's big questions and know exactly what path I'm supposed to take. If I knew this was in store for me, perhaps I wouldn't have looked forward to it so much.

It's barely seven in the morning, and I lay in bed, staring up at the ceiling with Allie snuggled right up beside me on my pillow, her soothing purrs right in my ear. Today is a good day . . . Well, mostly. Every other day this week, I've woken up feeling miserable, more tired than when I went to bed, but today, I'm feeling alright.

There's energy pulsing through my veins and a sense of accomplishment booming in my chest, though I don't really understand that. Perhaps it's because I've made it to my eighteenth birthday, and a small part of me was starting to wonder if I would.

There are still another few weeks before I'm due to start radiation therapy, but honestly, I can feel myself starting to decline. It's as though someone put me at the top of a snowy mountain, shoved a sled under my ass, and pushed me before I was ready. Only, instead of steering myself peacefully down the mountain, I hit a bump, and now I'm tumbling out of control, heading toward a ferocious crash landing.

I'm terrified that I'm not going to have the strength to get through the radiation therapy. I spend most days in bed with the occasional visit downstairs, but damn . . . the trek down the eighteen steps is exhausting. To be completely honest, everything is exhausting. I've never felt so flat in my life. I'm lethargic all the time, and the dizzy spells . . . shit. They're horrendous, but as long as I'm not stuck in that treatment center getting intense chemotherapy, then I consider it a good time.

Hazel comes to chill with me every afternoon when she gets home from school. She finds a movie, brings popcorn, and then goes ahead and talks the whole way through it, but I love every second of it. I wouldn't have it any other way, even if I always fall asleep before the end. Hope is the same. She comes over as much as she can, sometimes even during her lunch hour when she should be at school, and I appreciate it more than she could ever know. Both of them give me something to look forward to each day, and it's that kind of excitement that's keeping me strong.

As for Noah, he's doing everything he can. Most nights he sleeps right here beside me then makes the trip back to campus when he has exams or assessments that can't be avoided. Sometimes I wonder if he's just as exhausted as I am. This disease is putting so much strain on him. He's doing everything he can to be here with me, to give me what I need, but despite his encouraging smile, I know he's dying inside.

He's ready to break, and I hate that I'm the one doing this to him.

I think he can see that I'm not getting any better, and just like mine, his hope is beginning to fade. There have been multiple times when I've woken in the night to a cold bed, only to find him out in the yard, barely hanging on. Seeing him like that is killing me faster than this cancer ever could.

If I lose this battle and my heart stops beating . . . I don't know how Noah is going to survive it. He broke when we lost Linc, and then to lose me too . . . shit. Every day, the mere thought of it sends me into a sheer panic.

Allie wakes next to me and instantly rubs her head into my cheek when my phone rings on my bedside table. Reaching over, I scoop it up and smile to myself, seeing Noah's name across the screen. Then hitting accept before it rings out, I quickly bring it to my ear.

"Good morning," I say, my smile lingering on my lips.

"Hope I didn't wake you," he says, his tone so deep that it sends goosebumps sailing over my skin.

I snuggle deeper into my bed, pulling my blankets right up to my chin as Allie scooches even closer. "No, I was already up."

"Good, in that case, get your ass out of bed and open your window."

"Huh?" I grumble. The idea of climbing out of bed doesn't sit well with me right now. "My window?"

"You heard me, Zo," he rumbles. "Walk that fine ass of yours across your room and open your window."

Curiosity gnaws at me, and I reluctantly throw my blankets back before gripping the bedside table to help steady me as I get to my feet. Then the second I'm stable, I cut across my room to the window and peer out before breaking into a laugh.

A delivery driver stands at the curb, struggling to get control of his drone, a single pink tulip dangling below it.

My heart swells. Every single day I was in the treatment center during my second round of chemo, Noah brought me a tulip, knowing they're my favorite. When I finished my treatment and was discharged, I figured he would stop, but he didn't. And every day, he's been having to find new and creative ways to have my tulip delivered. It's the sweetest and most hilarious thing I've ever seen. Though I have no idea where he's getting all of these tulips from. My home is overflowing with them, but I wouldn't have it any other way. I love the way Noah loves me. It's everything I've ever needed.

Yesterday, my tulip was delivered via paper airplane. It was a complete disaster, but it was hilarious. Today though, this is a whole new level of insanity.

"Oh my god, Noah," I laugh, reaching up to unlock the window before the delivery guy accidentally flies his drone right into it.

I get it open just in time for the drone to storm into my room, terrifying the absolute life out of Allie. The tulip is dropped a little too soon and crashes to the ground, but I quickly scoop it up, needing to brace against my desk to keep me from tumbling over.

The drone is gone in seconds, and by the time I have the tulip in my hand and I'm straightening up, the delivery driver has the drone on the ground and is walking to pick it up. He offers me a quick salute before turning his back and making his way to his car. "Thank you," I call after him before clutching my window and pulling it closed again.

"You got it?" Noah asks.

"Yes," I laugh. "You know you're absolutely insane, right?"

"Insane?" he questions as I hear the sound of his engine revving, sending him sailing back toward campus for his exam today. "I call it being a genius."

Rolling my eyes, I move across my bedroom and add the tulip to the ever-growing bunch I have in the vase on my bedside table before dropping my ass back to the edge of my bed. "Thank you," I tell him. "I love it, but I love you more."

"I know," he says with a smile in his tone. "It's because I'm so fucking irresistible."

"Yeah," I scoff. "And not egotistical at all."

Noah laughs, and the sound brings me the sweetest kind of peace. "You wouldn't have it any other way," he tells me before a short silence lingers between us. "Are you still planning on going to school?"

"Are you going to give me another lecture if I say yes?"

"Would I be me if I didn't?"

I groan and scoot back down into my bed, pulling my blankets up to my chin as Allie makes herself comfortable, but it won't be for long. She'll be demanding her breakfast any minute now. "I thought I explained all of this last night," I say. "I don't want to be the cancer girl on my birthday. I just want to have a normal day and be just like everyone else who has to suffer through a shitty day at school."

"Babe," he groans.

"It's not like I'm going to be participating in PE and volunteering for the debate team. I just want to sit in class with the other assholes and pretend that I'm normal," I tell him. "Besides, I know my limits. If it's too much, I'll get Hope to drive me home."

"You know I'm going to be worrying about you all day."

"I know, but you don't need to," I say, pulling the phone away for just a moment to check the time, making sure I'm not already running late for what's probably going to be one of my last days of school . . . ever. "I'm still seeing you after, right?"

"I wouldn't dream of being anywhere else."

A soft blush creeps over my cheeks, and the smile that accompanies it is the one I reserve for only him. "Can't wait."

I can practically hear his smile through the phone. "Alright, Zozo, I have to go," he tells me. "And so do you if you plan on getting to school on time."

I groan and throw my blankets back, already regretting my decision to try and have a normal day. "Fine," I grumble. "I suppose I could get up."

"I'll keep my phone on if you need me, okay? And Zo," he says, pausing for just a moment, his voice lowering. "Happy birthday."

I don't know what it is about his tone, but those two words make my cheeks flush the brightest shade of pink. "Thank you," I whisper, knowing damn well he knows what he does to me.

"Love you, Zo. I'll see you this afternoon."

"Okay," I say. "I love you, too."

Noah ends the call, and my hands fall into my lap, more than aware that I could have spent the rest of my life listening to the sound of his voice, but in reality, I'd prefer to spend what time I have left wrapped in his strong, protective arms.

Realizing he was right about my morning schedule, I put my phone down on the bedside table and get my ass ready for school, taking much longer than it ever has before.

By the time the bell sounds through the school for homeroom, I'm standing at my locker with Hope, my hands in my wig, making sure it's straight. "Is it alright?" I murmur, being as discreet as possible. "Do you think people can tell?"

"They will if you keep pulling it like that," she whisper-yells, scolding me and smacking my hands away.

"I can't help it," I argue. "It's itchy."

"I mean, you could have always stayed at home," she mutters, looping her arm through mine and helping me through the throng of students scurrying to homeroom.

I roll my eyes, leaning on her a little more than I should. "And spend my birthday alone in bed, just waiting for someone to have a spare minute to text me back? No thanks. I'd rather face the jungle otherwise known as East View High. Besides, there's only so much Netflix and chilling one girl can do, and honestly, the chilling part of it isn't quite as exciting when I'm alone."

Hope scoffs. "I don't need to know what activities you participate in when you're all alone in bed."

My jaw drops, and I gape at my best friend. "You are too much for me."

"Girl, you've got no idea," she laughs, stepping through the door of my homeroom and delivering me right to my table. "If you had any idea the kinds of things I have to bite my tongue on to preserve your little innocent mind, you would be horrified."

Rolling my eyes, I take my seat and shake my head at her. "You're trouble."

"I know, but you love it," she says with a cheesy grin before slipping out of my homeroom and hurrying to get to hers before it's too late.

The day drags on just as I knew it would, and by lunch, I'm practically falling asleep on my feet. My body isn't handling it, and I'm quickly starting to crumble, but I'm determined to see it through, too stubborn for my own good.

I've had a million texts from Noah making sure I'm doing alright and that I'm not pushing myself too hard, and considering the big exam he has today, I don't know how he hasn't gotten in trouble yet. But nonetheless, I've responded to every single one of his messages so he wouldn't worry.

Making my way into the cafeteria, my face scrunches at the noise. I just need to find a table to sit at to quickly eat something and then maybe I'll let Hope talk me into spending the rest of the lunch break sleeping in my car. If she's lucky, I might just let her convince me to drive myself home and call it a day.

But there's only two hours of school left to go. Surely, I can make it, right? I'll be fine. Though I hope Noah doesn't have anything big planned for tonight because I'm going to crash hard the second I get my ass home.

Scanning the cafeteria for Hope, I find her at our usual table, and I give her a small smile, silently letting her know I'm okay. As I make my way toward her, my gaze shifts around the room and falls on the table I used to call mine.

Tarni and Cora talk between themselves, but I can't help but notice Abby's gaze locked on me. Her brows are furrowed as she scans over my face, my fake hair, and down my body. The longer she stares, the more concerned she looks. I can only imagine what she's seeing—my pale skin, my sunken cheeks, the bags under my eyes, and the too-thin frame.

She leans over toward Cora and murmurs something in her ear, and within seconds, both Tarni's and Cora's gazes snap up.

Shit.

I let out a shaky breath and avert my gaze, focusing on Hope's table across the cafeteria. The last thing I need today is some bullshit showdown with Tarni. I'm just lucky Shannan's been too preoccupied with forcing her tongue down some loser's throat to even notice I'm here today.

Taking my seat opposite of Hope, I pick at my lunch, feeling the weight of the day really settling into my bones. "Are you sure you're alright?" Hope questions as she reaches across the table and curls her fingers around my wrists in concern.

"I don't know," I tell her. "I really thought I'd be able to handle it, but I'm starting to have second thoughts."

"It's okay if you don't finish the day," she tells me. "It's not like you're being graded on whether you make it to the final bell or not. I can drive you home if you—"

Her gaze snaps above my head, and just as I go to turn around to see what's caught her attention, a shrill laugh breaks through the cafeteria.

Tarni Luca.

"Oh my god," Tarni laughs at my back, her tone loud enough to gain the attention of everyone around us, and I reluctantly turn to face her, preparing for the worst. "Who the hell are you trying to fool? A wig? Really? Are you that desperate to fit in?"

Her laugh chills me to the bone, and I try to force myself to appear indifferent, that her comments don't bother me in the least, but the fact she's drawing attention to my wig puts me on edge.

"Fuck off, Tarni," Hope seethes, spitting through her teeth as she stands, more than ready to throw hands.

Tarni barely spares Hope a single glance as her gaze slices right back to mine with disdain. "Where's your fucking backbone?" she throws at me. "How humiliating. You can't even fight your own fights anymore. Are you that pathetic now that your boyfriend is gone? Shit, I don't know what he was thinking wasting all that time with you. What was I thinking? I wasted years being your friend, but turns out you're the type of girl to throw everything away because of good dick. Do you have any idea how dull it was to listen to your drivel day in and day out? You have the personality of a blank wall."

Not prepared to waste what little energy I have left on Tarni's shit, I turn back toward Hope and brace my elbow on the table before leaning my head into my hand. "Go and find someone else's day to ruin."

Tarni scoffs, and her hand snakes out, smacking my elbow off the table and causing my head to fall away, leaving me scrambling to catch myself. "I'm fucking talking to you, bitch."

Hope launches herself right over the table, anger flashing in her bright blue eyes as she drops right down between me and Tarni, ruthlessly shoving her away from me. "Touch her again, *bitch,*" she spits, mimicking Tarni's tone. "And I'll fucking end you."

"Holy shit," Tarni booms, flicking her gaze between me and Hope. "I fucking knew it. You two are riding the fucking pussy train together, aren't you. It all makes sense now. Tell me, is it just the innocent scissoring shit, or are you hard-core? I bet you take strap-ons to a whole new level."

The whole cafeteria booms with laughter, but Hope isn't having it. "I told you to fuck off," she says. "I'm not going to ask again."

I put my hand up to Hope's arm. "She's not worth it."

Tarni scoffs, pushing around Hope. "Oh, I'm not worth it?" she spits. "Look in the fucking mirror."

With that, she reaches forward and grips the back of my wig, yanking hard and tearing it right off my head. My hands whip up to my head, trying to catch it and save myself the humiliation, but she's too fast, and the wig quickly drops to the ground.

My eyes widen in horror, feeling disgustingly exposed as Tarni sucks in a loud breath. "HOLY FUCK," she booms, the whole cafeteria pointing and staring right at me, their laughter already drowning me. "SHE'S BALD."

My heart races, and panic grips me around the throat, squeezing tight as my gaze darts around the room, feeling smaller by the second. My chest heaves, and as their taunting laughs get louder, I find it almost impossible to breathe.

Scrambling up from the table, I run. My feet carry me through the humiliation, and just as I reach the cafeteria doors, I glance back to find Hope taking Tarni to the ground with her fists swinging. Tarni's terrified squeal is the last thing I hear before I race out of the cafeteria and down the hall, my feet barely able to hold me up.

People stare at me, their brows furrowed as the sobbing bald girl races through the school. I stop at my locker to grab my things, stumbling with each step, but I push through it, the humiliation and devastation more than I can handle.

With all my things in hand, I keep running, straight through the front doors of East View High and down toward the student parking lot as the exhaustion quickly catches up to me. I was late, so my Range Rover is toward the back of the lot, and as I weave through the endless number of cars, falling against them as my knees start to give out, the dizziness reaches an all-time high.

I hurry to my car, desperately needing to block out the horror of the cafeteria, and just as my hand touches the back end, the dizziness claims me. The last thing I see is Principal Daniels racing toward me as my world fades to darkness.

Chapter 51

NOAH

My pen taps against the desk as I stare down at my exam papers. There's still forty-three minutes remaining, and truth be told, all I've managed to write is my fucking name at the top. It's Zoey's eighteenth birthday, very possibly her last birthday ever, and I'm sitting here instead of being with her.

If I'd somehow found a way to be with her today, I'm sure she would have been happy to pass on her ridiculous need to go to school. I understand her reasonings for wanting to go, but she's too fucking stubborn to know when to call it quits. She's not strong enough to endure a whole day at school. She needs to be in her bed resting, but she's determined to see it through and prove to herself that she can.

Fuck, she makes me so angry sometimes. I don't even care that I've been acting like a little bitch by blowing up her phone today. I need to know she's alright.

My phone buzzes in my pocket, and I shoot my gaze across the room to my professor, making sure he's still fully engrossed in the papers on his desk before slipping my phone out of my pocket, expecting a text from Zoey. Only it's Hope's name that flashes across the screen.

What the fuck?

I quickly unlock my phone and open the new text.

Hope: You need to get home. Now.

I'm out of my fucking chair so fast my exam papers fly off my desk, and I quickly scramble to pick them up before racing to the front of the room. I drop the papers on my professor's desk, barely sparing him a glance before racing for the door with my phone already at my ear.

It rings twice before Hope picks up. "You on your way?" she demands, sheer panic in her tone.

"Yeah," I grunt, hurrying across campus toward my car. "What the fuck happened?"

"Tarni," she spits. "She was already too exhausted to be there, I was trying to talk her into going home, but Tarni—that fucking bitch—she had other plans. She humiliated her in front of the whole fucking school, tore her wig off, and laughed about her being bald to the point they were all laughing at her."

"FUCK!"

"She's in the hospital now. I'm on my way."

"Wait. WHAT?" I demand, my eyes going wide. "How the fuck did she end up in the hospital? What happened?"

"Oh," Hope says, realizing she jumped too far ahead in her recap. "She took off. She got all her shit and ran to her car, but it was too much, especially after how exhausted she already was. Apparently, she collapsed in the student parking lot, and if Principal Daniels hadn't waited so long to tell me, I'd already fucking be there by now."

"What do you mean *apparently?*" I demand, throwing myself into my car and kicking over the engine, barely giving it a second before slamming it into gear and hitting the gas. "Where the fuck were you when this happened?"

The call switches over to the car's Bluetooth, and Hope's voice sails through my speakers. "I was too busy beating the shit out of Tarni," she tells me. "I got her good too. Think I gave her a black eye. It was fucking amazing. She won't be a problem anymore."

I scoff. Tarni will cease being a problem only when I'm personally through with her. "Just tell me Zoey is okay."

"I think so," she says. "I haven't been able to talk to her personally, but from what I understand, Principal Daniels found her in the parking lot and took her to the nurse, and then they called the ambulance. But apparently that was only for precaution. The lady in the student office said she was okay, but . . . I don't know. Apart from when she was having her chemo, I've never seen her so exhausted."

"Fuck. Okay," I say, trying to calm myself. "I'm two hours away, an hour and a half if I'm fast. If they let you in to see her, let me know how she's doing."

"Okay. I'll be there in ten."

Hope ends the call, and I try Zoey's cell but get nothing. I dial her mom next and check in. She tells me just about as much as Hope did, but unlike Hope, she's actually been allowed to speak to Zoey, which goes a long way in calming my fears.

It's almost an hour into my drive back to East View when my phone rings again, but this time, it's Zoey's name on the screen, and I quickly answer the call. "Babe?"

"I'm okay," Zoey says in a small voice as if she's already preparing for me to blow up.

"Zo, what the fuck?"

"I thought I could make it," she says, her voice cracking, and fuck, I can just imagine the tears in her eyes as her voice wobbles.

"Zo, you're fighting an aggressive cancer that's trying to kill you," I tell her bluntly. "I know you wanted some form of normalcy for your birthday, but you're *not* normal. You don't get to have normal right now, not until you're better."

She silently weeps on the other end, and I immediately feel like a dick.

"I'm on my way, okay?" I tell her. "Fuck, I need to hold you."

"They're discharging me soon," she tells me. "Can you meet me at my place? Mom is going to drive me home."

"Whatever you need, baby."

"I'm sorry," she finally says. "It was stupid. I shouldn't have gone to school, but I just—"

"You don't need to be sorry, Zo. I shouldn't have said that just now. I just hate this happened and I wasn't there for you," I tell her. "You fucking scared me, babe. When Hope called—"

"Hope was just scared. She overreacted," she says. "Besides, if I wasn't an idiot and used all my energy like that, I would have been okay. I just panicked and didn't know what to do, so I ran, and I—I thought I was going to make it."

"As long as you're good now," I tell her, though I say it for myself, needing to repeat the words a million times over. "You're okay."

"I am. I—shit. I have to go. The doctor is back to discharge me," she says. "I'll see you soon, okay?"

"You got it, Zo," I murmur. "I love you."

"Love you, too," she says before ending the call and leaving me gasping for air. I white-knuckle the steering wheel all the way back into East View, only able to focus on the road simply because I know Zoey is safe with her mom, back at home, and hopefully tucked in bed.

The drive feels as though it takes a lifetime, and as I speed through the very streets my brother was killed on, I find myself passing Tarni Luca's home. Her car is in the driveway, along with her friend's Lexus. I can never remember the names of the girls she hangs out with, but they were all shitty friends to Zoey when she needed them most.

Before I know what I'm doing, I hit the brakes and pull up over the curb, my Camaro screeching to a halt and tearing up her father's pristine lawn. The anger is like nothing I've ever known as I push my way out of my car and storm up to the front door.

I don't knock, don't stop to check who's home, simply bring my foot up and kick down the fucking door, breaking right through the lock. The door violently swings open, and as I cross the threshold, I hear the terrified screams of the girls coming from inside.

I follow the sound, my hands in tight fists at my side, and I walk through to find Tarni and her two sheep hovering around the kitchen island. Their eyes are wide and filled with terror, gaping at me as though I'm an ax-wielding serial killer ready to turn them into a statistic. And honestly, the idea sounds intriguing. There's nothing I wouldn't do for Zoey, but despite how I feel about these girls, she wouldn't want that. She's too fucking pure for her own good.

Recognizing me, they all let out heavy sighs of relief, one of the friends placing a kitchen knife back on the counter and shaking out her hand as though she was clutching it with a death grip, but my venomous stare remains locked on Tarni.

She gapes at me, knowing damn well this isn't about to go her way.

"What the fuck do you think you're doing?" she demands, trying to find courage, but she won't find it, not here. "You broke my door."

"You broke my fucking girl," I spit, walking straight into her and grabbing her arm, yanking her off the island stool and to her feet, needing to meet her stare straight on. "Do you have any fucking idea what you've done?"

Tarni scoffs. "Dramatic much?"

I can't fucking believe this bitch.

I know Zoey wanted to keep it quiet, but I can't anymore. Tarni needs to know exactly what it is she did today. I want to see the exact moment the guilt hits her, and I hope she drowns in it just like I do every fucking day.

"How fucking stupid can you be?" I roar. "You were there the first time. You sat at her side for eighteen fucking months while she went through her leukemia treatments."

"What the fuck does that have to do with anything?" she throws back at me.

I shake my head, unable to believe that she can't put the pieces together by herself. "Are you fucking kidding me? Do yourself a favor and think about it for once in your miserable fucking life. She's been gone for months at a time, coming back weak and slim and barely able to hold herself up. And now, she's lost her fucking hair, and instead of seeing the bigger fucking picture, you humiliated her."

One of her friends gasps, clearly putting it together faster than Tarni can, but Tarni just looks at me with a blank expression. "What . . . What are you saying?"

"Zoey is fucking dying, Tarni. That girl who stood by you for the past ten years, who had your back even when you didn't deserve it, *she's fucking dying.* You want to know why she hasn't been at school for months at a time?" I continue. "She's gone through two intense rounds of chemotherapy that have cost her way more than her hair, and for the record, the treatment didn't fucking work. So instead of getting better, the cancer is killing her from the inside out. But you, you worthless piece of shit, made her the laughingstock of East View

High when all she wanted was to have one normal fucking day for her birthday—probably the last birthday she'll ever have, and you fucking stole it from her."

Tarni gapes at me, her eyes wide and quickly filling with tears as the other two girls silently cry. "Her . . . Her leukemia is back?" Tarni asks.

"Congratulations," I say with a disgusted grunt, pushing away from her. "You must be so fucking proud of yourself."

Tarni sucks in a gasp, her wide eyes looking at her friends in horror. "What . . . What have we done?"

"*You*," I spit, reveling in the grief filling her eyes. "Don't even try to force your friends to carry that burden. You're the one who turned your back on her. You're the piece of shit who humiliated her. And you're the one who broke her fucking heart. You let her down, and when she needed you the most, you were dancing on her waiting grave."

And with that, I turn my back and storm out of there, desperate to get home to my girl, and as I slam the broken front door, the only sound I hear is guilt-ridden sobs behind me.

Chapter 52

ZOEY

My birthday sucked. There's no other way to put it.

After getting home from the hospital, Noah and Hope came over, and despite the fact that I was falling asleep on the couch, they stayed all night, doing what they could to help salvage the rest of my day, and I can't lie, it definitely helped, but the sting from the whole bald debacle at school refused to subside.

We did the cake thing while Mom and Dad forced smiles across their faces despite the fear in their eyes. Then afterward, once Hope had gone home, Noah took me up to bed. He gave me an infinity charm to hang on my necklace, identical to the matching tattoos we share, and then I unapologetically forced him to recite exactly what he'd said to Tarni three times, reveling in the image of him busting down her front door.

Then, even though I was exhausted, Noah made the sweetest love to me. After he'd somehow turned such a shitty day into a perfect night, I couldn't sleep, and so he sat out on the roof with me, holding me in his arms as we watched the stars sparkle against the dark Arizona sky.

When I couldn't fight the exhaustion a second longer, Noah took me to bed and held me until I woke up this morning, ready to put it all behind me. At least, I thought I was until Mom was called in for a meeting with Principal Daniels. She was told that I wouldn't be able to return to school until I have fully been cleared by my doctor—for my own safety.

It's a fair call, and after yesterday, I don't think I'd be foolish enough to return, but it still sucks. It's just another thing that this disease has taken away from me.

Noah was called in to meet with his professor after handing in a blank exam yesterday, and since then, I've been sitting here with my laptop, but the words aren't coming. So, instead of writing, I make my way up to my room to get dressed.

Not bothering with a wig, I tie a bandana around my head, making a knot in the back before finding a pair of shoes and heading downstairs. Mom would be pissed if she knew I was going out today. After everything that went down yesterday, everyone would be, but I don't see how it matters.

I'm starting to realize that the little bit of hope I had for radiation is a distraction meant to keep me in good spirits while I slowly fade away. And if this really is the end, if my time on earth with Noah and my family truly is limited, then I don't want to spend it holed up, suffering alone in my room.

Making my way downstairs, I stop by the kitchen and grab something small to eat, and just as I go to find my keys, I hear a soft knock at the door. My brows furrow, and I spare a glance at the clock. We're not expecting anyone today. I don't have any scheduled check-ups with the home nurses, and Noah and Hope have learned that if they bother to knock, they'll more than likely be left standing out on the porch. They quickly figured out the importance of walking right in.

Certain it's either the Girl Scouts, a salesman, or the antichrist coming to take me away, I brace my hand against the wall and make my way to the door. Everything seems slower now, more painful, and tiring. When I finally open the door, I find myself gaping at Cora and Abby as they stand in my open doorway with tears in their eyes.

I narrow my gaze on them, wondering what the hell they could possibly want when it hits me, they must have either been at Tarni's house yesterday afternoon, or Tarni has already started spreading the news. I let out a heavy sigh. "Who told you?"

"Noah did," Abby says, barely able to meet my eyes. "He broke down Tarni's front door and kinda screamed it at us."

Ah, so they were witness to Noah's performance yesterday. He must have forgotten to mention that part of his grand story. "Where's your leader?"

Abby presses her lips into a hard line. "She um . . . She couldn't bring herself to face you after everything that went down yesterday," she explains. "She feels like shit and hasn't been able to get out of bed all day. But if it makes you feel any better, your friend really did a number on her. She has a black eye."

I scoff. That actually does make me feel a little better. Though it's almost comical that *I'm* the one with cancer and am a victim of her bullying, yet *she* can't seem to get out of bed to face me. She has always been weak, and naturally, she's doing her part in playing the victim. Some things will never change.

I'm glad to never have to see her again.

"Yeah, look," Cora says. "We're really sorry. If we knew that you were sick, we never would have—"

"Oh, this is just great," I say, cutting her off. "Let me guess, you never would have humiliated me? Spent the last year ignoring me? Made me feel like complete shit?"

"Zoey—" Abby starts.

I shake my head. "No. What you're trying to tell me is that if I wasn't sick, you wouldn't be standing here on my front doorstep trying to apologize. That your behavior is justified because you didn't know I had cancer, like the way you've all treated me for the past year is somehow okay. But all you're doing is confirming that I was right to pull away from you."

"That's not fair," Cora says.

"Isn't it?" I argue.

She shakes her head, her brows furrowing. "No. It's not," she says. "We were friends before any of this, for years. Doesn't that count for anything? We were forced to pick sides, and you didn't even seem to care."

"I didn't seem to care?" I scoff, needing to grip the door handle to keep from swaying. "Not one of you had my back when Noah came back into my life. You were all too busy trying to get him in bed to even care that we had history. Not to mention, you were all too self-obsessed to notice the way your behavior was killing me. So yeah, you know what? You're right. I didn't care about reconnecting with you. Once Noah helped me see that I was worth so much more than all of your bullshit, I didn't even want to try."

"You really hate us that much?" Abby questions, looking as though I just slapped her across the face.

"Honestly, I really don't know," I tell her. "I was willing to try again and reconnect with you both after you gave me a lift home from that lake party last summer. But in the end, what it comes down to is that you were terrible friends to me, and I'm not comfortable being forced to accept an insincere apology because you're trying to clear your conscience before I die. It's not my responsibility to bear the weight of your shitty decisions and behavior. If you want forgiveness, then earn it. Be good people, and don't treat the next girl who needs help like shit."

"So, that's it, huh?" Cora questions. "You're just going to die and leave things like this between us?"

"Yeah. I think this is what we call living with the consequences of your actions," I say, reaching back to the entryway table to grab my car keys before stepping out of the house and locking the door behind me. "But let me put this into perspective for you. You just told me that you're aware I'm dying, and not once have you asked me how I'm feeling, how my chemotherapy was, or if there's even a chance that I might pull through. All you care about is how it affects you. But guess what? *I am dying*, and my time on this earth is limited, and the last thing I want to do is spend what little time I have left catering to your selfishness. I'm not interested."

I walk away, getting halfway down the path toward my car when Abby calls out behind me. "You know, that's really shitty of you, Zoey," she says at my back, waiting for me to stop and turn around. "We were just innocent bystanders most of the time. The real person you have a problem with is Tarni, and now you're just punishing us out of spite."

I scoff, having to step back against my car to keep myself from swaying too much. "I'm not punishing you," I tell them, already exhausted from this conversation. "I just no longer care. I'm too busy trying to spend every chance I have with the people who actually matter, the people who actually care and love me. I don't have the energy to work you two back into my life in order to make you feel like you somehow matter. And if I'm perfectly honest, I'm not even sure I'll make it to graduation. But for what it's worth, you're right. Most of the time, the nastiness came from Tarni, but not once did either of you step in and try to put a stop to it. Despite years of friendship, you allowed that bullshit to continue. So while the vile things that were said and done against me didn't come directly from you, you're both just as guilty."

And with that, I unlock my Range Rover and climb in, needing just a second to sit and catch my breath.

I watch as Cora starts to cry and Abby pulls her away, leading her back to her car that's parked behind mine, blocking me in, and I hope to God that they can use this as an opportunity to grow, to be better people. They drop back into the car, and it hits me that this could potentially be the very last time I ever see either of them, but despite how things were left, I don't seem to care how they feel.

Then as they both get in and Abby starts backing out of my driveway, I pull out my phone and work on a new text to Noah.

Zoey: *Middle finger emoji*
Resident Asshole: What the hell was that for?
Zoey: You failed to mention that Abby and Cora knew I was sick. They just bombarded me, begging for forgiveness.
Resident Asshole: Ah shit. How'd that go?
Zoey: Take however you think it went and make it ten times worse.
Resident Asshole: Fuck. My bad.
Zoey: It's fine, actually. I put things into perspective for them. Maybe they might have learned something for once. They didn't even bother asking me how I was doing. They only cared how it affected their guilty consciences.
Resident Asshole: Fucking bitches. Always knew you were better off without them.
Resident Asshole: I'm on my way back now anyway. Want me

to bring you cheesy fries?

Zoey: I'll forgive you if you add a burger to go with it.

Zoey: And a soda.

Zoey: OH! And some rock candy. I love that stuff!

Resident Asshole: That rock candy is gonna cost you!

Zoey: I'll give you a little peek at my laptop...

Resident Asshole: You're lying.

Zoey: Totally lying...but where does that leave us on the rock candy?

Resident Asshole: You're lucky you're hot!

Zoey: HELL YEAH!!!!!!!!

A wide grin stretches across my face, knowing without a doubt that Noah isn't just showing up with everything I asked for, but with everything and more . . . so much more. He likes to spoil me, and if that means making sure I eat as much as humanly possible, he'll buy it, even if it means putting a dent in his bank account. There's nothing he wouldn't do to make sure I'm getting everything I need. He's far too good to me. I just wish there was some way I was able to repay him for everything he's doing for me. Just the nights where he holds me is so much more than I've ever deserved.

How does a girl become so lucky as to be loved so fiercely by Noah Ryan?

With Noah already on his way back, I put my car into reverse and back out of the driveway before finally getting out of here. I drive down to the cemetery and park as close to Linc's grave as possible. It's a beautiful day, and since being sick, I haven't come down here nearly enough.

Making my way to his gravesite, I stand over him for a minute, staring down at the words on his tombstone and then gazing over the few pictures that have been left here.

Starting to get dizzy, I drop down into the grass, crossing my legs and leaning back on my hands. There's always been something so soothing about sitting here with Linc. Most of the time, I can picture him sitting right here beside me, chatting away as though he were never gone.

God, I miss him, but I know he's waiting for me, beckoning me to come and join him so that he doesn't have to be alone anymore. Hazel once told me she feared my sickness coming back was Linc's doing, that he needed me to be with him, and a part of me is starting to wonder if she was right. And if she is, how could I be mad at him for that?

Letting out a heavy sigh, I reach forward to the plastic folder that Hazel leaves here and start going through the messages that she leaves for Linc. I know it's wrong of me to reply to these and allow her to believe that it's really Linc talking to her, but it's gone on too long now. How could I possibly stop? But on the other hand, if this illness were to claim me and I was no longer able to respond to her letters, would she think that both Linc and I had abandoned her?

Shit. Perhaps Noah will respond to them for me, though he'd have to come up with an explanation as to why Linc's handwriting suddenly took a dive.

Finishing up with my response to Hazel, I settle the plastic folder right back where I found it before getting comfortable in the manicured grass. I kick my legs out, crossing them at the ankles before just sitting here in the sun, closing my eyes, and breathing in the sunshine.

I rarely get to do this now. Every day is the same four walls, but this right here . . . I feel so at peace.

I don't pay attention to the time, and before I know it, a familiar black Camaro pulls into the cemetery, driving right around until it pulls to a stop behind my Range Rover. Noah steps out a minute later, my lunch piled high in his arms, and with only one look at it, I know there's no way in hell I'll be able to eat all of that, but Noah is a machine when it comes to food. He could eat all day, non-stop, and still be hungry. I don't know where it all goes.

"You scared me for a minute," he tells me, striding up toward Linc's grave, his gaze shifting to the tombstone and lingering there.

"I knew you'd eventually find me," I say, knowing without a doubt that he would have stopped at the park before coming here as his second option.

Noah smiles and drops down beside me, handing me the extra-large soda. "I know you too well," he agrees.

A smile lingers on my lips, and I turn my gaze back to Linc. "I didn't think I was going to be here this long," I admit, "but I just kinda sat down and never left. It's peaceful here."

"That, it is. I've been coming down here more often," he admits. "You know, he would have turned fifteen this year."

I nod, having had that exact thought today and nearly blowing myself away. "It's insane how quickly time flies. It feels like yesterday that he died, and then I blinked, and suddenly, all this time has passed."

Noah nods and loops his arm over my shoulder before pulling me into him. On instinct, I tilt my head, resting it against his big shoulder, wishing so desperately that I never have to lose this. We sit in silence as we eat our lunch, and before I know it, the clouds have blocked out the warmth of the sun. It's certainly not cold during this time of year, but it's enough to have Noah glancing at me nervously.

"Come on," he tells me. "Let me get you home."

Not wanting to argue with him, I simply nod and allow him to pull me up, knowing he's right. I've been gone for longer than I anticipated, and soon enough, I'm going to need to lie down and replenish what little energy my body can work up.

Noah scoops up all of our trash from lunch and quickly jogs across the cemetery to get rid of it, and as I glance down at Linc's grave one more time, a soft smile spreads across my face. "I hope you're waiting for me, kid," I tell him when Noah is far enough away and unable to hear me. A single tear rolls down my cheek, and I hastily wipe it away, feeling my heart shattering into a million tiny pieces. "I'm going to be seeing you real soon, but I'm going to need you to guide me through. I'm scared, Linc. I don't know what waits for me on the other side, but I know with you holding my hand, I'm going to be okay."

As I let out a heavy breath, the smile falters on my face, and I make my way back to my car, knowing without a doubt that Noah will follow me the whole way home.

Chapter 53

ZOEY

It's a stormy Sunday afternoon, and I sit in my living room with my family. Allie sleeps soundly on my lap, and Hazel is beside me, curled up with a blanket as a movie plays, but truth be told, I haven't taken in even a second of it. When I woke up this morning, I just knew . . . I'm not making it through this, and it's all I can think about.

It's been a little over a week since my birthday, and if I'm honest with myself, I've known this for a while. I keep declining, too rapidly to be able to fight it much longer. My radiation therapy is due to start next week, but I just don't think I have the strength to go through it, nor do I want to spend what little time I have dealing with the discomfort that will come along with it.

I'm dying.

It's as simple as that. And when I go, I don't want to be in pain. I don't want to be locked in a treatment facility having my body constantly blasted with high doses of radiation for the small chance it might actually work.

I want to go on my terms. I want to be happy. I want to go in my own bed, holding Noah as I take my last breath and fade away from this magical life. I want to be surrounded by love and happiness, not the incessant beeping of machines and clinical smells of the treatment center.

The clock is ticking painfully fast, and I'm running out of time. A week, two, maybe three? I don't know, but I think it's time to start asking those hard questions. Time for me to sit down with Noah and tell him that I'm not getting any better, that this is going to be the end of the road for me.

He holds so much hope that I'm going to somehow magically survive this, but deep down, I think he knows just as I do. He's been watching me fade each day, watching me getting further and further away.

Tears well in my eyes, and as a shaky whimper escapes my lips, my family all stops what they're doing, their eyes coming right to mine. Hazel pauses her movie, her brows furrowed as Dad glances up from his phone. Mom though, her eyes search right through to my soul, and as if being on the same wavelength, her heart breaks right in front of my face, big tears forming in her eyes.

She quickly hurries across the room, throws herself down beside me on the couch, and pulls me right into her arms. "Oh honey," she cries, gently rocking me back and forth. "It's going to be okay."

I cry into her shoulder as Hazel scooches in closer. "I'm not going to make it," I tell them, absolutely terrified, breaking into deep, heaving sobs. "I'm not going to make it. I'm dying."

"Shhhhhh," Mom soothes, holding me so damn tight, it hurts, and yet she doesn't tell me I'm wrong or beg me to hold on just a little while longer. Deep down, we all know it's true. We all know this is the end of the road for me.

Hazel scooches so close that she's practically in my lap, shoving Allie out of the way, tears streaming down her face. "I don't want you to die," she wails, and the agony in her tone is the most excruciating thing I've ever heard, tearing me apart from the inside out.

"I'm sorry," I cry, desperately wishing there was another way. "I can't . . . I can't do the radiation like this. I'm not strong enough. It's only going to kill me faster, and I don't want to die like that."

"It's okay," Mom murmurs, her hand brushing down my hair as Dad sits forward in his chair, his elbows braced on his knees as he silently weeps into his hands. "It's going to be okay. You don't need to be scared, my sweet girl. I'm right here. I'll always be right here."

I cry into her shoulder, the despair, fear, and uncertainty crippling me as we all fall to pieces in our home—the very home that holds so many memories, so many good times, the home where I had my very first kiss from Noah and he whispered in my ear, telling me how much he really did like my stupid girl kisses.

How can I possibly leave this place?

I have so much more I want to do, so much life I want to live. I want to graduate high school and spend years at college with Noah. I want to fall so much deeper in love with him, every day falling harder until he's down on one knee, asking me to spend the rest of our lives together. I want to walk down the aisle and throw myself into his arms. I want to travel the world and be there for Noah as he accepts a contract with the NFL. I want to have a million little babies with Noah's dark eyes, and I want to watch as they grow and call him daddy. And then once our babies are all grown and moved out, I want to spend every day of the rest of our lives loving each other until we die of old age, only after living a full life, knowing it couldn't have possibly gotten any better.

Hours pass where I mourn the life I'm never going to have, the grief overwhelming me, and when the tears have finally started to ease, Mom promises that first thing tomorrow, we'll talk to Dr. Sanchez about our options and where to go from here.

None of us move even an inch, too afraid to let go, and just when I start to fall asleep on the couch, the door opens, and Noah strides in, his eyes so bright as he looks at me with that single orange tulip in his hand. But taking in the devastation in my eyes, the tulip drops to the ground. "Zo," he breathes, shaking his head. "No. No, no, no."

Pushing myself up from the couch, I shakily make my way across the living room and right into his arms, reaching up and cupping his face. "Come on," I whisper. "Let's go talk."

Fear flashes in his eyes, his chest heaving as I take his hand and pull him toward the stairs, not having the strength to pull him along like I used to, but he follows nonetheless, and every step up the stairs kills me, knowing what I have to tell him now.

I get halfway up the stairs when Noah sees just how much I'm struggling and scoops me up into his warm arms, holding me close against his chest before taking me right up to my room and lowering me into my bed.

As I reach for my blankets and pull them up, snuggling right into my bed, I catch sight of the photograph on my desk—the little six-year-old girl who pushed through the worst. She was a fighter, a freaking rockstar. She gave everything to give me the life I had, to give me the chance at a future, and I'm letting her down. She's so much stronger than I am, and I'm so grateful for the ten years she was able to give me.

Noah sits on the end of my bed, his elbows braced against his knees as if knowing that whatever I'm about to tell him is going to change his world forever. Fresh tears linger in my eyes, and I can't stand the distance. Throwing my blankets right back again, I scramble across my bed and climb into his lap, straddling him as my arms lock so tightly around his neck, our chests pressed firmly together.

"Noah," I breathe, my voice breaking.

"Just tell me," he begs, unable to bear it a second longer.

"The radiation therapy," I whisper as I take a shaky breath. "I'm not strong enough. I can't do it."

He closes his eyes, his forehead dropping to my shoulder as his arms tighten around me, and when I feel his tears dropping to my collarbone, I break all over again. "What . . . What does this mean?" he asks, the agony in his tone like nothing I've ever heard.

"It means . . ." I start, my bottom lip trembling. "They'll make me comfortable—"

"Don't fucking say that," he demands, lifting his head and looking straight into my tear-filled eyes. "There has to be another option, something else we can do. I'm not ready to lose you, Zo. You're my whole fucking world. You promised you wouldn't leave. I can't lose you."

"Noah—"

"Please," he begs, gripping my waist so tight that his fingers dig into my fragile skin. "Please, Zoey. For me. Fuck. Don't give up on me like this. I need you to keep fighting."

I crush myself back into him, my arms pulling him in even tighter as I curl my face into the curve of his neck, breathing him in. "I'm not giving up," I promise him. "I want to have another fifty years with you. I want to take your last name and build a life with you. I want it more than you'll ever know, and it's that vision that's allowed me to get this far, but every day, this disease kills me just a little bit more. I don't have what it takes to survive more treatments. I'm not strong enough, not anymore. Believe me, if I had what it took to push through and fight this, I would do it without question because I'm terrified of having to leave you, but I'm out of time. I'm going to die, whether we're ready for it or not, and when that happens, I want to do it right here in your arms, not in some hospital, filled with drugs that are only making me feel worse. I want to live what little time I have left, and I want to do it right by your side."

He shakes his head, taking my face and lifting it from his shoulder, his dark eyes lingering on mine. "This can't be the end, Zo," he murmurs, leaning in until I feel his lips brushing over mine. "I can't lose you."

"I'm sorry," I cry, tasting his tears on my lips. "I'm so sorry."

"What am I supposed to do without you?"

Not knowing what to say, I don't respond. Instead, I crush my lips against his and kiss him deeply, letting my emotions pour out of me. Letting him feel how deep my love runs for him. How terrified I am. How crippled I am by the fear of having to leave this world and leave him behind. How I'm grieving for the life we won't get the chance to live together, the children we'll never have, the marriage we'll never get a chance to screw up.

Noah kisses me right back, and I feel his overwhelming despair and agony with every swipe of his tongue over mine. When I finally pull back, we're both panting, and I tilt my forehead against his, content to just sit here with him until the end of time.

"How much . . ." he starts before pausing and clenching his jaw, needing a second to get the question out. "How much time do we have?"

I shake my head, and he reaches up to wipe the tears off my cheeks. "I don't know," I tell him. "We're going to see Dr. Sanchez tomorrow and see what she has to say, but I . . . I can't see this going on any further than a few months. Two, maybe three if we're lucky."

Noah closes his eyes again, and I can almost hear the rapid beat of his heart right through his chest. "Are you going to be in pain?"

I shake my head again. "No, I'll be okay . . . I think," I murmur, my fingers pushing up through his hair, almost as long as it was before he shaved it for me. "They'll make me comfortable, but it won't be long until my organs start shutting down, and when that happens, we'll be on the home stretch."

"Fuck, Zo," he breaks. "This isn't how this was supposed to go. We were supposed to have it all."

"I know," I murmur, trying to soothe him the same way Mom had done for me downstairs. "But it's okay. Fate has other plans for me, and when the time comes, I'll be going home to Linc. I'm not going to be alone, and I won't be sick anymore, and even though I won't get to be in the warmth of your arms, you know I'm always going to be with you. No matter what, wherever you go, I'll always be right here, watching over you."

Noah holds me tighter, and as his world burns to ashes around us, he lifts us off the edge of the bed before laying me down on my pillow and following me right in, not letting me go for even a second. He curls me right into his chest and pulls the blankets up, making sure I'm always warm and have everything I could possibly need. "I love you more than life, Zoey," he tells me. "I'm going to be right here, right 'til the end, and I swear, I'll never let you go."

Chapter 54
NOAH

Over the past three weeks, I've watched her deteriorate, watched as she slowly began to slip away. It's the most excruciating thing I've ever had to suffer through, but I've held myself together, knowing just how much she needs me. I won't allow her to fall, even if it means giving up everything I am in order to protect her.

Zoey James is my whole world. I breathe for her, and when she's gone . . . I don't know if I'll even be able to breathe at all.

Most of the time, she can barely get out of bed or stay awake long enough to listen to Hazel's stories, but she pushes through it, wanting to soak up every last second of the time she has left, and that includes senior prom. I really don't know how this is going to go, but when she stood before me, clutching my hands, and asked if I'd be her date to prom, how could I possibly resist the chance to make her smile?

She's been so excited about this, searching for the perfect dress and forcing her mom to video chat her through a million different stores to pick it out. It's kept her busy and happy, but I worry about the crash on the other side. It's as though getting to prom was a milestone for her, but what happens after that milestone has been met? What keeps her motivated to hold on then?

Dread fills my veins, but I push it aside. My only goal is to see her smile as much as possible before the inevitable end.

I stand outside her house in a black suit with my jacket open and the top few buttons of my shirt left undone. I know how she gets a kick out of seeing me all dressed up like this, and because it's her prom—maybe the only chance she has left to do something like this—I went all out. I'm even going to knock on the door and wait for her father to help her down the stairs before putting her corsage on.

If we're doing this, then we're doing it right, and I'm going to show her the best night of her life.

Glancing down, I make sure I have everything, not wanting to be that dick who accidentally leaves the corsage in the back of the car and then has to make an ass of himself by running out to grab it. I pat down my pockets. Phone, keys, and wallet are all there, but what does it matter? The only thing I truly need is Zoey.

Then raising my fist, I knock on the door and hear my mother's familiar tone coming from within the house. "Awwwwwwww, what a big cutie. He actually knocked on the door for a change."

Great. I was expecting a lot of things tonight, but for some reason, I hadn't prepared for my overbearing mother. She's about to make the next hour of our lives a living hell with all the photos and gushing. Though, maybe one day soon I might want all of these photos and be desperate to lay my eyes on Zoey's beautiful face, even if it's only through the screen of my mother's phone.

The door opens a moment later, and I glance down to find Hazel with her father quickly creeping in behind her. "Ewwww," Hazel says, a smirk pulling at her lips. "You look like one of those try-hard dudes out of a bad mafia movie."

I scoff and ruffle her hair. "You wish you could look this good."

She pretends to gag as Henry glances over me. "Not bad, kid," he says. "Who would have known you could scrub up so well?"

I roll my eyes as Mom and Erica barge their way through, starting the onslaught of over-the-top gushing. "You remembered the corsage, didn't you?" Mom double-checks, even though she can see it right here in my hand. "Tonight has to be perfect."

"Yes, Mom," I groan, holding up the corsage. "I've got everything I need."

"Perfect," Erica says, a grin from ear to ear. "I'll go see if she's ready."

Erica takes off, and I'm not surprised when Mom and Hazel hurry up the stairs behind her. Despite everything Zoey and I have already been through, I can't work out why the hell I suddenly feel so nervous.

Zoey's father remains by the door, his gaze coming back to mine as we hear Zoey's mom knocking on her bedroom door. "I always thought I'd be giving you the bring her home by midnight speech," Henry tells me. "But . . . just make sure she has a great night, something for her to hold on to. Make some memories."

I nod. "I will."

He gives me a tight smile, and I see the dread in his eyes, the same way it lingers in mine, and just as he goes to say something else, we hear Erica calling from upstairs. "Zoey, honey? Where are you?"

My brows furrow, not liking the tone in Erica's voice when I hear my mom. "I'll check the bathroom," she mutters to Erica before I hear her footsteps hurrying down the hall. There's a quick knock before I hear Mom's voice again. "Hey, my little warrior. Are you in here?"

There's the subtle creak of the door before Mom calls out again. "She's not here either," she says. "Where could she have gone?"

They check the rest of the house, but when they start making their way back down the stairs with furrowed brows, I realize I already know the answer to their questions. "It's alright," I tell them before they start to panic that she's passed out somewhere. "I know where she is."

With that, I turn on my heel and jog down to my car. "Let me know when you find her," Zoey's dad hollers after me.

As I unlock my Camaro and drop into it, I glance back toward the parents and give a firm nod, knowing without a doubt that they're going to worry until they know she's safe. Then hitting the gas, I take off down the street, desperate to get to her.

Pulling up in the park barely a few minutes later, I look out toward the swings and find her sitting in the moonlight, her silver gown sparkling with her subtle movements. She doesn't make a move to look back, but I know she senses me here.

Quickly shooting off a text to Zoey's dad, I let them know I've got her, and with that, I push out of my car and make my way across the park, my gaze lingering on my girl as she gently swings back and forth.

I plant myself right in front of her, crouching down as I grip the chains on either side of her, bringing her to a stop as I look up into those dazzling green eyes. She's fucking gorgeous, and my heart stutters in my chest as I take her in. "Fuck, Zo," I breathe, unable to take my eyes off her as a soft blush spreads across her cheeks. "You're breathtaking."

She smiles but it's only a small one, the exhaustion of her day already shining through. "I'm sorry," she says, her gaze eating me up as she checks me out in my suit. "You got all dressed up for me, but I don't think I'm going to make it. I'm just . . . I'm tired."

"It's okay," I whisper. "Seeing the way the moonlight sparkles off you in this dress is more than enough for me. I just want you to have a good night."

She shakes her head with sadness in her eyes. "You went through all that trouble getting Principal Daniels to let me go," she says, her voice breaking. "All I wanted was to dance with you at prom. Anything else would have been a bonus."

Releasing the chains, I brush my fingers down the side of her face and watch as she leans into my touch. "Who said you still can't dance with me at prom?"

Her brows furrow. "I . . . What?"

I grin, standing up and offering her my hand and getting the sweetest satisfaction as she delicately places her hand in mine. Closing my fingers around hers, I help her up from the swing, placing my other hand at her waist as her feet press into the sand.

I move us back to where the ground isn't so bumpy before lifting our joined hands over her head and gently spinning her before pulling her right in against my chest. "Just because we're not in some stale school gym with shitty decorations and a bunch of teenagers trying to get laid doesn't mean we can't have our own prom right here," I tell her. "Pick your favorite song and let me dance with you."

Her cheeks flush, and when the overwhelming happiness reaches her eyes, I could crumble right here in her arms. "You're going to dance with me right here in the middle of the park?" she asks, pulling her phone out of the hidden pocket at the side of her silver gown.

"There's not a damn thing I wouldn't do for you, Zoey James. And if you want to dance with me on your prom night, then we'll do that until our feet can't move a second longer."

Zoey tips her head up to me, pushing up on her tippy toes and brushing the softest kiss over my lips. "You need to warn a girl before you make her swoon like that."

"Never," I tease, my hand curling around her back and pulling her in even closer. "I'm a *live on the edge* kind of guy."

Zoey grins wide, rolling her eyes before finally hitting play on a song and carefully tossing her phone into the grass to free up her other hand. A cover of "Like I'm Gonna Lose You" by Jasmine Thompson starts playing through her phone speaker and my chest starts to ache as she folds back into me.

I avoid listening to songs with deep lyrics that force me to face reality, but if this is what she wants to dance to, then I'll suck it up and be the man she needs me to be, even as the words eat me alive.

Zoey and I move so perfectly together that it's clear we were made for one another. Her hand rests against my chest as we dance in the moonlight, my hand low on her back. "Tell me you didn't walk here," I say, my lips moving against her temple.

I hear the smile in her tone. "I can barely walk across my living room. I'm not stupid enough to try and walk all the way here," she tells me, gently lifting her head and meeting my gaze. "I stole Hazel's hoverboard and rolled my ass here."

I grin down at her, picturing this beautiful goddess in her silver gown flying down the street on a hoverboard. "You know, I would have paid to see that, right?"

"If you're lucky, I might just let you see it for free."

I can't help but laugh as I drop my lips to hers and kiss her as we dance through the park with the starry Arizona sky as the perfect backdrop.

When she pulls back and rests her head against my chest again, she lets out a heavy sigh, clearly deep in thought. "What's wrong?" I ask, my hand moving up and down her back.

"Nothing's wrong," she whispers in a small tone as if still considering whether she's going to say anything. "I was just thinking about you and me, and what I'll be leaving behind."

"Zo—"

"No," she says, cutting me off, gazing up at me with such a deep love in her eyes that it almost brings me to my knees. "It's just . . . After I'm gone, when you think about us and how we were together, I want you to remember us this way. Not the pain of losing me or the long days in that treatment center. I want you to remember these moments that were so unbelievably perfect that you took my breath away and left me feeling so overwhelmingly in love with you." She holds my gaze, pausing for just a moment. "Promise me, Noah. Promise me you'll *remember us this way.*"

Dropping my forehead to hers, I swallow hard, trying to gain some semblance of control over the wild emotions burning through my body. "You have to understand, Zo, I never planned on you being a memory. When you're gone, and I have to say goodbye, it's going to destroy me. I don't know how I'm going to survive it, but I promise, when the time comes that I'm able to think back and remember our life together, when just the mention of your name doesn't tear me to shreds, I'll remember us just like this."

Those beautiful green eyes fill with tears, and she pushes up on her toes again, kissing me gently before settling back into my arms. "Thank you," she whispers just as the song comes to an end and shifts into something new. *Perfect* by Ed Sheeran.

As the opening lyrics sound through the park, I feel Zoey's smile against my chest, and I realize just how well-suited this song is to this very moment. Every single lyric hits home. "I'm pretty sure this song was made for us."

Zoey laughs and snuggles in closer to my chest. "You're cheesy, Noah Ryan."

"Says the one who gave me the puppy dog eyes saying that all she wanted was to dance with me on prom night," I grin. "You knew what you were doing when you said that."

Her grin stretches wider across her face, and I realize just how right I was. I was taking a shot in the dark when I said that, but her grin is nothing but a blunt confirmation. No one's ever claimed that Miss Zoey James wasn't sneaky as all hell. She's a master manipulator in the best way, and I fucking adore that about her.

Two songs are all she can handle before we find ourselves sitting in the grass. Zoey sits between my legs, her back resting against my chest as my arm remains locked around her waist, holding her against me.

Her gaze lingers on the twinkling sky, watching the world pass us by. "Do you believe in reincarnation?" she asks.

I shake my head. "I don't know," I tell her. "I don't think I've ever really thought that hard about it."

"Yeah, me either," she says. "But I've been wondering about it these past few weeks, like if it were true, what I'd want to come back as, and I can't stop thinking that I'd want to come back as a bird."

A smile pulls at my lips, and I drop my head, pressing a kiss to her shoulder. "Out of all the things you could potentially come back as, you choose a pigeon?"

"No," she laughs, jamming her elbow back into my stomach. "Not a dirty pigeon. I want to be one of those real pretty ones with all the colors that can fly higher than any of the others," she says, pausing a moment. "I don't know, birds are just so . . . free. They soar through the skies, flying into the horizon without a care in the world."

"Sounds perfect," I murmur.

Zoey shrugs her shoulders. "I just think that after having to deal with everything that's going on right now, a life soaring through the skies sounds like a dream," she says, letting out a heavy breath. "What about you? What would you come back as?"

"I don't know. Is this a world where you're still alive, and I'm the one who's gone?"

"How does that have anything to do with what you're coming back as?"

"Answer the question, Zo. Are you alive or not?"

"Yes," she laughs. "I'm alive."

I grin, knowing she'd say that. "In that case, I'm coming back as your favorite pair of panties," I tell her. "And it better be a thong, too. Otherwise, I'd be pissed."

"Noah!" she screeches, ramming me in the ribs again, but all I can do is laugh as she pulls herself up and scrambles around until she's straddled over my thighs, having to hoist the bottom of her gown up to give her space to move. She flings her arms around my neck, and I brace a hand at her waist, hating how much she sways.

It's been a long day for her. I should get her home soon.

"You're trouble, you know that, right?" she says, her eyes sparkling with silent laughter.

I grin wide. "Not as much trouble as you."

Zoey rolls her eyes and leans into me, resting her head against my shoulder as I hold us both up. "Noah?" she questions, her voice barely a whisper. "Can I ask you something?"

"What's up, Zo?"

"How did you picture our lives?"

My brows furrow. "What do you mean?"

"If I never got sick, and we got to have everything we ever wanted," she explains. "What would that look like?"

My body sags, and I let out a breath. "Are you sure you really want to know this?" I ask. "I don't want to upset you."

"I wanna know," she tells me. "And don't even think about telling me that you haven't ever thought about it because I know you have. You've known since we were kids, and while I have my own idea of how I wanted to see our lives play out together, I want to know yours."

I force a smile across my face. She's right. I've been thinking about the future we could have together since I was a kid. I always knew we would end up together and grow old in each other's arms, but it wasn't until I was thirteen and realized what I felt for her was more than just a kid's crush. It ran deeper than anything I knew could exist, anything I'd seen in the movies. Our souls were entwined together, permanently connected as one, and I knew every step we took in life would be done as one.

Since then, it's been almost impossible not to imagine what kind of life we would build together. But now, knowing that dream is never going to happen, that every day we get closer to having to say goodbye, thinking about that future does nothing but hurt.

"It's simple," I say, brushing my fingers over her creamy shoulder. "The second I could, I would have made you my wife and given you the grand wedding you've always deserved. Then while we were away doing the whole NFL thing, I'd have your belly swollen with our babies. Four—"

"At the same time?" she gasps.

"No," I laugh. "Two boys. Two girls. Just like you, me, Linc, and Hazel. It would have been a new generation of musketeers."

"The boys older," she whispers in a dreamy state, "so they could always protect the girls, just like you've always protected me."

"Of course."

"I'm sorry," she tells me, a heaviness lingering between us. "You don't know how badly I wish we could have had all of that and more. I think I first started dreaming about marrying you when I was ten, maybe eleven."

"Really?"

"Uh-huh," she says, sounding a little sheepish. "Nearly every night for a year straight, I would have these vivid dreams about being yours, whether it was some grand proposal, our actual wedding, or leaving for our honeymoon."

My heart thunders in my chest, desperately wishing for some kind of window into her mind to see what she saw in those dreams. "You never told me that."

"I was so young," she says. "I was embarrassed, and we were still in that awkward stage where *we* didn't know if we were more than friends. I didn't want you to think I was crazy. Besides, you were the older, cool football protégé, and I was such a nerd. On some level, I knew you would never turn your back on me, but I was also terrified that one day you'd realize that I was nothing more than an obsessed kid and start putting distance between us."

"You really thought that?"

"Right up until Linc died and you actually did," she admits, a strange tone in her voice, both of us still hurting over that time apart despite how far we've come. "I figured one day you would just fall deeper with your football friends, and I'd get left behind. But you never did. You always showed up for me."

I press a kiss to her cheek, a smile pulling at my lips as I wonder just how much I can still offer her before she finally passes, if I can somehow make just one of her dreams come true. "I'll never stop, Zo," I tell her. "I will forever show up for you."

Chapter 55

NOAH

My palms sweat as my heart booms right out of my chest. I always knew this day was going to come, but I never expected it to be so soon, and certainly not under these circumstances. Sitting out in the park with Zoey tonight and hearing how she always envisioned our lives together only made me realize just how right this is.

She didn't last much longer dancing in the park, and she had me find Hazel's hoverboard out in the grass before letting me help her into my car. I brought her home, and she was out cold within five minutes. It's been a big day for her, and despite being so exhausted, I'm glad she pushed through and was able to enjoy our version of prom night.

It's not exactly how she always planned senior prom, but it was everything to me.

Before Zoey got sick, I never realized just how much I'd taken our time together for granted, because I always believed that we had a whole lifetime together, but with a clock on our time, I'm doing everything I can to make every second count. Which is exactly why I'm sneaking out of her bedroom and gently closing the door behind me.

I blow out my cheeks, shaking out my hands. I'm so fucking nervous, but not a damn thing is going to stop me now.

Rolling up the sleeves of my suit shirt, I make my way downstairs and straight toward the internal door of the garage. I pass Mom and Erica, both of them drunk out of their minds in the living room, giggling like little schoolgirls, but shit, it's nice to hear their laughter rather than the crying I've grown accustomed to.

They eye me as I walk past and all I can offer is a small smile, too fucking nervous to even speak. I don't even feel nerves like this when heading into a championship game. But Zoey James . . . fuck. She brings it out in me.

I hear both our moms whispering, already curious about what I'm doing, but I don't stop to answer their questions as my grip tightens on the door handle, and I push through to the garage.

Zoey's father is bent over his Mustang, fucking around with the twenty-year-old engine. He's spent a lot of time out here since Zoey's been sick. I think it gives him something to think about apart from the fact that his baby girl is only weeks away from taking her final breath.

It's not unheard of for me to come and chill with him in here, but when I close the door behind me, he glances up, his brows furrowed in question. "She alright?"

"Yes, sir," I say, swallowing hard and sounding way too formal. "She's asleep in bed."

He nods. "Did you ever make it to prom?"

"Not exactly," I say. "But she still had a good night."

"Good," he says with a heavy breath, bracing his hands against the rusted frame of the Mustang, staring down at the broken engine as though it holds the answers to all his questions. "That's all I've ever wanted for my little girl."

"That's why I'm here," I say, not willing to pussy-foot around this one, even if it means standing here as he tears me to shreds first. His head snaps back up again, his gaze locked and loaded on mine. "Sir, I—"

"Ah, shit," he says with a heavy sigh, tossing his wrench back toward his workbench. "I knew this was coming, but truth be told, I didn't expect it for another few years at least."

I nod, knowing exactly what he means. "With all due respect, Zoey doesn't have the kind of time we always thought she would, and I want to make her happy now. I want to give her everything she's ever wanted. I want as many of her dreams to come true before . . ." I trail off, not able to finish that sentence.

I let out a shaky breath, needing just a moment to compose myself before continuing. "I know you've had your reservations about me after I broke her heart when Linc died, but Zoey means more to me than anything. I love her. I've always loved her, and even after she's gone, I'll still be doing everything in my power to make up for the hurt I caused her."

He nods, closing the hood of the Mustang and leaning up against it as he turns to face me straight on. "I know you will, Noah. But Zoey forgave you a long time ago. Her heart's no longer broken. You don't need to continue to beat yourself up over it."

"If I knew how to stop, I would," I tell him. "I lost three years with her because I couldn't come to terms with a lot of things, and in hindsight, knowing what I know now, I hate myself for that. Three fucking years. I could have made her smile every single one of those days, and I'll always regret that I didn't. But she only has a little time left, and I want to give her the world while I still can. There are so many things that time won't allow me to give her, but there is one, sir," I say, getting choked up. "With your blessing, I would like to marry your daughter."

He blows out a heavy breath, holding my stare as my heart thunders in my chest, desperate for him to say yes, despite knowing that I will still ask for her hand in marriage even without his approval. I will marry her come hell or high water, but it would mean the world to both of them if he got to walk her down the aisle before she slipped away.

"Are you sure about this?" he asks. "You're still just a kid. You will be a nineteen-year-old widow."

I nod, holding his stare and letting him see just how ready I am. "I'm all in," I tell him. "And while I might be a nineteen-year-old widow, I'll also be the man who got to marry the love of his life and give her a day that she'll always cherish. Getting to give her this will forever be my greatest achievement. No championship trophy or NFL contract will even come close."

He watches me a moment longer, pressing his lips into a hard line before pushing off the edge of the Mustang. He crosses his garage, moving toward his small workbench before pulling out a little drawer and taking something from inside.

Making his way back over to me, he positions himself right in front of me before taking my hand and placing a diamond ring right into my palm. I look down at it, my brows furrowed, something so familiar about it.

"It's the ring you stole from your mother when you were a kid."

"The one I proposed to Zoey with when we were kids?"

"The one and only," he tells me. "I didn't even know she still had it until she launched it out the window about six months after Linc passed. When I found it in the grass, I tried to return it to your mom, but she said I should keep it just in case this day ever came."

A soft smile pulls across my lips. Those first few months after Linc died were the hardest, and I was terrible to Mom, but she never gave up on me. She never stopped trying. "Even back then, Mom always knew Zoey and I were going to find our way back to each other."

"We all did, son," he says, looking at me with nothing but pure fondness in his eyes. "Now go and make my little girl's dreams come true."

Chapter 56

ZOEY

Hazel sits in my bed, curled into my side as she tells me about some guy from school who is definitely not good enough for her, but the way she lights up has me wondering if maybe I should bite my tongue just this once. I'm sure she's been strutting around school with her eyes closed just so she can't see his blazing red flags, and I hate that I'm not going to be around to teach her this stuff. Not that I really know much about it. I fell in love with the first boy I ever saw, and while he has more than his fair share of red flags, those flags don't fly around me.

Noah will be there though. Once I'm gone from this world and Hazel is experiencing life at a million miles an hour, he'll be there to guide her through it. He won't let her fall. I just wish I could be there as she grows to see the beautiful woman she'll become.

I picture her falling deeper into makeup and having a glamorous life, maybe becoming a makeup artist for runway shows or a stylist. She loves that stuff, and I hope that whatever she chooses to do with her life, it's rewarding, and she gets to smile every day.

Hazel gets distracted, and her recap of her latest crush somehow turns into a story about some girl named Molly who's apparently a nasty, hoity-toity cow simply for also having a crush on the walking red flag. Then just as I go to give her all the advice in the world about the company we keep, a soft knock sounds at the door, and I glance up, finding Mom. "Do you girls feel like going for a drive?" she asks, her gaze lingering on me, her smile brighter than I've seen in weeks.

I smile right back at her, making the most of all the time we have left. "Can we get ice cream?"

"OH!" Hazel cheers, scrambling up onto her knees. "Yes! With choc-chips?"

Mom rolls her eyes. "Fine, but we need to sneak," she says. "I don't want your dad to know we're getting ice cream without him."

"HELL YEAH!" Hazel cheers, throwing herself off my bed and racing to her room to get dressed. It's been another long day, but after my private prom night with Noah last night, I've opted to stay in bed for most of the day, and apparently Hazel classified today as a pajama party for the ages. But she was more than ready to bail on our pajama party the second ice cream was mentioned. I suppose loyalty only goes as far as her stomach.

Mom strides into my room and offers me her hand. "Come on, my sweet girl," she says. "Let's get you dressed."

She helps me out of bed, and the second my feet touch the ground, she places her arm around my waist, taking my weight as we walk, not that there's much weight left to carry. I'm getting slimmer by the day. I've had to borrow Hazel's shorts because mine keep falling off.

Mom walks me into my closet and picks out a nice dress before helping me into it. "How are you feeling today?"

I shrug my shoulders, not willing to lie to her. "It's getting harder,"

I whisper. "I'm tired."

"Oh honey," she says, drawing me into her arms and holding me tight. "I know it is, and as much as it kills me to see you going through this, knowing that I'm going to have to say goodbye, you can celebrate that it's almost the end because once you reach it, a whole new adventure will be waiting on the other side. There won't be any more pain. No more doctors and hospital beds. You'll be free to run. And when my time finally comes, and I see you in heaven, I'm going to run right into your arms and hold you while you tell me all about the grand adventures you've been having."

Tears well in my eyes, and I bury my face into her shoulder. "I'm not ready to say goodbye."

"We'll never be ready," she tells me, her hand gently roaming up and down my back. "Now, what do you say we sneak out of here before your father figures out I've kidnapped you?"

"I don't think it counts as kidnapping when you're my mom."

She gives me a wicked smirk. "For today, let's pretend it does."

As if on cue, Hazel barges back into my room ready to go, complaining about us taking so long. Apparently, even after three servings of spaghetti and meatballs, she's so starving she could eat a cow. Only then she mentions that the cow might just be named Molly.

Taking my time down the stairs, we make our way out of the house, and before I know it, I'm buckled into the front of Mom's car. We start driving toward the creamery and are halfway there when Mom turns to me. "Where's Noah today? He disappeared this afternoon."

My gaze lingers on the street, watching the world as we pass. "One of the seniors on his team had a baby this past weekend, so Coach Sanderson is hosting a full team baby-pushing party in the spirit of team bonding. He should be back in the next hour or so."

"Oh, that's lovely," she says. "But tell me Coach Sanderson didn't actually call it a baby-pushing party?"

I laugh, a smirk pulling at the corner of my lips. "I honestly don't know," I tell her. "That's just what Noah said when he got the message this morning."

"You know what? I've been with your father for over twenty-five years, and I'm still completely baffled by the opposite sex."

Hazel scoffs from the backseat. "Don't worry, Mom. I know everything there is to know about them," she says. "I'll walk you through it."

Mom and I both roll our eyes, and the rest of the way to the creamery, we listen to Hazel's long, drawn-out explanations of how a man's brain works, and honestly, I think she's got it down. Maybe I won't need to worry about her as much as I thought I would.

Choosing the right flavor is the biggest challenge I've ever had to face, and considering the two failed rounds of chemotherapy, that's a strong statement to make. I mean . . . okay, maybe I'm exaggerating a bit. Nothing is worse than chemo, especially that second round. That shit was brutal. Just the thought of it sends chills down my spine.

I end up with a strawberry and white chocolate swirl on a cone, and as we wander back to the car, Mom takes a deep breath, breathing in the warm evening. "Perhaps we should drive down to the lake and eat our ice cream there? Have you ever been there at night?"

I scoff as we reach the car and get back in. "Mom, I've not only been there at night, but I've been wildly drunk and partying like nobody's business there at night, and well into the morning, too."

She gapes at me, her jaw dropping. "You've done what?"

I laugh and bat my eyelashes. "You think that's bad?" I say. "Did I ever tell you about the night Hope and I snuck out and shared a joint? Noah had to carry my ass home. I couldn't see straight for days."

"What's a joint?" Hazel asks from the backseat.

I laugh a little harder, having to clutch my stomach when it starts to hurt.

"Nothing," Mom says, shaking her head as she pulls out of her parking spot and takes off toward the lake, but I see a glimmer of happiness in her eyes, and despite the reckless things I'm admitting to, I know she's glad that I've had my chance to walk on the wild side, that I haven't spent these past eighteen years being an overly good girl who never got a chance to really live. But since the second Noah stormed back into my life, he's made sure that I've lived so enormously that it'll be enough for a million lifetimes, and yet, not nearly enough for just this one.

We pull up at the lake a moment later, driving through the twisty dirt road to get in. Then, instead of having to get out to walk, Mom drives straight past the parking lot and right up to the water. "Should we get out and sit by the water?" Mom asks, despite all of us already finished with our ice cream.

It's a no-brainer, and we all pile out of the car, tossing our shoes aside so we can stroll right down to the water's edge. I stand with Mom, her arm around my waist to hold me up as Hazel pulls up her pant legs and walks calf-deep into the water.

As I search for a log to sit on, a throat clears behind us, and the sound is all too familiar. I whip around to find Noah standing a little further down the lake, looking just as sexy as last night. Instead of the black suit he wore to prom, he's in a gray one, and the top few buttons are undone just the way I like it.

He looks amazing, and as much as it kills me to have to let him go so soon, I hope he's able to move on and find something incredible with a woman who inspires him to be everything I know he can be. But on the down-low, I hope he doesn't love her quite as much as he loved me.

A smile pulls at my lips as he walks toward me. "What are you doing here?" I ask as he steps right into my arms, taking my weight from my mom. "How'd you know we were here? No, better yet, why are you in a suit? Was the baby-pushing party that fancy? I thought it was a casual thing."

Noah just laughs, and as his fingers brush up and down my arm, he leaves a trail of goosebumps everywhere our skin touches. "Walk with me," he murmurs in that deep tone that makes me believe that nothing bad could ever happen in this dark world.

We make our way a little further down the lake, my feet barely skimming across the water's edge. "You're being awfully shady, Noah Ryan," I say. "Explain yourself."

"Can't I just do something nice for my girl?"

I narrow my eyes. He knows how I feel about surprises. I like giving them, love it even, but the whole receiving thing has always been a sore point for me, and over the past few weeks, the surprises just seem to keep rolling in.

He takes me around the bend in the lake, and when I glance up and peer out into the opening, my heart swells bigger than it's ever been. My eyes instantly fill with unshed tears. "Noah," I gasp, clinging on to him with everything I am.

Hundreds of long-stemmed red roses have been planted into the ground to form a large semi-circle with dozens of candles scattered among them. Fairy lights hang from the trees above, creating a beautiful canopy over the rose-lined circle below, and if that weren't enough to take my breath away, the words MARRY ME are written in giant light letters, creating the most stunning backdrop.

I fall into him, my knees going weak. I knew he might try to make some grand gesture over the next few weeks, but never in my wildest dreams would I have imagined that he'd propose.

My heart has never beat so fast, and as he takes my hand and leads me toward the rose-lined circle, my whole body goes weak, but for the first time in months, it's not because of the cancer or medications pulsing through my veins.

We enter the semi-circle, and as he leads me right into the middle and turns to face me, I take a quick look around, which is when I see my whole family—Mom and Dad standing in each other's arms, tears in my mother's eyes, while my dad . . . God, he's never looked at me with such pride before. Aunt Maya is here, her arm around Hope's shoulder, and damn it, I'm going to have to have a word with her about secret keeping, but it can wait because all that matters right now is the man standing before me.

He clutches my hands, his thumbs rolling over my knuckles. "Zo, you've been my world since the day I first met you. You've been my everything. My *bestest friend*, my partner in crime, my salvation when the world was closing in on me, and through it all, you've been the love of my life. I'm proud that you've allowed me to be the man by your side right from the beginning, and you know that I'll be right here, holding your hand until the end. Getting to see you grow from the scrawny little kid who went mud diving with me into the radiant, incredible woman you are today has been and will always be my greatest honor. And Zo," he says, pausing a moment. "No words will ever be enough to express just how in love I am with you, and while I know our time is limited, I want to be able to give you everything you've always deserved."

Tears flow from my eyes as I clutch his hands tighter. His words play on repeat in my mind, and my heart has never been so full. "Just having you by my side for the past eighteen years is more than I could have ever asked for, Noah," I tell him, my voice breaking over the lump in my throat, my lips starting to tremble. "I love you more every day, and getting to walk this life with you has been the greatest gift of all."

He smiles and leans into me, gently brushing his lips over mine. "Always, Zozo," he murmurs. "You'll always be the other half of my soul. Without you, I'm not whole, and while having to learn to walk this earth alone is going to be the hardest thing I'll ever do, I want to treasure every last moment I have with you."

With that, he inches back just a bit, putting space between us as he drops to one knee. Releasing one of my hands, he pulls a small velvet box from his pocket. He holds it up toward me, and my hands shake as he opens the lid, revealing a beautiful diamond ring—a diamond ring that I'd recognize anywhere.

I suck in a gasp, my eyes lifting to his. "Is that?"

"The same one I proposed to you with when I was seven," he confirms.

"But how did you—"

"Your dad found it," he says, squeezing my hand. "He kept it for you—*for us*—because even back then, they all knew we'd make it right here."

"Noah," I breathe, the tears graduating from a steady flow into a raging river.

"Zo," he says, his voice shifting, a seriousness wrapping around us and closing us into this beautiful private bubble for this moment I've always dreamed about. "You had me wrapped around your little finger from the day I first met you, and every day since has led us right here. I've always known that this is the path we would take and that you would be the one I would give myself to, vowing to love you in front of all our friends and family for as long as we both shall live. And I've been so lucky and grateful that you've opened your world to me and loved me in return, even when I didn't deserve it. Every piece of me belongs to you, Zoey James, and though we won't have as much time as we always dreamed of, nothing would make me happier than to be your husband."

He pauses, holding my stare, those dark eyes so full of undeniable, overwhelmingly pure love. "Zoey, will you marry me?"

A wide smile stretches across my face, and I fall right into his open arms, our bodies colliding as tears stream down my face. "Yes," I whimper. "Yes, of course I'll marry you."

Noah holds me so damn tight as our family cheers for us, and honestly, I'd forgotten they were even there. He crushes his lips to mine, kissing me so tenderly, and even through our kiss, it's impossible to wipe the smile off my face. I've never been so happy.

Over the past few months, I had to come to terms with the fact that marrying Noah Ryan was only ever going to be a dream for me. But the fact that Noah is willing to get down on one knee and ask me to marry him, despite the heartbreak he knows is coming his way, fills me with the most genuine, unadulterated, pure kind of love.

When we finally break apart, Noah takes my hand and slides the ring into place, right where it's always belonged.

He kisses me again, and with that, we're swarmed by our family, each one of them crashing into us and wrapping us into their warm arms, not a single dry eye to be seen. Noah doesn't dare let go of my hand, keeping me right by his side as our family offers us their congratulations.

It's an incredible night, easily the best one of my life, and as Noah drives me home after all is said and done, I can't help but smile. His hand lingers on my thigh, the weight of my illness not welcome here tonight. As I gaze at him, his elbow resting against the driver's door, his fingers carelessly draped over the steering wheel, my heart flutters. Things could not be more perfect.

This incredible man is going to be my husband.

Right from the start he was mine, and now I'm going to walk down the aisle to marry him before he inevitably walks me through to the end, our hearts entwined until the end of time.

Chapter 57

ZOEY

The beautiful Arizona sun peaks above the horizon, welcoming a new day and turning the sky into brilliant shades of dazzling gold. It's a perfect day, more than I could have ever asked for because, in a little more than an hour, I'm going to marry my best friend.

It's been a week since Noah proposed at the lake, and while I know this is all happening so fast and not typically how this would go down, I wouldn't have it any other way, especially considering the circumstances. We want to make the most of every second, and if that means getting to marry the man who makes me the happiest woman in the world in a short, private ceremony while the sun still rises in the dewy morning, then that's exactly what we're going to do.

I stand at my bedroom window, not brave enough to crawl out onto the roof. At this point, I don't even think I'd have the strength to haul myself out through the frame. While this past week has been incredible with Noah getting to plan our wedding and Mom helping me choose a dress, I've also continued my steady decline, which is part of the reason why we're doing this so early in the morning.

By the time the sun is just reaching the top of the sky, I'll be too exhausted to even stand, and by the time it lowers back down to the horizon, I won't be able to keep my eyes open. If we opted for a starlight ceremony like I'd always imagined, I would have only been able to enjoy it for an hour or two. This way, I get to take my time and soak up every last second—even if it means asking my family to wake up before dawn.

A soft knock sounds at my door, and I turn to find Mom beaming at me with glassy eyes. "Are you ready to start?" she murmurs, her voice filling my room with nothing but unconditional love.

I nod, glad that I get to relax and sit down through this part. "Born ready," I tell her as butterflies dance through my stomach.

I make my way back to my bed, knowing Hazel is about to come in and bombard me with makeup, and as I drop down, I can't help but glance toward Noah's empty side. He stuck to tradition and snuck out early so he wouldn't see me the morning of our wedding, and while I love that about him, I also hated not waking up in the warmth of his strong arms. It's daunting that I don't know how many mornings I have left to open my eyes to him, but I know from this day on, I will never have to wake up alone again.

Just as expected, Hazel shows up only moments later and doesn't waste a single second. She dives straight into my makeup, going the extra mile to make sure I'm pampered at the same time. Hope turns up halfway through makeup, and seeing just how gifted Hazel is in this department, demands that she does hers too, which Hazel is more than happy to cater to.

Without hair to worry about, getting ready doesn't take long, and before I know it, Mom and Hope are helping me into my dress as I gaze at myself in the mirror. It's a beautiful silk gown with delicate beaded straps and a plunging back, soft and flowy, that perfectly accentuates what little curves I have left. The gown trails down to a small train, the material gathered at my feet, and while it's not exactly the extravagant gown I pictured for myself, it's beautiful all the same.

I always wanted something covered in beading with a long train, but I'm simply not strong enough to bear the weight of a gown like that anymore. Looking at myself now, taking in the subtleness, the soft lace, and the headband veil that falls like a gentle summer breeze over my face, I realize that nothing could have been better. It's absolutely perfect, but what makes it better is knowing that this will be the dress Noah always remembers me in. This very moment will live in his memories, treasured and cherished until the end of time.

When I'm ready, my dad appears at the door, his soft intake of breath drawing my attention. I glance up, peering at my father across the room, a small smile stretching across my glossy lips. "Hi Daddy," I whisper.

A single tear falls from his eye as he wanders toward me, not stopping until he's standing right in front of me. He gently collects my veil between his fingers and lifts it over my head, letting it fall back behind me. "You're absolutely breathtaking," he tells me, his fingers gently brushing over my cheek. "You truly are an angel sent from the heavens."

I smile up at my father, willing myself not to cry. "You're walking me down the aisle, right?"

"There's no greater honor for a father than to give his daughter away on her wedding day," he whispers. "There's no place I'd rather be."

My cheeks flush, and for a fleeting moment, I feel like that same little girl who used to dress up in Mom's old wedding gown without a single care in the world. I would make Dad walk me down the aisle and give me away to Hazel, who was forced to step in as the groom when Noah had enough of playing weddings. It's surreal to think that we're right back there again, only this time, it's for real, and no one is playing.

"You won't let me fall?"

"Never," Dad murmurs before reaching back around me and gathering my veil once again. He leans in and presses a soft kiss to my cheek before meeting my eyes. "I love you, Zo. You're always going to be my sweet angel, my little girl."

I can't keep the tears from falling and he hastily wipes them away before finally lowering my veil back into place. "Let's go get you married," he says, and with that, he steps in beside me, his arm folding right around my waist. I place my hand over his, and as Hazel collects the bouquet of tulips, made out of the dozens Noah has gifted me over these past few weeks, one each and every day without fail.

The nerves and excitement creep in, but I can't wait. I've never been so ready in my life. We make our way down the stairs, and Dad holds on to me tighter than ever as Mom and Hope follow behind us.

Dad opens the door of the fancy limousine, and I can't help but laugh to myself. This is insane. I've never ridden in a limo before, but it's absolutely everything and more. I feel like a princess. This has Hazel written all over it, and I love how she put her two cents in to make sure today is absolutely perfect for me.

We all climb in, and after we all get settled, the driver hits the gas, and we're sailing down the road, away from East View and out toward the countryside. I have no idea where we're going, only that I'll get to see Noah when we get there.

The second Noah found the place, he decided he wanted to keep yet another surprise. It's been bugging me all week, but I know whatever he's chosen is going to be amazing.

It's a thirty-minute drive before the limo turns down a long, winding road, and as he does, my eyes light up with an array of breathtaking, vibrant colors. Beautiful shades of reds, pinks, yellows, oranges, and whites fill the rolling hills of the tulip fields before me.

I sit up straighter, my eyes so wide as the morning sun glistens off the dew lingering on the delicate petals. It's the most incredible thing I've ever seen. "Oh my gosh," Mom whispers, her hand falling to my thigh and gently squeezing. "I knew it was going to be beautiful, but I never could have imagined this. It's breathtaking."

I've never heard truer words in my life, and my eyes start to water. It really is breathtaking. I didn't think anything could outdo Noah's incredible proposal, but this is so much more than I ever dreamed.

We drive through fields and fields of vibrant tulips when the driver finally eases onto the brake, and as I twist to gaze out the opposite window, I finally see him—Noah Ryan, my *bestest friend* and the love of my life—waiting for me among a sea of beautiful colors.

His smile is brighter than I've ever seen, and the way my heart races is something I've never experienced before. It's overwhelming, pure, and filled with the most adoring, eternal love, and I know with every fiber of my being that my purpose in life, every single moment I've ever experienced, was a path leading straight to this.

My reason for being was to be with this man, to teach him how to love, how to grow, and to be the light that's always led him home.

I've never felt so at peace, never felt so perfectly right.

He stands under a gorgeous wooden arch with drapes of white chiffon that sway in the morning breeze, but despite its beauty, my gaze remains locked on him. He's so ruggedly handsome, and that sparkle in his eyes has me ready to barrel out of the limo and fall straight into his strong arms.

Despite the dark window tint, his piercing eyes collide with mine, holding my stare as that tether between us solidifies and turns into the most indestructible kind of metal, entwining right around our souls and holding us there. Not even in death will this bond falter.

He will hold me up, right through till the end of time, and when we finally get the chance to meet again, it'll be like a sonic boom, the stars aligning as everything falls right back into place, right where it was always supposed to be.

I take a shaky breath as the limousine driver walks around the car and opens the back door. Dad gets out first, offering his hand to all of his girls, even Hope because my nana raised him to be the perfect gentleman—though sometimes I think he forgets that.

From within the car, I can hear the subtle music playing through the tulip field, and my heart sings. He really has thought of everything. When it's my turn to get out of the car, my father offers me his hand, and I gingerly take it, beaming up at him as he smiles right back. "I won't let you fall," he promises.

Stepping out of the car, Mom and Hope fix my veil, making sure everything is just right, and as the celebrant strides through the beautiful tulips and takes his place by the corner of the arch, I turn to face Noah.

The wide smile on his face falls into a gasping breathlessness, gazing at me in complete, overwhelming awe, his eyes conveying the words he can't speak. My heart races and booms like thunder among the rolling clouds.

It's so much more than I thought it could be, so undeniably perfect.

Mom, Hazel, and Hope make their way through the small rows between the tulips, meeting with Aunt Maya and the small handful of friends and family that are gathered around us, and as the music shifts to *From This Moment* by Shania Twain, my father offers me his arm.

We walk toward the beautiful arch, and with every step I take, my gaze remains locked on Noah's. My father holds me up, his strong hands ready to take me right to the end as he tells me how much he loves me.

Each step brings me closer, and as my heart races so much faster, I pick up my pace, unable to wait a second longer. My feet stumble to a stop in front of Noah, and my father leans in to wrap his arms around me. "Always my little girl."

My eyes sting, but before my tears can fall, Noah takes my hand and pulls me right into him. It's just the two of us existing in this moment, and the world fades away. His fingers entwine through mine as he drops his forehead, the two of us locked in pure bliss. "You're so beautiful," he murmurs, his voice thick with emotion. "I love you."

"I love you," I whisper right back, our hearts synching and beating as one.

The celebrant steps forward, and as the music fades out, he commences the ceremony, welcoming our family and friends and giving a brief rundown of our story so far. And with every second that passes, Noah's dark gaze remains locked on mine, both of us absolutely captivated.

I breathe him in, wanting to revel in this moment, not willing to miss a damn thing. I want to save it all to my memory, the feel of his hands in mine, the way my heart races, the heavy pulse in my ears. I want to remember the way he smells, the way his hair falls forward into his eyes and dances in the morning breeze.

I want to remember the sound of my mother's soft cries as my father holds her at his side, the overwhelming scent the tulips create around us. I want it all. I want to drown in this moment and feel it lift me right into the sky.

When it's time to say our vows, Noah's hold shifts on my hand as he places a gold wedding band at the tip of my finger. "Zo," he starts, holding my gaze as though it's the only thing keeping him breathing.

"It's simple. I will love you. I will love you today, tomorrow, and every day until the heavens and the earth no longer exist. Whether you're here by my side, sharing our lives together, or watching over me from above, I will love you. You're my everything, Zoey James, and as long as my heart continues to beat, it will beat for you."

Tears roll down my cheeks as he gently pushes the gold band into place on my finger, and when it's my turn, I take his hand, just as he did mine, looping the gold band around the top of his ring finger. "You're my person, Noah. I've walked my life with you, side by side, right from the beginning, and as a little girl, I couldn't have imagined the type of roller coaster loving you was going to take me on," I breathe. "You've consumed me, have owned me in every possible way. So for me, today isn't about giving myself to you because I've always been yours, and I will continue to be yours until the end of time. My heart has always belonged right in the palm of your hand, just as yours has belonged in mine. We're twin flames, and while I won't be here to give you another fifty years, to build our lives together, or to build a home filled with love and laughter, I promise you that our souls will never part. I will always be with you, always love you with everything I am, even as I watch over you from the heavens."

Noah drops his forehead to mine as I slide the wedding band into place, then before the celebrant has a chance to tell him that he may kiss his bride, Noah lifts the veil over my head and pulls me into him, wrapping his arms around my waist as his lips come down on mine.

Our family and friends applaud as the celebrant officially announces us as husband and wife, but all that matters to me is the feeling of Noah's warm lips moving against mine.

Husband.

Noah Ryan is my husband.

Our family rushes us, congratulating us as the celebrant tries to pull us away to sign the documents to make this official. And once all is said and done, we spend the rest of the day celebrating. Coach Sanderson and Noah's teammates hired out a whole restaurant just for us as a wedding gift, and after a magical day filled with love, family, and undeniable happiness, Noah finally gets me in the car, and I'm more exhausted than I've ever been in my life.

Dusk is just starting to fall over East View when Noah brings his Camaro to a stop outside the fanciest hotel in town. My brows furrow as I look toward him. "What are we doing here?"

"It's hardly romantic spending our wedding night under your parents' roof," he tells me. "Especially considering that they'll know exactly what we're doing."

My cheeks flush, and I try not to think about just how right he is. The fact that we're spending the night in a hotel is even more of a reason for my parents to know what we're doing. But we're married now, and nothing is going to stop me from getting to spend my wedding night with the man I love. *My husband.*

"Thank you," I tell him. "Now hurry up and take me to bed. I haven't been able to kiss you the way I really want to kiss you with everyone's eyes on us all day, and if I don't get to put my hands on you soon, there's no telling what I might do."

Noah gapes at me for a moment. I've always been forward when I needed intimacy with him, but it usually comes with flushed cheeks and a shy smile, but not tonight, not now.

Noah helps me out of the car and hands his keys to the valet before sweeping me right up into his arms, the delicate train of my dress hanging below. He carries me right into the elevator, his lips on mine the whole way up to the thirty-fourth floor. And when he slides the keycard into the reader and opens the door, a soft gasp slips between my lips.

The room is incredible, but it has nothing on the city views out the floor-to-ceiling windows, and I have to pull away from Noah, needing a moment to take it all in. He sets me on my feet, making sure I'm balanced before allowing me to step out of his strong arms. I make my way across the room and right over to the impressive window as I gaze out at the sunset dancing across the windows of the high-rise building around us. I've never seen anything like it.

I'm taking it all in when I feel Noah's warm fingers at my shoulder, gently brushing over my skin, trailing all the way down my elbows to my hands. My fingers catch his and then his lips are at the base of my throat, and I tilt my head, opening up for more.

His other hand takes my waist, and he turns me until those lips are coming down on mine. Fire burns through my veins, and I push up on my tippy toes, needing to be closer to him. He fingers the beaded strap on my gown, pushing it down over my shoulder, his fingers so sensual over my skin. I need so much more.

He takes his time, kissing me deeply and worshiping every inch of my body as I reach up between us and start unbuttoning his suit shirt.

My dress falls away, and as I free him from the confines of his pants, his hands skim over my ass, effortlessly lifting me. Wrapping my legs securely around him, I hold on for dear life as he turns and walks us over to the massive bed, and as he lays me down against the pillow, he pulls back from our kiss. "I love you so fucking much, Zoey," he tells me. "This right here, with you in my arms as my wife, I'll always remember us this way."

Tears form in my eyes, and I nod, absolutely breathless. "I know," I tell him, my hand sliding down from his shoulder to his chest, feeling the way his heart beats beneath my palm. "Remember us just like this."

He nods, his lips coming back down to mine, and when he reaches out over the bed to grab the small foil packet, I shake my head. "Not tonight, Noah," I murmur. "I just want to feel you."

He holds my stare a moment longer, and while I'm sure there are a million reasons why we shouldn't, there are also a million reasons why we should. What it really comes down to is that I love this man with everything I am, just as I told him in my vows, and with only a handful of weeks left, I want to spend every single moment I can feeling the way he makes me come alive. Feeling him and only him.

Noah nods, and not a moment later, he reaches down and grasps my thigh, hitching it high over his hip, and with that, he pushes inside of me, his lips moving over mine.

Chapter 58

ZOEY

Newly wedded bliss has consumed me over these past few weeks, and it's been so much more than I thought it would be, but I can't lie, I know my time is coming soon. I can feel it in my bones. I'm almost at the end, and having to watch Noah's heart break every time he walks into my room is tearing me to shreds.

The pain has taken over, and it's worse than I was prepared for, even more so now that my organs have started to surrender. They're giving up, and every day, it only gets harder.

It won't be long now. Maybe a few days, and I've never been so scared. I'm not ready to leave this world without him. I don't want to be just a memory.

Getting out of bed has become a chore too challenging to tackle until it's absolutely necessary, and when I do, I need Noah right there holding me up. And in those times when it gets too much and my mind clouds with fear, Noah makes love to me until all I know is the all-consuming bond we share.

I can't lie. I'm terrified of what waits for me on the other side. Will I see Linc? Will I slip away into nothingness? Or will there be a whole world waiting for me with all the adventures Mom promised? But I'm also terrified of what I'm leaving behind. Mom and Dad will be devastated, crushed, and broken beyond repair, but they'll hold each other up. Noah and Hazel on the other hand . . . Every time I think about it, my world burns to ashes around me.

I've spent the last few weeks immersed in my laptop, writing away, only over these past few days, I haven't had the strength to finish it. Or perhaps it's the courage I'm lacking. I know what comes next, but I don't know how to put that into words.

Kelly—my home care nurse and my nurse from the treatment center—finishes checking my vitals, and the sad, encouraging smile on her face tells me that tonight is not the night. She's been with me right from the start of that first round of chemo, and since then, we've somehow developed some kind of silent way to communicate. I know exactly what she's trying to tell me by just the simplest flicker in her honey eyes. She was really rooting for me. She really wanted me to be able to pull through this, and over these past six or so months, she's become family.

Finishing up with her usual treat for Allie, she strides out of my room, closing the door behind her. As she gives my parents an update out in the hallway, I do what I can to block out their muffled voices. I can't bear to hear how I only have a few days left.

Instead, I pull out the pen and notepad I've been busy writing in and get back to work, wanting to leave a little something for the people who mean the most to me.

Tonight's letter—Hazel.

Noah sits beside me, giving me the privacy I need to write, but I'm not going to lie, I see the few times he peeks over my shoulder, reading the words I'm writing to my little sister. He just can't help himself, but when the time comes for me to pick up this very notepad and write the words *Dear Noah* at the top, I don't know how I'm going to get through it.

It's well after nightfall when I stuff the five-page essay into the envelope and scrawl Hazel's name across the front, and I'm exhausted. I can barely hold my own head up, but as I glance over at Noah, watching the way he watches me, I know I have to do this now because come tomorrow, I don't know if I'll have the strength to even try.

"Noah," I say, my voice croaky as a lump forms in my throat.

His eyes are instantly wide, scanning over my face, about ready to launch himself off my bed and race for help. "What's wrong?" he rushes out. "Are you okay? What do you need?"

"I'm . . . I'm okay," I breathe, my words getting harder to string into complete sentences. "I just . . . will you take me . . . out to the roof?"

"The roof?" he questions, already shaking his head. "Baby, I don't know if that's a good idea."

"There's some things I want to talk to you about," I say, taking a deep breath and trying to ignore the pain, but truth be told, it's not so bad right now, not after Kelly just dosed me up. "And I just . . . I want to sit in your arms and . . . and look at the stars."

His brows pinch in concern, and I see in his eyes as he wars with himself over what to do, but ultimately, he's not going to tell me no, not now. "Okay," he finally says, taking the blanket and easing it back off my thin legs. "You're not to let go of me."

I nod, knowing that's not even going to be a problem because he'll be the one holding on to me, refusing to let me fall.

I scoot to the edge of the bed, and he takes my hand before thinking better of it and scooping his arm right under my legs and lifting me against his chest. Then turning toward the window, he takes a few strides before placing me down on my desk. He unlocks the window and opens it wide before climbing right through. Then reaching back, he scoops me right off the desk and out onto the roof of my family home.

Noah settles back against the brickwork and holds me between his legs, his hand on my thigh as his thumb brushes back and forth. His other hand wraps around my waist, and I clutch on to it, my fingers weaving through his as I feel the night breeze blowing against my face.

I breathe it in, closing my eyes and enjoying the night, wondering if this is the last one I might ever experience. "This is perfect," I tell him. "It's a beautiful night."

"It's always perfect with you," he murmurs, dropping his face to press a kiss to my shoulder.

Gazing up at the stars, I watch as they twinkle against the dark sky as if winking right at me, enticing me to join them, and I suppose I will. "You've always loved watching the stars," Noah comments.

I nod, swallowing over the lump in my throat. "When I was a little girl, I always dreamed that one day I'd dance among the stars," I say softly, finding it easier to talk in whispers, "jumping from one to another like little sparkly stepping stones, and I guess . . . maybe I can."

"No, Zo," he murmurs, bringing his hand up to cradle my face, turning it back to meet my stare. "You were never supposed to be one of the many stars. You're the whole damn sun."

My bottom lip trembles, and I tilt my head, raising my chin just enough to kiss him. "In that case, every morning when you wake up and see the sun rays peeking through your blinds, you'll know that's me. Or when you're running up and down the field, winning games and that blazing sun is making you sweat, you'll think of me."

"Always, Zo. Every day I'll think of you. Morning. Noon. Night.

You'll always be right there, and anywhere I go, I'll be able to take you with me."

"Noah, I . . . I need you to do something for me."

"Anything."

"I need you to watch over Hazel," I tell him, pausing to catch my breath as tears trickle down my face like a silent river flowing through the night. "She's going to need you more than ever. You're all she has left."

"You know I will," he vows. "I'm not going to let her fall."

I nod, turning in his arms to rest my head against his chest. "I'm scared."

"I know, Zo, but it's going to be okay. Kelly will make sure you're not in any pain and—"

"No," I murmur. "I don't mean that I'm scared about that. Well, I am. I'm terrified of letting go and never seeing your face again, but what really scares me is what I'm leaving behind."

Noah fights back tears, his hand cupping the back of my neck, holding me so damn close. "How do you mean?"

"I'm terrified that you're going to fall into the darkness like you did after Linc died," I admit, my tears staining his shirt. "You can't let that happen, Noah. We didn't suffer through those three years and claw our way back only for you to fall again. I'm not going to be here to pick you back up. Promise me, Noah. Promise me you won't let it happen. Your mom and Hazel need you too much, and I can't go until I know that you're going to be okay. *I need you to be okay.*"

"Fuck, Zo. I—"

I shake my head, needing to get the words out while I still can. "I want so much for you," I cry, diving deep into the darkest corners of my heart. "I want you to find love again. I want you to get married and have the big house on the hill with the picket fence and a million kids running around. But more than that, I want you to know that you're deserving of that love, and while it hurts to think about you ever loving someone else the way you've loved me, I don't want you to feel guilt for opening yourself up again."

His tears fall, his voice all choked up. "Zoey, I . . . I can't do that," he tells me. "I don't want to love anybody else. I don't want a child running around who doesn't have your eyes. I don't want to move on, Zo."

"Don't say that," I beg, clutching him as though he were the one slipping away. "I know it's going to be hard, excruciating even, but you're going to make it through the other end. Then one day, when it doesn't quite hurt so bad and you can think of me without your world crumbling around you, you'll find that you're ready to try."

He shakes his head. "Don't, Zo. Don't make me picture the life I always wanted with you, with someone else. I can't do it."

"Not yet," I whisper into the night. "But one day. You're so strong, Noah. You've held me up all this time and given me the most wonderful life. You've given me so much and taught me what it truly meant to love with everything I am. I took your last name and have gotten to call myself your wife. On top of that, I've been the only woman you've ever looked at with love in your eyes. You don't know how much that means to me, Noah. Just having you in my life as my bestest friend has been the greatest gift of all, but nothing would make me happier than being able to watch over you and see your world filled with happiness. I want to watch you tackle parenthood. I want to see you agonizing over paint swatches for the home you'll build for your family. I want you to have it all, Noah. You deserve it all. And I know it's going to take some time, but when you're ready, I'll give you a sign and let you know that everything's going to be okay."

He crushes his arms around my frail body, holding me tighter than ever before, his face buried in my shoulder. "I don't know how to do life without you."

"You won't," I promise him, resting my hand against his heart. "I'm always going to be right here, guiding you through."

He's silent, and the only sound is the soft spring breeze rustling in the leaves. "These past six months, you've gotten me through the worst. You've held me through chemotherapy and given me the strength to keep going, but it's my turn now. Let me hold you up the way you've held me."

"I fucking love you so much, Zoey," he says, lifting his broken gaze to mine.

Reaching up, I cradle the side of his face, looking deep into those eyes that I've loved my whole entire life. "You've been my whole world, Noah. Don't ever forget how much I've loved you."

"Never," he vows, and with that, he brings his lips to mine in the most tender kiss—the sweetest goodbye.

Chapter 59

NOAH

My fingers clutch the single stem of the pink tulip I just picked up from the East View Florist, and I hold it to my chest as I pull up at my mom's house. Her car's gone, and I let out a breath of relief. This isn't exactly a conversation I want to have with her listening in.

This shit is already hard enough.

It's been three days since Zoey sat out on the roof with me, pouring her heart out and telling me her hopes and dreams for the future I'm supposed to have without her. She made me promise that I wouldn't fall back into the darkness that consumed me after Linc died, and while I couldn't get the words out that night, I'm going to do everything in my power to try and keep my head above water. If she needs me to promise her this one thing, then I will. Besides, how could I possibly let her down like that? She's fought so hard to get this far, so the least I can do is allow her to leave this world with the knowledge that I'm going to be alright.

There's nothing I wouldn't do for Zoey, for my *wife*.

These past few days have been gut-wrenching. Her organs are quickly succumbing to her illness and shutting down, and while she smiles for me every time I walk into a room, I know she's in agony. Her fingers are swelling, and she can hardly move, hardly keep her eyes open, and while I want to hold on to her forever, keep her here for my own selfish needs, I need to let her go so she can finally be at peace.

She doesn't have much longer. I overheard Kelly mention to Zoey's parents that it could be as soon as tomorrow, which is exactly why I'm here.

Clutching the single pink tulip, I push out of my car and make my way up the familiar path to my mom's front door before welcoming myself in. I walk into the small foyer and cross through the living room before heading down the hall.

I stop at Linc's bedroom as the heaviness weighs down on my shoulders.

How the hell did we get here?

This isn't how this was supposed to play out. She's only eighteen. She's barely had a chance to live. I was supposed to give her the world, build a home together, and watch her belly swell with our growing babies. And now when I stare up into the stands on game day, I'll be looking at nothing but an empty seat.

Pushing past the threshold of Lincoln's bedroom, I take a deep breath, positive I can still smell him in here. It feels as though a lifetime has passed since I last saw his face, yet it also feels like it was just yesterday.

It's funny how grief can come up and sucker punch you right in the gut. Just when you think you're doing okay, something happens and you're all the way back at square one, down on your knees, unable to breathe. That's what it feels like mourning my little brother. It's been almost five years, and while it's gotten easier to get through each day, it still hurts all the damn time.

Fuck, I can't even wrap my head around how much it's going to hurt to mourn Zoey.

Walking around Linc's room, my fingers skim across his desk, scanning over the papers and photographs I've looked at a million times before finally dropping down on the edge of his bed, Zoey's tulip still clutched tightly between my fingers.

Bracing my elbows on my knees, I lean forward, taking shaky breaths and willing myself not to cry—not here, not in this room. "Linc, I . . . I know I'm not in any position to be asking favors from you. I was never the greatest brother. I let you down over and over again, especially after you were gone. I hurt the people I love, Zoey more than anyone," I say, clenching my jaw and needing a minute to find just a shred of strength to continue. "I know you're watching over us. There are times when I feel you and it's as though I could swear you were right there in the room with me. I know you see what's happening with Zoey. It won't be long, and she'll be up there with you, and despite how much I want to hold on to her, she needs to go to be free. She's in pain, Linc, and it fucking kills me seeing her like that, but I need to know—" I pause, my voice beginning to waver. "I need to know that you're going to watch out for her. She's scared. Fucking terrified. She doesn't know what's coming for her, but you can help her. Take her hand and guide her through it. Please. Help her find her purpose in this next life, help her to let go, help her to know peace."

Tears well in my eyes, and I hang my head, taking a few short breaths when my phone cuts through the silence. I dig into my pocket, pulling it out to find Henry's name flashing across the screen, and my heart contracts as I bring the phone to my ear.

"What's up? Is everything okay?" I rush out, not bothering with formalities.

"Noah, I . . . It's time," he tells me, his voice thick with grief. "You need to come home to her."

My phone falls away, clattering to the ground as my hands start to shake.

No.

No, this can't be right.

I'm not ready.

We were supposed to have another day. She was supposed to spend the day in my arms so I could tell her over and over again just how much I've loved her all of these years. I need to tell her how my heart races every time she looks at me, how her smile alone could bring me to my knees, and how much I'm going to cherish the time we spent together.

We were supposed to have more time.

I don't remember leaving Linc's room, but one second I'm on the phone with Zoey's father, and the next, I'm racing down the street, pushing my Camaro to its limits. All I know is that she's dying, that it's time for her to go, and I'm not there holding her hand like I always promised.

I drive on auto-pilot careening through the morning traffic until my tires screech to a stop outside Zoey's home, and then I'm running.

My feet pound against the pavement, sending me flying toward the front door when I grasp the handle and throw it open. I'm up the stairs in seconds, and just as I reach her bedroom door, I pause, terrified of what I'm about to see.

The door is open, and I hear Erica's muffled cries, but when Zoey's pained tone fills the room, it puts me back into motion. "Where's Noah?"

"I'm here, baby," I whisper, striding through the door and taking her in.

Those green eyes I love so fiercely are dull, quickly fading as Hazel lies in bed with her, the two of them snuggled in close. Zoey's parents hover on her other side, and as I walk in beside her bed, Hazel pulls out of Zoey's arms, giving me space.

"Come on," Erica sniffles, her hand on Hazel's shoulder. "Let's give them a minute."

Zoey's eyes don't leave mine, and I can only imagine what she's seeing there. Pain. Despair. Agony. Heartbreak. Emptiness.

Zoey's family walks out, but I hear them hovering by the door, not wanting to go far as I climb right into Zoey's bed, pulling her into my arms and holding her to me, struggling to keep myself together. She doesn't need to see me break. I need to be strong for her. I need to give her the strength so that she can pass on with peace, knowing that I'm going to be alright.

"I'm sorry," she cries.

"You have nothing to be sorry for, Zozo."

"I . . . I think . . . I think it's time," she tells me, her voice breaking.

"I know," I say, holding her even tighter, my hands gently brushing over her skin, desperately trying to soothe her. "You're going to be okay, Zo. I don't want you to be scared."

Her tears soak into my shirt, and they destroy me as the grief doubles down, constricting around my chest like a vise. "I'm terrified," she whispers. "I'm not ready to let you go."

"You won't. I'm going to be right here, holding you the whole time. I'll never let you go," I vow to her, my voice trembling. "And then when you close your eyes and feel peace come over you, Linc will be waiting. He'll guide you through."

"Do you really think so?"

"I know so," I promise her. "He's going to watch over you until I get there, but just know that when I do, I'm going to run to you, Zo.

I'm going to run so fucking fast, right back into your arms, and we'll be together, just as we were always meant to be."

She nods against my chest, reaching up to wipe her tears. "*Not goodbye*," she whimpers. "*Just see you later.*"

"Exactly. It's never goodbye."

She takes gasping breaths, her crying making her even more uncomfortable, and I try to soothe her the best I can, but I'm breaking, feeling her beginning to slip away. She reaches back against her pillow before taking something in her hand.

She turns back to me, those fading eyes gazing up at me. "I want you to have this," she says, taking my hand and dropping a long chain into it. Reluctantly pulling my gaze away from hers, I look down at my open palm and see the two rings that represent the short-lived marriage between us. They're looped through the delicate chain I gifted her on her seventeenth birthday, and I instantly curl my fingers around it.

"Zoey, I—"

"Don't," she says. "I know what you're going to say, and I don't want them buried and forgotten with me. I want . . . I want you to have them. These are the most precious things I have. They represent you and me, Noah. I need you to keep them safe for me. Treasure them the same way you've treasured me."

I nod, barely able to get the words out.

"I need you to be okay," she begs me. "Promise me, you won't fall into the darkness."

"I promise, Zo."

"And when you have kids," she continues in a broken cry. "Will you tell them about me? About how much you loved me?"

My hold tightens around her slender body as I press my lips to her temple, terrified to let go. "Every day of my life," I vow to her.

She whimpers, snuggling her face into the curve of my neck. "I .

. . I love you, Noah."

"I love you, too, Zo," I say, hot tears welling in my eyes as I struggle to hold on. "You're my *bestest friend*, right from the beginning. You've mesmerized me, held me captive for eighteen years, and been the other half of me. Just like you said in your vows, baby. We're twin flames, and I promise you, no matter where you are or what happens next, *I will find you*. Don't be scared, Zo. I've got you."

I feel her nod against my skin, and as she starts to relax in my arms, my tears flow over.

Her parents peer back into her room, and I nod, letting them know it's time to come back, that she doesn't have much time left—minutes maybe.

Her mom stands at her bedside, grasping her hand, her thumb brushing back and forth over her knuckles as her father drops to his knees, his hand resting against her thigh. Hazel stands between them, tears streaming down her face. "I love you, Zo," she croaks.

Zoey offers her a beaming smile. "I want you to fly, Hazel," she tells her. "You can be anything you want to be. Don't think about those silly boys who don't deserve you, don't settle for anyone unless you know he'd have Linc's stamp of approval, okay?" Zoey pauses, needing to catch her breath. "Live your life like it's the greatest adventure. Treasure every day just as much as I've always treasured you."

Hazel shatters, sobbing hard as she crushes herself into her mother's side.

Zoey closes her eyes, absolutely exhausted, and as I listen to her shallow breaths, I tell her all about our lives together, wanting her to go with love and happiness, remembering all the incredible times we shared together.

"Do you remember when you were eight, and I forced Mom to bring you on our family trip to the beach? You made me dig a massive hole, and just when I thought we were about to throw Linc into it, you pushed me right in and tried to fill it up before I could get out."

Zoey smiles and nods against my chest, taking soft, shallow breaths.

"I had the best day with you then. It's one of my favorites."

"Mmm, what else?" she whispers.

"When you were twelve and Huxley Brayford tried to kiss you—"

"You punched him so hard."

"Yeah," I say, remembering it all too well. "I punched him so hard I broke three of my fingers, and it hurt so bad, but I never told you that. I didn't want you to think I was weak. I spent that whole night in the emergency room, but it was worth it."

"You kissed me the next day," she murmurs, her hand falling from my chest, but I quickly scoop it up and hold it there for her. "A real kiss. Not one of those small pecks you'd always given me before."

"Apart from the kiss I gave you after we exchanged our vows, that's still one of my favorites because it was the day I realized that no other lips were going to be enough for me, only yours, Zo."

Over the next ten minutes, I recap every milestone of our relationship, remembering the day I realized that it was so much more than just a crush, the day I first told her I was in love with her, and the day I knew I was going to spend the rest of my life with her. I recall exactly how she looked in each of those moments, the way her eyes lit up when I whispered those sweet words to her, the way she clung to me, knowing that I would always protect her, right until we were old and gray. Even then as kids, we knew that what we had was rare. It was eternal, and we held on to it with everything we had.

Then as her breathing becomes so damn shallow that I can barely hear it anymore, I simply press my lips to her temple, my fingers laced through hers. "Remember to dance among the stars, baby," I tell her, desperately wishing that if she can't stay here with me, that I could somehow find a way to go with her, to run headfirst into our next adventure hand in hand. "Be the sun in the sky."

"Noah—"

"It's okay, Zozo. I've got you," I whisper over the lump in my throat, my chest constricting with the most horrendous, soul-shattering agony. "You can let go now."

She nods ever so slightly, and as I press my lips to hers in one final, agonizing kiss, her father's words fill the air. "Soar, my sweet angel. Be free."

With that, Zoey Ryan, the love of my life, my *bestest friend*, slips away, and that invisible tether that's existed since the moment I first met her is severed, and everything in my world just . . . stops.

Chapter 60

ZOEY

Noah clings on to me, his lips gently brushing over mine as the sweetest peace washes through me, the pain of the past few days fading to nothing. The brightest light shines through my childhood bedroom, consuming me with the most enchanting happiness, and suddenly, I'm no longer there on my bed, and my lips no longer linger against Noah's.

I'm high above, looking down as my family weeps over my body, my mom dropping to her knees in agony. My gaze lingers on Noah, and despite his promise to be okay, I know this is going to destroy him.

He's shattered inside—an empty shell, screaming out with overwhelming grief.

I watch them for a moment, desperately wishing I could stay, but a force has me turning. Realizing I'm not alone, I gaze upon a beaming white light and make out a familiar face, his eyes so dark just like his big brother's.

Lincoln smiles at me, a fondness brimming in his gaze as he holds out his hand toward me. "I've been waiting a long time for you, Zoey," he tells me in that sweet voice I've longed to hear for almost five years, so carefree and young.

"I know you have," I smile as I take his welcoming hand, never having felt so at peace, so painless, and light.

Linc tugs on my hand, pulling me away, but I stop, glancing back toward Noah, desperately needing him to be okay. But Linc tugs on my hand again, a soft smile lifting the corners of his familiar face. "He's going to be alright," he promises me. "He's going to hurt for a while, but he'll be alright."

I nod, knowing Linc is right. Noah promised me, and he's always been a man of his word, especially when it came to me. He's going to stand by his promise, and when the time is right, he'll dig himself out of the darkness and teach himself how to fly. And when he does, I'll be right there soaring beside him.

I'll be the sun in his sky, and every night when he's looking up at the stars, watching as they twinkle against the night sky, he'll know that's me, shining just for him.

"It's time to go, Zo," Linc whispers, his gaze dancing over Hazel's beautiful face with such immense fondness that it kills me they never got to have their chance.

"Okay," I tell him, and this time, when he tugs my hand, I go with him, letting him guide me as we fade away into nothingness, ready for my next adventure.

Chapter 61

NOAH

Agony sears through my chest as Kelly takes Zoey's wrist and presses her fingers against her pulse. A sad smile pulls at her lips. "She's gone," Kelly whispers into the room as Erica weeps over her daughter's body, and Hazel sobs on the ground.

Kelly's words ring in my ears.

She's gone. Zoey is gone.

My *bestest* friend, my confidant, my whole fucking world.

My wife.

Gone. Just like that.

I can't fucking breathe, and I clutch the rings tighter in my hand, vowing to never let them go as the tears pour from my eyes. I've never felt such despair, such excruciating, intense grief. It's like that vise around my heart has finally pushed through my limits and crushed me from the inside out. I need to scream. I need to run.

I need to get out of here.

The pain is unbearable, and as I look down at Zoey's lifeless body, the sobs heave from my chest. How am I supposed to do life without her? How am I ever supposed to be okay with this?

It hurts so fucking bad.

I try to suck in a breath, but it gets caught on the lump growing in my throat, and I gasp for air, feeling as though I'm choking on my own torturous grief. Her body is still warm in my arms, so frail and broken, but I hold her to me, not willing to let go, and with her like this, it's so easy to pretend she's just sleeping. But she's not. She's gone.

My Zoey is gone.

I've never felt an emptiness like this, and it quickly pulses through my veins like poison, filling every inch of me until there's nothing left. As the agony burns me alive, I have no choice but to pull away from her, to lower her sweet body back to her mattress, and run.

Busting out of the house and into the street, storm clouds let loose over me, rain pouring down as I race past my car and run, my feet pounding against the hard pavement. I push myself to my limits, heaving sobs until it becomes too much, and I tumble to the ground, my knees slamming against the road. I catch myself on my hands, the rain drenching me. I throw my head back and scream, the sheer agony tearing right from my soul as thunder booms through the skies above as though it can feel the excruciating pain in my chest.

Why did she have to leave? Doesn't she know how much I need her?

A car rolls to a stop in front of me, and I barely have the energy to look up, finding my mother's Audi, and I'm distantly aware that I'm outside my family home.

My mom gets out of her car, holding her hand above her head as if to protect her from the rain. "Noah?" she calls, her voice sailing across the distance. "What on earth are you doing?"

I look up at her again, and as her eyes come to mine, reading the devastation in my gaze, she crumbles. "Oh no," she breathes, and then she's running, not stopping until she crashes into me, her arms flying around my shoulders and holding me to her.

I grip on to her with everything I have, barely able to keep myself up as Mom sags under my weight, but she refuses to let go. She holds me as the agony continues tearing through my chest, eating me alive. "Why did she have to go?" I cry into my mother's shoulder. "I can't . . . I can't breathe without her. I need her, Mom. I love her."

"I know," she says, her hand roaming over my back, the same way she used to when I was just a kid. "I know you do." Then as the storm rages on and the pain permanently settles into my chest, creating my new reality—a reality where I'm forced to live without her—I burn into ashes, not having a damn clue what will remain once the dust has finally settled.

Chapter 62

NOAH

When someone as young and vibrant as Zoey dies so abruptly, the entire town feels entitled to pay their final respects. Not that the assholes pouring through the church doors had any respect for her while she was living.

Tarni, Abby, Cora, and Shannan are among the crowd of kids from school, leading the way into the church foyer with big, ugly sobs shaking their shoulders. Those tears aren't for Zoey, though. They led the mindless mob of students that made her school life a living hell. If anything, their tears are for themselves and the guilt they carry.

How the hell am I supposed to go in there? How am I supposed to say goodbye?

It's been a week of hell.

The second Zoey faded away, the agony grasped hold of my heart and refused to let go, but something told me that it would only get harder from there. The first night was excruciating, going to sleep alone and rolling over to hold her, to pull her against me and whisper sweet nothings in her ear, only to find her no longer there.

Who's supposed to hold me up? Whose eyes am I supposed to search for to pull me out of the darkness? She was my whole universe. We were entwined as one, formed together as part of the same soul, and having to slice that down the center, it feels like part of me died with her.

I don't know how I'm supposed to survive. Is it even possible?

Zoey's funeral is due to start any second, and despite knowing I need to be in there, my feet feel glued to the pavement. Once I go in there, once the funeral starts, I'll be forced to say goodbye, and it all becomes too real.

I'll have to face the fact that I'm never going to see her again, never going to feel her touch, never going to see the way those beautiful eyes light up when she smiles at me.

Her smell. Her warmth. The way we made love.

I try to tell myself how blessed I was to have her in my life. I had the chance to love her so fiercely, so purely, even if it was only for a little while, but it does nothing to take the sting away from the fact she's gone.

"You going in?" I hear a small voice beside me, and I glance to my right, finding Hope, looking just as broken as I feel.

I shrug my shoulders, my gaze sailing back to the church. "I know I should, but I can't bring myself to move."

She nods. "I know the feeling," she says. "This is my fourth attempt to get through the door."

I glance toward Hope, a small smile on my lips. "You were a good friend to her," I say. "I don't know how much she ever told you about high school, but you showed up right when she needed you the most, when I couldn't be there for her. Especially during those last few months. You made her smile, even through the hardest times. I don't think I've ever thanked you for that."

"There's no need to thank me," Hope says. "Because when it comes down to it, she was exactly what I needed too. Without her . . . I was heading down a bad path, and she opened my eyes to the important things in life. It's me who needs to thank her. She was like the sister I never had."

I nod, both of us gazing back toward the church. "We're going to regret it later if we don't go in," she finally says before letting out a shaky breath. "Come on. We'll go together and then after, we can get wicked drunk."

Fuck, that sounds good.

I blow out a heavy breath, feeling unsteady, and as Hope takes a step toward the church, I walk with her, somehow feeling as though there's an invisible hand in mine, pulling me along.

Hope sits beside me in the pew with Mom and Zoey's family on my other side, and when the funeral starts, Hazel shuffles across the pew and squeezes in between me and Mom, clutching on to my hand like her only lifeline, and it's that touch that keeps me together.

The ceremony is beautiful, classy just like she was. A few songs that Zoey had chosen are played, and fuck. They hit me right in the chest, especially as *In The Stars* by Benson Boone plays through the church.

I somehow find the strength to stand up and read the words I've written, each one of them describing the life we had together, the love we shared, and the rare friendship that became so much more. Then after another song that destroys me, Hazel stands up, and holding her father's hand with tears streaming down her face, she says a few broken words, telling Zoey how much she's going to miss her.

Once the funeral comes to a close, I take off, forgetting all about Hope's offer to get drunk. I know I'll end up that way by the end of the night, but as the funeral finished, and I was forced to face reality with the undeniable excruciating grief closing in on me again, I needed to be alone.

I find myself back at Zoey's house, pushing through the door of what's now one of the loneliest places I've ever been in. Mom stayed with Zoey's parents, preparing for her wake this afternoon, but I just don't know if I have the strength to stand around a bunch of people who didn't really know her, telling me how sorry they are for my loss.

Instead, I make my way up to her room, needing to feel that closeness, to smell her, to feel her around me, and the second I walk into her room, I do just that. It's as though she's right here, her arms wrapping around me, only this time, there's a gaping hole right where my heart used to be, leaving nothing but a hollow emptiness.

My gaze shifts around her room.

I've spent so many hours in here growing up. Chilling out on her bed while teaching her how to play video games, pretending the way my leg brushed against hers was nothing more than an innocent accident, pushing her up against the wall in her closet and really kissing her like I'd been desperate to do for years.

Dropping down on her bed, I take her pillow and hold it to my chest, breathing her in, when I notice an envelope peeking out from within the pillowcase. My brows furrow, and I curl my fingers around the edge of the paper, pulling it out to find Zoey's neat cursive writing across the front.

My name stares back at me, and my heart starts to race.

This is my letter, the one she spent the last few days of her life agonizing over. I sat with her as she wrote her letters for her family and Hope, but when she turned to a new page and scrawled my name at the top, she sent me away.

Over the past week, I've wondered if I would ever see this or if she even finished it. But now that I have, I don't know what to do with it. It's like one final piece of her, one final gift, and after I open it and read the words she's left for me, that will be it.

But these words . . . God. They're going to crush me, no matter how sweet they might be.

Flipping the envelope over, I slip my finger beneath the flap and break through the seal before taking the letter out. My hands shake as I open the papers, seven full pages of blue pen, smudged with the stains of her fallen tears.

I let out a breath, not prepared in the slightest for what I'm about to read, but my gaze drops to the paper, unable to wait a second longer.

Dear Noah,

It's almost comical how pathetic that sounds when you think of the insane journey we've been through together. "Dear Noah," barely sounds like enough.

Let me try it again!

Dear my bestest friend, my soul mate, my twin flame.

My first and only love, my universe, my partner in crime. My first and last kiss, my one great heartbreak. The man who taught me how to love. The man who taught me it was okay to fly. My lover. My fiercest protector. My overwhelming happiness. My forever valentine.

My heart. My world. My everything.

My husband.

There. That sounds better don't you think? It sounds right, and yet somehow still not enough. I don't think I'll ever find the right words to adequately describe just how much you mean to me.

I've agonized over what I was going to write to you. I've thought about it for days, having to start over and over again because nothing feels like it could possibly be enough. How could any words make this okay? How could I possibly take any of your pain away?

I've tried to put myself in your position and think about how I would feel if it had been you taken from this world, and I couldn't bear the thought of it. The pain alone would have eaten me alive, and I know without a doubt that I wouldn't have been strong enough to pull through. But you're different, Noah. You've always been strong enough for both of us. You've carried me through these past six months, and I'm so grateful. I need you to know that, and I need you to understand, without you standing by my side, holding my hand every step of the way, I wouldn't have made it this far. You've lent me your strength and given me the courage to hold on.

I feel as though I have so much I need to say to you, and I could honestly go on for pages telling you how much I love you and how every single time you smiled at me, I felt like I could fly. But you know all of this because you've felt it right along with me. You took my hand, and we ran through life together, full steam ahead, and you never let me fall. You were my protector. My warrior. And you fought for me, even when you didn't realize you were.

Ah, crap! Look at me crying all over the paper. I'm smudging everything! Though, somehow, I don't think you mind. You've always just gone with the flow, been so chill about everything . . . most things at least. I can count more than a few times that temper of yours proved you to be very unchill! But never with me. No matter how often I pushed your buttons, you were always patient with me, always kind. It's one of the reasons I love you so much.

I worry about you, Noah.

Right now, I hear you down the hall, sitting with Hazel. She's still so young, and yet I feel like my sickness has forced her to grow up before her time. I think you need each other. I can hear you talking with her, hear the subtle changes in your tone, trying to make it sound like everything is okay. And I know she will buy it, everyone always does, but I know you too well. I hear the pain in your voice. I hear the way you're hurting, and it kills me because I know it's only going to get worse before it gets better.

These next few years are going to be hard for you, but I need you to know that I'm going to be there every step of the way, just as you have been for me. I don't know where I'm going to end up or what waits for me on the other side, but I feel it in my gut that everything is going to be okay. I'm going to be okay.

Wherever I am, just know that I'll be free. I won't be hurting anymore or trapped in a disease-riddled body, and I want you to think about that when you're missing me, and it becomes too hard. I want you to know that even though I would give anything to be in your arms right now, I am where I need to be. Whether that's in heaven or some other form of afterlife, who knows. Maybe the whole reincarnation thing is real, and right now, I'm in the middle of learning how to fly. And if that's the case, I hope you always leave your window open for me because you know I'm coming back as a bird. And no, definitely not a dirty pigeon. Something beautiful. Something that can soar higher than the stars.

These past eighteen years with you have been a whirlwind, and if I had the choice to do them again, I would. I would always do it again because the feeling of being loved so fiercely by such an incredible, loyal, and pure-hearted man was the greatest experience any woman could ever imagine, and you gave it to me every single day.

I hope you know just how happy you made me.

I know you don't want to hear it, and that you're definitely not ready to have this conversation, but one day when the time is right, I hope you can find it in you to be happy. I want you to open your heart again and allow yourself to find love. Have a bazillion kids with those dark eyes and your quick temper, and for your mom's sake, I hope they give you hell, just like you and Linc gave her.

I know it's hard for you to see now, but your happiest times are still ahead of you. You have so much to look forward to. I want you to find hope, love, and joy. God, Noah. I have so many dreams for you. I want you to push through with college and do something incredible. Though, between you and me, we both know you'll be a superstar playing in the NFL. And when you are, when you look up at the stands, I want you to picture my face, picture the way I would cheer for you, and when you do, I want you to smile.

I want you to push yourself in your classes, push yourself in your personal relationships, push boundaries, and push good times. Go on all the camping trips, explore the world, and try new things. Build a dream home, and fill it with laughter, but don't forget to check in with your mom every day, especially during these years you're away at college.

Maybe set her up with a hot pool boy. She'll love that, but do yourself a favor and avoid my place on Friday night wine night. If our moms are going to be drinking and talking about hot pool boys, trust me when I say that's a conversation you're going to want to avoid!

I'm not really sure what else I should say.

I knew writing this letter was going to be hard, but I wasn't prepared for just how excruciating it would be. It's okay, though, because I know you'll be walking back through my door any minute now, and when you do, you're going to hold me so tight. You'll press a soft kiss to my lips and then you'll brush your fingers up and down my arm until I fall asleep.

You've always known exactly what to do. Which is how I know you'll be okay now. You need to trust yourself, trust that you're making the right decisions, trust your gut, and when in doubt, just take a moment to breathe.

I'm not ready to say goodbye to you, so I won't. Instead, all I'm going to say is the one thing that matters. I love you. I've loved you today, yesterday, and will continue to love you every moment until the end of time.

I will always be waiting for you, Noah.

Your Zoey
xxx

Now . . . down to the nitty-gritty. I've left you some things.
Under my desk, you should find a box (assuming Mom remembered to put it

there. Otherwise, you're going to have to go on a scavenger hunt through my house. But for the love of all that's holy, don't look under my parents' bed. I made that mistake once, and I've never been the same.)

In the box, you'll find a whole bunch of things, some of them self-explanatory, others I might need to talk you through.

On top, you'll find your old phone. You lent it to me when I first started chemotherapy, and it was filled with all the pictures of our life together. Only now, I've added a few things. Apart from every single photo we've taken over the past six months, from selfies of me and Allie to you kissing me on our park prom night, and of course, our engagement and wedding photos, I've loaded every single email we've ever sent each other, right down to the ones we sent when we were only kids. I've gone through it all, by the way, and trust me, we really were partners in crime!!!!

Now, here's the important part about your old phone, and it's going to take a little self-control on your part, actually . . . a LOT of self-control. I've added a voice note message for every birthday between now and your fiftieth birthday. Now, no judgment. The first ten were creative, but after that, I'm pretty sure they all started to sound the same, just rinsed and recycled. Among those voice notes, there are also a few messages, just random thoughts that have popped into my mind over the past little while, little nothings that somehow meant enough to me to put into words for you.

Next up, are two pressed tulips. The orange one is the very first one you gave me when I started my second round of treatment, and the second—the pink one— is from our wedding day. I'll never be able to express just how much these tulips meant to me. Seeing your insane ways of having these tulips delivered to me every single day meant the world to me. You put a smile on my face every single time, and because they meant so much to me, I wanted to gift you these two, the most important ones. They were so special to me, and now they get to be special to you.

There's a whole bunch of other things in there like the little velvet box my engagement ring came in and the infinity charm you gave me for my eighteenth birthday—the very charm that's identical to our tattoos. God, I loved the way you *spoiled me. And don't even think about giving me the whole "Oh, I can't take this stuff, it belonged to you" bullshit because I don't want it left here in this box getting dusty. I want you to have them because apart from me, you're the only one who's going to cherish them the way they deserve to be cherished.*

Now, here's the kicker.

My laptop.

I know you've been curious about this, and I've been keeping it close to my chest because I couldn't bring myself to show you or explain what I've been writing all this time, though deep down, I think you might know. You always know when it comes to me and you.

When you open the laptop, you'll find a document called Remember Us This Way, *and this is our story, from the beginning right up until now. But the problem is, it's not complete. These past few days, I haven't been able to type. I haven't had the strength to finish it, and while I know writing isn't really your thing, it would mean the world to me if you could finish our story for me.*

I know this is the furthest thing from your mind, but I want you to share our story with the world because it deserves to shine. I can't stand the idea of this journey stopping here with us.

I want to tell the world just how amazing you are, Noah Ryan, and these written words are me screaming from the rooftops. Let the world fall in love with you the way I have, and maybe one day, our story might give someone else the courage to find their own version of happiness.

Zoey's letter comes to an end, and I stare at her words, a lump forming in my throat, and immediately restart from the beginning. Then after my third full read-through, I lay the letter down on her bed, and my gaze shifts to the space below her desk.

Sure enough, a brown cardboard box stares back at me, and I get up on shaky legs, crossing her room before pulling her desk chair out of the way and picking up the box. I take it back to her bed, place it down, and lift the lid to see all the items she laid out for me in her letter.

I take the phone, swiping my thumb across the screen to see the familiar wallpaper image—me and Zoey grinning at the camera like complete morons. It's one of my favorite pictures of the two of us, but something tells me that the new ones she added, especially the images taken from our wedding, are going to hold the highest place in my heart.

I quickly scan through them, trying not to linger on any of them for long so I don't get all choked up again. When I open the voice notes and find one labeled 'HEARTBEAT' my brows furrow, and I click on it before the subtle *boom boom* of Zoey's heart fills the room.

I fucking crumble, dropping to my knees.

It's the sweetest sound I've ever heard, the sound I've craved to hear every day for the past week, and here it is. I've heard this soft beat a million times before. It's the sound I've lived and loved by. The sound that has kept my own heart beating, and now I have it right here in the palm of my hand, only it's never sounded so far away.

My back braces against the edge of Zoey's bed, and I close my eyes, just listening to her heartbeat play on repeat. Then as the late afternoon sun ducks behind the trees, I reach back up to the box and drag it down on the ground beside me.

I go through the few things she's left, each one breaking me just as I knew it would. Last but not least, I pull out Zoey's laptop. I stare at it a moment too long before finally finding the courage to open it and find the document that I know will tear open a gaping hole right in the center of my chest. But the second I do, it's impossible to stop reading her brilliant words. Right here on her bedroom floor, I read over every last word of our story until the bright morning sun beams through Zoey's bedroom window.

Then the moment I can, I scroll right back up to the beginning and start filling in the pieces of our story, telling it just the way she would have wanted me to.

Epilogue

NOAH

FIVE YEARS LATER

After walking through the home I've built in East View, right on a hill with a picket fence just for Zoey, I lock up behind myself, feeling good about its progress. It's just about done. It should get the big stamp of approval in a few weeks, then I'll be able to start moving in over the summer.

It's perfect. Maybe a little too big for just me, but it's everything Zoey and I dreamed of having for our home—the home where we always planned to have children and make memories. Maybe it's morbid of me to build my dead wife's dream home as if I could somehow entice her to come back to me.

Fuck. I miss her. Every day still hurts.

The few months following her death were the hardest, and some days, I felt as though I let her down. I was drowning, allowing the darkness to swallow me whole, but I fought through it. The only thing that kept me afloat was the words she'd written on her laptop. I would read it over and over again, taking in our story from her perspective until I'd memorized every word she'd written.

Filling in those last final days tore me to shreds. I would sit there for days on end, listening to the soft sound of her recorded heartbeat while diving into the most haunted remains of my soul, recalling those whispered, broken words that were spoken as I held on to her, and she slipped away from me.

God, even now, five years later, it doesn't get any easier.

I've kept myself distracted. When I have something to keep my mind running, I find I don't get lost in the darkness quite so easily, but it does nothing to ease the gaping hole Zoey left inside my chest. But fuck, I would do it a million times over, just to relive those eighteen years. I would endure the most brutal pain to hold her one more time. To smell her. To kiss her and hear the sound of her voice telling me she loves me.

Her birthday messages have been a godsend. I've looked forward to them every year, clinging to her words like a starved junkie desperate for his next hit.

Just as Zoey had always hoped for me, I was signed to the NFL straight out of college, and I kept my head down, pushing my limits and stretching the boundaries. It means this past year, I've had to be away more than I'd like to be. I've always tried to keep close with Hazel. Zoey was right, we needed each other, especially in those twelve months following her death. We helped each other through it, and she was able to lean on me, but I couldn't bring myself to lean on her. She was too young to have to deal with my pain too. But still, just being in her company and listening to her stories about Zoey was more than I needed from her.

Now, she's seventeen and more trouble than any of us were

prepared for. Linc would have loved it. She's rebellious, and for the most part, it's fucking hilarious, but her dad is going gray trying to keep up with her crazy ass. I promised Zoey I would watch out for her, and while Hazel is doing her best to push her own boundaries, sometimes I've needed to step in and make sure she's not getting herself in trouble.

Today, she's graduating, which is exactly what's brought me back to East View. I just need to swing by my mom's place, say hello and check in with Linc, and then I'll be heading over to Zoey's.

She hasn't been there for five years, and I still refer to it as her place. I don't think that will ever change.

All too aware of how much time I don't have, I get back in my car and head down to Mom's house. Not stopping to knock, I fly through the front door like always but stumble to a horrified stop when I see Mom and Principal Daniels making out on the couch like horny teenagers.

"Ah, fuck," I grunt, turning away and wondering how much bleach I'll need to pour directly into my eyeballs to be able to scrub that image from my mind.

Mom laughs and pulls herself off the couch as Daniels gets up and straightens his tie, neither of them looking the least bit sorry. They started seeing each other late last year after his wife ran off with her Pilates instructor, and honestly, my mom has never been happier. He's good to her. He was always good to me too, even when I didn't deserve it, and while I'm happy for her and wish them all the best, nothing will ever feel right about seeing your mother hooking up with your high-school principal.

"Noah, honey," Mom says, striding right into me and throwing her arms around my neck, pulling me in tight. "I wasn't expecting you so soon."

"What are you talking about? I'm late," I say, glancing over her shoulder at Daniels. "And if I'm late, that means you're definitely late."

His brows furrow, and as he glances down at his watch, his eyes widen. "Ah, shit," he grumbles, looking around for his suit jacket. "We must have lost track of time."

Mom chuckles and smirks at Daniels as she pulls out of my arms and scoops up his jacket, holding it out to him. "It was worth it."

He grins right back at her before leaning in and pressing a kiss to her lips. "Damn straight it was," he says, and then he's out the door, hurrying toward his car.

I pull the door closed behind him and stride down the hall, detouring to Linc's room and sitting with him for a minute before striding down to my old room. I haven't been in here for a while, haven't needed to, and for the most part, I try to avoid sleeping in any of the beds Zoey and I ever shared together. When I do, I've never felt so cold.

My hand closes around the door handle, and I push it open only to find my bedroom window wide open. My brows furrow, and I walk toward it, wondering why the fuck Mom would have left it open like that. She never does. Hell, she barely ever comes in here because most of the shit in here is filled with my memories of Zoey.

As I grip the window frame to close it, I'm knocked back a step as a massive fucking bird flies straight through. Its bright colors practically smack me in the face as it scrambles through my childhood bedroom, knocking shit over in a panic.

"Fuck," I grunt, trying to catch it, only it evades me with ease before finally coming to a stop on my bedside table, its big wings knocking over the framed photo of Zoey from our wedding day.

The bird watches me, and I hold my hands out as if to tell it I mean no harm, and then I slowly inch toward it, preparing to grab it and shove it back out the window. I mean, fuck. What kind of bird is it anyway? It's beautiful, but shit. I don't think I've ever seen one like it.

As I creep across my room, the bird suddenly jumps, launching itself over to my bed, walking across the bedspread until it's standing right on top of Zoey's book, the one I had published that she'd titled *Remember Us This Way.*

I go to shoo it off, not caring where the hell it wants to stand, just *not on that*, but it keeps moving its feet, up and down like the bird version of stomping, and I pause, wondering if it's trying to send me some kind of message.

Nah. That's fucking ridiculous.

I move a little closer, and as I lean toward it, the chain around my neck falls forward, both of Zoey's wedding rings dancing right in front of the bird's face, catching its attention. The bird leans in and knocks its head against the rings, and I pull back, staring at it in wonder.

What in the ever-loving fuck?

Maybe I've taken a few too many hits to the head during training because, right now, I'm starting to wonder if this bird is my dead wife. She told me that if she could be reincarnated, she'd come back as a big, colorful bird that could soar high through the sky, and then she reminded me of that in the letter she left for me, telling me to keep my window open.

So either this is a really weird coincidence or . . .

"No fucking way," I mutter, gazing at the bird, my heart launching right out of my chest.

The bird creeps toward me, and I hesitantly hold out my hand, certain it's about to bite the whole fucking thing off with its strong beak. Instead, it rubs its head across my hand before gazing up at me. I crouch down, putting myself eye-to-eye with the bird. There's something about it that tells me if this thing had a human face, it'd be smirking at me, smug as fuck.

"Am I crazy for thinking you're my Zoey?" I ask, my voice shaking.

The bird just tilts its head as if to say, Y*eah dude, you're fucking crazy,* and then it struts back toward my bedside table, jumping back onto it. Only this time, it settles right on top of the fallen photo frame.

I stare at the bird for a moment when I hear Mom making her way down the hall. "Noah, you're going to be late for Hazel's graduation," she calls, the sound startling the bird as it shoots back toward the window frame.

"No," I panic, racing toward the window as it goes to take off. Only it pauses, its head swiveling back to face me, and as the sun catches on its face and lights up its eyes, I could almost swear I see that same shade of green that I've loved so deeply for all these years.

And then it's gone, shooting out into the sky, and soaring high among the trees.

I gape at it, watching its beauty as it flies, knowing without a doubt that was my girl.

My heart races, filling with undeniable, bittersweet joy, something I never thought I'd ever feel again, and I smile, unable to take my eyes off it until it flies so far that it's not even a dot in the wide open sky. For the first time in five long years, I finally feel content. At peace.

Mom's head appears in my room, staring at me as though I've truly lost my mind. "Earth to Noah. You need to scram," she says. "Oh, and close that window. You're going to let out all the cool air."

My brows furrow, and I look back at her. "You didn't open it?"

"No," she grunts with a scoff. "You know how I feel about leaving windows open. You're going to have all sorts of rodents coming in." She mutters to herself about having to burn down the house if that were to ever happen, and before I know it, she's gone, leaving me staring out the window again.

Twenty minutes later, I sit in the field at East View High, the late spring sun shining over the graduates as I watch some kid in a blue cap and gown make his way up onto the stage, stopping to shake hands with Principal Daniels before receiving his high-school diploma.

I clap on cue with the rest of the audience as Zoey's father leans in. "That's Hazel's newest boyfriend."

My brow arches as I gape at the scrawny kid. "The fuck?" I mutter, my gaze sailing over him and knowing this guy is nothing but a fling to irritate her father. Linc would be rolling in his grave if he knew about this one. "What the hell does she see in him?"

"Who knows. The kid looks like he struggles to comb his own hair."

"Forget about combing his own hair," I mutter, trying to keep my voice down. "What if there was an emergency? How the hell is he supposed to carry her out of a burning building? He couldn't even lift his own dick. Hazel would have to carry him instead."

Erica leans around her husband and swats at us. "Shut up, the both of you. Flynn is lovely."

"I'm sure he is, but he's not gonna cut it," I tell her. "Don't worry, I'll talk to Hazel after. I'll set her straight."

Erica rolls her eyes, knowing I intend to stick to my word, even if it means going toe-to-toe with Hazel James, but it'll be fine. She's always respected my opinion . . . most of the time.

A few more kids get their diplomas before Hazel's name is finally called, and I sit up a little straighter, watching as a beaming smile cuts across her face. It tears me in two. She looks so much like Zoey. It's hard to believe that she's almost the same age as Zoey was when she passed.

A shadow passes overhead, and as Hazel makes her way up onto the stage and toward Principal Daniels, my gaze shifts to the trees, and as that same colorful bird settles onto one of the tallest branches, my jaw drops again.

No fucking way. I'm definitely going insane. Perhaps I really have taken a few too many hits to the head on the football field.

Despite not wanting to tear my eyes off the bird, I force myself to watch Hazel accept her diploma, and as the bird squawks from the trees above, I stand and clap, congratulating Hazel, just as I know Zoey would. A knowing smile spreads across Hazel's lips, and she glances up into the trees. I can't help but wonder just how many bedroom windows this bird has been flying through.

When the graduation ceremony comes to a close and all the graduates take off toward their loved ones, Hazel comes right for me, throwing her arms around my neck and squeezing me tight. "I wasn't sure if you were going to make it."

"Wouldn't miss it for the world," I tell her, pulling back and meeting her stare, the curiosity getting the best of me before I get a chance to reel it in. Or hell, maybe I just need to know if it's time to be checked into a mental institute. "Hey, when you were getting your diploma, what were you looking at?"

"Huh?" she says way too quickly, nervousness flashing in her eyes.

"You were looking up toward the trees," I say.

"Oh, um . . . nothing," she says awkwardly. "I, uh, gotta go. See you later."

She starts to scurry away, and I narrow my gaze at her back, certain she knows exactly what I'm talking about. "Don't think we're not going to talk about this Flynn kid later," I call after her.

Hazel pauses, whipping back around to glare at her father. "You told him?" she hisses.

"Of course I did," he scoffs, looking all too proud of himself. "How else am I supposed to get you to break up with him while thinking it was your idea?"

Hazel glares at her father. "Oh, we're going to have words about this."

"I look forward to it," he laughs, and with that, Hazel storms away, heading toward the very boyfriend who'll be nothing more than an ex within a matter of hours.

When all is said and done, I make my way back toward the parking lot, my hands buried deep in my pockets, when a feminine voice calls out behind me. "Noah."

I whip back, my brows furrowed as I search through the sea of people making their way toward the parking lot when I spot a familiar face. "Hope?" I ask.

She smiles wide. "I wondered if you'd be here today."

"Nowhere else I'd rather be," I tell her. "But the real question is, what the hell are you doing here?"

A stupid grin stretches across her face, and she shrugs her shoulders, holding her hands out wide. "You're looking at East View High's newest English teacher."

"No shit," I say. "Good for you. How do you like it?"

"Honestly, it sucks. The students think that because I'm young, they can mess with me or that I'll let them off the hook easier than other teachers would, but they're starting to learn that I'm not the pushover they were hoping for."

"Good," I say. "How's that boyfriend of yours? Or is he a fiancé now?"

She scrunches her face, cringing. "Yeah, he's actually not doing so well," she tells me. "He accidentally tripped and fell into his secretary's vagina."

"No shit."

"Yeah, it's fine," she says. "Well, not really, but it was six months ago, so it doesn't hurt quite as much anymore."

"Shit, I'm sorry," I say. "If you need someone to teach you how to slash tires, I can help with that."

"It's cute you think I don't already know how," she laughs before glancing back toward the school. "Listen, it was great seeing you, but I should probably get back. I volunteered to be on pack-up duty."

I laugh, and just as she goes to turn away, a flash of color catches my eyes, and I glance up just in time to see the bird swooping low, so close it forces Hope back, and she lets out a terrified yelp, gasping as she falls.

I race in, throwing my arms out and quickly catching her before she hits the ground. "You good?" I ask, helping her back to her feet and making sure she's balanced before letting go.

"Yeah, I'm sorry," she says, shaking her head, eyeing the bird hovering nearby in a peculiar way. "You know, it's the weirdest thing. This bird has been following me around all week."

"You don't say?" I mutter, eyeing the bird with a wide grin. It starts stalking toward us and Hope inches closer to me, her shoulder pressing up against my arm as she watches the bird with caution, clearly not as thrilled with the bird as I am. Only I lift my hand to Hope's lower back, trying to calm her, and the bird looks back to me, bowing its head, almost like a nod.

I gape at it, wondering if this is Zoey trying to send some kind of message. But what?

I'm struck by something she wrote in her letter, telling me that when the time came, when I was ready, she would send me a sign. She wrote *I want you to find hope*. But what if all this time, it's been a different kind of hope she's been wanting me to find?

Unease pounds through my veins, and I glance at the bird to find it holding my stare. It takes another step toward us, and Hope inches back again, her body now pressed right up against mine.

Is this really what Zoey wants? What she feels I need in my life?

The bird seems to nod again, as if reading my mind, and feeling the unease that pounds through my veins. It feels like this damn bird is silently daring me to take a chance, telling me that it's time to find my new happiness and live again.

Then taking that chance, I shift my hand a little higher on Hope's back, hoping like fuck I'm doing the right thing. "Hope, I . . . I know this is a little out of left field," I say, certain that I sound like a moron, but I've never had to put myself out there like this before. "I was wondering if you'd want to have dinner with me tonight?"

Hope inches back just a little, looking up at me with wide blue eyes, clearly just as shocked as I am. "I, ummm . . . yeah. I think I would."

"Yeah?"

She nods, the promise of a new adventure brimming in her eyes. "I've actually been meaning to reach out to you," she tells me. "After I kicked Brent out, I was going through a bunch of my things and found some old photos from senior year, and well, most of them are with Zoey, and I wondered if you'd want to see them?"

"Yeah," I tell her fondly, my gaze shifting back toward the bird. "I think I would."

Hope beams up at me, and as a soft blush creeps into her cheeks, my heart starts to pound just a little bit faster. Behind us, the bird squawks before launching itself back into the sky.

And with that, it disappears into the distance, soaring through the clouds and flying high, *flying free*. But something tells me that's not the last I'll be seeing of this bird, and as I gaze up toward the bright sun— *the sun in my sky*—the ache finally starts to ease in my chest, and I smile, welcoming a new tomorrow, but never forgetting my past.

Thanks for Reading

If you enjoyed reading this book as much as I enjoyed writing
it, please consider leaving an Amazon review to let me know.

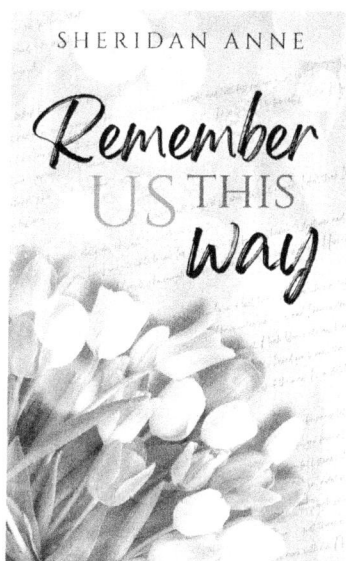

SHERIDAN ANNE

Remember US THIS *Way*

For more information on Haunted Love
find me on Facebook –

www.facebook.com/sheridansbookishbabes

Stalk Me

Join me online with the rest of the stalkers!!
I swear, I don't bite. Not unless you say please!

Facebook Reader Group
www.facebook.com/SheridansBookishBabes

Facebook Page
www.facebook.com/sheridan.anne.author1

Instagram
www.instagram.com/Sheridan.Anne.Author

TikTok
www.tiktok.com/@Sheridan.Anne.Author

Subscribe to my Newsletter
https://landing.mailerlite.com/webforms/landing/a8q0y0

Other Books By Sheridan Anne

www.amazon.com/Sheridan-Anne/e/B079TLXN6K

DARK CONTEMPORARY ROMANCE - M/F

Broken Hill High | Haven Falls | Broken Hill Boys

Aston Creek High | Rejects Paradise | Bradford Bastard

Pretty Monster (Standalone) | Haunted Love (Standalone)

Darkest Sin (Standalone) | Midnight Stage (Standalone)

DARK CONTEMPORARY ROMANCE - REVERSE HAREM

Boys of Winter | Depraved Sinners | Empire

NEW ADULT SPORTS ROMANCE

Kings of Denver | Denver Royalty | Rebels Advocate

CONTEMPORARY ROMANCE (standalones)

Play With Fire | Until Autumn (Happily Eva Alpha World)

The Naughty List | Remember Us This Way

PARANORMAL ROMANCE

Slayer Academy [Pen name - Cassidy Summers]

Printed in Great Britain
by Amazon